ONE
PRIV

Jem heard the sound of the door opening and heels tapping unsteadily on the floor. She turned her head to see a pair of black leather boots with thin stilettos. The boots, and their criss-cross lacing, continued tightly up a pair of long legs and were attached like stockings to metal clips on the end of chains that stretched tautly from a black leather corset. Above the collar, and framed by blonde hair, a pretty oval face was staring down in wide-eyed astonishment at Jem.

'Jem!' said the pretty oval face.

'Hello, Lesley,' Jem sighed. 'What's a nice girl like you doing in an outfit like that?'

ONE WEEK IN THE PRIVATE HOUSE

Esme Ombreux

First published in Great Britain in 1991
by Nexus
338 Ladbroke Grove, London W10 5AH

Reprinted 1991, 1992

Copyright © Esme Ombreux 1991

Typeset by Phoenix Photosetting, Chatham, Kent
Printed and bound in Great Britain by
Cox & Wyman Ltd, Reading, Berks.

ISBN 0 352 32788 X

This book is sold subject to the condition that it
shall not, by way of trade or otherwise, be lent,
re-sold, hired out or otherwise circulated without
the publisher's prior written consent in any form of
binding or cover other than that in which it is
published and without a similar condition
including this condition being imposed on the
subsequent purchaser.

PROLOGUE: *SATURDAY*

Julia awoke slowly from a blissful dream. Stealthily, reality intruded and overlaid the sylvan images flitting through her mind: the morning sunlight was dappled not by a canopy of woodland leaves, but by the patterns of the lace curtains; the insistent pressure between her legs was the work not of the tongue of a wild-eyed woodman, but of her own fingers; the clamour in her ears was not the call of forest creatures, but the raucous snoring of her husband Gerald, sound asleep in the bed next to hers.

Julia sighed, and teased her pubic curls with her fingertips, trying to recapture the sensation of running her hand through the tousled locks of the golden-tongued lad who had surprised her bathing in the tree-shaded pool. But the dream had dissolved. She folded her hand round the wet entrance of her sex and inserted one finger, and then another. She clenched her thighs tightly about her hand as she rolled on to her side and suppressed a loud groan of pleasure. Her other hand slid down the cleft between her buttocks, and she pulled gently at the tiny sensitive hairs surrounding her anus; but Gerald's relentless snores infiltrated her every thought. She turned on to her back, and brought her syrupy fingers to her face. Momentarily overwhelmed by the scent of her own secretions, she closed her eyes and ran her fingertips across her lips, opening her mouth to lick and then suck the sweet moisture. And then, after staring at the ceiling for several minutes, she threw back the damask-covered quilt, swung her long legs out of the bed, and padded across the white carpet towards the bathroom.

Showered and lightly talcumed with Chanel, Julia

studied her reflection in the wall of mirror tiles as she towelled her black hair. I don't *look* thirty-two, she told herself; in fact, I look about twenty-five. I don't weigh any more than I did when I married Gerald. I'm still a size ten – well, sometimes I need a twelve for trousers, but I don't want to look like a boy, do I? A few lines and dimples at the edges of my eyes and mouth; but they add character, I think. If I were happier I suppose I could call them laughter lines. Nothing sagging: no extra chins, and my face – which I still think looks rather French – is as firm as ever. My tits are bigger than they used to be, but they used to be almost non-existent, and they're certainly not big enough to start sagging. And do my little brown nipples still respond to even the lightest touch? Oh yes . . . yes, they like that. But the rear view is still my best: if I turn round, and lean forward slightly, and stick my bottom out, and look over my shoulder . . .

Julia saw, looking back at herself, a reflection of sensual beauty. This pose displayed nearly all of her best features, her long slim legs, her tight but rounded buttocks, separated by a valley of black curls leading down to a large, dark, swollen, inviting split prominence hanging between her thighs, her narrow waist, and the dark golden expanse of her unblemished back. Her tangle of black hair fell haphazardly across her shoulders and her large, dark lustrous eyes peered through a fringe of curls. Any man would want me, she thought; and quite frankly, the way I feel at the moment, any man could have me, any way he wanted me. She dabbed perfume behind her ears, round her nipples, and along the crease at the tops of her thighs where her buttocks flared outwards. Even if Gerald has another woman – which is far-fetched enough – he would still be interested in my body, wouldn't he, she wondered. I almost wish I could be taken back to – but no; that would be unbearable, really. I'll go and wake Gerald with a kiss.

She folded aside the quilt and looked down at her still-snoring husband. Gerald had had such a wonderful body, she remembered, when she had first known him; flab had accrued gradually, in unnoticeable increments, but the shape she had loved was still just visible – the broad chest, the short, muscular limbs, now shrouded in fat and dominated by a mountainous paunch. She knelt beside the bed and placed her mouth over the nearer nipple while her hand stroked down his torso to grip his flaccid member. The snores faltered, and Julia felt his flesh beginning to swell in the palm of her hand. His eyes opened.

'Jules! Oh, that's nice. Mmm, yes, don't stop . . . Sunshine. It's morning. What time is it?'

Julia felt her heart sink. She closed her eyes and nibbled the hairs on his chest while rubbing the tip of his half-erect penis.

'Hold on a sec, Jules.' Gerald was trying to sit up. 'God, look at the time. London's already open. Let me just have a quick look at what's been going on in Tokyo.'

Julia remained kneeling, her face buried in the sheet, while Gerald hauled himself upright and strode towards the computer terminal in the corner of the room. She held back her tears of frustration as she heard him switching the machine on; she tried to shut out the too-familiar sounds of the computer's insidious whine and the clattering of Gerald's fingers on the keyboard.

'Gerald,' she said in a muffled monotone, 'there are more things to life than the bloody international money markets.'

'What? Oh, yes, dear. I know. But I put through a deal in the Far East last night. Got to keep tabs on it, haven't I?'

'Don't you ever get tired of making money out of money, Gerald? Don't you ever want to spend any of it?'

'I thought that was your speciality, dearest. Just joking! But this is my job, you know. It pays for all this.' He waved a hand to indicate the Sanderson decor of the bedroom, and resumed his study of the numbers glowing greenly on his screen.

'Couldn't we at least live in town? You'd find things to interest you . . .'

'We've been through all that, Jules. Many times. I have to have an offshore base, as you know very well. And it's peaceful here on the island; no distractions. You can go to the mainland whenever you like, can't you? Spend weekends in the flat?'

3

It's not the same, Julia thought. But all she said was: 'I'll go and tell Maria to prepare breakfast. On the terrace, I think, don't you?' There was no reply.

When Gerald, wearing his towelling bathrobe, emerged through the patio doors, Julia was still staring at the letter that she had dropped amongst the crumbled remains of her croissant. The envelope was in her left hand; she could feel the hard edges of the small transparency that was taped in the deepest corner of the manilla, but she had no need to prise it out and look at it. She knew what the photograph would show her.

'Success!' Gerald announced. 'The deal went through. No trouble. Now I could do with some coffee. Maria! Where is that damned girl? Maria! Anything interesting in the post, Jules?'

'What? Oh. Yes. A pile of letters for you. Next to your plate. Some faxes came during the night, they're there too. The usual dull stuff.'

'What's that you've got? Anything good? Maria, there you are. Coffee, and toast. And marmalade without lumps in this time!'

'It's just an – an invitation. You remember I went to a – well, a sort of health club, on the mainland, a few years ago? They want me to go back for a couple of weeks.'

'Sounds alright. How much?'

'How much what? Oh, yes – seven and a half thousand.'

'What? Julia, that's outrageous. You can't possibly.'

'Gerald, you make ten times that much every night while you're asleep. The money's nothing, compared to . . .'

'Alright, alright. If you really want to go.'

Julia managed an ironic laugh. 'It's not a matter of wanting to go. I think I have to.'

'When will you go? I seem to remember we've nothing much on after the middle of July.'

'Tomorrow.'

'Tomorrow? You're joking. We've got dinner at the Villiers', and then next week Harbottle's coming over to stay while I grill him about Singapore, and – '

'Tomorrow, Gerald. They say it's the only available

4

date. I'll have to go. One doesn't ignore one of these invitations. It's a very select club.'

'Well if you ask me they go about things in a bloody fishy fashion. What sort of place is it?'

'The Private House? Gerald, it's like another world. It's like stepping back in time. I think I'm almost looking forward to it.'

DAY ONE: *SUNDAY*

The doorbell rang just as Jem was forming her lips into a circle to accommodate the velvet hardness of the penis that had been nuzzling her face.

'Leave it, Rudi,' she murmured, stretching forward to catch him in her mouth. But he had already pulled away, and was trying to wrap himself in his silk kimono in a way that would conceal his upright manhood. 'Rudi! Where are you going? You can't – !' But he was already heading for the door.

'It's Sunday,' he said nonchalantly, turning in the doorway. 'Stan's day off. Wouldn't do to leave a visitor standing outside on the street, would it, old girl?'

'Rudi, you bastard! Get back here!' Jem stopped protesting when she heard him talking into the intercom. Even in a fix like this, she thought, a girl has to maintain her poise. She allowed her head to drop forward, giving the muscles of her neck some much-needed rest. It was just about the only movement she could accomplish, and she reflected that when you choose to spend an afternoon having fun with a bondage fanatic, poise is about all you can maintain. No point worrying about dignity or modesty. I have to thank my stars, she thought, that Rudi's taste in interior design runs to expensive German furniture: the shapes may be a little odd, but at least the upholstery's comfortable.

The chair to which Rudi had tied her was not much use for sitting in; but the sloping seat and tubular steel frame made it ideal as a support for a kneeling fellatrix. Rudi was, Jem had to admit, not a subtle kind of guy, and she had only herself to blame: she had, during her one previous visit to the apartment, pointed out the suitability of the chair, and

7

had even provided the strips of black velvet – to match the cushion cover – with which she was now secured.

She tugged at her wrists, but had no expectation that she would be able to free them. Two uprights connected the seat frame to the minimal headrest; her head and shoulders protruded between the uprights, through the space where an ordinary chair would have a back. Her wrists were tied, above her shoulders, to the sides of the headrest. She stretched her head up and backwards, and felt the topmost curls on her head touching the back of the headrest; she tried to move her feet, but remembered that Rudi had tied her ankles, one crossed over the other, so that, as he put it, she couldn't help making an exhibition of herself. Not that there's any hope of doing otherwise, Jem thought, with my knees a yard apart and tied to the front legs of this stupid chair.

She let her body go limp, so that her weight was supported, from her ribcage to her pelvis, by the sloping and well-cushioned chair seat. This is quite comfortable, under the circumstances, she said to herself; at least Rudi's not a sadist. He could have tied me to a bare table. And in this position, with my face and tits sticking out through the back of the chair, and my arse sticking out at the front – well, I guess I look as though I've been prepared for a beating. Jem shivered as she imagined Rudi's leather belt landing on her outspread buttocks. 'Frankly,' she said out loud, 'anything would be more fun than just waiting here.'

The front door opened. Voices whispered in the hall, but Jem couldn't catch any of the words. She heard doors opening and closing, and then there was silence.

Only two weeks ago, Jem mused, Rudi had been nothing more to her than a potential customer of Executive Environments, the office furnishing company for which she was Home Sales Manager. She had met him for the first time in the deserted foyer of the Grantham Tower, the thirty-storey glass and concrete block that his architectural practice had designed. He and his partners were going to occupy one of the penthouse office suites. Over the telephone he had suggested a working lunch in the empty building, and she had interrupted her taxi journey across the city to buy smoked salmon sandwiches and a bottle of champagne.

Jem remembered standing at the foot of the brand new tower, looking anxiously to right and left while she waited for an answer to her ring on the door phone. She hated to be late for appointments with clients, but on this occasion she had started to wish she had delayed her arrival. If the architect was not in the building, she would have to wait outside; and already her tailored suit, short skirt and pillbox hat had started to attract the attention of the grimier elements of the local population. But the architect had arrived before her; the door had buzzed, and she had pushed through the revolving doors before any of the slack-jawed slatterns had had time to hurl more than abuse.

Rudi had been standing, large, relaxed, and smiling, wearing a crumpled linen suit, next to the reception console that was the only item of furniture in the cavernous foyer, and a sudden lurch in Jem's heartbeat had told her that once again she had fallen in lust at first sight.

His handshake had been warm and strong; he had smelt of lemon-scented aftershave and fresh sweat. It had seemed perfectly natural to hold his hand while entering the lift, and by the time they had reached the top of the building her lips had been pressed against his, and his big hands had been clasping her buttocks. The lift doors had opened to reveal lawns, flower beds, and gravel paths.

'This is the roof garden,' Rudi had said. 'It's a jolly nice day, and I thought we could eat al fresco. Ideal for sunbathing, too, of course; we're miles above the slums, can't be overlooked. I rather think you ought to let me take your clothes off.'

And Jem had simply replied: 'If you like.'

Standing in the shade of the ornamental birch, Jem had surveyed the shimmering, smog-shrouded cityscape while Rudi had undressed her. He had removed her jacket and skirt, and had then stood back to appreciate the peach-coloured underwear that clung to her curves. She had posed, half-turning away from him, one hand holding her hat on to her auburn curls, one knee bent, her eyes glancing at him over her shoulder.

'Good Lord, Miss Darke,' he had exclaimed, 'you're a real looker and no mistake!'

It had been at this point that Jem had started to realise that Rudi's conversational skills were perhaps not as thrilling as his muscular body and his deep brown eyes. But what the hell, she had concluded, I'm here for a picnic, not an intellectual debate.

Rudi had almost torn the lace-trimmed bra in his eagerness to get at Jem's breasts. 'This will have to come off,' he had said, and then, 'What lovely little pink nipples! May I touch them?'

'Go right ahead,' Jem had sighed, 'they're all yours. Maybe you'd better tear my knickers off, too.'

'I most certainly will. But I think I'll leave the stockings; I don't need them. I can use your bra to tie your hands together behind your back.'

'Excuse me?'

'Like this. It's all right. I won't hurt you. See? Now you look even sexier.'

'Maybe I do,' Jem had replied, 'but how am I supposed to eat my sandwiches?'

'Don't worry. I'll feed you. We've got plenty of time, and we won't be disturbed up here. Later on, I've got something else to put in your mouth.'

And so they had spent the afternoon sprawled on a rooftop lawn in the shade of a tree. Jem had been naked except for stockings and suspender belt; Rudi had been fully dressed except for his linen jacket and his unbuttoned flies. After the meal, and after Rudi had spent half an hour lying on his back while Jem had sat squirming on his ceaselessly moving mouth and tongue, Rudi had untied Jem's hands. But he had tied them again immediately, using Jem's bra and his tie to bind her wrists to the back of the waistband of his trousers. Then he had sat with his back against the trunk of the tree and had stroked Jem's copper-brown curls while she licked and kissed the prodigious organ that protruded from his flies.

They had stayed like that for hours. Jem was no sexual

novice. She had allowed other men to tie her up from time to time, but Rudi's prick was not only big and handsome, it also tasted delicious, and the knowledge that she couldn't escape from this position, that she was constrained to have her face pressed against his hard manhood, only added to her pleasure. The sun had shone endlessly, the bright green leaves had rustled in occasional breezes, the roar of the traffic had been only a muted buzz, and Rudi's hands had roamed across her body, making her shiver with delight when he caressed her breasts or squeezed her nipples. It had been an afternoon to remember, and, in her few moments of coherent thought, Jem had decided that in spite of his personality deficiencies Rudi would be a very satisfactory partner – at least for a few weeks.

At last the shadows had started to lengthen, and Rudi had clearly started to have difficulties controlling himself. 'Jem,' he had gasped, 'I can't stand this much longer. You've done this sort of thing before, haven't you? Do you mind awfully if I come in your mouth?'

'Be my guest,' Jem had replied. 'You can do this as often as you like – as long as you tie me up first.'

Which is how I come to be in this fix, Jem thought. Her reverie was interrupted as Rudi returned, carrying two cameras on tripods. Jem watched him as without a word of explanation he moved the chrome and glass furniture to the edges of the room, leaving Jem and her chair isolated in the centre of the geometrically patterned carpet. He seemed to be avoiding Jem's eyes.

'Rudi,' she said, in as conversational a tone as she could achieve, 'would you like to tell me what's going on? Why are you are moving the furniture? Who was that at the door? Why did you turn on the spotlights? And why are you training those goddamned cameras on me, you pervert?'

Rudi concentrated on adjusting the legs of one of the tripods. He frowned, his dark brows almost meeting above his broad nose. 'I'm sorry, Jem, old thing,' he mumbled, 'but it was sort of your idea. Well, you said you wouldn't mind, anyway. You know, it's dashed difficult talking to you when you're – well, like that.'

'You think it's difficult! I'm the one trussed up like a Thanksgiving turkey with boobs and a bottom. Anyway, don't change the subject. Which of the many things that I've said I wouldn't mind are you referring to?'

'You know, the group thing. More than just me and you. You said you wouldn't mind – '

'I can think of more convenient occasions for you to have sprung this on me, Rudi. Whom have you invited? A football team? And whose idea was it to record our activities on film for posterity?'

Rudi shrugged off his kimono and, with a sudden grace that belied his large frame, dropped to the floor to sit cross-legged in front of Jem. She looked into his dark eyes, uncertain whether she should allow herself the frisson of excitement caused by her inability to prevent him from reaching out and idly caressing her left breast with one of his big, hairy hands. Cursing her lack of self-control she felt her eyes half-closing as the tips of his fingers circled inwards towards the pink button of her nipple. 'We've got to go through with it, Jem,' said Rudi, his voice matching the gentle motions of his hand. 'I owe a favour to this fellow. Business. He put a lot of work my way. Including the Grantham Tower. Also put money into the practice. Loads more where that came from, he says. But he wants a favour in return, and – '

'And you thought I'd do your whoring for you! You shit! If that prick of yours gets any closer, I'll bite it off! Rudi, I never thought – '

'No, Jem, no! You've got the wrong end of the stick. He's not here. It's not him. I get the impression he doesn't need me to pimp for him. No – it's me he wants. I mean, he wants me in photographs. He wants photographs of me doing it. Now do you understand?'

'Not really. Who's our visitor? And where is he?'

'In the spare room, changing. And he's a she. Well, you said you'd prefer me and a woman, rather than me and another man.'

'Very considerate of you, Rudi. You don't think it might have been polite to ask me first?'

'You've got gorgeous tits, Jem. Your little nipples have

12

gone all puckered up. Shall I give them a pinch – like that?'

'Ow! Oh, yes, alright. Do it again. Mmmmm. But don't change the subject. Who is this other woman?'

'I don't know her. I mean, I do now, of course, because I've just met her. She was found for me by this same, um, business associate. She's very attractive. Look, I really couldn't say no. This chap's got me over a barrel, honestly.'

'And he's got me over your damned chair.'

'I'm sorry I had to get you involved, Jem. But he insisted on photographs of something a bit kinky, and so . . .'

'And so you immediately thought of me. Thanks a bunch.'

'The thing is, Jem, nothing turns me on quite as much as seeing you tied up. You're rather special, you know.'

'You mean you weren't confident of your ability to perform for the cameras without me. Well, I suppose I should be flattered. But just a minute. You said a bit kinky. How kinky, Rudi?'

'Ah. Well now. I – oh. Here she comes.'

Jem heard the sound of the door opening and heels tapping unsteadily towards the carpet. She turned her head to see a pair of black leather boots with thin stilettos. The boots, and their criss-cross lacing, continued tightly up a pair of long legs and were attached like stockings to metal clips on the end of chains that stretched tautly from a black leather corset. Large white breasts with wide aureoles were cradled in half-cups at the top of the corset, and the half-cups were supported by four chains that converged on a studded black collar. Above the collar, and framed by blonde hair, a pretty oval face was staring down in wide-eyed astonishment at Jem.

'Jem!' said the pretty oval face.

'Hello, Lesley,' Jem sighed. 'What's a nice girl like you doing in an outfit like that?'

'You two know each other!' Rudi said, but both women ignored him. Lesley was the secretary of the Managing Director of Executive Environments, and Jem was wondering how she could ever show her face in the office again. But then, she thought, I guess Lesley's wondering exactly the same thing.

'Now, Lesley, maybe you'll believe me when I tell you that sometimes I'm all tied up and can't come to the phone,' Jem said. 'What are you doing here, girl? And – perhaps more importantly – why are you carrying that mean-looking piece of wood?'

'I couldn't help it, Miss Darke. I had to come here. There would have been hell to pay if I'd refused. I'm supposed to whack your bottom while you're sucking off this bloke here – if you'll pardon the expression.'

'I see. Rudi, untie me. This has gone far enough. And stop doing that to my nipples. You're quite obviously excited enough already.'

Rudi stood up. Jem felt his fingers trail along her spine and down the exposed cleft of her rear. The boss's secretary can see my arsehole, she thought, moaning and trying vainly to squirm away from the questing fingers.

'I'm awfully sorry, Jem,' Rudi was saying, 'but how was I to know you and this other girl would know each other? It's just a silly coincidence. But we can't back out now – can we, Lesley?'

'Not a chance,' Lesley confirmed. 'For one thing, it took ages to get into this leather gear. For another, everyone at work says you like this kind of carry-on anyway – I'm sorry, Miss Darke, but that's what I've heard. But mainly, if I don't do what I'm told this afternoon – well, I don't like to think about what'll happen to me.'

'And that goes for me too, Jem,' Rudi added. 'And I'd say that I'm not the only one getting a bit excited about this – am I?'

'Damn you, Rudi, get your fingers out of there. Alright. You win. I'm in no position to stop you, anyway. But no photographs!'

In unison, Rudi and Lesley insisted that the photographs were essential. Each of them, it seemed, had promised to take compromising shots of the other, and both were terrified of the consequences of failing to do so. Jem thought they were both crazy, but didn't try to argue; her neck muscles were beginning to ache again from the efforts of looking up at them. She dropped her head and gazed at the legs – two leather-clad, two naked and hairy – lined up before her.

14

'OK,' she said, 'you can take the photographs. But only if I'm disguised. Gather my hair in a scarf, or something, and pull it down over my eyes. I don't see how anyone could recognise me that way.'

This compromise was greeted with general approval, and Rudi even managed to find a large square of black silk to match the rest of the tableau. Lesley was given the task of concealing Jem's hair and eyes, and while the girl's uncertain fingers gently tugged and prodded Jem's wayward curls, Jem felt Rudi's large, hot hands stroking her thighs and buttocks. She could no longer see: the black silk had been drawn across the bridge of her nose, beneath her ears, and tied at the nape of her neck. She was aware only of Rudi's left hand, moving in circles and dipping into the wet channel between her legs; of his hard member, teasingly entering her and then withdrawing; of his right hand resting on her right buttock, the thumb pressing insistently into her puckered anus. She felt Lesley's fingers toying with stray strands of her auburn hair and heard the creak of her leather boots, and smelt their spicy, sensual smell. She arched her back, and shuddered as the first small climax of the afternoon came upon her unexpectedly.

Rudi and Lesley moved away, and whispered together. Jem heard metallic clicks: Rudi was setting the cameras to shoot pictures at regular intervals. Then hands were between her legs again – not Rudi's hands, she realised, but Lesley's, with long fingernails that were following the contours of her outer lips, pulling gently at her pubic curls before smoothing them aside, opening her ever more widely. Lesley had big, soft lips with which she was now placing timid, velvety kisses on Jem's rounded cheeks; Jem felt her hot gasps of breath. 'I'm sorry, Miss Darke,' she heard Lesley stammer, 'but I've got to do it. This is where I'm going to whack you in a minute or two. I hope it doesn't hurt too much.' And, with much creaking of leather, Lesley installed herself on her knees behind Jem and began to lick and kiss every inch of the area she intended to punish.

In spite of the occasional click of a camera shutter, Jem began to lose herself in an ecstasy of little thrills. The sharpness of Lesley's fingernails combined with the insistent softness of her mouth to produce ripples of pleasure that spread from her outthrust bottom to the extremities of her limbs; and, when she tried to jerk her hands or legs in a sudden shock of pleasure, the unexpected reminder of her helplessness caused another tremor of guilty enjoyment. I'm tied up and at the mercy of the boss's secretary, she thought, and it's absolutely heavenly.

Something touched her face. A hand, Rudi's hand, lifting her chin. His lips met hers; she opened her mouth, her tongue twisting against his. He pulled away, but she kept her back arched and her mouth open, blindly inviting him to return. Then she smelt the salty, musky odour of his prick, and a camera clicked, and her lips closed round the huge plum. She started to move her head backwards and forwards, sliding her tongue from side to side against the twin curves on the underside of the helmet.

'Oh Jem,' Rudi breathed, 'Jem, that's bloody marvellous, but you've got to stop moving. I mustn't come until you've been thrashed. Lesley, for God's sake get on with it.'

Jem heard Lesley getting to her feet. Suddenly, her bottom felt very cold and naked, and for the first time she began to struggle against the bonds that held her knees and ankles. Almost for comfort, she started to suck the bulb of hot hard flesh that was fitting so perfectly into her mouth; but she stopped as she heard the whistle of thin wood cutting through the air. She waited for the pain, but the blow didn't fall. Lesley had merely been testing her weapon.

'I'll bet this stings,' Lesley said, thoughtfully. 'You know, you look really lovely like that, Miss Darke. All tied up and with a bloke's thing in your mouth, and showing off everything you've got. This is all making me feel ever so sexy. This leather gear's alright, too, after a while. There's something nice about being dressed up too tight, with these chains and buckles, and all my bumps hanging out all over the place. I wouldn't mind letting someone have a go at me with this thing. I'll bet it stings like anything.'

Jem, hardly daring to breathe, felt the long cool strip of wood touch her right buttock, then her left. Then it slid between her cheeks, paused to pass back and forth across her arsehole, and came to rest in the cleft between her swollen labia.

'Can I whack her anywhere?' Lesley asked, and Jem's heart jumped to her throat.

'Yes, if you like,' she heard Rudi say, 'just get on with it. We're only doing this for the cameras.'

There were no more words; there was just another whistling rush of air, and Jem felt a stinging fire across her bottom.

She gasped, jerked her head forward, and almost choked as Rudi's rod of flesh slid to the back of her throat. He swore hoarsely and withdrew his member until only the tip was resting within the circle of her lips. Whispering reassuring words, he placed his hands on each side of her head to steady it. Unable to speak, see, move, or hear, Jem almost sobbed with relief as she realised that Rudi intended to employ all his much-practised skill to fuck her mouth as considerately as possible. She sucked on his familiar hardness and pulled it in to fill her mouth.

Another slashing pain stung her bottom. It was less terrible than the first. Another followed quickly; then another. Jem concentrated on the warm hardness in her mouth, alternately licking and sucking it, trying to encourage the little involuntary spasms that presaged its climax. And she tried to imagine the scene from Rudi's viewpoint: his massive member moving in and out of its favourite orifice; his lover naked, helpless and bound before him; his lover's buttocks striped, glowing, convulsing each time the thin rod thwacked against them; his eyes roving over the leather-clad body of the pretty girl wielding the rod.

Jem now scarcely felt the separate blows; her arse was an undifferentiated area of blazing fire, and the steady rhythm of the rod served only as a sharp repetitive impetus to the movement of her tongue.

Are they looking at me, she wondered, or are they looking at each other, smiling conspiratorially as Lesley's relentless efforts behind me result in Rudi's grunts of pleasure at my front end? He's going to come very soon, she thought, and although his hands suddenly tightened against the cloth over her ears, she heard him cry out.

The whipping stopped. Jem sucked hard. The shaft of flesh thrummed against her lower lip. And as the first spurt of Rudi's salty sperm shot into Jem's throat, Lesley produced her *pièce de résistance*. Four vicious vertical cuts of the rod landed in quick succession, slicing into the valley between Jem's tortured buttocks, the tip of the rod flicking into her wet and gaping sex. She wanted to scream, but all she could do was swallow the spurting floods of semen. Rudi withdrew and Jem allowed her head to drop; she cried out only weakly as Lesley administered a final six strokes to the underhang of each of her buttocks.

Some time later, Jem felt Rudi's strong fingers tugging at the velvet knots at her wrists. When her hands were free she tore off the black silk scarf and shook her hair. Lesley had gone; the cameras had gone. She cursed her hands for shaking as she pulled on her stockings and ignored Rudi's solicitous questions. She shrugged on her jacket, checked her seams, picked up her handbag and made for the door, followed by the pathetically pleading Rudi.

'All I have to say,' she announced as she opened the apartment's front door, 'is that I intend to get my own back on that girl.'

'I really wouldn't try anything like that, Jem old thing. She was only following her instructions.' Rudi seemed genuinely worried. 'And if you try to get your revenge on her – well, I wouldn't like to think of the consequences. I should steer clear of her if I were you.'

'Rudi, she works in the same building as me. Two offices away from mine. I'll see her tomorrow morning, assuming I can walk straight by then.'

'Oh dear. How was I supposed to know you'd know each other? It wasn't my fault – '

'Spare me. You were just following instructions, I know. You're crazy.'

'Will I – will I see you again, Jem?'

'After this? Rudi, you really are crazy. This is goodbye.'

DAY TWO: *MONDAY*

Inspector Lucy Larson, on her way to the police computer centre in Hendon, lounged on the back seat of the Rover Sterling. It was a long drive, and she had plenty of time to congratulate herself on her rapid rise through the ranks and into plain clothes, and on her choice of car and driver.

There is something special about cars with leather seats, she thought, tugging at her skirt so that the cool hide touched her skin above her stocking-tops. And there's definitely something special about young women in uniform. She studied the back of WPC Pritchard's neck, where wisps of long blonde hair, even lighter than her own, were straying from under the constable's cap. Lucy transferred her attention to the small hands, relaxed and confident, that held the steering wheel. She looked up to the rear view mirror, and watched the driver's eyes intent on the road ahead. Suddenly Pritchard's blue eyes flicked upward, towards the mirror, and their gazes locked for an instant.

'Constable.'

'Yes, Inspector?'

'I'm getting bored with this motorway driving. We have plenty of time. Take the next exit – we'll find a cross-country route.'

'Yes, Inspector.'

Lucy liked to hear her driver's voice, with its soft Welsh lilt and slight lisp. She watched Pritchard's hands and eyes as the WPC took the car up a slip road, round a round-about, and into a lane that ran between tall hedges. It was early morning, and there were few other vehicles.

'Watch your speed, Constable.'

'Sorry, Inspector.'

19

And there was certainly something special, and something sensual, about the combined sensations of speed and power. Lucy felt her erect nipples tingle, and a tickling between her legs.

'Pritchard.'

'Inspector?'

'Are you glad I picked you for secondment to my team, Constable?'

'Very glad, Inspector. Very happy. There's not much of an opportunity to get on in the valleys.'

'Nothing but traffic duties and occasional riot control, I imagine.'

'That's about it, Inspector. I've wanted to get more involved with crime detection ever since I joined the Force.'

'You sound like an old-timer, Constable. But you're just a kid.'

'I'm twenty-two, Inspector.'

'As old as that? You'll have to move fast to catch up with me.'

'But you're exceptional, Inspector, if you don't mind my saying so. An inspiration to all of us WPCs.'

'Is that so? Well, I'll help you to get along, Constable, if you perform well.'

'I'll do my best to please, Inspector.'

'Will you, now? We'll see. Let's stretch our legs, shall we. Take that road – the next on the left, through the woods. And pull up somewhere quiet.'

The Rover purred to a halt on a verge of dry leaves. Pritchard switched off the engine. Only the wind in the topmost branches of the surrounding trees broke the silence.

'Get out, Constable. Stand by the car.'

Inspector Larson stretched, and opened one of the rear doors. She ignored Pritchard, who was standing uncertainly by the bonnet of the car, while she reviewed her make-up and filed a fingernail. Leaving her handbag on the seat, she stood up to remove the jacket of her dark blue suit. At last she walked round the front of the car to face her driver.

'It's getting hot already, Constable. You can take off your cap and your jacket.'

'It's alright, Inspector, I don't mind the – '

'Take them off, Pritchard.'

'Yes, Inspector.'

'Put them on the front seat.'

'Yes, Inspector.'

'Now then. That's better, isn't it? Unpin your hair.'

'Inspector?'

'Unpin your hair, Constable. That's an order.'

Lucy watched WPC Pritchard's fingers fumbling with the hair clips, and felt a surge of sexual pleasure like a jolt of electricity as the long, near-white hair fell about the Welsh girl's freckled face. Pritchard's cheeks were glowing and she kept her big blue eyes downcast, not daring to meet the Inspector's gaze. But she knows what's going on, Lucy thought, and she knows she'll have to play the game.

'Now then, Constable.'

'Inspector?'

'You wouldn't like to have to go back to the valleys, would you?'

'No, Inspector.'

'Then we understand each other. Time for a clothing inspection, I think. If you and I are going to be working together – close together – you'll have to pay attention to the rules. I'm not lax about matters of discipline. I imagine I could be particularly strict with you, if necessary. So: everything by the book. Including the uniform. Unbutton your blouse, Constable.'

'Inspector, I can't – '

'Pritchard. That hair of yours is much longer than regulations permit. I don't want to have to make you have it cut off . . .'

'No, Inspector. Not that, please.'

'Then get on with it. I want to see everything you're wearing.'

With a little sob that Lucy thought quite delightful Pritchard plucked at the buttons of her blouse. Then, at Lucy's impatient gesture, she held the garment open, averting her face to hide her eyes behind the long veil of her hair.

Lucy was enthralled. WPC Pritchard had milk-white skin peppered with freckles, a slim, incurving stomach, and a pair of small round breasts barely concealed by a thin lace-trimmed bra. Lucy's eyes drank in the sight of the anxious rise and fall of those two pert orbs and the sweep of ethereal hair that hung down to a point between them. With her head half-turned and her arms lifted to hold open her blouse, the Welsh girl seemed a perfect vision of wanton surrender. It was several minutes before Lucy regained her composure.

'Pritchard. Come here.'

Now the Welsh girl was only inches away. Lucy resisted the urge to touch her. Make her do it herself, she thought. Get her used to it.

'That bra contravenes regulations,' she said. 'It hardly covers your nipples. Well? Don't just stand there. Where are your nipples?'

Lucy could see the large pink aureoles very clearly through the thin material, but she still felt a thrill at the sight of Pritchard placing a tense fingertip on the point of each cup of the bra.

'Very witty, Constable,' Lucy sneered, pretending that her shaking was the result of suppressed anger. 'I know where they are, you stupid girl. I want you to show them to me!'

With trembling hands, Pritchard pulled aside the flimsy cups of the bra, exposing her firm, white, freckled, pink-tipped breasts. And at last she dared to look shyly up into the Inspector's face.

'Very good, Constable,' Lucy snapped. 'Leave them like that. Lift your skirt. Higher than that, you little fool. Up to your waist. And keep those tits uncovered.'

Pritchard's stockings were black and seamless, held up by a plain black suspender belt. Her panties were of black cotton. The flesh between her stockings and her panties looked, by comparison, completely white and smooth. Lucy was seized with a desire to fall to her knees and kiss that cool pale skin, but she mastered herself.

'Don't squeeze your legs together, girl, you'll fall over. Come on, knees apart. Wider than that. That's better. Now then: what do you mean by wearing knickers on duty?'

'But – but surely . . . I mean – well, goodness gracious, it can't be against regulations to wear a pair of knickers, now, can it?'

'Constable, are you trying to tell me I don't know the rules? Well?'

'No, Inspector.'

'Just as well for you. I've got regulations specific to my team, Constable. One of which is that my driver doesn't wear knickers. Understood?'

'Yes, Inspector.'

'Well don't just bloody well stand there, Pritchard. Get them off!'

Lucy couldn't decide where to look: at the slowly-revealed bush of blonde curls, with the hint of a pink slit showing as the girl struggled to step out of the black panties; at the little breasts, jiggling so prettily; or at Pritchard's face, with its flaming cheeks, tear-filled eyes, and perfect upper teeth biting into the lower lip.

I can't let her off the hook, Lucy thought, but it's time to let the line run out a little. 'Very good, Constable,' she said. 'Clothing inspection over. Button yourself up, and we'll be on our way.'

'Knickers, Inspector?'

'Knickers to you, Constable. Leave them here – no, we mustn't litter the countryside. Give them to me. You won't be needing them again until you go off duty. Regulations must be obeyed. And what are you doing with your skirt? Did I tell you to put it back? Lift it up again – right up. You'll stay like that until we reach Hendon; you'll look perfectly respectable sitting behind the wheel. I'm sure you'll get to like the feel of leather on your bare bottom. Now jump to it!'

They had returned to the motorway, and had driven in silence for some time. Lucy leant forward, blew gently on the back of her driver's neck, and ran a scarlet fingernail along her driver's stockinged thigh. The Rover swerved, then straightened.

'Steady, Constable,' Lucy whispered. 'You've got to pay

23

attention if you want to succeed with me. And you do want to succeed with me, don't you?'

'Yes, Inspector.'

'Good girl. We do understand each other, then. And, of course, you understand that I'll have to punish you for wearing knickers on duty?'

'But Inspector, I didn't know – '

'Ignorance is no excuse, my dear.'

'But I've got a clean sheet, Inspector. I've never had a disciplinary report before, and – '

'Calm yourself, Constable. I'm sure we can avoid that outcome. I have a rather less drastic form of punishment in mind.'

'Oh, thank you, Inspector.'

'I think we might both rather enjoy it. Come to my office after we've got back from Hendon.'

'Of course, Inspector.'

A thick file labelled *Grantham Tower* dropped into the waste paper bin. Jem sighed. So much for the biggest potential account; the only worthwhile business on the horizon, in fact. She stood at her desk absent-mindedly rubbing her bottom and watching the computer screen as the cursor ran down the names of the few sales leads remaining in her database. She became aware of the sounds of the other employees of Executive Environments arriving in their offices; her secretary would arrive at any moment. There must be time for one more look, Jem thought, and, twisting her head over her right shoulder, she used one hand to pull up her pleated skirt and the other to squeeze her knickers into the crease between her buttocks. The lines had almost disappeared; the smooth, rounded inverted heart of which she was justly proud looked as good as new.

The telephone rang; automatically she picked it up.

'Sales office,' Jem said, readjusting her clothes.

'Jem, is that you? It's Mike.'

'Yes, Mr McKenzie, it's me.'

'Are you alone?'

'Yes – yes, Tracey hasn't showed yet.'

'Good. I need to see you. Right away.'

24

'In your office?'

'No. I'm in the car park. I'm calling from the car. Can you get down here straight away?'

'Sure thing, MM. I'll be right there.'

Jem took a swig of black coffee, turned off the computer, fluffed her hair, touched up her lipstick, and made for the door. When the Managing Director wants you in his office first thing Monday morning, it's important, she thought. But when he wants you in the car park, it's serious.

As Jem stepped out of her office, she saw Lesley threading her way between the seating units that were artistically scattered across the carpeted reception area. Lesley looked demure in a pink pencil skirt and a white cardigan.

'Good morning, Lesley,' Jem called out. 'I'm glad to see you've decided to forgo your weekend taste in clothes.' Jem felt immediately guilty as the tall blonde blushed, stammered a greeting, and fled into Mike McKenzie's outer office. Maybe I should tell her she looks great in leather, Jem thought as she continued towards the smoked-glass front doors.

'Hold it there.' Inspector Larson interrupted the civilian boffin, who was beginning to expound on the theoretical relations between fields of data that had been stored under differing software applications. 'Let me get this straight. You were operating outside the parameters of your brief, right?'

'Strictly speaking, yes. But I did it in my own time, and – '

'Never mind about that. Who else knows about this?'

'No one. Your Chief Inspector didn't seem particularly interested.'

'He told me it was a wild goose chase. I think perhaps he was wrong. Let's get back to the cases. All missing persons. All unrelated. So what's interesting about that? If they're unrelated – '

'Apparently unrelated,' the young man broke in, his spectacles wobbling excitedly on his nose. 'That's the whole point. I was trying to use the relational aspects of

HOLMES 2 to discover a pattern behind apparently unconnected data.'

'And you found one, I take it.'

'HOLMES found it. Correct me if I'm wrong, but I get the impression that missing persons are often investigated a little less . . . I mean, sometimes you don't really bother to . . .'

'We've got better things to do than to waste our time looking for runaway kids, bored husbands, and people who probably don't want to be found anyway.'

'Exactly. No one looks at the old files, of course. Closed cases. And you're right – I've asked HOLMES to check – most of the missing persons are teenagers, old people, recidivist criminals, middle-aged men. HOLMES couldn't find a pattern there.'

'But?' Lucy was becoming impatient.

'But there is a pattern within one particular sub-group of missing persons. Women, aged twenty to thirty-five, married, social group AB. Not a large sub-group. So far HOLMES has printed out details of only three individuals.'

'And every single one of them . . .?'

'Every single one of them has paid at least one visit to a health club known as the the Private House.'

'It's serious, Jem.' Mike McKenzie was slumped against the door of his Daimler; he was haggard and unshaven, and for the first time Jem considered that he looked as old as his forty-three years. 'Sorry to drag you down here, but I can't talk inside. Walls have ears. Even company cars can be bugged.'

'It's another fine day, MM. You sit on your company Daimler, I'll sit on my company Golf. What's the problem?'

'You mean you haven't noticed?'

'Oh. That problem. New business drying up, debtors reluctant to settle their accounts, suppliers screwing down our credit limits, the bank calling in our overdraft, and nasty rumours about us in the trade press.'

'Very perceptive. Some of that information is supposed to be confidential. If there was any point worrying about it,

I'd start worrying about the ambitions of my over-intelligent Sales Manager. But there isn't any point, so I'll ask her a favour instead.'

'What sort of favour?'

'Dirty work. I want you to be my secret agent.'

'Tell me about it.'

'Where do I start? Jem, the company's in a mess. Starting about three months ago, everything went wrong at once.'

'Last year was good. Sales up fifty per cent.'

'I know. A lot of that was your doing, too, Jem. We were maybe overtrading a little, and that hasn't helped now the crunch has come. Suddenly we're being attacked on all sides – contracts cancelled, customers not paying, suppliers not delivering, rumours flying all over the place. At first I thought it was coincidence – just a patch of lousy luck.'

'And now?'

'Now I've been approached to sell the company. For a ludicrously low figure.'

'Don't you own the shares?'

'I have the largest slice. My brother has some, also my wife. The executive directors have a few each. And a big chunk of the equity is held by the bank. If I sell, the company changes hands, that's for sure.'

'So who is making this offer you can't refuse?'

'Jem, you'll never believe it.'

Inspector Larson minced no words when telling the bespectacled boffin that he had wasted his own time and, even more reprehensively, that he had dragged a senior plain-clothes policewoman down to Hendon on exactly the wild goose chase that her Chief had predicted. But she took the print-outs and made a mental note of the address of the Private House before she stormed out of the computer centre.

She commandeered a vacant office in the nearby Police Training School, and had lifted the telephone before the door had had time to slam behind her.

'That's the address, Bert. Now give me the name that goes with it. And I don't want the name of the sitting tenant, or the holding company, or the caretaker's dog – I want the name of the man who owns this Private House, OK? . . . It's *who*? Terence Headman? *The* Terence Headman? . . . Well, I'll be damned.'

'You've got it, Jem. *The* Terence Headman. He made the bid through one of his subsidiary companies, of course, but I did some homework. He's behind it.'

'What does a property tycoon want with Executive Environments, MM?'

'Beats me, Jem. But his interests are wider than the press reports tell us. I've been digging up information about him. The trouble is, I can't dig up any dirt.'

'And you think he's behind the problems we've been having?'

'His representatives as good as admitted it. Bragged about it. They seem to know about every move I make. That's why I'm so paranoid – why we're talking out here. I'm almost convinced my office is bugged. It's like Headman has someone looking over my shoulder all the time. And he's certainly got the clout to bugger up our business. I'm sure it's him. And if he keeps up the pressure, we'll go under. We can't last much longer. I'll be forced to sell.'

'So you want me to dig up some dirt?'

'I don't know that there is any dirt, Jem. That's why I have to ask you to do this as a favour. It's a little deli- cate . . .'

'Spit it out, MM.'

'Well – you're single, am I right? And unattached? And you're also, in my humble opinion, the company's most attractive employee. In fact, Jem, I think you're just about the sexiest little vixen I've ever seen. You don't mind me saying that, do you? Good. And well, I get the impression that you're not exactly – what I mean is, you seem to be fairly broadminded, easygoing, and . . .'

'I get it. The badger game.'

'Pardon?'

'Entrapment. If I can't find any dirt stuck to Headman, you want me to create some. Get him *in flagrante*, and make off with some hard evidence.'

28

'Exactly. Excellently put. Will you do it, Jem? This is my last resort.'

'What's Headman like?'

'Wealthy, of course. Fortyish. Single. He's been seen in the company of a few ex-debs, so he's unlikely to be homosexual. There's never been a hint of scandal. He seems to be a regular clean-living chap.'

'This assignment sounds like a piece of cake. Of course I'll do it. When do I start?'

'Immediately. This morning I used a call box to phone an old acquaintance of mine. She's a journalist, and she's just gone to Brazil, incognito, to do a TV report. Her name's Jemima Fawcett, but she calls herself Jem – so you don't even have to get used to a pseudonym. Here's her NUJ card, driving licence, credit cards. I don't think anyone can connect her with me. So from now on, you're her. You're working freelance – her employers, the TV company, certainly won't be prepared to tell anyone where she really is – and you're after a story about Headman. Profile of the successful entrepreneur, that sort of thing. As a journalist, you'll be expected to carry a camera and a tape recorder. Use them, Jem – get Headman in a compromising situation, and get him on tape or film. There's a directorship waiting for you if you pull this off.'

'What if he refuses to talk to me?'

'Use your natural talents, Jem. Unless he's made of reinforced concrete, he'll jump at the chance.'

'No, Larson. Absolutely not. Terence Headman is one of the wealthiest businessmen in the country. And a thoroughly respectable one. I can't authorise an investigation. You haven't got a shred of evidence.'

'But I am owed two weeks' leave,' Lucy said, smiling sweetly at the Chief Inspector as she crossed her legs and fluttered her eyelashes, 'and I can't think of a better place to spend a fortnight away than an exclusive health club – can you?'

'If you get much fitter, Lucy, you'll develop pectorals that are even bigger than your – well, never mind. Of course I can't stop you trying to get inside the Private House – but remember, you're on your own!'

Julia had had two pink gins on the aeroplane, and was feeling a little light-headed as she walked from the airfield's one runway towards the small cluster of airport buildings. She was worried about her underwear and her travelling bag: she had had to leave with both, to prevent Gerald becoming suspicious, but knickers and personal possessions were unnecessary – and disapproved of – at her destination. Once inside the almost deserted lounge, she made straight for the public conveniences.

Locked inside one of the cubicles and seated on the lavatory she felt safer, less flustered. These are down, she said to herself, lifting her high heels out of her cream silk camiknickers, and so they might as well come right off. She picked the sheer material off the floor, held the knickers to her cheek, and then stuffed them into her Liberty-print travelling bag. She rummaged through the few other items of clothing that the bag contained, making sure that none of them was labelled, and inspected her make-up and toiletries – all unremarkable brands, nothing unusual. She emptied her handbag on the tiled floor, and checked every compartment for anything that might carry her name. There was nothing to identify her except for two crumpled, handwritten shopping lists and the passenger copy of her air ticket – these three items she flushed down the toilet. Smiling ironically as she refolded the bundle of banknotes that Gerald had insisted she should take she refilled her handbag and stood up to place both bags on top of the cistern. A nice surprise gift for the next lucky lady to use this loo, Julia thought. I just hope Gerald has no cause to ransack my writing-desk while I'm away – he'll get dreadfully excited if he finds I've gone without my credit cards and cheque book.

One last check, Julia said to herself. Shoes: I think the heels are high enough. Stockings: black, that's always a safe bet, very sheer and with seams – which are straight. Suspender belt to match stockings, and I think the lace trim will be permitted. Skirt: full, pleated, light cotton. Blouse:

matches the skirt, unbuttons at the front, cap sleeves. No bra. No jewellery – almost forgot! I'm still wearing my wedding ring! Change it to the other hand, hope they let me keep it. Hair tied back with a red ribbon, matching lipstick and nail varnish – I hope they appreciate that touch. More make-up than I usually use – more blusher, mascara and eye-liner – but that's the way they like it, even though I think it makes me look a bit like a Parisian tart. Perfume in my armpits, between my breasts, between my legs, between my buttocks – they say that applying perfume should always sting, and this morning I shrieked so much I almost woke Gerald. Anything else? Nothing. No possessions, no identity. Just one final adjustment, in case something happens straight away. They'll want me to be ready, so . . . Two hands under the skirt; one at the front, one at the back. That perfume's almost overpowering. Not too fast: just touch the pubic hair, tease it a little, and meanwhile push forward from the back, thumbnail against arsehole, fingers into the warmth and softness – I'm already wet, I can't believe it, just from thinking about what they'll do to me . . . Oh, that's nice, fingers from the back pushing in and out, fingers from the front going back and forth, and there's my little clit, peeking out, asking to be fiddled with – no, I must stop. They won't like it if it's obvious I've been enjoying myself. Wipe fingers on a piece of toilet tissue – can't get rid of the perfume smell, it's all over my hands. Never mind – time to go.

Julia emerged from the Ladies and saw a young man in old-fashioned chauffeur's livery. He hadn't been in the lounge when she had walked through it earlier. Her eyes met his and he raised a questioning eyebrow; she nodded. He turned and made for the glass doors, holding one of them open as she approached. She stopped in the doorway, and looked up into his grey eyes; she ran a fingernail along his square jaw.

'The car is just outside, madam,' he said, placing a gloved hand on her waist and pulling her towards him. She placed her hands against his tunic and then, amazed at her own bravado, she reached beneath it to find, as she expected, that the front panel of his stiff trousers consisted

31

of only a sort of codpiece of thin material through which she could feel every contour of his swelling prick. 'Steady on, madam,' the chauffeur whispered, 'we're not at the Private House yet.'

'Silly!' she replied, giving him a peck on the cheek. 'One is never really away.' There were several cars on the tarmac outside the airport buildings, but only one of them was a vintage Rolls Royce; Julia walked towards it, followed by the chauffeur.

They had driven through leafy country lanes for about half an hour before Julia decided to speak to the chauffeur again. 'Are we going straight to the House?' she said. 'I can't wait. It's odd, but I'm quite looking forward to it.'

'That was anticipated, madam,' the chauffeur replied in a level voice, 'and therefore the answer is, of course, no. I have been told to make a stop *en route*. In the woods.'

'And what are we to do in the woods?' Julia was excited and nervous at the same time, but did her best to replicate the chauffeur's measured tones.

'I have been told to make you cry, madam. "Clear evidence of copious weeping" is the exact requirement.'

Julia took a deep breath. 'And what will you do to make me cry?'

The chauffeur smiled at last. 'Whatever is necessary, madam. I have been told to use my own discretion. Perhaps you could offer a suggestion? Or should we abandon subtlety and go straight for the riding-crop? I think this is a suitable spot.'

The ancient car jolted to a stop, and the chauffeur held open Julia's door. 'Come along, madam,' he said. 'We're getting close to the Private House now.'

DAY THREE: *TUESDAY*

There were no filing clerks and no cabinets full of files, no typists and no word processors with beeping screens, no frantic executives and no rooms in which crisis meetings could be held. Terence Headman's private office was furnished as a tastefully-decorated, little-used luxury apartment on the top floor of a smart mews house – which is exactly what it was.

Terence Headman's personal assistant was curled on a *chaise longue*, reading not a confidential report but what appeared to be a paperback novel. The only sounds were the ticking of a grandfather clock and an occasional rattle of crockery from the direction of the kitchen. Miss Morelli looked up, smiled vaguely, and resumed her urgent scanning of the book. She did not, in Jem's opinion, look much like the personal assistant of a notoriously hard-working corporate predator; from the razor-cut spikes of her black hair to the golden patent-leather sandals that were about to drop from her lazily swinging stockinged feet, she looked more like a model taking a mindless break between photo-sessions.

Jem was becoming impatient. It had been surprisingly easy to make an immediate appointment to visit Headman's private office; but since then nothing had gone according to plan. Jem had taken care to dress in formal clothes, as she had expected to meet Headman in a formal office, but she had done her best to ensure that her appearance broadcast the correct seductive message. She had augmented the natural curls of her hair, and then pinned it up so that the cataract of auburn froth fell like a curtain behind her pixie-like ears; she had spent an hour over her make-up, carefully applying nail varnish, lip gloss, and face powder, and outlining her eyes and lips with painstaking precision. Her blouse was snow-white, and sheer enough to display the delicate lace tracery of her wispy bra; her skirt was short enough to reveal a glimpse of stocking-top whenever she crossed her legs, and tight enough to emphasise the curves of her bottom-cheeks. Her ankle-strap shoes, with heels even higher than those she normally wore, had been chosen to create a sensational arse-wiggle with every step she took.

But she had had no need to bother with these subtle variations on the theme of a businesswoman's suit: Headman's private office wasn't a real office at all. And looking seductive had been a complete waste of time: she hadn't met Headman, and in any case his personal assistant, apparently wearing nothing but a black lace tunic and black lace stockings and enough gold jewellery to wipe out the national debt of a small Third World republic, made Jem feel both overdressed and dowdy. She recrossed her legs and leant forward.

'Excuse me,' she said firmly. Miss Morelli frowned, sighed, and looked up. 'Excuse me, but I didn't come here to write a piece about the interior decor of Terence Headman's apartment and the reading habits of his personal assistant. When will I meet Mr Headman himself?'

'Only when I'm sure that Mr Headman will want to see you, Miss Fawcett. There are at least two hurdles to clear before you have any hope of meeting him. But here comes Darren; we'll find out whether you've passed the first test, shall we?'

Darren appeared in the doorway that seemed to lead to the kitchen. He was tall, bronzed and muscular, with wavy blond hair and a square jaw that was so clean-shaven that it gleamed. He was wearing nothing but white training shoes and a pair of tight white shiny shorts. Carrying Jem's camera and briefcase on a tray, he padded across the carpet and stopped deferentially in front of Miss Morelli. A Californian-style beach god, Jem marvelled; more than a little out of place in the inner city.

'Darren's one of my boys,' Miss Morelli said proudly.

'Isn't he a hunk? Well, Darren – is this a bone fide Miss Fawcett?'

Darren blushed, and spoke hesitantly in an accent that originated south of the river. 'Yeah, she's OK, Miss Morelli. She checks out. This gear's a bit iffy – I mean, the Boss doesn't like cameras and tape recorders and that, does he? But it's all straight stuff, nothing hidden in it.'

'That's good, Darren. But Mr Headman isn't *the Boss*, is he? We call him Mr Headman, or the Master, don't we?'

'Yes, Miss Morelli. Sorry.' Darren's face was bright red, and Jem was sure that she detected a twitch beneath the taut material that barely covered the young man's bulging crotch.

'Well don't just stand there, boy. Return that equipment to Miss Fawcett, and ask her if she'd like a cup of tea.'

Darren turned, and with a ripple of muscles bent forward to place the tray on the seat next to Jem. She dragged her gaze away from his perfect torso and found herself staring into his wide ice-blue eyes. 'Earl Grey, Miss?' he asked, in a hoarse whisper. 'Or China?'

'Earl Grey, please,' Jem managed to say, letting her gaze rest on Darren's groin as he straightened up. She was sure the bulge was growing, and it seemed to cause him nothing but embarrassment.

'Come here a moment, Darren,' Miss Morelli ordered in silky tones. He took a step and stood rigidly to attention beside her chair, flinching slightly as she ran her fingers across the tight curves of his bottom. 'He's a good boy, Miss Fawcett, but rather over-demonstrative. Aren't you, Darren?' she added, flicking a fingernail against the unmistakeable erection that threatened to burst the fabric of his shorts. 'Run along now and make the tea.' The discomfited beach god mumbled a reply and fled into the kitchen.

Miss Morelli tossed her book aside, and with a jangle of gold bracelets stretched her slim arms above her head. She stood up, smiling smugly as Jem surveyed her tall lissome body, very little of which was covered by the black lace camisole top and matching G-string and suspender belt. Jem tried hard to retain her grip on reality. This is the office of a business tycoon, she told herself. I'm here to interview

35

him; this is his personal assistant. 'Miss Morelli,' Jem said flatly, 'I would very much like to meet Mr Headman, and – '

'Perhaps you will, Jem. You don't mind if I call you Jem, do you?'

'Not at all. What should I call you?'

'You must address me as Miss Morelli, of course. I think that you have still not grasped the situation. Mr Headman is a very busy man. He has many interests. He never lets anyone see him. Occasionally he will ask to see someone. He delegates that authority to his assistants. On matters of property, finance, share dealings and so on his assistants are accountants, brokers, business managers. In matters touching his private life, I am his assistant. Mr Headman might ask to see you – if I recommend it. Is that clear?'

'No. But I'll play along, I guess. Can we move things along a little?'

'By all means. As you have heard, Darren has been making enquiries about you, and checking your belongings. The results are positive. Next we have to consider you personally. Stand up, Jem. That's right. Now: I think you're rather overdressed, don't you? Start taking your clothes off, my dear.'

Scented oils filled the wood-panelled room with a heady mixture of jasmine and patchouli. The Asian girl hummed softly as she continued her ineffectual but very relaxing massage. Lucy surrendered to the gentle caresses but fought off her inclination to doze: she was determined to review everything she had so far discovered about the Private House.

It had all been very easy; almost too easy, Lucy thought. She had telephoned yesterday. Yes, there were immediate vacancies; the club's facilities were extensive, and could provide a tailor-made regime for each member – anything from a weekend's peace and quiet to a month-long intensive fitness and dieting course. Fees were high, but not extortionate.

The place was less grand than Lucy had expected. She had driven through winding tree-shaded country lanes to reach the entrance, a vast pair of wrought-iron gates set in a high stone wall; but the Private House didn't live up to the promise of its gateway. The main building was a Jacobean manor-house, very charming but much smaller than Lucy had anticipated. It was surrounded by more modern buildings and a few acres of attractive formal gardens. Beyond the encircling wall lay the panorama of parkland and copses that Lucy had glimpsed while driving, and which she had assumed were the grounds of the club; now she realised that, even if the land had once been the estate of the Jacobean country house, it must have been sold off long ago. The Private House seemed to be no more than it claimed to be: an expensive, classy, health and fitness club. Turn left for car park; all major credit cards accepted; please do not leave valuables in the changing rooms; special menu for slimmers.

And yet, Lucy reflected as she tried to ignore the insistent fingers playing on her vertebrae as if they were piano keys, there are peculiarities. Not enough rooms, for instance: she'd already counted fifteen guests, and there were only about fifteen bedrooms; did the staff sleep in a dormitory in an outbuilding? Or were they from nearby villages? Come to think of it, there were no nearby villages. And the staff behaved oddly, too. They were very friendly with the guests – almost off-hand, in fact – but addressed each other only in the most formal speech. And they all wore uniforms that were outrageous replicas of those worn by nurses and dosmestic staff a hundred years ago.

If you want information, Lucy decided, you have to ask questions. She propped herself on an elbow and looked up at the Asian girl. Large dark eyes met hers. 'What's your name?' Lucy asked. 'Mine's Lucy.'

'Asmita,' the girl replied, with a devastating smile.

Lucy felt a familiar tingle of interest. There really is something about young women in uniform, she thought, as she let her gaze take in the crisp white button-through dress that clung tightly to every curve of the girl's brown body. 'Tell me, Asmita,' she began, 'do you come from these parts?'

'From round here?' Asmita giggled. 'Oh no. From the Midlands. I'm not really a masseuse, you know. I'm just . . .' she giggled again, 'moonlighting, I suppose. It's good to get away sometimes.'

'I see. What about the other staff? Are they part-timers too?'

'Some of them. Some are here all the time. But we all love our work. Do you like this?' Asmita had started to rub oil into the backs of Lucy's thighs, stroking her fingers higher and higher up Lucy's legs with movements that were far too gentle to have any effect on muscle tone but which were playing havoc with Lucy's nerve endings.

'It's quite nice,' Lucy said in a level voice, but she allowed her head to sink back on to the folded towel.

Asmita's hands stopped moving; they had reached the tops of Lucy's thighs. Then Lucy felt the hands gliding from her hips to the small of her back, skirting her bottom. One hand stayed resting on her coccyx; the other skimmed her right buttock, lifting the tiny invisible hairs. Lucy heard her heart beating; she remembered to breathe.

'Now I'll massage you here,' Asmita said lightly, 'if you ask me to.'

'Alright,' Lucy said in a voice that sounded unnecessarily loud. 'You can do that.'

The Asian girl giggled. 'No, no,' she said, 'you don't understand. I'll only stroke your bottom if you ask me to. You have to ask me nicely, or I won't do it.'

Lucy swallowed. This wasn't the sort of situation she was used to. Asmita's warm fingers were making little movements at the perimeter of her arse-cheeks, and Lucy found that she couldn't resist the urge to wriggle slightly, at the same time parting her thighs as unnoticeably as she could. She took a deep breath.

'Asmita,' she said with a slight tremor, 'would you please massage my bottom?'

'With pleasure, Lucy,' Asmita replied, moving her hands in diminishing circles that ended with her fingertips tickling the smooth sensitive areas on the lower inner slope of each buttock. 'Perhaps, in a few minutes,' she added after a while, 'you would like to ask me to smack your bottom?'

'Mmmm, yes,' was all that Lucy could say.

'And after that, if you ask me very nicely and remember

to say please, perhaps, I'll do the same things for your titties?'

Lucy sighed. In for a penny, in for a pound, she thought. Perhaps I'll find out some more about this place. And anyway, this feels heavenly. 'Yes, please, Asmita,' she said. 'Please smack my bottom.' She spread her legs apart and lifted her arse off the bench. 'Do anything you want, but please don't stop doing it.'

When Darren returned with tea on a tray, Jem was posing in her underwear. The semi-transparent bra barely covered her small but well-rounded breasts and the matching briefs hid only her triangle of dark red curls. The lace that trimmed both garments and her narrow suspender belt added a subtle touch, she thought, and her fortuitous choice of white undies perfectly complemented the black of Miss Morelli's brief garments. Jem was standing as Miss Morelli had directed, with one leg bent and her arms raised, her hands tousling her auburn curls.

She pouted at the muscle-bound boy. The tea-tray trembled.

'Well, Darren,' Miss Morelli said, 'what do you think?'

'Very nice, Miss Morelli. Should I put this down?'

'Yes, yes, of course. Stupid boy. On the table. That's right. Now back to business. I want your opinion, Darren.'

'She's a bit of all right, Miss Morelli, she really is. A bit on the small side, I suppose, if she weren't in them heels, but not dumpy, not at all. Nice slim legs, beautiful bum, tits aren't very big but they're a lovely-shaped couple of handfuls, if you see what I mean.'

'Yes, Darren, thank you. Very graphic. And what about her face? Her hair?'

'Beautiful hair, Miss Morelli. I think Mr Headman would go for that. And he'd like her boat race, too. She looks sort of cocky – cheeky, I suppose. It's a good face – small and round.'

'Heart-shaped,' Jem broke in, 'is the usual description. Are you both through dissecting me?'

'No,' Miss Morelli said bluntly. 'Turn round. Is that a tattoo on your hip?'

'Only a little one,' Jem said, 'and it doesn't say anything naughty – not unless you know what the letters stand for.'

'I'm really not interested, Jem. My only concern is whether Mr Headman will object to it. I don't think he will. You'll do, I think, in terms of appearance. Now we'll do some practical exercises. Come here; kneel on the floor in front of me.'

Jem opened her mouth to protest, but then she remembered that she would never meet Terence Headman unless she satisfied his tall, supercilious assistant. Anyway, she thought, as she sank to her knees and found herself gazing at the triangle of lace that covered Miss Morelli's prominent mount of Venus, this might be interesting.

'Put your hands behind your back, Jem,' Miss Morelli said, stepping forward so that her crotch was only centimetres from Jem's face and her thighs remained slightly parted. 'That's right. And you must remember to say "Yes, Miss Morelli" each time I tell you to do something.'

'Yes, Miss Morelli,' Jem said, breathing in the heady mixture of spicy perfume and body scents that emanated from the junction of the two long tanned legs before her.

'Darren,' Miss Morelli ordered, 'go and stand behind Jem. That's it. And now I want you to play with those titties you like so much. One in each hand. Keep your arms behind your back, Jem dear. I don't want you interfering with Darren's games. That's a very lovely little bra, isn't it, Darren? But surely you can play more roughly than that? Give those breasts a proper working-over, Darren. Keep those nipples erect!'

Jem bit her lip. Darren's thick fingers were kneading her breasts, returning incessantly to rub and pinch her upright nipples through the flimsy fabric of the bra. It was not an altogether unpleasant sensation, but it made concentration difficult.

'Now, Jem,' Miss Morelli said, her voice a little hoarse, 'I want you to remove this G-string I'm wearing – without using your hands, of course.'

Jem moaned, and tried vainly to shake herself free of Darren's relentless fingers. She knew she could move her hands, but they remained behind her back as though tied together. 'Yes, Miss Morelli,' she remembered to say, and leant forward, her forehead brushing the satin skin of Miss Morelli's flat belly and her lips searching for the strip of elasticated lace that held up the black triangle.

Miss Morelli smelt wild and exotic. Her skin had a warm, earthy odour; the perfume that rose from her tightly-curled black pubic hair was heavy and sophisticated. As Jem's lips pulled down the tiny garment and her nose slid deeply into the slowly revealed bush of black curls, she became more and more aware of the tangy smell of womanly sex that underlay all the other odours. There's no point in hurrying this, Jem thought, shuddering slightly as Darren squeezed both of her breasts simultaneously; she pulled the thin waistband away from Miss Morelli's pelvis, released it suddenly with a snap that made the tall woman flinch, and proceeded to plant a series of little kisses in the warm furrows between Miss Morelli's crotch and thighs.

She felt Miss Morelli's hand on her head, playing with her hair. 'Very good, Jem,' Miss Morelli said in an uncharacteristically gentle voice. 'You show initiative. But really, my dear, you should attend to the main business. I think I can undress myself from here. Both of you, stop what you're doing.'

Darren's hands were removed from Jem's mauled breasts. She watched as Miss Morelli slid the G-string down her long legs and stepped out of the black circles of lace. Jem felt a pang of disappointment as the tall woman stepped backward, removing her enticing body from the vicinity of her eager lips.

Miss Morelli arranged herself on the *chaise longue* with one golden sandal on the floor and the other on the seat, and rested one crimson-nailed hand between her widely-parted thighs. 'Now I'm going to watch,' she said. 'Let's see how hot you can make me, shall we? Jem darling, stay where you are, but turn to one side a little. And Darren, come and stand in front of her. Perfect!'

Jem found herself nose to crotch with the muscular lad. The bulge in his shorts had grown to an alarming size, and he was having some difficulty keeping still. 'The same procedure, Jem,' Miss Morelli called out, 'but this time it's freestyle. Let's see what you can do with a big boy's equipment.'

Jem raised her head, grasped the waistband of Darren's shorts between her teeth, and pulled down. An arc of skin, paler than the suntanned stomach, was revealed. Jem shuffled sideways and repeated the procedure. Darren, anxious to be helpful, began to turn round in small increments so that Jem was not obliged to circumnavigate him on her knees. Soon the shorts were half-way down Darren's hips. His pale, hard-muscled buttocks were protruding cheekily above the waistband, and Jem had not resisted the temptation to kiss and nibble them at every opportunity, drawing embarrassed shivers and whimpers from the boy.

Now Jem was faced with a problem. She was unable to drag the shorts any further down Darren's legs: at the front the waistband remained hooked over the boy's hard protuberance, and yanking at the stubborn garment with her teeth only caused Darren to writhe in pleasurable discomfort. She mastered the urge to unclasp her hands, and glanced towards the *chaise longue*. Miss Morelli lifted a languid eyebrow and moved her hand from her crotch as if to demonstrate that Jem's efforts had so far failed to arouse her.

Jem returned to her task. The front of Darren's shorts, supported by his burgeoning pole, had become pulled away from his groin. Kneeling as tall as she could, Jem peered down into the gap between flesh and nylon and saw, in the darkness, the thick set of the youth's penis emerging from a mass of blond hairs. So much for the expensive make-up job, she thought, and pushed her face in to the chink. Her left cheek pressed against the hard smoothness of the concave stomach; her right cheek was abraded by the waistband of the shorts. Her nostrils were assailed by the mingled odours of talcum powder and male sex. She pushed on, using twists and turns of her head to widen the gap between groin and shorts, until her lips made contact with the pulsating rigidity of Darren's prick. Then, almost lifting the youth from his feet as she stretched the waistband to its limit, she jerked her head away from his body until the shorts were clear of the end of his imprisoned member. The elastic waistband snapped back around the tops of his thighs, capturing his testicles in its firm embrace. With commendable restraint, Darren merely uttered a low groan of pain; his unfettered penis, apparently unaffected by this assault, stood proudly to attention only a few inches from Jem's face.

'Bravo!' Miss Morrelli commented, a little ironically. 'Well done, Jem. Now what?'

The next bit's easy, Jem said to herself; I've had more than enough practice with Rudi during the last few weeks. And, regardless of previous instructions, she raised hands to yank down Darren's shorts and clasp his tight buttocks. With deliberate care she pulled his thick truncheon inch by inch into her mouth, simultaneously insinuating a finger into the crinkled orifice of his bottom.

Who's a big boy, then, she thought, as Darren's prick touched the back of her throat before her lips had encountered even a stray hair of his pubic bush. And who's got an easy-access arsehole, too? I wonder who's been up there on a regular basis? Terence Headman? Or is the Morelli woman a dildo freak?

She pulled away from him until only the velvet plum was in her mouth and only the tip of her finger was encircled by his anus; she lapped with her tongue at the underside of his helmet, and vibrated her fingertip. She felt his body jerk, and realised that he wouldn't be able to stand that sort of treatment for long, so she pulled him deeply into her mouth again, even more slowly than before, and pushed two fingers into his arse.

He's going to come soon, Jem thought; I wonder what Miss Morelli would consider a suitable finale? I can fix my make-up, but I really don't want spunk in my hair. Then she noticed the odour of Miss Morelli's heavy perfume, and glanced to one side to find that the long-limbed woman was kneeling next to her.

'Very good indeed, Jem,' Miss Morelli said in a conspiratorial whisper. 'He seems to be enjoying this. Please carry on; I don't think he's quite ready for his climax. He has very sensitive testicles, but as you seem to have your

43

hands and mouth rather full, I'll deal with his balls. You just keep sucking, my dear.'

Leaving two fingers firmly in Darren's arse, Jem slid her lips to the end of his pole and gently licked and kissed the little slit at the tip. In this way she was able to watch Miss Morelli's hand close around the youth's bulging, wrinkled sac, and appreciate the sudden muscular spasm that accompanied his desperate groan.

'He loves this,' Miss Morellil said, in a voice that suggested command rather than mere comment; she started to flick her fingers against the bottom of his scrotum, almost as if she were chucking a baby's chin. Jem wriggled her fingers inside the youth's anal passage, and circled his helmet with her tongue while she watched the increasingly violent movements of Miss Morelli's fingers, which were now slapping upwards with regular sharp smacks that made Darren's balls bounce all over the place, eliciting loud cries of distress. 'Now,' Miss Morelli shouted, 'now, Jem, suck him off!'

Jem closed her lips around the shaft, pressed the helmet against the roof of her mouth, gave flickering licks to the flanged edge of the plum, and then sucked. Darren gave a long, ragged wail, and during it Jem realised that her fingers were pushing in and out of his arse at exactly the same rate and with much the same violence as Miss Morelli's fingers were smacking against his balls. And then a flood of semen burst into her throat, and then another, and another, so close together that she had difficulty swallowing them. She began to pull away, but Darren pre-empted her. With a cry that was almost a sob, he turned and fled from the room.

Jem was left on her knees, swallowing to dilute the salty taste of semen that filled her mouth. Beside her, Miss Morellli was kneeling too, with one hand still between her wide-spread thighs.

'Oh dear,' Miss Morelli said, turning to look at Jem with bright eyes, 'Darren is such a naughty boy. I'll have to punish him for running away like that.'

'I expect he'll enjoy it,' Jem said.

'Oh yes, I'm sure he will. And so will I. I've certainly

enjoyed your performance. Look.' Miss Morelli lifted her hand and, surprisingly coyly, moved her legs together. Jem saw that her fingers were wet from tip to palm; she inhaled the strong smell of female secretions. 'I'm very pleased with you, Jem. I only wish I could keep you here. But I'm sure Mr Headman will ask to see you. I'll give you a glowing report. Now then: would you like to suck my fingers clean? There's a good girl. Do you like the taste? Excellent. You'll find there's plenty more where that came from.'

It had not taken long for Julia to re-adjust. The chauffeur had had to tie her across the bonnet of the Rolls to prevent her moving while he alternated between spanking and caressing the dark and succulent fruit between her legs; but once she had accomplished the arduous climb to orgasm – which came at last with screams and laughter and, as required, copious weeping – she felt that she had reached a plateau from which she had no desire to descend. Laid out before her was another country: a wild, unpredictable place, exotic and mysterious, and yet a landscape in which she felt completely at home.

After that, she enjoyed every minute. The Private House seemed unchanged since her last visit; she recognised some of the other staff. Her room had oak wainscotting and furnishings of brown and gold fabrics; from the east-facing window she saw an avenue of chestnuts that disappeared into a belt of woodland beyond which, she realised, was hidden the health club that had been for her, as for so many others, the first experience of the Private House. At the edge of the panorama, not far from her window, she could see just the easternmost tower of the old castle, ivy-covered and mysterious, ominous and yet picturesque. Her little room already felt like home, and she was so delighted that she hugged the buxom maid who had escorted her there. Then, remembering where she was, she laughed, and changed the hug into a passionate embrace; she pulled the giggling girl by the nipples towards the four-poster bed.

Half an hour later the maid said that it was time for Julia to prepare herself to report for duty. 'I seem to be undressed already, Maxine,' Julia said, 'but do please stay and help me on with my things.'

With much tickling and kissing, Julia first dressed Maxine. The maid wore the standard uniform that Julia remembered: a black voile blouse with white collar and cuffs, and a short flared skirt of stiff black satin, both worn over a black waist-length corset with open bra cups and long suspenders to hold up black fishnet stockings. Pointed-toed ankle boots and a head-dress of white lace completed the outfit.

It's quite wrong for her, Julia thought. I'd look marvellous as a French maid, I've got the right sort of looks. But she's lovely anyway.

She turned Maxine to face away from her, buried her face in the girl's mass of deep brown hair, and reached forward to cup the huge and heavy breasts that jiggled so delightfully beneath their thin covering of voile.

'Don't be starting all that again,' the maid said. 'We've still to dress you in your finery. Although I don't know that a maid's uniform wouldn't suit you best of all.'

'I'll be your maid, Maxine. Would you like that?'

'Don't tempt me, Miss. Let's get you dressed.'

It was only as Maxine was pulling tight the laces of Julia's boots that Julia's fears about the Private House started to resurface. She inspected her reflection in the wood-framed full-length mirror and wondered what her role would be. She had been looking forward to a few weeks of continuous sexual activity, but she knew that the courtesans were usually clothed in gloriously-coloured silks and satins; she didn't understand her new uniform at all.

The black lace added a touch of refinement, she thought, but it was only a touch: apart from the full-length gloves, which consisted only of black lace, the material was used elsewhere merely as a decorative frill. The tunic was of black leather, as were the thigh-length boots, the rather uncomfortable choker, and the wide belt that constricted her waist as tightly as any corset. The entire ensemble isn't even very sexy, she complained to herself; the tunic can be buttoned all the way up my neck, it's got this ridiculous tall stiff collar, and it almost covers my bottom. If it weren't for the cutaways at the thighs no one would be able to see any of my naughty bits.

She ran her fingers along the choker, and swore. The pointed studs were really quite sharp. And she was not at all happy about the sturdy metal rings that were inset all round both the choker and the belt.

'Maxine,' she said, 'I've got a nasty feeling about this uniform. It doesn't look as though it's designed for having fun, does it? And I'm sure I've seen it somewhere before.'

'Well of course you've seen it before, you big silly. You've seen it here. And you're right to say it's not for having fun. That's the uniform that the Security wears. It looks like you're in the private army of the Private House this time.'

'The Private House is a specific place, Jem – or, to be more accurate, it is several specific places. But it is also an institution and a frame of mind, and so in a sense it is everywhere. Mr Headman has invited you to the Private House as his special guest, and I don't think I can adequately emphasise that such an invitation is an unusual honour. But be warned; if you accept, and go to the Private House, you will find it very difficult to leave, and you will certainly not be permitted to make public anything that you find there.'

Such were the terms of Miss Morelli's offer. Jem had accepted, of course, and had kept her reservations to herself. I'm a reporter, she had protested inwardly, or at least I'm pretending to be one, and Mike McKenzie's depending on me to save Executive Environments by publicising something scandalous about Terence Headman. Mixed with Jem's exultation at her success in gaining access to Headman's inner sanctum were other emotions: intrigue and excitement about the mysterious Private House, to the extent that she had to admit to herself that she would have accepted the invitation even if she had had no ulterior motives. She had the disquieting feeling that the more she seemed to be closing in on Headman, the more their places were really reversed.

Jem had had plenty of time to think and no opportunity to ask questions. Naked but for a fur-lined one-piece flying suit, she had been whisked in a limousine from Headman's office to his city heliport, where a small two-seater helicopter had been waiting for her. The pilot, wearing an expensive pin-striped business suit and an incongruous crash helmet, had said nothing as Jem clambered into the cockpit and had glanced at her only once, when handing her a crash helmet similar to his. He had said nothing since; conversation was in any case impossible, because the all-encompassing helmets blocked out every sound except for the dull chatter of the rotor blades.

The helicopter had sped westward, towards the setting sun. Soon the glass towers of the city were replaced by the neat lines of suburban roofs, densely-packed at first but then no more than brick-red tendrils lying across green fields; and at last there was nothing unrolling beneath the helicopter but a rural carpet of woodlands, farms and villages.

Jem had pulled open the Velcro strap at her left wrist before she remembered that her watch, along with her clothes and all her equipment, was locked in a strongbox in the helicopter's tiny hold; she wondered when she would see it again. She wondered how long she'd been airborne. It wouldn't help to know, she realised; she didn't know how fast the helicopter flew, and in any case the pilot had been following a zig-zag course that Jem suspected was designed to disorient her and to avoid recognisable landmarks such as motorways and large towns.

The helicopter was descending gradually, heading towards a dark green landscape of motley woods and parkland. Something crackled electronically next to Jem's ears – a radio built into the crash helmet, she realised, just as the pilot's deep voice boomed from the speakers.

'Welcome to the Private House, Jem. We're approaching the edge of the estate. Better take off that silly jumpsuit you're wearing – not the right sort of get-up at all.'

Jem was getting used to undressing on demand. She unbuckled her safety belt, tore apart the strips of Velcro, and wriggled out of the flying suit. Naked but for the crash helmet and a pair of sandals, she strapped herself into her seat, crossed her legs, and turned to look at the pilot. Her gaze met eyes as blue as hers. His face looked weather-beaten, and his thin lips were set in a half-smile that appeared habitual.

'You're Terence Headman,' Jem exclaimed, the words blurting from her lips as soon as the idea had sprung into her mind.

'As my guest, Jem, you have certain privileges,' said the amused voice in her ears, 'but at the Private House I am Mr Headman at the very least, and usually addressed simply as "Master". Is that understood?'

'Sure. I mean, yes, Master. So is that the Private House?'

The helicopter was swooping over the moss-encrusted slates of a Jacobean country house surrounded by a walled garden.

'That is one aspect of the Private House, certainly. Don't cross your arms; I want to be able to see your breasts. That's better. That property is the health club known as the Private House; it occupies one corner of the estate. I believe it was once a gate-house.'

'So all of this is still your spread, er – Master?'

'Indeed it is. It extends almost as far as you can see in all directions, and it includes woods, pasture, a few farms, various other buildings and, of course, the House itself. You can see the rooftops over that avenue of oaks.'

'Are we going to land there?'

'No, the airfield is further west. Jem, you must learn to sit properly. You are a delightfully attractive young woman, and clearly very talented, but I expect more than just a pretty face and a ready wit. You are here at my pleasure, Jem, and I expect you to take the trouble to look sexually provocative at all times. There is no turning back now. Understood?'

'Yes, your Mastership.'

'Very well then. Back straight; head up; hands together at the back of your neck. Chest out; tummy in; legs apart – more than that! – and feet pointing down with toes touching the floor, so that your thighs are clear of the seat. That's much better. Now stay like that until we land. And no more talking!'

The landing-strip was lined with aircraft and vehicles.

Along one side of the tarmac, ranged in front of a complex of modern buildings, were several Land Rovers, a Porsche, various estate cars, two Cessna light aeroplanes, and commercial vehicles in a range of sizes; on the other, symbolically separated from the up-to-date machines and nearer to the site of the House, was a working museum of antique cars and lorries, including a 1930s Bentley sports car, a vintage Rolls-Royce, and a number of trucks that would have been obsolete in the Second World War.

Jem was helped from the helicopter by a young man in chauffeur's livery who removed the crash helmet from her head. With some difficulty, because of the swirling winds caused by the still-spinning rotor, he wrapped a long black cloak around her, and led her into the glass-fronted reception hall and into the waiting arms of Terence Headman.

Jem, feeling suddenly very small and helpless, looked up into Headman's ice-blue eyes. He smells nice, she thought, and he's got strong arms and a very tasteful silk tie and black hair which is going a little grey at his temples which are attractively high and very white teeth . . .

'Jem,' Headman said, 'kiss me.'

Jem lifted her head and pressed her open mouth against his lips. His tongue touched hers just as his left hand moulded itself round her right breast; she pressed her body against his, and shivered as his thumb flicked back and forth across her nipple. He raised his head and spoke to the chauffeur above Jem's tousled curls.

'You received the fax? And the video transmission of Jem's audition?'

For a fleeting moment Jem wanted to protest, but Headman hugged her to his chest while using the hand that he had insinuated inside the cloak to caress her back and buttocks. The idea was for me to get him on tape, she reflected, not vice versa; but she found it difficult to maintain a sense of disappointment. Headman lifted her chin, kissed her lightly, put his arm around her shoulders, and led her along a passage into another building.

Here, at last, was something like a real office. Young men in tail-coats looked out of place in front of computer terminals; young women festooned with chains and leather thongs answered continuously-ringing telephones. Through the smoked-glass windows Jem saw the contents of articulated trucks being unloaded into cavernous warehouses. A short woman with tightly curled red hair put down her telephone and stepped forward to meet Headman. She was dressed like a St Trinian's schoolgirl, with a skirt short enough to reveal that she was wearing no knickers, but given the general state of undress in the room, she looked almost respectable.

'Master,' she said, 'it's good to see you again.'

'It's good to be back, Rhoda. The city's getting less and less bearable. But soon we'll be able to handle almost everything from here. And I've brought back a prize: this is Jem.'

'I'm very pleased to meet you, Jem. She's lovely, Master; prettier in the flesh even than on video. Wherever did you find her?'

'You know my methods, Rhoda, but in this case I must admit that Jem found me. Is everything running smoothly here?'

'Of course, Master.' Jem was sure she detected a note of flustered exasperation in Rhoda's voice. 'We're moving out of construction, and showing a good profit on every transaction. We're keeping the personal handles, of course, in case we want to move back in. The office services operation is almost complete; we've still to mop up one or two of the companies that were doing well against the trend. Robert and his team have started on life-style retailing: it's going through a bad patch, and there are several big players who would benefit from our particular brand of commercial investment.'

'That sounds reasonable, Rhoda – although I haven't seen a proposal paper from Robert. He's getting almost too keen. Remind me to have a word with him. And I'm not happy about office services; I wanted that finished by now. I want a schedule of the current position first thing tomorrow morning.'

'Of course, Master.'

'Don't sulk, Rhoda. You've done well. Jem – give Rhoda a cuddle to make her feel better.'

Jem stepped uncertainly towards the plump redhead. She and Rhoda were the same height, and as their eyes met they both grinned suddenly. Rhoda slipped her arms inside Jem's cloak and clasped Jem around the waist, one hand sliding unerringly into the furrow between Jem's buttocks and delving into the moist hollow between her thighs. Jem gasped, and her mouth sought Rhoda's as the redhead almost lifted her off her feet. Headman's voice broke in.

'That's enough, Rhoda. You've got your own staff to have fun with. As for you, Jem – you're incorrigible. Rhoda, have the wardrobe department found something for Jem?'

'Yes, Mr Headman,' said Rhoda, giving Jem a final kiss on the cheek and a pinch on the bottom before thrusting her back into her Master's arms. 'Everything's ready for her in room one-oh-nine of the hospitality suite.'

'Then I'll take Jem through myself. We both need to relax and change. Would you tell John that I'll need the Rolls in about an hour?'

'Handcuffs.'

'Yes, Chief.'

'Chain.'

'Yes, Chief.'

'Holster.'

'Yes, Chief.'

'Air pistol.'

'Yes, Chief. Chief, I don't know how to – '

'I know, Julia, I know. That what your training's all about. Marksmanship's included, as well as unarmed combat and all the rest. Hypodermic darts.'

'Yes, Chief.'

'Buzzer.'

'Yes, Chief. Chief, what is this buzzer?'

'Very useful, your buzzer is. Delivers an electric charge – adjustable from a little tingle right up to a jolt that'll knock a horse flat. Comes in very handy for impromptu interrogations, although I'm told some of the lads and lasses use their buzzers on the lowest setting for purposes that are, shall we say, therapeutic. Flicker.'

'What, Chief?'

'Your flicker. Your flexible friend. That swishy number made of plaited leather. No, don't stick it in your belt; put the loop round your wrist and carry it at the ready. Perk of the job, isn't it, dishing out little flicks to all and sundry.'

'Is it?'

'Course it is. You're in the elite now, Julia my darling. The Security Corps reports direct to the Master, through me. You can use your flicker on anyone you meet.'

'Can I now?' Julia said, experimentally slicing the air with the thin whip. 'Well, I suppose there has to be some compensation. I don't think I'm cut out for Security, Chief. There must be younger people who'd enjoy it more than I will.'

'No doubt; and I don't want them in my force.' Chief Anderson sat down heavily in his swivel chair and watched Julia as she disconsolately took her equipment from his desk and clipped each item to the correct hook on her belt. 'You're about right, as far as I'm concerned. Not too eager, a mature head on your shoulders, and coming up to the age when you could do with the exercise.'

'My body's in good shape,' Julia protested.

'I can see that. Now's the time to make sure it stays that way. And Security training'll teach you all the physical jerks you'll need, you mark my words.'

'So is that all I'm going to do, Chief? Just training?'

'Training and drill in the mornings; in the afternoons I've got some real work for you. Undercover work.'

'That certainly sounds more interesting. Is that why I haven't seen many Security people when I've been here before? Because they work incognito?'

'Partly that's it; and partly because a lot of our work's out on the estate, patrolling the grounds; and partly because we can see without being seen, thanks to the surveillance kit; and partly because Security often operates beyond the estate – although that's always in plain clothes, of course.'

When I was here before, Julia thought, Security wasn't much more than a rumour. There were obviously wheels within wheels: entire layers of the organisation of the Private House of which she had been unaware. Rumour had whispered that the Security Corps remained within the crumbling walls of the old castle, but here she was in Chief Anderson's office, and beyond the door was the Rotunda, the circular cellar of the Round Tower, beneath the very centre of the House, packed with computer terminals and video screens and efficient-looking Security personnel.

'So what's this special job, Chief? Tell me about it.'

Anderson pressed a button on his desk console. After a few seconds, there was a knock on the door. 'Enter!' he shouted.

A young woman with coffee-coloured skin and long black hair stepped into the room. She smiled at Julia and then looked questioningly at Anderson. He nodded, and the girl walked up to the side of his desk, put her hands behind her back, and pulled open the overlap of her sari. She bent forward, allowing the sari to hang on either side of her rounded bottom, and reached across the desk to grip its far side with her outstretched hands.

'This is Asmita,' Chief Anderson said, standing up and placing his left hand on the small of her back. 'She's on duty in the club, pretending to be a masseuse or some such nonsense. As you can see, she's been here before. She knows all about the flicker, don't you, Asmita? How many would you like today?'

The Asian girl's face was turned towards Julia, who saw her purse her lips in thought. 'Five please,' she said at last, 'but only if they're not too hard. I don't want any marks, you see.'

'Get your arse up, then,' Anderson said, fondling the bulge that was threatening to burst through the thin layer of gauze at his crotch. 'That's the best thing about the flicker,' he added. 'It stings, but it doesn't mark. Much better than the riding crops we used to have. Now hold still, darling.'

Asmita's light brown bum-cheeks were large and round, bisected by a cleft that was so dark it was nearly black. Almost unconsciously Julia moved a few paces to the side, so that she could see the whole expanse of the twin globes, and she was slightly disconcerted to see Asmita had turned her head to watch her. Anderson's flicker whistled, and landed with a loud crack across the tops of Asmita's thighs.

The girl flinched, and lifted her bottom higher into the air. The dark red stripe that appeared on the nut-brown skin was broken where it crossed the black grotto within which Asmita's hidden split could just be discerned.

'That's right, girl,' Anderson muttered, urging Asmita's bottom upwards with little taps of his flicker, 'you keep your arse up or you know what you'll get.' He emphasised his point with a upward flick into the dark cleft, whereupon Asmita, on tiptoe now, merely grinned more broadly and waggled her hips.

Julia was enthralled. She had watched – and participated in – plenty of punishment games during her previous visit to the Private House, and she realised that she had not lost the taste for them during her long absence. Now the mere symbols – the bent body, the taut muscles of calf and thigh, the rounded, outthrust buttocks, and the raised whip – were enough to make her randy. Conscious of Asmita's eyes on her, she slowly parted her legs and pushed two fingers into her hot, wet channel. The flicker swished again.

Asmita yelped. A second line appeared, parallel to the first and a couple of inches higher. Anderson wiped his brow. His face was flushed. 'That's set the parameters,' he panted, 'now the final three have to be equidistant and between the first two. And sharpish, too, before they start to fade. I always like to set myself a challenge, Julia, and that's a fact.'

Anderson accomplished his self-imposed task with an accuracy that hinted at long years of practice. He sank into his chair while Julia helped Asmita up, all the time caressing the smooth globes of flesh and anointing the hot stripes with the juices from her own body. The Asian girl tossed her hair and laughed as she disentangled herself from Julia's embrace. 'Chief,' she said, 'do you want me to talk about this customer or not?'

'What?' Anderson said with a start. 'Oh, yes – of course. Tell your story again, my dear, for Julia's benefit.'

'I think you tell me to repeat my story for the benefit of your flicker,' Asmita replied, 'but OK – here it is.

'I'm working in the Health Club at the moment; it's a

bore, but someone has to do it I suppose. Anyway, there were some new customers today, and one of them has been asking a lot of questions. She's taken a liking to me, and so the Chief thinks that I can find out who she really is, and what she wants.'

'And, Asmita, you'll report back to Julia here. I want the two of you to work together. I'll get you a posting to the Club, Julia, so you can get to know her too. She's calling herself Lucy Larson, although she's got no identification with her – and that's fishy by itself. We've got her on video, of course.'

Anderson pressed another button on his desk, and one of the many screens that lined the walls burst into colourful life. On the screen was a bedroom; and in it a tall young woman with golden blonde hair, an open, fresh face, and a lithe suntanned body was taking her clothes off. She discarded her blouse, and was now wearing only white briefs and a white bra. It was clear that she was slim and fit, and Julia was disappointed that she didn't release her heavy breasts or reveal the golden curls between her legs. Instead, the young blonde glanced suspiciously about her, as if she knew that she was being watched, and began to search the room, opening every drawer, moving everything moveable, inspecting every cranny.

'She didn't find the cameras, of course,' Anderson said, 'but I'd love to know what sort of customer sets about ransacking an empty bedroom as soon as she arrives at a health club.'

'A paranoiac,' Julia suggested.

'Or a spy,' Anderson said. 'And I want to know which she is. Right then, you two – you've got your instructions. Julia, my sweet, I think you'd better pretend to be a fellow customer. So change back into your ordinary clobber, go round the front way to the Club, get yourself booked in, and start chatting up this Lucy Larson. Now I've got work to do: the Master's on his way. Both of you report back here first thing tomorrow – and I'll be expecting some ideas.'

'Or else we get a flicker, I suppose?' Julia asked.

'I think we'll get that anyway,' Asmita said as they left,

'although with two Security flickers and three people we can at least ring the changes a little, can't we?'

The hospitality suite was very hospitable, Jem decided. Room 109 contained everything she could have asked for, except the answers to any of her questions. She had wallowed in the circular bath, and had then turned on the jacuzzi to restore her vitality. She had had a glass of the Dom Perignon, and had eaten with it a little of the *salade Niçoise* and warm bread. She had plundered the dressing table and had smothered herself in scented talc and Magie Noir perfume spray before carefully applying make-up to the same high standard as that which had been ruined by her foray into Darren's shorts.

She left the curtains open and watched the last red arc of the sun slide below the horizon before she switched on the discreet lights that surrounded the full-length mirror. She looked at her naked reflection. I feel beautiful, she said to herself, stretching and pirouetting. They'll be watching me, that's for sure, but who cares? So far, I'm having a whale of a time. Now let's go see what they want me to dress up in.

It was a costume of wine-red satin. The top consisted of little more than a pair of wide padded shoulders; at its back the yoke divided into two strips of gathered material which crossed each other and then curved down Jem's back and ribcage to meet again just below her navel, where they buttoned to the waistband of a short skirt. At the front similar wide strips of satin descended from the shoulders, narrowed as they parted, covering and separating Jem's tits, and then left her stomach bare as they curved down to the small of her back, coming together at the top of the cleavage between her buttocks where they too buttoned to the skirt waistband. From front to back the skirt's waistband sloped downward – its highest point was Jem's belly-button, and it ran diagonally across her hips to its lowest point, resting on the upper slopes of her bum. The skirt's hemline mirrored this slope: at the front it was merely a short skirt, the softly-pleated satin reaching the mid-point of Jem's thighs; but the hemline rose diagonally across the sides of Jem's hips so that there were only a few inches of material draped across the upper half of Jem's pert bottom.

Jem studied herself in the mirror. All very well, she thought, but as soon as I lift my arms, or stretch – there you go, the skirt lifts half-way up to my neck and the whole effect is ruined. This can't be right. What else have they stashed in this box of goodies?

She pulled at the drifts of white tissue paper in which the costume had been wrapped, and almost failed to notice the two short lengths of ribbon. They were soft and elasticated, wine-red to match the dress; each had a small hook, like those found on bras and suspender belts, at each end.

Where there are hooks, Jem reasoned, there must be eyes for them to hook into. She ran her fingers along the inside of the skirt waistband until she found the four corresponding fastenings. There were two at the back, close together, and two at the front that were wide apart, almost at the sides of the skirt. She hooked the ribbons on to the hooks inside the back of the waistband; the two red strips protruded, an inch apart, only a little below the ridiculously short skirt.

I know where they're supposed to go, Jem thought, but they don't look long enough to me. She leant forward, reached between her legs with both hands, and gripped the hanging ends of the ribbons. Then she pulled hard. With some difficulty she managed to drag the taut strips up to the inside of the waistband at her hips and to clip the hooks into the fastenings. Then she lifted the skirt and looked in the mirror.

The ribbons didn't exactly hurt; but they weren't exactly comfortable, either. Seen from the front they formed a wide V that enclosed Jem's tangle of red-brown curls and seen from the back . . . Seen from the back, Jem thought, I'm on display in this outfit. If I'm leaning backwards this skirt just about covers me; at all other times – I'm a walking invitation.

The two ribbons converged, but did not touch, as they entered the cleft of Jem's peach-like arse. The strips of tense elastic held apart the round cheeks, exposing and framing the puckered pink hole between them and, below it, the split swelling and its rich covering of hair.

Jem stretched and turned, watching her reflection in the mirror. The ribbons served their purpose: the skirt remained in its position, resting on Jem's hips and arse, whichever way she moved, and the strain was taken by the slight stretchiness of the satin material that criss-crossed her torso. And whenever she moved, she felt the taut ribbons between her legs and buttocks, and the soft satin sliding across her breasts. As long as I'm wearing this number, she thought, it's going to be difficult to wrap my mind around anything but sex.

In the bottom of the tissue-filled box Jem found a pair of wine-red shoes with wedge heels and satin bows at the heels; and three more satin ribbons with ready-tied bows, which she fastened round her wrists and her throat. I look like a chorus girl from an Eddie Cantor movie, she thought, except that even chorus girls were allowed to wear knickers.

Behind her, the door opened.

Terence Headman was no longer wearing a pin-striped suit. He no longer looked like a city businessman. He was dressed in the uniform he had created for his role as Commander-in-Chief of the Security Corps, and therefore his costume resembled the one Julia had changed into only a few hours earlier. He had no lace gloves, but gauntlets of black leather that matched his boots and tunic. And unlike Julia's, his outfit included gold-braided epaulettes and a black codpiece of extraordinary dimensions. Hanging on a loop round his right wrist was a length of plaited leather, and he was carrying a cloak over his arm.

'Why, Master,' Jem said, 'what a big cricket box you have.'

'All the better for impressing the staff,' Headman replied with his usual half-smile. 'You look as stunning as I anticipated, Jem. Turn round and bend over. Legs apart, hands on knees.'

Jem bent forward, but lifted her head to watch him in the mirror as he approached. His icy eyes surveyed her body; his fists clenched and unclenched as he walked, highlighting

59

the muscles in his bare arms. Jem was more aware than ever of the tight strips that were pulling apart her buttocks. She flinched as a gloved finger touched the lips of her sex, and started to move into her, pushing the lips aside to reveal the moist interior.

'This is an exceptionally eloquent costume, Jem,' Headman said thoughtfully. 'What, do you imagine, is it saying to me?'

The finger was wriggling forward; it was almost at her clitoris. She could not help the movement of her hips. 'I guess – ah! – I guess it's saying, Fuck me, Master.'

'I think it probably is,' Headman said, sliding his finger backwards between Jem's labia and up to the stretched hole of her anus. 'What else might it say, Jem?'

Jem took a deep breath. 'Fuck my arsehole, maybe,' she suggested.

'That's also very likely,' Headman went on, resting his gloved palm on the roundness of Jem's right buttock. 'What else?'

'What's left? Whip me, Master? Is that it?'

'I expect so, Jem. I expect we'll try all three, later on.'

'But not necessarily in that order,' Jem said. 'I'd like to get the whipping over with before I start having fun. If that's OK with you, Master. Can I stand up now?'

'Yes, it's time to go to the House. This cloak is for you.'

'Thanks, Master. What happens at the House?'

'The usual welcome-home party, I imagine. I like to celebrate on my first evening home. There will be a banquet, followed by various entertainments, considerable over-indulgence in alcohol and other narcotics, and then a general sexual mêlée, I should think. You will sit beside me on the top table, of course.'

'Sounds like a good time.'

'I think perhaps that for once I won't want to stay to the end. I want to respond to your earlier suggestions, my dear; and I don't want to share you with others, as yet. Shall we go?'

'By all means, Master. Hey – how'd your hand get in there?'

'A design feature of your cloak, Jem. The slit seems to be in exactly the right place, wouldn't you say?'

Headman's right glove, and his whip, were in his left hand; his right hand was inside Jem's cloak, and much of it was inside Jem. 'You know, Jem,' he said, 'you really are quite special.'

Jem said nothing, and squeezed her muscles around his fingers and thumb. But she was thinking: Soon you'll find out just how special, Terry baby.

DAY FOUR: *WEDNESDAY*

Never again. I must never again pop amyl nitrate while drinking champagne, particularly after a six-course meal. This resolution was the one fixed point in Jem's whirling thoughts as she struggled to open her eyes.

Why did I have to stay to the end of the banquet, she asked herself plaintively. Because I wanted to drink Headman under the table, she told herself sternly as her consciousness reasserted itself. And it had worked: I kept him interested all evening, but by half-past one this morning the only bedroom activity he could manage was to fall asleep.

Jem snuggled under the quilted eiderdown and tried to remember everything that had happened the previous evening. The banquet had been held in the Great Hall – an appropriate name for the vast vaulted room that occupied most of the ground floor of the Round Tower. Headman, with his right hand still nestling between Jem's thighs, had entered the hall like an emperor with a captive queen. The doors had been thrown open to a fanfare of trumpets, and the procession had marched into the already crowded room.

First had come a double line of naked young men, each one holding aloft a flaming torch with a right arm as stiff and upright as his tumescent cock; then a Security Corps squad, black leather uniforms highly polished and glinting in the torchlight. Behind them came a team of slaves, six slender women with long blonde hair, thigh-high boots of red leather, and naked except for the red harnesses strapped across their torsos; they had been pulling the open coach in which Headman and Jem had been standing. A deafening roar had exploded from the crowd in the hall as the coach had crossed the threshold; Headman had acknowledged the greeting with an inclination of his head and a private smile. Jem had almost forgotten about the delicious sensations that his fingers had been causing under her cloak as she had gazed in awe at the magnificence of the thronged hall.

Headman had lifted his gloved left hand to demand silence, and had made a short speech, at the end of which he had introduced Jem as his latest acquisition. His left hand had unfastened Jem's cloak and had swept it from her shoulders, whereupon a gasp of appreciation had arisen from the crowd. Only when the hubbub had faded had he slowly pulled Jem towards him, revealing to the spectators Jem's exposed arse and his right hand embedded inside her; as his lips had met hers, a thunderous cheer had erupted and echoed from the stone vault.

Headman had lifted Jem into his arms and had carried her from the coach, and they had made their way across the flagstones towards the raised platform on which stood the Master's table. They had made slow progress: Headman had stopped at each of the lower tables to chat to his staff and to display Jem. Some of the revellers, overcome either with affection for their Master or with the wine that had already been freely flowing, had offered their bodies to Headman; he had addressed a passing remark to one particularly striking beauty with waist-length black hair, and she, at a loss for a reply, had torn open her bodice and begged him to use his whip on her mountainous white breasts. One of the waiters, a youth with his sexual equipment displayed on the wooden tray that was tied round his hips, had thrown himself at Headman's feet and had asked very courteously if he might suck the Master's cock. Headman had availed himself of some of these offers, and meanwhile other guests had been availing themselves of Jem.

She had lost count of the number of embraces she was pulled into; the countless hungry mouths that had sought her lips, the countless hands, some rough and some gentle, that had roamed across her body, pinched her nipples,

64

slapped her bottom, and fumbled at the wetness between her legs. She had surrendered to every caress, her mind reeling with the constant stream of compliments and lewd suggestions whispered into her ears, her body responding with small, trembling orgasms as the Master's minions vied to touch his latest consort.

At last they had reached the dais, and Jem had lowered her tingling sex on to the velvet cushions of the seat that had been reserved for her alongside Headman's ornate throne. At last she had had a chance to survey her surroundings, and she had found herself gazing down at a sea of semi-naked revellers. It had seemed as though every inhabitant of the Private House had gathered for the party. Hundreds of men and women, clad in colourful, exaggerated, revealing costumes, had been seated at long tables; many more, wearing even fewer clothes, had been scurrying between the tables with trays of food and wine, or standing to attention as human torch-bearers at the bases of the stone columns, or waiting in the side-aisles to make their appearance during the entertainments.

For the first few hours, while the main courses of dinner had been served, a sense of decorum had been maintained. The waiters and waitresses, certainly, had been treated as fair game from the very start of the banquet, and the diners had missed no opportunity to grab and caress the breasts, bottoms and penises that the waiting staff could not help but offer whenever they had approached a table to ladle soup or pour champagne. The diners themselves, however, had taken their lead from the top table, and had restrained the urge to indulge their passions to the full.

The entrance of the entertainers had proved to be the turning point. Jem, who by this time had moved to sit on Headman's lap and had been busy manipulating the prodigious length of his tool while nibbling a strawberry that he held between his teeth, had suddenly noticed a lull in the cacophony. Turning, she had watched the entertainers, cloaked in scarlet, as they had stepped in silent procession to the clear space in the centre of the hall. In the gallery musicians began to play, quietly at first but with a pulsating beat. And the first of the entertainers had started to disrobe.

The striptease had been artfully contrived; the tall creature who had removed every item of clothing, except for a bow tie, black boots, and a red G-string, was the master of ceremonies, and Jem had been unable to tell which sex he or she belonged to. Some of the other entertainers had been easier to classify as they had slowly revealed their bodies at the start of each act: one of the men, a short, curly-haired satyr, had had an organ of massively priapic proportions; two of the women, apparently identical twins, had proudly revealed quivering breasts the size of footballs supported by shelf-like corsets that narrowed to impossibly thin waists. Most of the entertainers had simply been beautiful: lithe, muscular young people who had performed sexual gymnastics of increasingly bewildering complexity.

Audience participation had been encouraged: both guests and servants had been drawn into the entertainers' antics. There had been several games: the master of ceremonies had urged guests with agile tongues to attempt to excite the clitoris of a haughty-looking Amazon he called The Ice Queen, and a queue of men and women had come to kneel before her throne and bury their faces between her spread thighs. In another competition, waitresses had been lined up and instructed to remain still while a team of clowns inserted vibrating dildos into their vaginas; the winner had been the waitress whose tray had rattled least, and her prizes had been the dildo and a seat at the top table.

The acts had become more and more convoluted. As the waiters had cleared the tables, and the guests had begun to improvise their own tableaux of interlocking bodies, the master of ceremonies had announced a lion-taming act. Six flame-haired gymnasts, their bodies painted with leopard's spots, had been put through their sexual paces as the music rose to a crescendo.

The orgy had paused when the music had suddenly ceased. And the master of ceremonies had announced the climactic act of the evening – a human sacrifice. He had asked the audience for a volunteer: he wanted a young woman, he had said, who would be flogged into insensibility and then ritually stabbed. And then he had looked straight towards Jem.

Safe now in her bed, Jem still shuddered as she remembered the chill that had gripped her heart at that moment. Have they discovered me, she had thought wildly. Do they know I'm a spy? Are they really going to execute me?

But the master of ceremonies had merely been looking towards the Master for approval to continue; having received a nod from Headman, his eyes had started to rove across the audience. There had been volunteers: women had shrieked, torn off the remains of their gaudy gowns, and scrambled forwards. The master of ceremonies had ignored them. He – Jem was sure now that he was a man – had stalked among the silent guests, searching out the shrinking violets, the youngest, prettiest women with downcast eyes and shivering limbs. He had wanted, it seemed, only a truly unwilling victim. He had stopped in front of a cowering beauty; and had grasped a handful of her long blonde curls.

She had started to scream only when two muscular youths had started to chain her to the wooden frame that had been wheeled into the centre of the hall. By the time she was spreadeagled, her feet barely touching the floor and her arms stretched above her head, her sobs had been the only sounds that could be heard in the electric silence. The executioner, a huge black man with muscles that rippled beneath his oiled ebony skin, had then made his entrance. His face had been concealed behind a black mask, and in his hand he had carried a snake of black leather.

For ten minutes, while the blonde writhed desperately in her chains, the executioner demonstrated his skill with the whip. He had cracked it back and forth above his head, each report as deafening as a gunshot and each echoed by a yelp from his prospective victim. He had used the whip as a lasso, and had plucked bottles from the hands of inebriated revellers. He had flicked the whip with such accuracy that he had extinguished cigarettes with its tip. Each demonstration had drawn cheers and applause from the audience, and the clamour had quietened only when the masked giant had at last positioned himself at the side of the wooden frame. He had waited until the entire audience had remembered his deadly intention; he had waited until, once again, the only sounds in the hall had been the sobs and pleas of the blonde captive. Then he had raised the whip and struck.

The girl had screamed; several people in the audience had screamed too. But as far as Jem had been able to see, the girl's body had not been marked. As the whip had whistled again, and again, and the blonde had flinched and yelped at each stroke, and yet no angry stripes had appeared on her, Jem had begun to suspect that the whole thing was a charade. Some of the audience, too, had started to catcall and whistle.

And then Jem had seen it: a deep pink blush had started to suffuse the blonde's undulating buttocks. The big black man had been employing all of his considerable skill merely to skim and flick those rounded, tempting, swivelling targets. The girl had stopped yelling, and each stroke had begun to elicit a gasp of shock instead of a cry of pain. With sweat streaming down his torso, the masked man had shifted his position, delivering a series of upward cuts that had grazed the undersides of the girl's breasts. And then he had moved again, to stand behind her, and he had continued the upward strokes, each of which had flicked between her widely spread legs so that the tip of the whip had just touched the insides of her thighs, and the undersides of her buttocks, and the soft flesh of her sex. The hall had been silent but for the barely audible swish of black leather and the girl's regular moans. The executioner had been killing her with kindness, and the raucous crescendo of gasps that had started to issue from her throat had seemed to indicate that she had been near to orgasm. At that point the master of ceremonies had intervened.

'The flogging is satisfactory,' he had announced. 'A round of applause, please, for the masked executioner . . . Thank you, thank you, ladies and gentlemen. And now – the ritual stabbing. As you will see, the executioner has a formidable dagger. Shall he plunge it into the body of our sacrificial victim? Yes? Or perhaps . . .' and here he had paused, and opened his arms to indicate the top table, '. . . perhaps you, Master, would care to deliver the *coup de grâce*?'

And as Terence Headman had started to rise from his throne, Jem had realised that unless she acted immediately, she might lose whatever slight influence she had gained over him. She had tightened her grip on his upright manhood. 'This dagger's mine,' she had whispered as she bit his ear, 'and you can do all of that to me – later.'

Headman had hesitated, but Jem had not stopped fondling the engorged bulb at the top of his stem; he had laughed quietly, and had made a gesture to indicate that the executioner had his permission to continue. As the giant, urged on by the cheers of the crowd, had stabbed his dagger of black flesh between the blonde's reddened arse-cheeks, Jem had matched his strokes with the movements of her hands, and had whispered into the Master's ear a vivid description of how she would spread her legs and stick out her bottom for him and for him alone.

The strategy had worked. From that moment there had been no doubt, if there had been any previously, that Headman desired to do with Jem every single one of the sexual exercises that they had watched during the banquet. In fact the problem had turned out to be preventing him from carrying her off immediately to his chamber. Jem had reasoned that she would have to ration herself: Headman must not be allowed to slake his lust for her, in case he then abandoned her, thus preventing her from carrying out her undercover operation. And so Jem had prevaricated, insisting that she wanted to stay until the banquet ended, pointing out that Headman had a duty to stay too, suggesting that they should have just one more little drink, and giving many little kisses and squeezes to his ever-erect prick.

Towards the end of evening, long after midnight, when most of the revellers had disappeared under the tables in an indiscriminate jumble of sexual activity, a waiter appeared beside Headman's throne. Jem, on her knees between Headman's legs, had looked up: the young man, his face flushed and his nipples bright red from the tweakings they

69

had received, had pushed his pelvis forward. His hands had been tied behind his back and, like many of the waiters, the tray that he had been carrying had been secured to the front of his thighs by straps that ran over his shoulders, round his waist, and up the cleavage of his bottom. His penis, half erect and glistening wetly from the recent attentions of one of the guests, had lain twitching on the hairy sac of his scrotum, which in turn had been resting on the surface of the tray. Surrounding his manhood Jem had seen an array of glass phials, screwed-up papers, and fat cigarettes – an assortment of soft drugs. Jem had reached up to fondle his left buttock, and had pulled back her head to release Headman's organ from her mouth. 'Master,' she had said, as seductively as she could, 'this will feel even better if we both try a little amyl.' And before he had had time to protest she had squirmed on to his lap, and had kissed him, and had broken open an ampoule under their noses.

And after that, Jem thought, I really don't remember very much. But we didn't do anything except fall asleep, which means that Headman hasn't had me yet, and so – I hope – he still wants me, and therefore – I think – everything's going according to plan.

She threw back the covers and looked at her room for the first time. In shape it was a quarter-circle, with windows in the curved wall. The Round Tower, Jem thought; it seems to be where Headman hangs out, and I guess this room's part of it too. The walls are made of stone blocks; can this be part of a medieval castle? Is all of the House as old as this? Only one way to find out, Jem told herself, and jumped, naked, out of bed.

She crossed an expanse of Persian carpet to inspect her face in the dressing table mirror. She didn't like what she saw, but the dressing table contained an arsenal of cosmetics, and she set about repointing the cracks in the facade. Through the arches of the window she could see, stretching away to right and left, the rooftops of the two main wings of the House; they looked old, but more recent than the stonework of the tower. Between them, in the distance, were the manicured lawns and flower beds of a formal garden, crisscrossed with gravel paths and dotted with summerhouses, fantastic pavilions, pergolas and banks of shrubs. Brightly-dressed figures meandered along the paths in the hazy sunshine.

Jem set off on another expedition across the chamber, and reached a door. She opened it and peered out into a deserted corridor. That was no good; she'd been hoping for a bathroom. She went to the other side of the room, and tried the only other door: this one led into a bathroom. It was a thin room, and much smaller than the bedchamber; only about as large as a normal bathroom, in fact.

When she returned to the bedchamber, the room was no longer deserted. A maid with downcast eyes and clasped hands was standing in the middle of the carpet. Jem could tell she was a maid by her uniform: the white mob-cap that failed to contain her light brown hair, and the white apron that she wore over her short black skirt. She looked up as Jem approached, and gave a hesitant smile and a quick curtsey.

'Good morning, Ma'am,' she said. 'I'm Jenny. Is there anything I can do for you? Breakfast?'

'Orange juice,' Jem replied decisively. 'And coffee. Maybe a piece of toast. And some clothes? I want to get out and look around.'

'There are clothes in the wardrobe, Ma'am. I can find others if they're not suitable. Will you take breakfast here in your room? Or shall I help you to dress first?'

'I can handle getting dressed. Just bring me the breakfast – and fast, OK?'

'Yes, Ma'am,' Jenny said, and fled from the room.

Jem opened the door of the vast rococo cupboard to reveal an array of coloured silks and satins. Most of the garments were underwear, and Jem selected a bra that consisted of little more than two triangles of apricot silk, a matching suspender belt, and pale cream stockings. There were few clothes that were suitable for exploring a country estate, but Jem found a pair of black ankle-boots with almost sensible heels, and a black leather jacket that was long enough to just cover her stocking-tops. She laced up the boots and draped the jacket over her shoulders. There was a knock on the door.

71

'Enter!' Jem called, and arranged herself comfortably on one of the tapestry-covered settees. Jenny, carrying a tray, pushed open the door and stood uncertainly on the threshold, scanning the room for a table. Jem watched the maid's half-open lips and her wide dark eyes darting back and forth; she looked like a lost puppy. Jem spoke as if to a wayward pet.

'Here, girl! Put that on the floor, just here. Now kneel next to me. That's right. Now pour me some juice and coffee.'

Jem sipped her orange juice and looked down at the maid. 'Jenny!' she said, and the girl jumped. 'What are you wearing under that uniform?'

'Nothing, Ma'am. Is that alright?'

'We'll see. Get undressed! Did I tell you to stand? Stay where you are. I can see well enough.'

Jenny pulled the cap from her head and shook her wavy brown hair so that it fell to her shoulders. There's nothing very sexual about this, Jem thought as the maid unbuttoned her blouse to reveal small high-nippled breasts; the thrill is in having the power to make her do it – to make her kneel and expose herself while I sit and enjoy my breakfast. I've never felt anything quite like this before; this place of Headman's must be getting to me. Executive Environments? It seems a lifetime away. Just an unimportant part of a large operation; an annoying little company doing well against the trend; small fry that can't hope to evade Headman's net for very much longer. Does Headman really care what happens to Mike McKenzie? Do I?

The girl was naked. She had a small, slim, pale-skinned body, with very rounded buttocks. Jem bit into a slice of toast. 'Come here,' she said, 'and kneel in front of me. No, the other way – facing the door. I want to see your arse. Keep your legs apart and lean forward.'

Now this is getting sexy, Jem thought as she spread her own legs, nudging Jenny's ankles further apart with the tips of her ankle boots. The maid's sex-pouch was almost hairless, and the puckered skin of her deep anus was dark brown. 'Now, Jenny: put your right hand between your legs,' Jem said steadily. The girl lowered her head until her

72

hair was brushing the carpet. Jem saw a timid hand appear between Jenny's slim thighs to cover the split flesh. She drained her coffee cup.

'Don't hide it, Jenny. I want to see. Open yourself, girl! Show me your cunt. That's better. And now put your fingers inside . . . Very good. Play with yourself, Jenny. Make yourself wet. This is more interesting than breakfast television, that's for sure.'

As she watched the maid's fingers move in and out of the increasingly moist slot, Jem found her own hand straying into her lap. Her fingertips came to rest at the apex of her slit, pressing very gently on the area above the hood of her clitoris. She shivered.

'Your left hand, Jenny,' she ordered, 'put it behind your back . . . And now slide it between your buttocks – and put your thumb up your arsehole. Quickly!'

The maid groaned as her thumb disappeared into the dark opening. Jem rose from the settee and stood astride Jenny's back, clenching the girl's ribcage between her knees. She leant and seized the girl's left nipple between finger and thumb. 'You're a well-trained servant,' Jem whispered, twisting the nipple savagely as she spoke. 'I'm going out in a moment, and I want you to bring yourself off before I leave. So keep those fingers moving, OK?'

Jem stood back to watch the maid's performance and to listen to the growing harshness of her breathing and then turned and went into the bathroom.

When Jem emerged, Jenny was lying on the carpet in a foetal position. Her head was thrown back, her eyes were closed, and her lips were parted, moist, and moving slightly. Both hands were still trapped between her thighs. Jem zipped up the leather jacket and left the room.

As needles of hot water drummed against her skin and the cubicle became filled with warm steam, Julia found that she was able to think about something other than the muscular ache that seemed to extend from her neck to her toes. And the first thought that floated into her mind was the rueful realisation that being slim is not at all the same thing as being fit.

She felt half-dead. The warming-up exercises had left her exhausted, and then there had been circuit training, and weights, and a cross-country run. And the morning was still only half-way through. She would have to endure two hours of unarmed combat before she could dress herself again in her Security leathers and report to Chief Anderson. Compared to a sweaty track suit and muddy plimsolls, even a stiff, creaking Security uniform seemed comfortable, and a session with the Chief and his flicker would be infinitely preferable to charging across cow-fields followed by Instructor Peterson bellowing orders from his Land Rover.

Julia shook water from her eyes and turned off the tap. As she towelled her tired limbs, she thought that she could already detect a firmness, a definition of the muscles that had not been noticeable the day before. She felt suddenly proud of herself, and reinvigorated. The prospect of bending over Chief Anderson's desk and responding to the flicks of his flicker and the thrusts of his member was now quite definitely more attractive than worrying.

'Trainee squad!' It was Instructor Peterson's roar. 'Get yourselves out of those showers and report for unarmed combat now! Instructor Goltz is waiting for you in the gym! It's the building at the base of the Sallyport Tower. Get moving!'

Julia wrapped her towel about her body and joined the half-dozen other weary trainees who were scurrying out of the shower block and into the inner bailey of the old castle. I hate to admit it, Julia said to herself, but I think I'm beginning to enjoy this.

The receptionist – a middle-aged man in a uniform that looked like a Hollywood costume for the part of Jeeves – was very polite, but really was unable to say where the masseuse Asmita might be found this morning. Would Madam like him to procure the services of an alternative masseuse?

Lucy, equally polite, declined the offer: she had already spotted Asmita's name and room number written in the register behind the reception counter. She ambled across the hall, turned past a vast parlour palm, looked back to make sure that she couldn't be seen, and pelted up the stairs.

The room was at the end of the first floor landing. Lucy didn't bother to slow down: her shoulder hit the venerable panelling with a power born of years of police training and drug busts. The door, which had not been locked, flew open, and Lucy landed on her hands and knees on the carpet.

She looked up to meet the amazed stare of a naked man. He was sitting astride both a long, narrow table and the head of the woman strapped to the table top. His hands were covering her breasts, and his hairy buttocks were obscuring her face, but Lucy instantly recognised Asmita's lissome brown body.

'You filthy bastard!' she growled and launched herself at him.

The man had no time to move. Lucy's left fist sank into his midriff; her right arm locked around his neck. His spectacles flew across the room and he managed only to gasp a few feeble protests as he fell to the foor. Lucy landed on him with all her weight, pinioned his arms behind his back, and began to push his face into the deep pile of the Axminster.

Filled with rage and with the familiarity of police training, Lucy had almost suffocated her victim before she heard Asmita's anguished appeals. She stood up, delivered a final kick to the man's ribs, and turned to rescue her adored masseuse.

'Lucy,' Asmita said with a broad smile, 'what on earth do you think you're doing?'

Lucy put her hands on her hips, recovering her breath as she gazed down at the prone body of her friend. Asmita was secured to the table with leather straps across her ankles, her thighs, her waist and forearms, and her shoulders; only her head could move. 'Rescuing you, of course,' Lucy panted at last.

'Close the door,' Asmita said.

Lucy started to cross the room, and then turned back; she realised that Asmita wasn't responding as she'd expected a damsel saved from distress to respond.

'Go on!' Asmita urged. 'Close the door before someone comes.'

Lucy shrugged and closed the door. 'This bloke – ' she started.

'It's alright. He's a customer. He likes to tie me up when we do sixty-nine. That's alright, isn't it?'

'Is it?' Lucy was dumbfounded. 'I mean, well, yes, if you say so. I mean, no, it isn't. What do you mean, a customer? He pays you? Is that what this Private House thing is a cover for – just a knocking shop?'

Asmita sighed and shook her head. The man, having dragged himself across the carpet to retrieve his glasses, was now huddled in a corner of the room and staring fearfully at the blonde Amazon. Lucy had forgotten him. Her anger had dissipated, and she found that the sight of the Asian girl's imprisoned limbs was stirring feelings that distracted her train of investigative thought.

'What is this place, Asmita?' Lucy said, stroking the girl's long dark hair and her soft brown throat. 'Tell me the secret of the Private House. This isn't just a health and fitness club, is it?'

Asmita sighed again. 'I can't tell you, Lucy. Really, I can't. I don't want to, but even if I did . . . Anyway – what about you? There's more to you than meets the eye, I think. I've never come across a customer here who knows how to flatten someone the way you just did. That looked very professional.' She flashed the mischievous grin that never failed to melt Lucy's heart.

'I'd better stop you talking,' Lucy whispered, and lowered her mouth on to Asmita's smiling lips. 'I can kiss you all morning, and you can't do a thing to stop me.'

'That's – mmm – very – ohh – very nice,' Asmita gasped in the spaces between Lucy's determined kisses, 'but – mmm, Lucy, stop a minute! – I want more than this. Kiss me with your other lips, Lucy, please. That will keep my mouth occupied, won't it? I'd love to lick you. Get undressed and sit on my face.'

Within seconds Lucy was naked and straddling the table. All thoughts of investigating the Private House had, for the moment, fled; her mind was occupied with the sensations of Asmita's snub little nose nestling into the cleft between her arse-cheeks, and Asmita's tongue darting in and out of her lower mouth. Lucy shivered, and ran her hands up her stomach to cup the hard mounds of her tits. She tossed her head, and suddenly caught sight of the naked man sitting in the corner. Her eyes were bright and owlish behind his spectacles, and his hands were gripping his vertical member. Lucy frowned, but Asmita's tongue had parted her inner lips, and Lucy suddenly didn't care who was watching. She rolled her arse and then leant forward to press her love button against Asmita's pearly lower teeth. The Asian girl produced a muffled moan.

'What's that, Asmita my sweet?' Lucy said, her fingers rolling the girl's large, dark aureoles from side to side. 'You'd like me to squeeze your nipples? Of course I will. Harder than that? Oh yes – with pleasure, my darling . . . Just don't stop licking . . . Yes . . . Just there . . . I think I'm going to come . . .'

When Lucy opened her eyes, the man had gone. Reluctantly, she lifted herself from Asmita's face. She knelt beside the table and started to undo the strap around the girl's shoulders, all the time tenderly licking her salty juice from the smiling features she so dearly loved. 'I'd like to ride your face all day,' she whispered, 'but then you'd never be able to answer any questions. This is the strangest health club I've ever been to. You must tell me what's going on here, my little brown darling.'

Asmita raised her freed arms and hugged Lucy, flattening the blonde's soft breasts against her own smaller cones. 'I can't tell you anything about the Private House, Lucy. Really I can't. But I will tell you one small secret. I'll whisper it: there is someone else here who is perhaps on your side.'

'What do you mean? Who?'

'Another guest. She arrived this morning. Like you, she seems – I don't know – a bit different from the usual guests. And she's asking a lot of questions.'

Lucy's thoughts whirled. Who could this be? Another police officer? Was there an official investigation going on?

Was that why the Chief Inspector had tried to persuade her not to come here? Or was this a private detective? Whoever she was, this woman might be an ally. 'What's her name, Asmita dearest?'

'I don't know. But you'll like her – she's very pretty! Maybe I shouldn't have told you.'

'Never fear, my little dark angel. She couldn't replace you. But what does she look like?'

'She's very slim, with dark eyes and dark curly hair. She looks like a sort of petite gypsy. About your age, I suppose. You'll be able to spot her. She's the only new guest who's arrived today.'

'Thank you, Asmita. You're wonderful. Will you get into trouble for telling me about her?'

The Asian girl glanced from side to side, as if there might be eavesdroppers behind the furniture. 'Oh no,' she said, 'I don't think so.' And she gave a secretive smile.

The oak-panelled corridors were almost deserted. Jem glanced through the few open doorways, and occasionally disturbed servants at their chores – folding linen, polishing furniture, carrying trays of drinks. Each maid bobbed a curtsey, and each manservant bowed. Seems I'm a VIP, Jem said to herself; and then she saw a face she recognised.

The previous evening, at the banquet, Jem had noticed a hawk-nosed, patrician-looking gentleman sitting a few seats distant from her at the high table. Then he had been wearing the frockcoat and lace cuffs of a Restoration dandy, and with an aloof manner he had required several of the waiters and waitresses to service his rampant desires; now he wore nothing but a dirty apron, and he kept his gaze downcast as Jem strode towards him. He cringed as Jem halted in front of him, and he answered her questions in a quiet and respectful voice.

'Yes, Ma'am, I was at table with you last night. Yesterday a nobleman, today a servant. That's how it is in the Private House. How are the mighty fallen, one might say. And who am I to question the Master's whim?'

'What did you do to incur the Master's displeasure?' Jem asked, realising as she did so that she was beginning to ape the archaic language that the servants, in particular, seemed to use.

'Nothing, Ma'am, of which I am aware. But I had enjoyed the privileges of a guest for many months. Perhaps it was time for a change.'

'Does everyone change places, then, from time to time?'

'Everyone except the Master, Ma'am. I used to be the Chief Systems Engineer; I installed the new stock control and accounting software at the control complex.' A note of pride had crept into his voice.

'The buildings on the far side of the airstrip? The warehouses and offices?'

'Exactly so, Ma'am. Forgive me for speaking of such things in the House. And now – now I'm in charge of polishing the silverware.' A worried frown creased his forehead. 'I have no complaint, Ma'am; I mean no disrespect.'

'Don't worry, chum. I get more of a buzz from software than silverware myself. But you mean I could get you into trouble, talking to you about this stuff?'

The man scanned the ceiling beams with his deep-set eyes. 'Not here, Ma'am: I know the location of all the microphones that were on the system when I did some work on the Security computer, and the nearest is in yonder candelabrum. I don't think any more have been planted since then. So unless you intend to report me to Security . . .'

'Not right now.'

'Thank you, Ma'am. It has already been a trying morning. Several of my former rivals, having been informed of my diminished state, have already summoned me to their rooms and have exacted their particular forms of revenge.' He turned away from Jem. His naked back was streaked with lash-marks; his buttocks were fiery red; and a thick metal shaft, held in place by three tight chains, protruded from between his arse-cheeks.

He turned back and gave Jem a twisted smile. 'My services have already been called on several times this morning, Ma'am, but if there is anything I can do for you . . .' He gestured towards the front of his apron, which was beginning to rise upward. 'As you can see, it is difficult to resist the charms of so beautiful a Mistress.'

'What's your name, chum?'

'Sebastian, Ma'am.'

'I like you, Sebastian. Let's talk again – if you can show me another place with a microphone deficiency.'

'I'll be happy to oblige, Ma'am. Might I suggest . . .'

'Suggest away, Sebastian.'

The servant's voice dropped to a murmur. 'I suggest, Jem of the sea-blue eyes, that we'd have fun fucking each other senseless even if we weren't in this crazy establishment, but,' he resumed his deferential tone, 'on a more practical note, if you want to see the estate you'll need a vehicle. The Master's fleet is parked in the north courtyard, between the west wing and the old castle wall. Through the door on the right at the end of the corridor, Ma'am.'

'Why, thank you, Sebastian – for both of those lovely suggestions.' Jem stretched up to place a kiss on his nose, and marched off to find a car.

It was only when she reached the courtyard that Jem began to appreciate the size and antiquity of the Private House. The cobbled yard was as wide as a football pitch, but nonetheless gloomy because buildings surrounded it on three sides. Jem zipped up her leather jacket. Behind her the west wing of the House rose in a confusion of galleries and gables that indicated the many styles and stages of building that the House had undergone over the centuries; from the westernmost corner of the edifice a high brick wall encrusted with outbuildings stretched away for about a hundred metres. To Jem's right the courtyard narrowed almost to a point; but where the apex of the angle should have been there was instead a section of curved wall with a heavy door set into it. Looking up, Jem saw that the curved wall was a small part of the massive circumference of the Round Tower.

She gazed in awe at the huge cylinder of stone. It dominated the courtyard; it was twice as tall as the rooftops of the west wing of the House. It was the biggest castle tower Jem had ever seen.

Half-way up the sheer column she saw mullioned windows like the one in her bedchamber. My room is on the other side, she thought, but it must be on the same level as those windows, because from my room I can see southwards across the rooftops of the House. How many floors are there below mine? The Great Hall takes up most of one level, immediately below mine; then what? A ground floor, maybe a crypt, too? And above my floor – another two storeys, and then the battlements? I guess that's Headman's private quarters. He sure lives in one hell of a phallic symbol!

Opposite Jem, more sheds and single-storey structures clung to a decrepit wall that ran westwards from the Round Tower and ended, about fifty metres away, at a smaller, ruined tower. Jem realised that she was looking at part of the curtain wall of a medieval fortress.

The ruined tower marked the end of the courtyard: beyond it a tarmac track humped over a small bridge and ran parallel to the tall brick wall, forking into two roads as it ran out of the wall's shadow and into the sunshine.

Well, I'd like to know what goes on within the old castle walls, Jem thought; but I'll save it for later. For now, let's go cruising in one of these buggies.

The courtyard was a museum of ancient motor vehicles. Jem finally chose a little black roadster with wire wheels and a soft top: an MG TC, looking only a little less immaculate than when it had been first driven in 1946. Jem turned the ignition key, pulled out the choke and twisted the starter; to her surprise, the engine caught first time, and with a grin she hauled on the wooden steering wheel and pointed the long bonnet towards the sunlight at the end of the courtyard.

Now this is what I call motoring, Jem yelled into the wind as the little car bounced over the bridge that crossed a sluggish stream; the roar of the engine, the breeze in my hair, and the cool roughness of well-used leather upholstery pressing against my bare bottom.

The car sped out into summer sunshine, and Jem braked and turned left at the fork in the road. To her left, the high brick wall continued southwards; she guessed that it enclosed the formal gardens she had seen from her window. Between the wall and the road a wilderness garden sloped down to a distant shimmering lake. To Jem's right was dense woodland.

Within seconds Jem had reached another fork in the road. The MG screeched to a stop. The left-hand track zig-zagged downhill, southwards to the far side of the lake and the meadows beyond it; the right-hand track went westwards, into the woods, along the ridge that overlooked the low-lying farmlands, and towards two isolated towers. Jem spent a few minutes trying to memorise the lay-out of the panorama, and marvelling at the extent of Headman's estate; then she turned right.

With no plan in mind other than to look round Headman's domain, Jem drove towards the first building she saw: she glimpsed chimneys through the tree-tops, and swung the car up the gravelled track that ran between the trees.

In a clearing in the woods, the track widened into a square courtyard enclosed on three sides by brick buildings. Jem parked the MG between an Austin Seven and a lime-green coach from the 1950s.

The two side buildings were long and low, with regularly-spaced sash windows; they were connected by a larger, two storey structure in the same style but with three open doorways in the facade and a belfry on the roof. The buildings reminded Jem of something – an old-fashioned hospital, perhaps – but when she walked towards the central structure she saw the signs engraved on the stone lintels of the doorways, and she knew where she was. Above the central doorway was the word *STAFF*; the two smallers doorways were labelled *BOYS* and *GIRLS*. Back to schooldays, Jem thought as she skipped up the steps and into the staff entrance.

Floor polish and chalk dust. I didn't even attend a school like this, Jem thought; those smells must be part of the collective unconscious. She crossed the lobby, pushed open the double doors, and peered into a long corridor. Polished parquet, cream-painted walls, dust motes in the sunlight, indistinct and distant voices, a bluebottle buzzing at one of the windows – it was a perfect replica of a small grammar school. She turned back and noticed the brass plaque on the other door that led from the lobby: *NO ADMIT-TANCE. STAFF ONLY*. Jem hated to be told where not to go. She opened the door.

At the top of a flight of stairs Jem opened another door and found herself in a room full of recording equipment. A young man in Security leathers was staring at an array of video screens. As Jem's heels clicked on the floorboards he swivelled his chair to face her. His hands were clenched round a massive erection.

'What the blazes are you doing up here?' he hissed. 'This is a restricted – oh. I'm sorry. You're, um – you're the Master's . . . um . . .'

He was a pretty, dark-haired young man, with a slim body and full red lips. Jem walked up to him and held out her hand. 'Call me Jem,' she said. 'Whatever you're watching, it must be pretty good.'

The man took his right hand from the tip of his penis, hesitated, grinned, and offered it to Jem. 'I'm Dave,' he said, his left hand blatantly caressing his hard shaft as Jem shook his right and then raised it to her lips. 'There's only one lesson today – in Room Six. I'm taping it.'

'Can I watch?' Jem asked.

'Be my guest,' Dave said, 'but there's only one chair.'

'Oh dear. Guess I'll have to sit on your lap.'

Dave leant back and lifted his hands to stroke Jem's buttocks as she lowered herself on to him. She clasped his upright member between her thighs, placing one hand at the back of his neck and the other around the bulbous red helmet that protruded in front of her red-brown pubic curls. He unzipped her jacket and cupped her left breast in his long slim fingers. 'You're gorgeous, Jem,' he said, and lifted his face to meet her kiss.

For several minutes they were still, except for their constantly moving hands and tongues. Jem began to squirm as Dave's fingers roamed across her breasts, alternately caressing and pinching, sending tickles and stabs of pleasure through her body. At last Dave freed his lips from Jem's. 'Let's watch some TV,' he said, shaking his head. 'If we carry on like this – well, I have to be very careful not to get spunk on the console.'

Jem laughed. 'OK. Can we have the sound up?'

'Sure.'

Four of the video screens were in operation, showing four views of the same classroom. On the first screen Jem saw the whole room as if she were sitting in the back row of desks: half a dozen male pupils, wearing maroon caps and blazers, were seated at desks near the front of the class, facing away from the camera and towards the dais on which stood a table, a blackboard, and a schoolmistress.

The second screen gave a close-up view of the teachers' dais; and the other two displayed pictures that must have been generated by cameras positioned at the two sides of the room. The teacher was a young, dark-haired woman with luminous, wide brown eyes. She was wearing a mortarboard, a black gown, and white stockings and suspender belt. The pupils were middle-aged men, ridiculous in short trousers and too-tight blazers, with peaked caps perched on heads of greying hair.

They were not a well-behaved class. The teacher's big brown eyes filled with tears as the pupils ignored her ineffectual pleas for silence. Paper aeroplanes swooped past her head; howls and catcalls greeted her every word. Above the cacophony Jem heard shouted suggestions: 'Miss! Miss! Can you show us physical exercises again, Miss?' and 'Miss! I've hurt my willy, Miss! Come and kiss it better, Miss!'

Jem nuzzled Dave's neck as she felt his thumb exploring the valley between her buttocks. 'Those men . . .' she said.

'The schoolboys? They're crazy, aren't they?'

'But I know some of them. I mean, I've seen them, I know of them. That one there – the one who's got his prick out – he was on the cover of *Marketing* just a few weeks ago. He's a director of – one of the High Street multiples. I can't remember his name . . .'

'Don't worry about it. Everyone here is someone else outside. He seems to be enjoying himself. Even the guests who have to be persuaded to come here soon forget about the outside world. I'll bet you're different outside.'

'Wrong – ah!' Jem vibrated inside as Dave's thumb penetrated her anus and his fingers slid into her sopping sex. 'Outside, I'm just like this,' she purred.

'Look,' Dave said, nodding towards the screens, 'the Head's turned up.'

A figure in a billowing black gown swept into the classroom. The Headmistress was as old as the pupils, but tall and slender. Her grey hair was pinned in a tight bun and her black corset gleamed; the microphones picked up the swish of her cane in the silence that fell as soon as she stormed through the door.

'Quiet!' she bellowed, unnecessarily. 'Class 4B! Have you taken leave of your senses? I will not tolerate this kind of behaviour!'

The pupils cowered as she scanned the classroom with a malevolent stare. The Headmistress turned to the teacher. 'Miss Howard,' she said through gritted teeth, 'how many times must I tell you to keep your class under control? Come to my office at lunchtime. I can see you still need more practical instruction in the matter of discipline.'

The young schoolteacher blushed and hung her head, and the schoolboy who had exposed himself sniggered loudly. The Headmistress fixed him with a murderous glare. 'You!' she barked. 'Yes, you, sonny. The one with exhibitionist tendencies. Stand up. What's your name, boy?'

'Smith, Miss,' said the grey-haired executive, managing a convincing impersonation of a snivelling urchin.

'You're a filthy little child, Smith. What are you?'

'A filthy little child, Miss,' he stammered, his apparent distress belied by the twitching of his engorged member.

'Do you know what happens to filthy little children, Smith?'

'They – they have to be punished, Miss,' Smith ventured, unable to keep a hopeful note out of his voice.

'Indeed they do, Smith. And you will be punished most severely. Come to the front of the class! Quickly, boy! And take down your shorts!'

Jem started giggling hysterically. Smith – if that was his real name, which Jem doubted – was a portly gent with a

85

silver moustache, and he looked more than a little silly in his ill-fitting maroon school uniform with his trousers round his ankles, his penis wagging as if it had a life of its own, and his face red with excitement.

The Headmistress prodded him with her cane. 'Lift those shirt-tails, Smith. And bend over the table.'

Jem's gaze flicked from screen to screen. One gave her a close-up view of Smith's plump, white, hairy bottom, quivering with anticipation; another displayed him from the front, with his arms outstretched across the desk and the two schoolteachers standing behind him.

'The boy seems somewhat over-excited,' the Headmistress commented to Miss Howard in a voice that suggested that the younger teacher was to blame. 'Would you be so kind as to look at the state of his lewd parts.'

'Yes, Headmistress,' the young woman said, and removing her mortar board and gown, she ducked under the table. The screen which showed the entire classroom was now the only one on which Jem could see her: Miss Howard had become a small silhouette, squatting under the table and reaching out for Smith's rigid organ.

'Well?' the Headmistress demanded.

'It's still very hard, Headmistress,' said the meek voice from under the table. 'His testicles are hanging very loose, and his penis seems very big indeed. And it's hot. And it's sort of leaking a bit at the end.'

On another screen, Smith could be seen perspiring and open-mouthed with wordless delight.

'The disgusting wretch!' the Headmistress exclaimed. 'Clean him up, Miss Howard. I can't punish him in this condition.'

'Shall I lick where he's leaking?' the small voice said.

'Yes, yes. Of course. Give him a good hard suck if you like. It might be for the best if he spends his filth in your mouth. It might calm him down.'

There were several minutes of silence. Jem could see the young teacher's head moving back and forth under the table and Smith's knuckles whitening as he grasped the table-edge in his growing excitement. From time to time the Headmistress would deliver a half-hearted stroke of the

86

cane to his trembling buttocks, and then she would wander among the other pupils, lashing them at random with her tongue or with the thin wooden rod.

Just when it looked as though Smith was ready to explode, Miss Howard drew away from his engorged equipment and emerged from under the table. 'It's no good, Headmistress,' she said, 'he's being very obstinate. He just won't come.'

'I abhor obstinacy,' the Headmistress intoned. She put all her strength into a blow that landed across the backs of Smith's thighs. 'Keep still, boy! I'll teach you to be obstinate, you disgusting, perverted child! I'm going to thrash your bottom until you spurt your filthy stuff out of that horrible big thing of yours. What do you think of that?'

The question was rhetorical, but Jem could see from Smith's face that he was delighted at the prospect.

'Miss Howard,' the Headmistress said as she removed her gown and flexed the cane and her muscles, 'I think you had better hold him down. Quickly, girl – on the table!'

Miss Howard scrambled on to the table and sat with her stockinged legs dangling over the side. Then, with a surprising show of strength, she pulled Smith's head into her lap and pinioned his wrists behind his back, pushing his face into the mass of dark curls at the junction of her thighs. 'Ready, Miss Howard?' the Headmistress shouted. 'Then hold on tight; and here we go!'

Jem was astonished at the speed and severity of the punishment. She flinched more than Smith did as red lines appeared with remorseless regularity across the vast globes of his buttocks. The only sounds were the fearsome hiss of the cane, the bestial grunt that the Headmistress produced as she concentrated her strength into the final vicious flick of each stroke, and the loud thwack as the cane sliced into the fleshy mounds. When no tiny area of Smith's buttocks had escaped the cane, and purple weals were beginning to appear across the bright red expanses of flesh, the Headmistress stopped. She took a deep breath and rubbed the muscles of her arm. 'Miss Howard,' she said, 'would you look below and tell me whether this boy has disgraced himself yet?'

Miss Howard leant forward, crushing Smith's face still more deeply into her crotch. 'I'm sorry, Headmistress, I don't think anything's happened. His thing's still big and hard.'

The Headmistress appeared to be on the verge of apoplexy. 'Incorrigible wretch!' she yelled. 'Do you see, Miss Howard, how wilful and stubborn a little boy can be? Stand up, both of you. You, Miss Howard, are partly to blame for this. Spare the rod and spoil the child, Miss Howard. I have no doubt your own upbringing was too lenient. And as for you, Smith – ' she grabbed his up-thrusting organ and pulled him towards her, 'don't think I'll let things rest here. You're full of disobedience, boy, but I'll beat it out of you if it takes all day!'

Smith couldn't have looked happier, but he did his best to appear dejected. 'I can't come, Miss,' he mumbled, 'my bottom hurts too much.'

'You will come, my boy, you mark my words. And if you think your bottom's sore now, you've got another think coming. Miss Howard, I'll need your help again. Would you lie on the table – with your legs apart, you silly girl!'

With a resigned expression the young teacher stretched herself across the table. Smith, encouraged by the Headmistress's slaps, scrambled between Miss Howard's open legs, and the young teacher sighed and looked away as Smith lowered his paunch on to her body. She wriggled her hips, and closed her eyes as his prick found her opening and slid into her slick interior. She lifted her legs and crossed her ankles at the small of his back and the Headmistress, now with unobscured access to the whole of Smith's lower regions, flexed her cane and took up a position behind the coupled pair.

Smith remained motionless until the first blow fell; then he jerked his body and thrust into Miss Howard. As he pulled out of her, the Headmistress's arm was descending with her second stroke. Another line of fire appeared across the dull pink globes of flesh, and Smith thrust forward again.

Seen on the video screen, his face was distorted with pain and lust, the regular lashes producing barely a flicker of emotion across his face which was already as red as his arse and twisted into a rictus of frenzied glee. Jem was enthralled, her hand slowing almost to a standstill as she petted the gaping little mouth at the tip of Dave's thigh-held stalk. How much more of this can Smith take? she wondered, and at that moment he halted in mid-thrust, and his mouth opened as if in surprise.

'This is it, Headmistress,' Miss Howard shouted. 'I think he's almost ready!' And the Headmistress redoubled her efforts, no longer paying any attention to maintaining the rhythm of her strokes nor to the tresses of hair escaping from her bun. She lashed fast and mercilessly, concentrating on the tops of his thighs and throwing in short vertical strokes that landed at random between his buttocks, on the insides of his thighs, or even across his swinging scrotal sac. Smith's frantic movements echoed the swishing of the cane as he pistoned in and out of Miss Howard with renewed vigour, and at last, with a wild howl of pain and blessed relief, and with a great shudder that shook his large frame and the table, he shot his spurts of seed into Miss Howard, and collapsed on top of her like a dead whale.

'Ow!' Jem's hand flew to her tweaked nipple. 'What was that for?'

'Concentrate on me, please, not the TV,' Dave said. 'You can watch that over and over again, if you want. Shall I make you a copy of the edited highlights?'

'No thanks. Just do that again, only more gently. That's better. Do they know they're being filmed?'

'It's hard to tell. The ones who have been here before know, of course; some of the others must guess. But what can they do? If they're here, in the Private House, they're already in too deep to get out. In for a penny, in for a pound: they might as well lie back and enjoy being captured on videotape. The field operatives know which guests are newcomers, of course.'

'Field operatives?'

'Ye gods, you're persistent.'

'Tell me or I'll stop playing with your lovely big knob.'

'You win. Emma and Clarice are field operatives – Miss Howard and the Headmistress. They organise the routines;

I just film the show, and I'm on hand to jump in if anything goes wrong.'

'You're certainly on hand today, Dave. How much more of this treatment can John Thomas take?'

'I don't know, Jem. Perhaps you'd better give him a big sloppy kiss.'

'What a wicked idea. Are you sure you wouldn't like me to spank your bare bottom, you naughty boy?'

'Quite sure, thanks. And we're going to have to kiss and say goodbye, anyway. I have to adjust all the gear for shooting a history lesson in Room Nine. Come on – get up, Jem, I have to move.'

Jem kissed him, stood up, and made for the door. 'So long,' she said, 'I guess I'd better continue my tour of the estate. See you around!'

'I hope so,' Dave said. 'If you want to know the time, ask a Security man.'

Security, thought Jem as she descended the stairs and walked back to the MG. Where would I find the Security headquarters? Inside the walls of the old castle, that's where. Let's go and take a look.

She pointed the little roadster back towards the House, but instead of turning towards the courtyard she continued along the track that led north alongside the stream and towards the mound on which stood the battered remains of the castle's square keep. At the base of the mound the road turned sharply to the right, and the MG stopped at a gap in the castle's curtain wall. A wooden barrier extended across the gap, but the Security sentry recognised Jem, lifted the barrier, and waved her on, into a vast hexagonal yard full of huts, vehicles, and leather-clad Security personnel. She was inside the walls of the oldest part of the Private House.

Julia sat on the wooden bar and plucked at her sweat-soaked garments. She was alone in the gymnasium, which was one of several in the sports complex that sprawled at the base of the old castle's Sallyport Tower. In the distance she could hear the shrieks and laughter of her fellow trainees in the showers, and from elsewhere the erratic ricochets of a ball game.

Unarmed combat training had been surprisingly enjoyable, she reflected. Instructor Goltz was a hard taskmistress whose plimsole-slap was as vicious as her tongue, but she had taken a lot of trouble to explain and demonstrate the techniques to Julia, and Julia had found that she had rapidly picked up the rudiments of judo throws and the disarming of attackers. Although she was the newest recruit, and was smaller, slimmer and older than most of the rest of the class, she had found that by the end of the session she had been throwing her opponents more often than they had been throwing her. Instructor Goltz had commented on her progress, and in the last few minutes it had been Geoffrey, a skinny lad with a slight stammer, rather than Julia who had been the victim in the game of 'chase and kick' that, the other trainees told Julia, was a regular feature of Goltz's class.

Goltz had told her to stay in the gym for some individual tuition; and Julia had been rather pleased with herself until several of the trainees had whispered comments like "tough luck" as they had escaped to the safety of the showers. Now, as she cast her eyes round the bleak and clinical walls, she wondered what the Instructor had in store for her; and then she spotted a figure standing in the viewing gallery.

How long's she been up there? Julia wondered. That's not a Security uniform . . . I know! It's the Master's new consort. She looks terrific. I wish I could get out of here. I don't know what Goltz is up to, but with that woman watching . . . It's going to be so humiliating! Oh God, she's definitely seen me; she's waving.

Half-heartedly, Julia returned the greeting. The auburn-haired beauty in the gallery grinned. Julia turned away. Instructor Goltz crashed through the swing doors.

Goltz was a big woman, tall and athletic and full of energy. She fixed Julia with a steady stare and advanced slowly towards her on the balls of her feet. In her right fist she continuously flexed the battered plimsole that was never out of her grasp. Julia stood up and stepped hesitantly backwards.

'Don't run away, little one,' Goltz said, smiling broadly.

'We're going to have some more fun. You've still a lot to learn.'

Julia stood still, trying to control her rising panic. Goltz was so much bigger and stronger than her; Goltz could do anything. Julia didn't dare to look across to the gallery; she just prayed that the Master's consort had gone and that no one would witness her fear and weakness.

Goltz's helmet of cropped blonde hair advanced relentlessly. The Instructor stopped in front of Julia and stood with her plimsole-flexing hand behind her back. 'Now then, girlie,' she said, 'it's just you and me. And I'm one-handed, see? So come on – attack me!'

Maybe it will be alright, Julia thought. Maybe she just wants to teach me some more moves. And Julia reached for Goltz's collar and swept her right foot towards Goltz's legs.

The Instructor had moved; she had side-stepped and advanced and turned before Julia could begin to regain her balance.

Julia felt herself being lifted into the air as Goltz's hand grabbed the waistband of her track suit trousers and Julia flailed her arms, attempting to stay upright. There was a sound of tearing cotton and Julia was sliding head-first towards the mat, naked from the waist down, leaving her trousers in Goltz's clenched fist.

Julia lay on the floor. There was an ominous silence. She lifted herself to her hands and knees; Goltz's plimsole splatted against her buttocks and sent her sprawling. Tears filled her eyes.

'Come on, girlie,' Goltz said through gritted teeth. 'On your feet! I haven't finished with you yet; not by a long way. Up! And come at me again.'

Julia dragged herself to her feet, turned, and stepped towards the Instructor. Goltz jumped aside, tripped Julia's feet, grabbed her arm as she fell, and twisted her wrist up to the back of her neck, clutching a handful of Julia's black curls in the same fist.

Julia screamed. Her shoulder and the roots of her hair were competitive centres of agony. She staggered as Goltz thrust her forward, bending her over the wooden bar that crossed the gym; once again the plimsole crashed against her bare backside, shaking the bar with the force of the blow.

Goltz's hands released her. She shook tears from her eyes and breathed deeply, hanging limply over the bar. She felt the plimsole probing the crease between her buttocks. 'Lovely bum,' Goltz said. 'I think you need a great deal more training, girlie. Stand up or I'll whack you again.'

You'll whack me anyway, Julia thought, and threw herself backwards towards the sound of Goltz's gloating voice. The back of her head struck something hard. She reeled, and her eyes focused at last on Goltz, standing with her hand to her chin and a dazed expression on her face.

Julia moved backward, warily, a step at a time. The exit was on the far side of the gym, beyond the Instructor. A look of concentrated malice replaced the surprise in Goltz's glittering blue eyes. Julia ran.

Made it! she thought, as her hand touched the door. And then a hand grabbed her shirt and she found herself whirling in a circle that ended in a collision with the wallbars. She dropped to the floor, and felt herself being dragged to the centre of the gym. She tried to stand, but her legs were kicked from beneath her. An arm went under her torso, and lifted her to her knees. She tried to scurry away – and the plimsole slammed upwards between her legs, lifting her and then propelling her face-down across the floor.

She lay still. The pain was so all-encompassing that she hardly felt it. She was past hope, but past desperation too: nothing mattered anymore, except to get away, curl up, find somewhere warm. She started to drag herself across the floor.

A foot stood on her spine. 'Oh!' Goltz said, in a friendly voice. 'You'd like some more, would you?' And Julia could only wail helplessly as she felt the arm around her waist lifting her to her knees again. She didn't try to move; she waited for the blow to fall.

The plimsole didn't hit her. Instead, she felt the shock of something landing on the gymnasium floor, and heard a voice shout 'That's enough!' She lifted her head to see the Master's consort standing, hands on hips, below the gallery.

Instructor Goltz was advancing towards her. 'Get out!' Goltz said. 'This is a private training session.'

The leather-jacketed redhead didn't move; she just smiled. 'Do you know who I am?' she asked.

'No, sweetheart,' Goltz replied, 'and I don't care. You could be the Queen of Sheba but if you don't get out of here now I'll give you a lesson too. Understood?'

Julia managed to sit up. The Master's consort was looking decidedly less confident as Goltz strode towards her, fists swinging. She raised her hands as if preparing a karate strike, and Goltz laughed softly. She started to circle the room towards Julia. Goltz pursued her steadily.

Julia felt hands grasping her under the arms. She moaned. 'Stand up, for God's sake,' whispered a voice in her ear. 'This woman can make mincemeat of me, but if you can clobber her while she's not looking, we might both get away.'

Julia staggered to her feet to find Instructor Goltz only an arm's length away, staring at the auburn intruder. 'I know you now, sweetheart,' Goltz said. 'You're the Master's new tart. He won't save you if you tangle with me. He appointed me personally. I'm a volunteer, not like most of the scum in this place. Get out now or I'll bruise your bottom for you.'

The Master's consort backed away. 'I'm not going without her,' she said, 'and if you lay a finger on me Terence will flay you alive.' And in the moment of shocked silence that followed her use of the Master's real name, the leather-jacketed young woman hurled herself at Goltz in a whirlwind of pointed toes and clawed hands. The Instructor took a step back – and Julia had only to extend her foot and pull the back of Goltz's shirt. The tall woman toppled backwards like a felled tree, and Julia twisted her as she fell, using all the remaining strength of her two arms to force the Instructor's right hand up towards the back of her neck. Julia collapsed across the woman's back, pinning her to the floor, and as if in a symbolic gesture of defeat, the Instructor's hand relinquished its grip on the plimsole. With an expression of distaste, the Master's consort lifted her leather jacket and sat with her naked hindquarters imprisoning the Instructor's head.

94

Julia felt gentle fingers stroking her hair, and looked up into smiling blue eyes. 'I'm very grateful,' she said, 'you really shouldn't have put yourself out for me – '

'Cut that out. You're damned lucky I happened to be here. I'm Jem, by the way. Pleased to meet you.'

'Hello. I'm Julia. Security trainee. This is my first day.'

'Some introduction! What shall we do with Miss Universe here?'

'I don't know. If we stand up, she'll kill us.'

'We'll immobilise her. I'm sure glad I decided to wear nylons today. She'll be a whole lot less trouble with her hands tied behind her back.'

Jem elicited a grunt of pain as she altered her position to sit astride the Instructor's neck. She ran her hand across the small patch of spikey blonde hair that was visible between her legs. 'Never fucked a hairstyle before,' she said as she rolled down her stockings. 'It's tickly, but kind of nice. Now let's get those hands trussed together.'

With her hands pinioned behind her back, Instructor Goltz seemed to have lost her enthusiasm for unarmed combat. She lay still when Jem and Julia stood up, each keeping one foot on the prone body.

Julia found herself facing a blue-eyed, lighter-complexioned mirror image. The Master's consort was only a fraction shorter than her, and had the same slim build, pert breasts and bottom, and long lustrous hair, but her skin was golden and lightly freckled, her eyes sparkled with mischief, and she had the most kissable bee-stung lips that Julia had ever seen. She understood why the Master had selected Jem to be his concubine; she also suddenly realised that Jem was returning her gaze. They smiled at each other, and Jem's glance strayed to the battered plimsole that lay abandoned on the floor. 'Revenge is sweet,' she said.

Jem's other stocking and several skipping ropes were pressed into service to secure Instructor Goltz to the bar. The big blonde had struggled and kicked, and Julia and Jem were exhausted when they stood back to admire their work. Goltz was bent double over the bar; coils of rope secured wrist to ankle and elbow to knee, while other ropes ran round each muscular thigh, beneath the bar, and were drawn tight around her waist. Jem's stockings were now tied around Goltz's ankles, which were secured to the ends of an upturned bench. The Instructor could hardly move a single one of her well-developed muscles; and her firm, round, widely-parted buttocks, and their blonde-haired underhang, were prominently displayed.

After a few moments Julia began to tire of beating her tormentor. Goltz's buttocks were bright pink, and the pattern of the plimsole's rubber sole was clearly visible on the glowing flesh. Julia began to think that Jem, who had positioned herself between Goltz's legs and had concentrated on titillating the Instructor's innermost recesses, was providing a more humiliating punishment for the sadistic blonde.

'Jem,' Julia suggested, 'shall we stop now? I'm exhausted.'

'Whatever you say, Jules. You know, this little hole is very definitely beginning to feel wet. But you're right; this could take all night, and what's the point?'

So, after one final whack of the plimsole that set the bar shuddering and echoed from the gymnasium walls, Julia stood back, dropped the plimsole and turned – to be greeted by cheers and handclaps.

'Jem!' she called. 'Look! The gallery's full of people. All the other trainees are there, and some of the Instructors!'

'Don't worry,' Jem replied, 'it looks like they're on your side. Something tells me the blonde fuzzhead wasn't popular in these parts.' Jem picked up the plimsole, waved it at the crowd, and placed it on the small of the Instructor's back. Then she took Julia by the arm and led her out of the gym. 'They'll either untie her – or play with her some more, I guess. For now, you need a shower and some gentle loving care.'

'That sounds wonderful, Jem. You're awfully good to me.'

'Why don't you spend the rest of the day with me? I'm just poking my nose around the estate.'

'I'd love to, but I'm on duty this afternoon. And what about the Master? Won't he want you to be with him?'

'You're in Security, Julia honey. You ought to know that I can't walk ten yards without appearing on some camera somewhere. If he wants me, he'll find me. For now, I want to massage your poor little bruised butt.'

'That's fine with me, Jem.'

Absently stirring an insipid infusion of herbs and yearning for a proper cup of tea, Lucy watched the other guests entering the dining-room.

She spotted the newcomer immediately: a petite, black-haired woman, exactly as Asmita had described, carrying a plate of salad and scanning the room for an empty table. Lucy caught her eye, and waved. After a moment's hesitation, the woman walked delicately towards her.

'Hello there,' Lucy said. 'You're new here, aren't you? Me too. Take a seat. My name's Lucy.'

'Pleased to meet you. I'm Julia,' said the black-haired beauty. She winced as she lowered herself on to the chair.

'Tough massage this morning?' Lucy asked.

'Pardon?'

'You look a little stiff. And whacked, too, if you don't mind me saying so.' Lucy thought she detected a flicker of a smile on Julia's lips.

'That sums it up perfectly,' Julia said. 'Are you enjoying it here?'

'It's OK.' Lucy considered her strategy. How much should she reveal about her suspicions? 'The facilities are excellent, aren't they?'

'It seems so,' Julia replied. 'And the house is so old and interesting.'

'Very interesting. In fact, I find the place a little strange.'

Julia's dark eyes flashed a look of intense interest. 'So do I,' she said. 'Did you have an appointment with the doctor when you arrived here?'

'No,' Lucy replied, genuinely surprised. 'Why did you want to see the doctor?'

'I didn't. That's just the point. It was arranged for me. And the doctor – it was a woman, thank goodness – gave me a very thorough examination, if you know what I mean. Especially down there.'

'And what did she say? Do you need treatment?'

Julia laughed quietly. 'She said I wasn't getting enough sex. Can you believe that? I was speechless. And another thing – '

Lucy had become rapt in contemplation of Julia's small white teeth and crimson lips. 'Oh – sorry. Yes, what else?'

'Well, don't you think there's something funny about the staff? It's not just the old-fashioned uniforms. They're so formal with each other, but I'm sure they're – well, they seem very intimate, too. Do you know what I mean?'

'Precisely,' Lucy said. 'I've noticed it too.'

'I'm sure there's something funny going on.' A delightful frown appeared on Julia's brow. 'And do you know, I'm determined to get to the bottom of it!' Her fingertips, for emphasis, rested momentarily on Lucy's forearm.

Lucy surrendered to the shiver that ran from her arm into the depths of her insides. And I'm determined, she thought, to get to the bottom of you. She covered Julia's hand with hers; the dark-haired woman smiled uncertainly and looked quizzically at her, but didn't pull away.

'I agree,' Lucy said. 'Shall we join forces and do some investigating?'

'Sounds exciting,' Julia replied. 'What shall we do first?'

'We can't talk here. Too many staff about. And anyway, you're walking wounded.'

'I am frightfully sore,' Julia said with wide eyes. 'What do you suggest?'

Lucy had no intention of recommending Asmita's services; she suspected the little Asian girl of having designs on the new guest anyway. 'None of the staff here know anything about massage,' she said. 'Let's go to my room, and I'll see what I can do for you.'

'You're very kind. Are you sure it's not too much trouble?'

'On the contrary, Julia. It will be a pleasure.'

Julia was lying tummy-down on the bedspread, her arms wrapped around the pillow which was covered by the soft fan of her long black hair.

Lucy gazed down at her, stroked her hair, and leant to

place the gentlest of kisses on the lobe of her ear. Julia smiled, sighed, and closed her eyes. Lucy pulled her T shirt over her head, stepped out of her jeans, and waited. She wanted Julia to see her golden body, her welcoming big breasts, and the golden curls between her lithe thighs. Julia opened her one visible eye, and smiled again. 'You've taken your clothes off,' she giggled.

'All the better to make you feel better. I should unbutton your dress, don't you think?'

'Mmmm. Please do.'

Lucy sat on the bed, her hip touching Julia's bare arm. Slowly and carefully, folding aside the material after each button, she exposed a widening V of Julia's back. Julia's skin was perfect, she thought; lighter than Asmita's, but more tanned than her own could ever be.

She stopped unbuttoning when she reached the slope of Julia's arse; she could no longer resist kissing that flawless bronzed skin, and she brushed aside the black curls to press her lips against the back of Julia's warm and spice-scented neck. Julia murmured. Lucy slid her lips downward, kissing each vertebrae, until her mouth was exploring the entrance of the dark valley that ran between Julia's buttocks. Her fingers recommenced their work on the buttons.

'You're not wearing any knickers,' Lucy said, her voice indistinct as she placed kisses on the firm rounded hillocks that she was revealing centimetre by centimetre. 'There are bruises all over your poor little botty.'

'Kiss them better,' Julia murmured, moving her legs apart as Lucy unfastened the final button. 'I told you the doctor was weird.'

Lucy stood up, walked to the foot of the bed, and knelt between Julia's overhanging feet. She wanted to hear more about Julia's experiences of the Private House Health Club, but the vision before her drove all other thoughts from her mind: the two half-spheres of Julia's arse were separated by an inky chasm that invited investigation, a cave of such dark, secret depths that it had to contain hidden treasures. Below it, as swollen and dark as an over-ripened fruit splitting open with the pressure of the sweet juices within, Julia's sex-pouch pressed against the bedspread and filled the wide space between her thighs.

Lucy restrained her passion. After all, she had known Julia for only half an hour. Perhaps her well-spoken new friend was simply naïve and trusting, and expected no more than a kiss and a cuddle. The thought only added to the turmoil in Lucy's loins.

She placed her hand on the back of Julia's thigh. Julia sighed, and shifted her position; her dark fruit lifted a little from the bed, and split open a little more widely. Lucy's hand moved forward, her fingers brushing across the smooth curve of Julia's right cheek and coming to rest in the topmost part of the furrow between her buttocks. Lucy rested her other hand between Julia's thighs. Her fingers moved and momentarily touched the fringe of black curls; she retracted them and then touched again. Julia murmured wordlessly.

'Should I kiss you here?' Lucy said, her heart in her mouth.

'Oh,' Julia said, sleepily, 'that's rather naughty, isn't it?'

'Is it?' said Lucy, her fingertips tracing the edges of Julia's parted lower lips.

'I don't know,' Julia said in a small voice. 'That does feel nice. But I'm not, you know, that way inclined. Not since I was at school . . .'

'Don't worry. I won't hurt you. It's going to be lovely.' And Lucy leant forward, her breath catching as her nipples rubbed against the bedcover, and her breasts squashed against her ribs, and her senses filled with the musky odour of Julia's sex.

Slowly, slowly does it, Lucy told herself; I mustn't startle her. I want to taste her now, immediately, but we'll do this in easy stages.

As lightly as she could, she rested her hands on the twin globes, allowing her thumbs to follow caressingly the velvet skin as it curved inwards towards the silk-smooth hollows at the tops of Julia's thighs. She moved her thumbs upward again, pressing into the yielding flesh and widening the central divide. She stopped as she caught her first glimpse of the brown puckered skin, and fought the temptation to plunge her face between the ovate cheeks and touch her tongue to the unfathomed orifice. She averted her face, and pushed her lips into the warm cushion of Julia's left buttock.

Lucy couldn't wait any longer. Her thumbs advanced through soft, tight curls of hair and met at the bursting seam of Julia's sex. They pushed forward, encountering little resistance; Julia groaned and Lucy's thumbs entered a tropical cavern of pulsating wetness. 'You're sopping, you beautiful thing,' she said, lifting her lips from Julia's skin only long enough to whisper the words before trailing her tongue along the dark valley and into the tiny hole she so much desired.

She loved Julia's anus. She loved its musky, bitter smell, its texture of crinkled silk, its little palpitations and contractions as she forced her tongue deeper and deeper into the secret recess. She was dimly aware of her fingers paddling with a life of their own in Julia's subterranean fruit-juice lake, and of the slow writhing of Julia's hips, but her tongue was hunting for paradise in a slick, vibrant tunnel, and she returned to the outside world only when her jaw began to ache.

'I'm sorry,' she said, breathing hard. 'Got a bit carried away . . .'

'It's alright,' Julia sing-songed, 'it was absolutely heavenly. Come here and cuddle me.'

Lucy crawled up the bed, her limbs still weak with desire. 'You've got to kiss my tits,' she breathed, 'and suck my nipples hard. Please, please . . . Oh, yes, like that . . .'

As Julia's knuckles pressed against the hood of her clitoris and engendered a spasm that shook her from head to toe, Lucy resolved to tell her delicious bedmate every one of her suspicions and discoveries about the mysterious health club. Together, she thought tenderly as Julia's nibbling teeth began to lift her towards another climax, together Julia and I will be invincible.

Jem brought the MG to a halt in the shade of the trees at the edge of the woodland clearing. She re-read the dossier that the Security agent had given her at the castle, checked her make-up in the mirror, stepped out of the car and made for the ornate structure at the centre of the clearing.

It was an oriental temple: an extravagant folly with spiral columns and onion-shaped domes, its rooftops and doorways decorated with gold and turquoise paintwork. Jem pushed aside heavy, brass-studded doors and walked along a gloomy corridor with sky-blue floor tiles that glowed in the shafts of sunlight that dropped through occasional light-wells in the ceiling. She stopped at a door marked *Private*; knocked, and waited for permission to enter.

It was a quiet, peaceful room. Light filtered through the climbing plants that had colonised the sills of the small, high, triangular windows and illuminated the erotic tapestries that hung on the white walls. Chinese carpets were scattered across the tiled floor, and white leather couches were arranged in a semi-circle facing an antique desk inlaid with lapis lazuli. Behind the desk was the only discordant element: a modern table on which stood a video cassette player and a large television screen. Terence Headman was seated at the desk. Jem strolled across the room towards him.

'Reporting for duty, boss,' she said.

Headman watched her approach. 'That is not the correct mode of address,' he said, his moustache twitching as he failed to restrain a smile. 'Shall I punish you now or later?'

'Later, your Masterliness. I thought we had chores to do this afternoon.'

'You're right. It's always later with you, Jem.'

'Such are the burdens of responsibility, I guess. And partly it's because I want to keep you interested. I'm enjoying myself too much to let you finish with me just yet.'

'You're having fun here? I'm pleased. I, on the other hand, have been working all morning. Or trying to. But you've bewitched me, Jem. You're quite extraordinary. I couldn't get you out of my mind. So, in the end, I decided to have you with me. I see you've changed your outfit.'

'Aha! So you have been watching me! I thought you wouldn't be able to resist keeping tabs on me. I laddered my stockings, so I thought I'd find something else. Do you like it?'

Jem pirouetted, casting aside the cape that she had been wearing to keep her warm while driving. She was in powder-blue and silver. Her red-brown curls were tied back loosely with a blue silk bow; from a square-cut blue yoke across her shoulders fell a short net of fine silver strands through which her nipples peeked as she moved. A skirt of fine silver chains hanging from her waist failed to cover a blue cache-sex which was held in place by a silver chain that ran between her buttocks; each pale blue stocking was held up by a silver chain that ran from beneath the skirt to the outside of each thigh. On her feet were high-heeled laced blue shoes.

'Magnificent, Jem!' Headman seemed genuinely impressed. 'Wherever did you find that costume?'

'You haven't spent all morning spying on me, then,' Jem laughed, swaying her hips as she moved towards him. 'You remember that Rhoda took a fancy to me yesterday? I went over to see her at the airstrip. We did a fashion show for the guys in the clothing warehouse, and this little number came out tops.'

'The Reception Centre is out of bounds, Jem. And you know that. But I have to admire Rhoda's taste. You look almost too lovely to touch.'

'Almost?' Jem said, pressing the front of her thighs against the arm of Headman's chair.

'But not quite, of course,' Headman said, reaching behind Jem to run the back of a fingernail down the chain links that disappeared between her arse-cheeks. Jem leant forward to meet his kiss, pushing her tightly-covered sex against his fingers.

'Now it's my turn to postpone our pleasure,' Headman whispered. 'Duty calls. Are you ready for the interview?'

'Aye, aye, Master. Let it roll.'

Headman removed his hand from between Jem's thighs and pressed a button beneath the desk. Jem spread her legs and sat on the arm of the chair, moving from side to side until her buttocks were suspended in curvaceous freedom on either side of the armrest and she could feel the silver chain pressing into her anus. Headman leant back in the chair, cupped her nearer buttock in his hand, and decided to remain in the same position to impress his interviewee. Jem smiled: she understood the little erotic elaborations that Headman appreciated. She put her hands behind her head and pushed forward her silver-netted breasts. The door opened.

A young woman entered the room, bowing her head to the Master. She was short and slim, with bobbed and wavy blonde hair. A crimson mask covered most of her face, revealing only a wide mouth with full, crimson lips. She was wearing a one-piece red catsuit that clung to her figure; ragged holes had been torn in the material to expose her small, high breasts, her fuzz of blonde pubic hair, and the outswelling pears of her buttocks.

In her right hand she carried the end of a length of rope; stumbling behind her, his hands tied together with the other end of the rope, came a naked man. He, too, was slim, but much older than the woman. His hair was greying, but he was tanned and carried no excess weight. Jem guessed that he was probably older than he looked. His eyes were covered by a blindfold, but he retained a dignified bearing as the crimson-mouthed blonde led him to one of the leather couches and pulled him on to it alongside her. At a signal from Headman, she removed the man's blindfold and untied his hands.

He blinked, and found himself staring at the masked girl. Her red-nailed hand crept up his thigh, and her lips smiled suddenly as she grasped his wrinkled member. He smiled in return. 'More games, my dear?' he murmured, leaning forward to kiss her. She shook her head, and flicked her eyes towards the desk – and the man realised that they were not alone.

Jem admired his sang-froid; he didn't bat an eyelid as he turned to face the Master.

'So,' the man said, his voice carrying a trace of a Scottish accent but no hint of concern, 'it's you. I have to say I'm surprised. What is all this in aid of?'

Headman removed his fingers from Jem's bottom and placed both hands flat on the desk. He paused before speaking, and avoided the question. 'I trust you've had a pleasant day, Morton.'

'I would have preferred not to have been drugged and kidnapped and blindfolded and held prisoner; but apart from that, things haven't been too bad.'

There was another long pause. Morton and Headman looked at each other, both reluctant to commit themselves and both ignoring the two shamelessly-attired women. Jem was enjoying the subtle moves in the power game between the two men; the masked girl gazed at Morton, her hand moving gently and ceaselessly in his lap.

'The entertainment was to your liking?' Headman asked at last.

'This bonny lass has been very – er, amenable. As were her equally bonny friends. No doubt you have the entire performance on that video machine over there. I'm surprised you think that a film of a bit of hanky-panky will give you any kind of a hold over me. I've survived worse, you know. So don't bother to show me the tape. You're wasting your time.'

Headman nodded once. 'Jem,' he said, 'would you remove the first cassette from the machine and insert the second?' Jem thought she saw a momentary widening of the eyes behind the woman's mask; she stood up with a tinkling of silver chains and changed the videotapes.

'Do you know what I want, Morton?' Headman barked suddenly.

'Money, I imagine. Although I would have thought your property dealings provided you with an adequate income. Have you fallen on hard times, perhaps? Is that why you're reduced to these pitiful blackmail attempts?'

'I want your companies, Morton. Every one of them. Every last share you own.'

Morton laughed. 'This is madness. I'm sitting stark bollock naked in some architectural nightmare in the middle of God knows where, I've been screwed senseless by a bunch of gorgeous girls one of whom is still hard at work on my poor tired private parts, and now this whizz-kid financier wants me to donate everything I've got to him – and all on the strength of a dirty video.'

'Not donate, Morton,' Headman said. 'I've no wish to drive you into penury. You can keep your properties. And I'll give you a hundred grand for your stockholdings. Seed money: you can start again.'

'A hundred – ! My companies are worth millions, man!'

'It seems unreasonable, doesn't it? But you see, I've got more than just a dirty video. I've got your daughter.'

'Flora?' Morton at last looked concerned. 'What do you mean? Flora's in Italy.'

'No,' Headman said. 'She's on tape. Jem, would you switch on the machine and run the second cassette?'

Jem flicked the switch and resumed her perch on the arm of Headman's chair, which he had swivelled to face the huge screen. Light flooded the room as the television flickered into life.

FLORA MORTON, said the message that appeared on the screen as guitars flowed on the soundtrack, followed by *in HOLIDAY ROMANCE*. The music continued as the titles were replaced by an aerial shot of a Mediterranean coastline; the camera panned across villa-strewn cliffs and crowded beaches before zooming in towards a rocky headland. The film cut to a middle-distance shot of a white-walled, red-tiled villa perched on the summit of the crag, and then cut again, to a close-up of the villa's wrought-iron gates and the lawn-sprinkler within.

The guitars faded as the picture changed again to reveal a white-walled, brick-floored courtyard in which a young woman lay sunbathing. Jem stared at the screen: the terra-cotta pots looked Italian, but the plants they contained would have thrived in almost any climate. Jem suspected that from this scene onwards the film had been shot on location in the grounds of the Private House.

The young woman in close-up: lying face-down on a white towel, long black hair in a pony-tail, naked but for yellow briefs that barely contained rounded buttocks that seemed almost too generous for her otherwise slender frame. She turned over, to face the camera, and opened blue eyes.

Jem heard Morton's stifled exclamation. The poor bastard's recognised her, she thought; I hope he doesn't go through with this.

Headman might have had the same thought. 'Do you want to see any more?' he asked.

'This proves nothing,' Morton said wearily. 'You've been snooping round her villa, that's all, and you've managed to get some – what do you call them – some candid shots of my daughter. I expect you'll tell me you've got some compromising film of her. Well, she's an adult now, and her life is her own affair. If she's been fooling around on her holidays, that's her business.'

On the screen, Flora Morton stood up and cupped her small, pink-tipped breasts in her hands. She looked into the camera and smiled. 'I'm so frightfully bored,' she said, her voice clear and actressy on the soundtrack. 'I wish something sexy would happen. Oh look! Here comes Antonio the gardener with his great big garden hose!'

The picture expanded to include a curly-haired bronze-skinned youth in dazzling white trunks that matched his delighted grin. He was dragging a length of green hosepipe and holding the dripping nozzle in front of his bulging crotch. Flora stepped back in mock alarm, and the hose suddenly spurted into life, producing a spray of water that sprinkled her with droplets from neck to feet. She squealed and giggled but remained in the spray as her nipples visibly hardened and her yellow briefs became transparent. The gardener threw the hose aside. 'Very sorry, *signorina*,' he said, still grinning. 'I make you wet.'

'You certainly do,' Flora gasped. 'You'll have to take my knickers off, you naughty boy, they're soaking!' She caressed her breasts with the palms of her hands as Antonio knelt in front of her and eased her briefs down her legs, pausing at intervals to lick drops of water from the bush of dark hair he had revealed. She stepped out of the wet garment and stood with her legs apart and her hands on the young man's head as his face disappeared between her thighs. There then followed close-up shots of Flora's fist clenched in Antonio's hair, of his face and extended tongue, briefly withdrawn from between her quivering thighs, of his hand squeezing her rotund arse and exploring its dark recesses and of her face flushed and wide-eyed in ecstasy.

The picture dissolved and re-formed to reveal Flora on her knees before Antonio, struggling to lower his trunks over the massive bulge they contained. 'What a big hose you've got!' she exclaimed, with a wink towards the camera, which moved in for a series of loving close-ups of Flora's full lips and wide mouth as she kissed, licked and sucked the thick brown shaft. Jem studied the screen, and decided that she could detect no trace of unwillingness in the girl's expression or behaviour; on the contrary, she seemed to be enjoying her performance, and glanced frequently towards the camera to make sure that her every lick and nibble was being recorded on film. Jem reached down at her side, into Headman's lap, and her fingers met a rising hardness.

On the screen the picture had changed again. Flora was on her back on the towel, writhing and laughing as Antonio tried to tickle her between the legs; whenever she prevented him from doing so, by turning on to her stomach or holding her hands over her sex, he would give a playful slap or pinch to whichever of her breasts or buttocks came within reach. 'Stop it, Antonio!' she shrieked. 'We're going to have to find somewhere to put that big hose of yours, aren't we?'

The youth watched as the young woman lifted her legs into the air, bending her knees so that her thighs were drawn up to her shoulders. Her arse was taut, rounded, and open; her raw split and the puckered hole beneath it were stretched wide, on display. The camera lingered over her body before zooming in to her face.

'Do you want to put your hose in here?' she asked, her blue eyes sparkling. She slowly inserted two fingers into the O of her lips. She withdrew the wetly glistening fingers, then plunged them back into her mouth as far as the knuckles. The camera followed her hand as she moved it from her face, across her breasts, down her ribs, and round her tightly-bent hip.

'Or would you like to put it here?' her voice teased as the screen showed a close-up of her fingertips sliding up and down the slick lips of her sex – and then her fingers slowly disappeared into the slit, emerged again, went in again more quickly and more deeply, and then began to move in and out at an ever-increasing rate as her amplified voice on the soundtrack gasped and moaned to a crescendo.

'Or perhaps,' her voice whispered after a pause, 'perhaps you'd like to put your hose in here.' And her lubricated fingers slid from her sex-channel and came to rest in the crater of her arsehole.

'Stop! Stop the damned thing, for the love of God!' Morton was almost sobbing. Without waiting for Headman's nudge, Jem jumped up and switched off the television. Morton was sitting slumped on the couch with his head in his hands; the masked girl was next to him, sitting upright and very still. Jem tried to smile encouragement at her, and returned to the arm of Headman's chair.

Morton lifted his head. 'What was the point of that?' he pleaded. 'What have you done to my Flora? And why? She's not much more than a child. Why did you have to involve her? What do you hope to achieve?'

'I want your shareholdings,' Headman said, reaching up to fondle Jem's breasts through the silver net. 'I want you to sell me the lot – for a hundred grand.'

'Why the hell should I?' Morton roared.

Headman turned his gaze to the crimson-lipped blonde, and held out his hand. The girl rose, walked slowly round the desk, and lowered herself on to Headman's lap. Headman kissed her cheek, whispered a few words, and then removed the all-enveloping mask from her face.

'Hello, Daddy,' she said.

Morton stared. When at last he spoke, his voice was a ghostly croak. 'Flora?' he said. 'Your hair . . .'

Jem ruffled Flora's blonde locks. 'Dyed,' she said, 'You understand, Mr Morton, that we had to prevent you from recognising her.'

Morton was looking ill. 'Last night . . .' he gasped, and sat motionless with his mouth hanging open.

'I'm sorry, Daddy,' Flora said, squirming more from embarrassment than from the squeezing of Headman's fingers round her nipples. 'They made me do it – well, to start with, anyway. But they only want your silly old stocks

109

and shares. And I like it here now. Everyone's nice to me. Even when they're doing horrible things to me, they're being nice really. This is my home now, Daddy, you must understand, please!' Jem wiped a tear from the girl's cheek.

There was a long silence. At last Morton snorted an ironic laugh. 'I'm not a quitter,' he said. 'You've got a dirty video with me in it – use it! I'll say it's a fake. I'll admit it's genuine, if I have to. I don't care. You've got my daughter. You've seduced my poor wee Flora to your evil ways. But there's no helping it. She's a grown lass, and she'll have to live with what she's done. As for last night . . . I don't see that I have to blame myself for that. I did what I did unknowingly. That's no legal defence, I know, and I'll never forgive myself either. But it won't make me give up my shares, do you hear me? You've lost, Headman!'

Jem looked down at Headman. This, she knew from the briefing paper she had read, was as far as Headman had planned. He had no more cards to play. She guessed that behind his impassive features his mind was searching desperately for one more ace – and that he was failing to find it. She touched his shoulder, and leant to whisper in his ear. 'Look after Flora,' she said. 'She needs a cuddle. Comfort her. Leave Morton to me.'

Jem lowered herself on to the couch and looked at the man sitting beside her. He stared straight ahead, his eyes blank, his fists clenched. Jem pitied him; but she tucked her emotions into the back of her mind, and summoned a calm determination. This has to be finished, she told herself; and I know I can do it. She rested her hand on Morton's.

'Mr Morton,' she said, cramming each word with all the sincerity and concern she could muster, 'you still don't understand. Flora is ours now, I'm sure you see that. But you belong to us too. No one ever leaves the Private House; you can go outside, but you can never leave.'

Morton turned to her, his eyes once again betraying uncertainty. 'What do you mean?'

'You're right: the videos don't compromise you. You're compromised inside. You enjoyed last night; you revelled in everything you did. You'd do it all again if you had the chance. You know you would. And we'll give you the chance. Over and over again. Here, and at your office, and in your home.'

'You'll need more dirt than you've got here, young lady.'

'And we have more, Mr Morton.'

'I'm a strong-willed fellow. I can stand up to anything.'

'Anything, Mr Morton? Even the disclosure – with evidence – that you've sexually abused your daughter all through her childhood?'

Morton tried to laugh. 'But that's a lie. Who says so?'

'Look at Flora,' said Jem, turning her gaze towards Headman's swivel chair.

Morton's daughter was sitting in Headman's lap, leaning backwards against him, her eyes squeezed shut and her red mouth smiling as the Master nuzzled her neck and worked his fingers between her widely-parted thighs.

'She didn't wear her mask all the time last night,' Jem said, without having the slightest idea whether or not this had been the case. 'While you were – involved elsewhere about her person, shall we say, she showed her face for the benefit of the camera. I think a jury would recognise her.'

Morton shook his head from side to side. Jem steeled herself to continue.

'And do you think she would hesitate to swear that you've been tampering with her ever since she was a little girl? Look at her, Mr Morton. Look at her enjoying what the Master's doing to her.'

Morton pursed his lips. Jem could almost see the images that were going through his mind: the court appearances, the newspaper headlines, the cramped cell of a rule 43 prisoner, the disgust on the faces of family, friends, and colleagues, the resignations from directorships, the expulsions from clubs. 'All right,' he said at last, his voice calm and steady, 'you've got me.'

'I'll make it easy for you,' Jem said. 'You can set up a trust for Flora. You and the Master will be the trustees. Transfer everything into the trust. We'll help each other, Mr Morton: we don't want to ruin your companies – quite the reverse. We own more than you can possibly imagine, and we have the resources to make your companies more successful than you have ever dreamt. Join us!'

Morton nodded, his eyes revealing acceptance of defeat but also a re-awakened interest in the future. Jem offered him her hand; he shook it.

First rule of a successful negotiation, Jem thought, is always to leave the other fellow with the bus fare home.

'Can I ask a favour?' Jem said as she and Headman walked hand in hand through the woods.

'After that performance, Jem? You've given me Robert Morton. You can have anything you like – within reason.'

'There's a new Security trainee. She's been here before, but she's new to Security. Her name's Julia. And she's very cute. Can she be my bodyguard?'

'Do you need a bodyguard, Jem?'

'Of course not. But I want Julia.'

'Then you shall have her, my dear. I'll call Chief Anderson immediately.'

'So she's definitely a spy.' Chief Anderson switched off the video monitors and swivelled in his chair to face Julia and Asmita. 'You've done well, both of you – for a trainee and a field operative. Everything in your reports, and everything we've taped, points the same way: Lucy Larson is not what she seems.'

'And what is she really, Chief?' Julia asked.

'If I knew, I'd tell you. I've got people working on it, but until we can find out her real name we can only guess. She has to be from either the police or one of the intelligence agencies – unless she's a private eye working for someone who's looking for a missing relative. In a way, it doesn't matter which. What matters is that she doesn't find out the truth.'

'But if she goes outside again,' Asmita said, 'and talks about her suspicions . . .'

'We'll maintain surveillance,' Anderson said. 'Here and outside. We can deal with trouble if we have to. For the moment, we'll keep her on camera. And we'll rely on you, Asmita, a little longer. Go to her this evening. Keep her occupied.'

'A pleasure, Chief.'

'What about me, Chief?' Julia asked. 'Lucy will become even more suspicious if I'm absent from the Club.'

'That's too bad. I've new orders for you. You're to report to the Master's chambers this evening.'

'The Master!' Julia was surprised, excited, and more than a little nervous. 'What does he want me for? He doesn't know me. I mean, I've never actually met him – '

'Orders is orders, Julia. You don't question a summons from upstairs.'

Three pairs of eyes glanced upwards, as if they could penetrate the stone vault of the Security cellars, the lofty expanse of the Great Hall, the guest apartments above it, and into the Master's sanctum at the summit of the Round Tower.

'So that's it,' Chief Anderson said, rising to his feet and walking to the door. 'But as you're both here, and there's a few minutes before the end of the afternoon shift . . .' He turned the key in the lock and returned to his desk. 'Watkins!' he called into the intercom. 'I'm not to be disturbed!'

Asmita, smiling mischievously, had already shrugged off her chiffon sari. Anderson picked up the short strip of plaited black leather that lay on his desk. 'Where's your flicker, Julia?' he said. Julia pulled an identical implement from her belt. 'Good girl,' Anderson said. 'Keep it always at the ready. It's time you had some practice with it. Not the desk, Asmita; I want you on my chair. Kneeling on it, you silly girl: face the back and put your knees on the arms of the chair.'

Chief Anderson's executive chair was a sturdy piece of furniture; it remained upright while Asmita mounted it, and its arms were wide enough to support her knees. Anderson instructed the Asian girl to lean forward so that her small, brown-capped breasts were perched on the back of the chair, and then he swivelled the chair so that Julia was presented with the delightful vista of Asmita's outthrust hemispheres, her taut thighs, and the swelling underhang between them.

'Ready, Julia?' Anderson said, unbuttoning the tight gauze covering his groin and releasing his already upright

113

member. 'Remember to start gently and build up slowly. When you get into your stride, don't get carried away: try not to leave marks, and ease up on any stroke that looks like it's going to land on her plump little cunt. I'll look after her tits. Alright?'

'Absolutely, Chief,' Julia said, and positioned herself slightly to the side of the chair. She rested her flicker across the middle of Asmita's cheeks, and allowed the thin leather cylinder to roll down the brown skin until its tip was resting against the dark slit in the hollow below her bottom.

The Asian girl turned her head and smiled over her shoulder. 'Go on,' she said, 'enjoy yourself.'

'I'll try not to hurt you too much, honestly.'

'That's all right. I like it, as long as you don't mark me. I'm more worried about what the Chief's going to do to my titties – oh!' Asmita's exclamation was of surprise, not pain: Chief Anderson had leant forward to take one of her large brown nipples into his mouth. He began to suck rhythmically, and Asmita threw back her head.

Julia watched for a few seconds, and then lifted her flicker. She took aim, and brought the leather down in a lazy stroke that landed with a soft slap across the centre of Asmita's right buttock. The girl glanced back, and hollowed her back a little more, inviting Julia to continue.

Julia delivered five more blows to Asmita's right buttock, each a little harder and placed a little lower than the last, so that the final one landed with a loud report along the faint indentation between cheek and thigh. She repeated the pattern on the left cheek, and this time the tip of the flicker also caught the very inside of Asmita's right buttock on each of the first five strokes, and on the sixth it tapped the dark swollen flesh of her sex.

Asmita shuddered, and her buttocks clenched involuntarily. Julia paused, waiting for Asmita to relax completely and revelling in the prickly sensation that had begun to pulse in her loins. Chief Anderson was standing close to Asmita, holding her head against his chest and idly fondling her breasts as he supervised Julia's progress.

Julia stepped forward to run her hand through Asmita's cascade of thick black hair, and then returned to her posi-

tion while running a fingernail down the dark girl's spine.
Her finger came to rest at the point where Asmita's
buttocks met to form their tight dark valley, and she left it
there until, with a muffled groan of acquiescence, Asmita
twisted her knees so that her feet trailed on the outside of
the armrests and her arse opened widely. Chief Anderson
nodded his approval.

Now Julia stood behind Asmita, experimenting with
quick, sharp, criss-cross strokes that landed across the
central divide and left small ticks of dull pink on the sensitive skin on either side of the sooty crinkled hole. Anderson, breathing deeply, released Asmita, who lowered her
head against the back of the chair and began to move her
hips in little back and forth impulses in time with the
regular cracks of Julia's leather on her reddened flesh.

Julia was hardly aware of Chief Anderson standing
beside her until she felt his fingers grasp her free hand and
guide it to the tip of his stiff prick. Without pausing in the
rhythm of her blows she started to squeeze it gently, and
she threw him a quick smile as she felt his hand lifting the
back of her tunic and delving into the moist pit of swirling
lust between her thighs.

The breathy gasps of all three participants now filled the
room, almost covering the increasingly erratic thwacks of
Julia's flicker. Asmita was pushing her hips so far back that
her arse-cheeks were like two perfect orbs; her dark sex
had split open to reveal pink glistening folds of wet flesh. I
know what she wants, Julia thought as she struggled to
keep her mind on the job, but I jolly well won't whip her
delicious big vagina, no matter how much she begs with it.
And she continued to strike all around the gaping mouth
until a glowing halo of punished skin surrounded Asmita's
proffered sex.

At last she stopped and, almost without thinking, she
pulled Chief Anderson forward by his twitching member
and inserted the purple tip into Asmita's cleft. Asmita
gasped with shock, and Anderson, placing his huge hands
on her hips, rammed his bulk against her raw backside.
Julia moved behind the chair and, grabbing a handful of
Asmita's long hair, pulled the girl's face up. Asmita's eyes

were bright with tears, but her face was flushed and her smile was as wide as ever.

'OK?' Julia said softly.

'Fantastic,' Asmita said, beginning to rock up and down as Anderson increased the speed of his thrusts, 'but you're a terrible tease, Julia. Kiss me. And play with my nipples, you'll make me come like that.'

I love this place, Julia thought as she happily complied with Asmita's requests, her tongue meeting Asmita's each time Anderson buried himself in the Asian girl and her fingers tugging at Asmita's soft but wrinkled brown titends. Her trepidation about being called to the Master's chambers vanished from her mind as she felt and heard Asmita and then Anderson reach a climax that threatened to shatter the chair.

Lucy glumly crunched the last corner of her ration of crispbread. She had extended her dinner for as long as she could, but with so little to eat it was difficult to find reasons to linger. She was ravenous, and Julia had still not appeared. Other guests, who had arrived even earlier than she, had long since nibbled their way through the assorted salads and departed towards their evening sessions. Evening sessions of what, Lucy wondered – aerobics or fornication? How could she find out? And where was Julia? Had they abducted her? Who were *they*? Lucy sighed and folded her napkin into a small triangle. The waiters were beginning to stare at her, she was sure of it. Perhaps she should return to her room. No point in drawing attention to myself, she thought; I've still got two of the apple turnovers I smuggled in yesterday.

With a final glance along each of the portrait-lined corridors that led from the reception hall, none of which contained Julia, Lucy climbed the staircase and made for her room.

Once inside, she checked the long blonde hairs that she had pulled from her head and placed as if at random across the drawers and cupboard doors. Not one had been disturbed. They haven't rumbled me yet, then, she congratulated herself, so I've got nothing to worry about.

She unzipped her light cotton dress, stepped out of it,

116

and stood in bra and panties before the built-in wardrobe mirror. She patted her flat stomach, reflecting that on the Health Club's diet she hardly needed exercise to keep her in shape. But regular habits have a momentum of their own, and she started her warm-up routine, touching her toes, stretching her spine, and flinging her arms backward in time with an imaginary tune.

Warm-up completed, she paused to catch her breath, and caught sight of the golden curves of her breasts rising and falling in their underwired cradles of lace. Who'd be an hourglass, she thought smugly, when you can have a finely-honed wedge-shaped body like mine? Men go crazy for my chest – she filled her lungs and her bulging torpedoes almost burst from their restraints – but there's not another surplus centimetre of flesh on me. She admired the reflection of her taut ribcage, inswept stomach, slim hips, round buttocks and long, tapering legs and realised with a start that she was wasting exercise time. Leg lifts, she told herself, and lowered herself to the floor.

She failed to hear the door open, and was on her back with her legs pointing straight up at the ceiling when she became aware of the intruder. Slowly, she parted her erect legs and saw her beloved Asian masseuse staring down at her prone body.

'What a lovely sight,' Asmita giggled, her eyes fixed firmly on the taut gusset of Lucy's knickers. 'Hello, Lucy!'

'Asmita!' Lucy said, allowing her legs to fall to the floor. 'I didn't think I'd see you again. I was a bit rough with you when you wouldn't tell me anything about this place.'

'That's alright. I forgive you. I told you about Julia, anyhow.'

'Yes. Yes, you did. She's a – useful lead.'

There was an awkward silence. Asmita's cheerfulness seemed almost artificially bright, Lucy thought; perhaps her own guilty conscience was causing her to imagine things. Only a few hours ago she had seduced Julia in this very room; she allowed her eyes to wander to the bed, and blushed when she realised Asmita had been following her gaze. But Asmita couldn't possibly know she'd been unfaithful, could she?

'It's too early for bed,' Asmita laughed, and Lucy's worries dissolved. 'It would be fun, of course; but you have to finish your exercises.'

'Finished!' Lucy said, starting to lever herself up from her prone position, but Asmita descended on her in a flurry of silk sari, surrounding her face within a curtain of scented black hair. Lucy could have thrown her off in an instant, but instead she sank back to the floor, gazing up into her lover's deep dark gleaming eyes. 'Oh, my dark angel!' she sighed, and left her lips open to receive Asmita's kiss, surrendering to the hands that wriggled into her bra, eased it up to her neck, and attempted to encompass the freed mounds of her breasts.

'Exercises!' Asmita said between kisses. 'I want to see these titties bouncing up and down. But to start with: let's carry on with stretching your legs.' She twisted round, and as she did so her sari dropped from her body. Lucy pulled the sheer material away from her face to find Asmita sitting on her stomach again, but this time naked and facing towards her feet. The Asian girl glanced over her shoulder. 'Knickers off!' she said. 'Lift up your legs, like before.'

Asmita's fingers were already tugging at the elastic waistband. Lucy straightened her long legs and lifted them steadily into the air, until her toes were pointing straight up to the ceiling. She was rewarded with a closer view of Asmita's delightful bottom, as the girl slid her arse back from Lucy's raised hips and leant forward to pull the knickers up Lucy's vertical thighs. Asmita lifted herself away from Lucy's ribcage to tug the knickers from the tips of Lucy's toes, and Lucy feasted her eyes on the dark swollen sex-lips on which she so dearly wished to feast her tongue. She raised a hand and trailed the backs of her fingers across the forested hillock of black curls.

'Hands off!' Asmita said, slapping away the hand and squashing Lucy's breasts as she sat down again firmly. 'That's for later – your prize for doing your exercises. Now then: let me see you spread these legs.'

Lucy felt her muscles tremble as she tried to keep her movements smooth and steady. Little by little she moved her legs apart, biting her lip as she resisted the temptation to hurry, determined to allow Asmita only a gradual view of the blonde treasure at the apex of her straining thighs.

There was a tickling between her knees; as the gap between her legs widened, Asmita was leaning forward and lowering her face into the growing V. Lucy could feel the soft fringe of black hair descending between her thighs, and watched hungrily as Asmita's bottom lifted and brought the dark underhang closer and closer to Lucy's face. Lucy pressed her arms against the carpet and raised her head; Asmita stopped moving.

'Not yet,' Asmita said. 'Legs very wide, please, first.' She pecked a kiss on the inside of each of Lucy's thighs. Lucy groaned and let her head fall back to the floor. The muscles in her legs and neck were aching abominably, but she wanted to please her dark-skinned darling; she drew on her experience of years of police training, and summoned the willpower to widen her legs little by little, until the angle between them was greater than ninety degrees, and each foot felt like a lead weight that she could barely support.

'Beautiful,' Asmita breathed. 'Now keep very still.' And she swept aside her long tresses and lowered her face into the yawning angle between Lucy's trembling legs. At the same time she wriggled her hips backwards, capturing Lucy's overflowing breasts between her thighs and bringing her sex, at last, within reach of Lucy's eager lips.

Lucy was in heaven. With the tip of her nose touching the stretched silkiness of Asmita's anus, she could smell only the earthy, bitter-sweet odour that she adored and that was subtly heavier than the tangy aroma of Julia's arse; with her lips covered by the moist prickly softness of Asmita's sex she could do nothing but let the girl's salty musk drain into her mouth. Asmita's tongue darted about her throbbing clitoris, sending shivers through her insides that grew into explosive tremors only to subside into more shiverings. .With each tremor that shook her spine she extended her tongue more deeply into Asmita's hot, wet interior; each time she thrust her tongue upwards, Asmita's cruel hands closed more tightly around the febrile hardness at the tips of her imprisoned breasts.

She had no idea how long she remained in this paradise,

nor how many tremors and quakes racked her body; she opened her eyes to find Asmita kneeling beside her.

'Naughty girl,' Asmita said, 'you didn't keep your legs straight. You need more exercises.'

'What? Asmita, my sweetness, I'm shattered. I can't – '

'Press-ups next, I think.'

'Press-ups?'

'Come on, turn over. On your front. That's it. But wait a moment. If you lift your front up – that's right – I can lie in front of you, like this.' Asmita positioned herself face down, lying in the same direction as Lucy with her hips between Lucy's hands and her legs spread wide apart.

'My bra – ' Lucy began, as, although she had lifted her torso to the full extent of her arms, her heavy breasts were almost touching the carpet between Asmita's legs.

'It'll be nice,' Asmita said, looking back over her shoulder. 'Every time you lower yourself, your big hard nipples will be crushed against the carpet and you'll be able to push your face right into my rude places.'

Lucy experimented. 'Oh yes,' she said in a muffled voice as her breasts were compressed between her ribs and the prickly velvet of the floor, and her face sank between the soft brown cushions of Asmita's arse. 'But I won't want to lift myself up again, will I?'

'It doesn't matter,' Asmita laughed, 'we've got all evening to do your exercises, haven't we?'

This is it, Jem said to herself. I won't be able to hold him off tonight. Let's hope I can pull off a virtuoso performance – and tire him out quickly, too.

She was standing beside Terence Headman as he worked at his desk in his study, an octagonal room that occupied the attic of the Round Tower. A shaft of red evening sunlight entered through one of the skylights that pierced the Tower's conical tiled roof. Occasionally Jem heard the pacing of the Security guard who circled the battlements.

Like the rest of the Private House, the Master's study was furnished in antique style. The walls were lined with books, the desks were of oak inlaid with cherry, and the chairs were covered in fine red leather. Even the telephone, a modern push-button device with conferencing and call-back and every one of the latest improvements in telecommunications, was disguised within an old-fashioned black bakelite shell. And although Headman referred continually to the glowing, digit-filled computer screen that sat incongruously on the french-polished woodwork, he wrote his notes on fine bond paper with a fat Waterman fountain pen. From time to time he would lift the telephone to demand information about certain trans-actions or to insist on changes to plans; the red-haired Rhoda, it seemed to Jem, was on the receiving end of most of these calls. But when he wanted to instigate new pro-cedures or to issue important new orders, Jem noticed that he would write them by hand, in his plain, upright script, and would seal the folded paper with red sealing-wax; and he would mark the molten wax with his monogram, a cursive capital M, using either the signet ring on his right hand or one of the identical rings that lay in a tiny ivory tray on the desk.

The computer was not the only improbable element in the antiquated study. The narrow brass bed was not in itself unusual, but the leather straps and metal buckles that hung from its sides gave it a disconcerting appearance, as did the upholstered A-frame that lay propped against it, waiting to be fixed in position. Still more remarkable were the con-tents of the glass-fronted cabinets behind the bed. In one there was a display of whips, crops, canes and tawses, while the other contained a sparklingly clean array of vibrators, dildos, handcuffs, complexly linked lengths of chain, shiny metal spheres of various sizes, and other objects the func-tion of which Jem could not guess without a closer view.

Headman doesn't look much like a vintage businessman, either, Jem thought. He was wearing only black leather boots over black leggings that extended to his thighs and were tied around his waist; his groin and buttocks were not covered. The hair on his body – a thick covering across his powerful chest that narrowed to a line down his flat sto-mach and then expanded again into a bush from which his half-erect member sprouted – was dark, but attractively speckled with grey. When Headman was deep in thought

Jem would reach out and run her fingers across his torso, smoothing the curls, and Headman would look up at her with his familiar ironic smile. Jem would try to read the expression in the glacier-blue eyes that looked at her from beneath his hooded lids, and would find love and pity mingling with the distaste she felt for the cold and calculating tyrant. What a waste, she would say to herself, sighing as she caressed his neck and his fingers thrust into her, what a pity he's not as wonderful as he looks.

And if Headman looks out of place, Jem thought, I look like a freak. And I smell like an oriental bazaar. Once again she surveyed her body, coated with a film of glistening oil the spicy scent of which almost overpowered her senses. Her hair was coiled on her head and held in place with bejewelled pins; apart from her shoes, with heels so thin and high that she hardly dared move for fear of falling over, her only garment was a red corset that had been laced so tightly she felt she would snap in two. The corset flared out from her hips with a flounce of ruched red silk, emphasising the swelling of her backside and the nakedness of her belly; and it was shaped to fit exactly below her breasts, tilting them slightly upwards. Clips, more insistent than the most ardent lover's fingers, gripped her nipples and were connected by slender chains to a diamond-studded necklace; if she stood straight, with her head held erect, her nipples were pulled upwards in an exaggeration of their normal pert readiness. This isn't comfortable, she thought, even if it is kind of sexy. What's Headman going to want this evening?

Headman flicked a switch and his computer screen faded. 'All work and no play,' he said, swivelling his chair to face Jem, 'makes your Master a very dull fellow. It's time to play, Jem.'

'You have a half-decent chess programme on that machine, Master?'

'No, I haven't. That's not a bad idea. But at this moment, Jem, I'm interested only in mating with my queen.'

'Oh, Master! And I thought I was just a pawn in your game!'

Headman smiled his thin-lipped smile. 'I like a courtesan

with an accurate idea of her status. Get on the desk, Jem. On your hands and knees. Facing towards me. Quickly!'

By the time Jem had manoeuvred herself into position, Headman had wheeled the front of his chair under the desk and had started to turn two handles at the sides of the seat. Jem watched his face rise in front of her as the seat of his chair moved upwards, like a piano stool, until his thighs were pressed against the underside of the desk's surface. His erect member protruded stiffly between his stomach and the edge of the desk.

'Is this going to be fun for me?' Jem asked.

'Of course not,' Headman said. 'Not yet. Later, perhaps, if you please me. It is the Master's privilege to take pleasure, and the duty of others to provide it. Now lean forward, push your arse up, that's right, and use your mouth. And do it very gently, Jem: I don't want to rush things.'

Jem was in a far from comfortable position, but she had to admit that Headman's prick was not an unpleasant lollipop. It was a long, tapering, elegantly shaped organ; the helmet was the shape and size of a plum, with only a narrow flange at its base, so that it was exactly the right size for Jem to hold in her mouth and roll her tongue around. She could take the whole shaft into her mouth, and although the tip then reached right to the back of her throat, she found she could still breathe quite easily. For several minutes she toyed with the hot hard flesh, discovering its shape and texture; then she started to draw back occasionally, to rest her mouth and to kiss and lick the wide-cracked tip. Glancing up, she saw Headman becoming more and more relaxed, his breathing deep, his eyes closed, and his fingers tugging gently at the taut chains that ran to her pinched nipples.

Jem returned to her task, sliding her lips down the length of Headman's rigid pole.

'The Devil finds work for idle hands, I see.' Headman's voice was stern. Jem stopped her movements. 'I saw you,' he continued. 'Your hands were being very busy between your legs. I said you were not to take your enjoyment yet, did I not? If you want something to occupy your hands, I'm sure I can find them some suitable employment. Stand up; go and select a dildo from the cabinet.'

Jem stifled a sigh of relief: her subterfuge had not been discovered, and now Headman was unwittingly assisting her. Pretending flustered contrition, she carefully descended from the desk and teetered towards the display of sex toys.

The cabinet contained row upon row of artificial penises of every size, shape, material and colour. There were double dildos with their twin shafts set at various angles to and distances from each other; and single cylinders of metal, latex, and polished wood, some smooth and others realistically sculpted, and some ribbed or covered in rubber nodules. Jem selected a smooth, pointed model made of soft fleshy rubber, and, taking tiny steps, returned to present it to the Master.

'That's rather small, isn't it, Jem?' he said. 'It's scarcely bigger than the real thing.'

Jem gave him a look of wide-eyed innocence. 'But Master, I've only got a little bottom!'

Headman nodded appreciatively. 'Small, but perfectly formed,' he said. 'How very thoughtful of you to choose buggery. Now: back on the desk, as you were before. Insert it as slowly as you can.'

'Thank you, Master,' Jem said, genuinely grateful. But before clambering on to the desk she pushed forward her russet-curled mound, and with a flourish, she lubricated the slender tube within the moist channel of her vagina. Her gaze locked with Headman's as she withdrew it again, glistening with her internal juices.

Headman's eyes devoured her as she resumed her position on the desk. Her lips closed around the hard knob of Headman's shaft as she reached behind herself to guide the tip of the dildo to the puckered entrance up her uplifted arse. She started to lap gently at the soft underside of the helmet, her tongue moving in time with her hand as it pushed the slick leatherly nub against her tight ring of muscle.

This is getting almost enjoyable, Jem thought as the ring relaxed and then closed around the head of the cylinder; if

124

only this desk weren't so hard and this corset weren't so tight. For Headman's benefit she allowed herself to utter little grunts of pleasure with each fraction of a centimetre that she insinuated the dildo into her anus.

By the time it was fully inserted, Jem had almost begun to believe her own propaganda. Her loins throbbed with a delicious feeling of fullness, and her stretched sphincter sent little jolts of excitement shooting towards her clitoris with every miniscule movement of the dildo. The problem was that Headman seemed no nearer to reaching a climax.

'Very good, Jem,' he drawled. 'Now move it in and out – faster than that, much faster. Give your arsehole a really fierce fucking, Jem.'

Jem pulled away, released Headman's prick from her tired jaws, and stretched upward, shaking her head. She had forgotten the nipple clamps: the chains rattled and pulled her breasts to and fro, sending stabs of near-pain through them. Headman appeared to find the display entertaining, and Jem forced herself to smile at him.

'I'll fuck my own bottom with the greatest of pleasure, Master,' she said, eyes glittering, 'but wouldn't you prefer to see it?'

'Perhaps . . . What do you have in mind?'

'You've had a busy day, Master. Why not relax on the couch?' She took his hand in hers, led him to the couch, and laid him on it. 'Come along, let's try it. Now if I start above your head, like this, and crawl over you, along the bed . . . Well, what do you know? I've found that ever-ready stiffie of yours, just waiting to be popped back into my mouth. And my little stuffed arse is hanging right over your head, so you can see exactly what I'm doing with it.'

'A courtesan with imagination! This is indeed an excellent arrangement. It requires only one extra element to make it perfect . . .' Without moving from his prone position, Headman fumbled beneath the bed and produced a thin, smooth length of cane which he swished through the air experimentally.

As Headman was considerably taller than Jem her hips were above his shoulders rather than his head, and he had an excellent view of her curved arse and the distended ring at its centre even after she had leant forward to apply her tongue to his trembling organ. 'Suck me very gently, Jem,' he admonished her. 'We have a long night ahead of us. I want you to use a slow mouth and an energetic hand. This isn't the ideal position from which to wield a cane, but I'm sure I'll be able to use it to encourage you if your self-sodomising begins to show signs of waning enthusiasm.'

Oh my, Jem thought, this is another fine mess I've gotten myself into. I just have to get out of this, and burn up a little of Headman's fuel, too, if I can.

She pushed her left arm under Headman's silk-clad thighs, as if to push his penis further into her mouth, and set up a regular rhythm with her tongue and her lips and the insides of her cheeks, very gradually increasing the pressure while making only half-hearted efforts with her right hand to move the dildo in and out of her anus.

'What's the matter, Jem?' Headman's voice taunted her. 'Is your arm getting tired?' Jem felt the cane tap against her buttocks. She released her hold on the dildo, and Headman made use of the opportunity to deliver a second, stinging blow; but Jem's hand searched for his, found it, and pulled it to the flanged base of the cylinder lodged between her cheeks.

'Why, thank you, Jem,' Headman said, his voice notice-ably less steady. 'How considerate. I'd love to fuck your bottom. But I'll be less gentle than you.'

Headman was as good as his word. Swift in and out thrusts of the dildo alternated with strokes from the cane. When he started to favour upward strokes that flicked into Jem's open sex-slot and knocked against the base of the deeply-embedded dildo, she almost lost her concentration on the action of mouth on prick. But Headman's participa-tion and her relentless sucking were beginning to have their effect, and Headman's hips were moving convulsively as his excitement mounted.

Jem judged that the time was right. She lifted Headman's thighs; moved her right hand to rest against his hairy, upcurving bottom; with her left hand grasped his testicles, and squeezed; pushed the index finger of her right hand into his arse-crack, and on into his warm rubbery anus; and pulled the head of his throbbing prick to the back of her throat, sucking mightily as she did so.

With a brief cry, Headman started to come. The cane flailed wildly as boiling salt fluid flooded Jem's throat.

Jem swallowed, sucked saliva into her mouth, swallowed again, and waited.

'Jem!' Headman's voice was weak.

'Yes, Master?'

'You know that was not what I had intended, Jem.'

'Yes, Master. But it was fun, wasn't it? and I wanted to move on to something else. I guess I just like variety.'

Headman sighed theatrically. 'If I thought there was the slightest point, Jem, I would send you to the dungeons from now until dawn. You'd find more than enough variety there, I warrant you. But there's no point. You're incorrigible. But yes, it was fun. So tell me: what would you like to do next?'

It was almost midnight when Jem, stiff, sore, and naked except for a long cloak of blue velvet, made her way down the wide curving staircase to her own chamber. Her escort was one of the Master's slaves; a timid blonde whom Jem might have described as wraith-like had it not been for the huge beige-capped globes that swelled out from the girl's narrow chest. She had clearly been some weeks in Headman's personal service: her tremulous manner suggested it, but a clearer sign were the gold chains that decorated her body, hanging from pierced ears to pierced nipples, from nipples to wrists and pierced labia, and from wrists to ankles. Jem was too exhausted to appreciate the aesthetic effect, and waved the girl away when they reached the door of Jem's room.

The quarter-circular chamber was in darkness, but Jem made out the slim figure sitting on the bed.

'Jem? Is that you?'

'Julia! Welcome to the Round Tower, sister. Lead me to a hot tub, pronto.'

'But why am I here, Jem? I thought the Master – '

'Because I asked for you, silly. No more questions until I'm lying in hot water, please. Come on into the bathroom.'

Julia remained silent until Jem was up to her neck in a bathful of bubbles. Jem found herself almost falling asleep in the steamy heat, and she forced herself to stay awake.

'Boy, this feels good,' she said, pausing between each word. 'OK, Julia, talk to me.'

'Have you been with the Master?'

'Uh-huh. We've been keeping each other occupied. He's a boy who likes a lot of action in the bedroom.'

'They say he usually has at least two courtesans, and they don't last long. And then of course there are his poor little slaves . . .'

'I should be getting danger money. I detect a look of awestruck gratitude when those slaves of his look at me. He won't have the energy to whip them tonight, that's for sure.'

'Oh Jem!' There were tears in Julia's eyes. 'Has he hurt you?'

'Don't worry. I'm not hurt any more than I can take. And I think I have more to come tomorrow.'

'Is there anything I can do?'

'Just be here, Julia dear. Look after me. Sleep with me tonight. And tonight I mean just sleep. Kiss me goodnight, put your arms round me, watch over me. Keep the ghoulies and ghosties away. Will you do that?'

'I'd love to.' Julia plunged her arms into the bath and hugged Jem to her. 'I'd do anything in the world for you.'

'Thanks. I hope you mean that, Julia. I may hold you to it one day soon. But right now I just feel delicate and vulnerable, and I've a suspicion I'll need to be neither tomorrow.'

'Well you look jolly comfortable in your bath. What's that on your finger?'

Jem put the encircled finger across her lips. 'Hush! It's a ring. A signet ring. I just pulled it from the very deepest recess of my private regions. I purloined it upstairs. Thought it might come in handy. Don't tell a soul!' She continued in her normal tone. 'Enough explaining. It's your turn to explain things to me.'

'What things, Jem?'

'Everything. Your new job in Security. Tell me all about that.'

Jem, with eyes closed, dozed in the water while Julia told her everything she needed to know: the organisation and methods of the Security Corps, Julia's assignment to watch over the suspicious visitor Lucy Larson, the helpful role played by the field operative Asmita, and the locations of the secret tunnels that ran from various parts of the estate to the small corner plot containing the Private House Health Club.

A beatific smile spread slowly across Jem's face as she soaked up the information. A plan was forming in her mind. Tomorrow would start like any other day in the Private House; but it would be a new dawn, if Jem's plan could be made to work.

DAY FIVE: *THURSDAY*

Barrel-vaulted passages pierced the five-metre thickness of the Round Tower's outer wall to connect the gallery that ran round the Great Hall to the upper storeys of the West Wing and the old East Wing of the House. These two much-altered edifices, the oldest parts of the House apart from the Round Tower itself and constructed in part in stone from the walls of the old castle, extended from the Round Tower to the south-west and south-east. Over the centuries more structures – another wing, a kitchen block, a stable block, and servants' quarters – had been added to the extremity of the old East Wing, which had been rebuilt as the central axis of the House. A corridor known as the Long Gallery ran along the entire length of its first storey.

It was only a little after dawn when Julia pulled aside the curtain at the end of one of the stone passages to find the Long Gallery flooded with yellow sunlight within which rippled the green refractions of dancing leaves. She stopped to peer through the lozenges of ancient, thick glass, but she hardly saw the stately, shadowed avenue of trees and the distant gilded rooftops of the old gatehouse, now the Health Club, within its walled enclave.

Her mind was teeming with thoughts of the Master's consort. Jem was her saviour, her confidante, her protegée, her friend; they had met only yesterday, but Julia felt they had known each other for years. She had thought she had grown out of schoolgirl crushes; she had never believed in love at first sight. But as the beautiful, dazzling, exhausted child-woman had fallen asleep in her arms, Julia had felt that her heart would burst. She had wept silent tears of overflowing affection, placed soft kisses on Jem's cherry

131

lips, and ran her fingers through the waves of russet hair until she too had fallen into sleep.

She had woken at first light, pulled on a cloak, and left without waking Jem. If she opens those blue eyes, she had thought, I'll never be able to leave her. She had intended to go straight to her own room, above the Long Gallery, where Maxine would be waiting and worrying; but now she wanted solitude and time to think, and she made her way down the central staircase to the other side of the building, and out on to the terrace.

The gravelled courtyard was cold and gloomy in the shadow of the House. Dew sparkled on the wide lawn beyond, and Julia left dark footprints in the grass as she hurried across it to the sunlit boulevard of cobbles that ran from the East Courtyard to the walled cloister and marked the edge of the formal gardens. She rested against the edge of the vast stone bowl of the fountain; Proteus and his sea-nymphs, scintillating under a shower of droplets, contrived a stirringly erotic tableau even without the assistance of the living statues who would be chained to the assembly during the course of the day.

The formal garden had been Julia's favourite haunt on her previous visit to the Private House. She set off aimlessly along one of the avenues of cobblestones, waving absently to a team of gardeners, the first people she had seen awake this morning, as they emerged from the cloister to inspect the box-bordered flower beds. Further from the House there were pools and fountains, rockeries, and arbours, convoluted hedges, copses of slender trees, and even artificial hillocks on which had been constructed wild woodlands and rushing waterfalls. Every place held a memory for Julia, and in particular she remembered every one of the pavilions and follies that blossomed in the shady nooks of the garden.

The architectural whimsies were empty now, but later in the day courtesans, gigolos and slaves would occupy them and exhibit their bodies for the entertainment of passing strollers.

On her last visit to the House Julia had slipped easily into the luxurious life of a courtesan. She had held court in one of the pavilions – which was it, she asked herself, shielding her eyes as she scanned the edges of the garden. Ah yes; there it was, deep in shadow, built against the east wall. It was a mock-Attic temple with white, fluted pillars. Julia had been dressed in a diaphanous robe of white voile, and she had been chained – very loosely, and for aesthetic appeal rather than for constraint – to the base of a cushion-strewn altar in the shadowy sanctum. A notice posted in the portico had encouraged passers-by to use her, the temple's priestess, on the altar, as the receptacle for their offerings to Aphrodite.

Those had been wonderfully carefree, relaxing days. Julia had received a stream of visitors of both sexes, each of whom would take her according to his or her own pre-dilections. Julia had found the experiences pleasant in almost every case, and nearly every one of her guests would stay to chat and gossip until another votary entered the temple and the previous visitor might leave, or might stay to watch. The Greek pavilion of Aphrodite had at times become crowded with people, some of whom had brought food and wine, and entire hot afternoons had been passed in the cool shade of Julia's temple: happy gatherings in which simple fare, sparkling conversation and languorous lovemaking had been enjoyed in equal measure.

What a life of ease Julia had led then! And how different this visit seemed. She had been here less than three days, and so far they had been more eventful than a normal fortnight in the outside world, and certainly less relaxing. But Julia had to admit that things were interesting; in fact, she felt more alive than she had for years.

And was she imagining that the House itself had changed, too? In appearance it was as she remembered it; but the safe routine of harsh initiation followed by unquestioning obedience to a life of lazy sexuality seemed to be disturbed. The atmosphere was electric rather than soothing. She would find huddled groups – guests, servants, slaves, courtesans, gigolos, and even Security staff and field operatives – deep in animated conversation rather than chattering idly. There was talk of unjustified punishments, although Julia knew that these were hardly unprecedented; of excessive demands being made on slaves and field operatives; of friction between the staff out at the airstrip; and, as an unspoken undercurrent, the hint that the pressures leading to these incidents came from the Very Top. Julia found it disconcerting but, like everyone else, she tried to concentrate on obedience and sexuality. Besides, she found the gossip exciting – and she had met the marvellous Jem.

Jem had been here as short a time as she had herself; surely Jem's arrival couldn't have anything to do with the air of unrest? No; others had told her of erratic orders that had been issued weeks earlier. And yet Jem's arrival remained significant to Julia; she saw Jem in her mind's eye with red-brown hair glowing like a halo round her wide blue eyes. Jem is a beacon, she thought, a light illuminating the Private House from a new angle . . . The vision faded. Julia wrapped her cloak around her body and returned to the House.

Maxine was lying on the floor at the foot of Julia's bed. Julia closed the door silently and watched her maid sleeping. The girl had thrown off a quilted bedcover and was now almost naked; her thin nightgown had ridden up about her generous hips and barely contained the rising and falling swell of her huge breasts. The tip of a thumb rested between her glistening red lips.

Julia threw her cloak on to the bed and knelt naked next to her maid. With careful fingers she untied the loose ribbons that held together the bodice of the nightgown and folded aside the flimsy cotton, revealing the voluptuous pink-tipped spheres of flesh. She curved her fingers and ran her nails from the undersides of the globes to the aureoles, delighting in the slow lifting of the heavy bulbs and the bright scratch-lines she was creating across their surface. Maxine moaned, and sucked her thumb. Julia continued to toy with the maid's breasts, lifting them and letting them fall, until the fluttering eyelids at last opened wide; and at that moment she smiled, and twisted both nipples between her fingers and thumbs.

'Ow!' Maxine said, her hands flying to her chest; and

then, recognising Julia, she drew her hands behind her back and pushed her breasts into the air. 'It's you, Miss. And it's morning. Where have you been?'

Julia needed to use both hands to contain just one of Maxine's soft mounds, and she squeezed them in turn. The maid lifted one side of her body and then the other, and each time she did so the unattended breast flattened and rolled and spilled into her armpit, from which haven Julia would drag it by pulling on the nipple. This game continued until Maxine's nipples were crinkled and as hard as jewels, and her pale skin was red with scratches and slaps.

'You're a wonderfully well-trained servant,' Julia said at last. 'And I can quite understand why all your menfriends want to rub themselves up and down between these gorgeous titties. But tell me, Maxine: how did you come to be here in the Private House?'

'I'm not supposed to tell, am I, Miss? What if Security – oh.'

'Exactly. I'm in Security, so you can tell me. Are you a volunteer?'

'Me, Miss? Not likely! I was conned into coming here. I'd just finished secretarial college, and I thought I'd temp for a while. The agency looked alright, perfectly ordinary place; but I reckon they knew where they were sending me. It was just an office in the city, but they weren't interested in my typing speed, I can tell you. But I was very young; naïve, I suppose. I let them take photographs, then they said they'd publish them in one of those girlie mags if I didn't agree to a holiday in the country. And I ended up here.'

'And then you found you were enjoying yourself?'

'You're joking! I hated it. I was a right tearaway, and I wasn't going to let other people tell me what to do. I spent most of my first visit in the dungeon, and even at the end of that I wasn't exactly a model of obedience. Then, right at the end, one of the courtesans saw me and persuaded Security to let me go and spend a day with her. Classic move, of course, like the cops using a hard man and then a soft man when they're questioning a suspect. But I fell for it, of course. I'd never really enjoyed sex until that day with Carla. And I haven't looked back since.'

'Are you on the permanent staff?'

'Almost. I don't like it outside any more. My Mum thinks I'm working in Dubai. I go back to see her every now and then; sometimes Security give me little jobs to do while I'm outside.' Suddenly the maid remembered her duties. 'But what about you, Miss? Where have you been? Is it time for you to report for training?'

'Don't worry, Maxine,' Julia said, helping her maid to stand. 'It's early. Plenty of time to get dressed. I've just spent the night in the Round Tower.'

Maxine's eyes widened into circles. 'With the Master! Oh, Miss, are you alright? You're not hurt, are you?'

'Not with the Master, Maxine. With his consort, Jem. She's chosen me to be her bodyguard.'

Maxine squealed and put her hand to her grinning mouth. 'Miss! Oh Miss! You? Her bodyguard? Oh, Miss Julia!'

'What on earth's the matter, Maxine? She's only a courtesan, of sorts, and a new one at that. I mean she's rather special, it's true – '

'Rather special, Miss? I'll say she is! She's amazing. She's so beautiful. Everyone's talking about her, you know.'

'Have you seen her, then?'

'Only from a distance, Miss. But she's got a lovely walk. And she's so slim and small and sexy. A bit like you, Miss, if you don't mind me saying so.'

Maxine blushed and looked away. Julia was terribly flattered, but she suppressed her smile of childish glee and pinched the maid's nipple to punish her over-familiarity. 'That's enough cheek!' she said. 'What is everyone saying about Jem?'

'Well, Miss, she's been all over the estate, and all in her first day here. They say she's made all the Security instructors look a bunch of right idiots – pardon me, Miss, but that's what they say. The Master's infatuated with her, by all accounts, and she's got him round her little finger. They say he's making mistakes, and that she's sorting out all of his problems for him. And she's got a kind word for everyone, even the slaves.'

'And would you like to meet her, Maxine?'

'Oh, Miss! I'd give anything. I'm so jealous of you, being with her all the time.'

'Not all the time, I'm afraid. But I'll see what I can do.' Julia couldn't bring herself to resent Maxine's unquestioning adulation of the Master's consort, as she had to admit her own feelings were as rapturous. 'But you'll have to be very good, Maxine. I expect impeccable service.'

'I'm always good to you, Miss.'

'Then stay undressed. I'll put my uniform on myself. Get on the bed and play with yourself. And don't take your eyes off me for a moment!'

How unseemly, Julia thought as she emphasised the sway of her hips on her way to the wardrobe, I'm putting on a show for my maid! She opened the door and spread apart her long legs as she bent to retrieve a pair of boots. She glanced back to see Maxine kneeling on the bed, one hand roaming across her breasts, the other between her plump thighs, and her eyes fixed on Julia's round bottom. Julia felt a tickling, seeping moistness in her loins, and decided that she must dress herself this way more often in future. She pushed back the door so that she could watch her reflection in the mirror and also see Maxine's slowly moving body on the bed beyond.

The leather collar seemed less uncomfortable than on the previous day. She fingered the bright metal studs and the rings of steel. She pictured Jem next to her, similarly naked but for a black leather choker; she imagined the two of them linked to each other by a short length of chain that obliged their faces to touch, their lips to meet constantly. Maxine gave a quiet groan of pleasure.

Julia next pulled on the long lace gloves, touching the material to her nipples as she crossed her arms to smooth the gloves against her skin. She turned away from the mirror, presenting her back to Maxine as she stepped into the boots and bent to tug the long leather cylinders round her calves and thighs, taking her time as she tightened the laces. 'Miss Julia, please come here, Miss Julia, please,' Maxine was calling to her, softly, but Julia merely smiled and stroked her hands up the taut black leather, from heels to thighs and across the rounded hillocks of her arse to her waist.

Today the soft leather tunic felt like a second skin. I look bloody marvellous, Julia said to herself as she lifted her long black curls above the lace-trimmed high collar and turned to look at herself in the mirror. Her breasts were contained within the shaped bodice, her bottom was almost completely covered by the tunic's stiff skirt, but the leather was cut away at the front of her thighs to frame her triangle of black hair. The wide belt had three buckles, and as she tightened them one after another she felt her sexuality throbbing more insistently with the increasing constriction of her waist. She was dressed. She gave Maxine a final display of her hindquarters as she reached into the wardrobe for her flicker; then she turned and strode to the bed.

Maxine had collapsed on the quilt, both hands clenched between her moving thighs, her eyes only half open as she watched Julia approach. 'Up!' Julia shouted, pretending the be angry with her voluptuous maid. 'On your knees. And keep playing with yourself!'

Maxine struggled into an upright position. Julia's eyes followed the maid's big breasts as they swayed from side to side. She slapped her flicker against her leather-clad thigh and, having enjoyed the sensation, she did it again, harder. She was definitely starting to have fun in Security, she thought, and pressed the strip of plaited leather into Maxine's trembling mounds.

'Where is your right hand, Maxine?' she said, tapping the girl's right nipple with the tip of the slender whip.

'Here, Miss,' the maid replied with a smile, 'between my legs.'

'And where are your fingers?'

'I've got two up inside me, Miss, and my thumb's just touching my little button.'

Julia used the tip of the flicker to push the maid's left nipple into its vast cushion of flesh. 'And your left hand?'

'In my arse, Miss. I've got two fingers up my bum.'

'Good girl, Maxine.' Julia allowed the nipple to spring back into position. She used the flicker on each breast in turn, stroking it upwards, lifting the heavy pendant bulbs of flesh, flicking the nipples and letting the breasts drop again with a bounce against the girl's ribs. 'I'd love to flicker your breasts properly,' she said, 'and watch you come at the same time. But I've got to do some more silly old training. I'll have to leave you here to enjoy yourself without me.'

'Thank you, Miss,' the maid said, red-faced and struggling to overcome the tremors in her voice. 'I'll tidy the room this morning, if that's alright. And Miss – don't forget you said you'd try to arrange for me to meet Miss Jem.'

'I won't forget, Maxine. And if I succeed, you naughty little thing, I'm going to give myself a reward. I'm going to give myself your great big breasts to play with. That's what the Master would call an incentive.'

Lucy had woken to find herself alone in her room. Asmita had gone.

There was still no sign of her at breakfast. Lucy, oblivious to the scandalised glances of the waitresses, was devouring a third grapefruit half when she noticed the man in the Jeeves outfit snaking across the dining-room. He was making for her table. When he reached it, he bowed. Lucy, who had been preparing for a verbal duel, found herself without an opponent. The man was even more obsequious than usual, and had removed all trace of his habitual half-concealed sneer.

'Madam,' he murmured. 'I'm terribly sorry to disturb your meal.'

'Don't worry. You can't really call it a meal anyway, can you?'

The man winced. 'My sincere apologies, madam, if the catering displeases in any way. I am the Under-Manager and of course I'll do my utmost to comply with any dietary requests. But first: there is an urgent missive for you at the reception desk. It arrived by courier; by very special courier, if you take my meaning. Please allow me to escort you.'

Lucy had no idea what the Under-Manager was talking about, but she was interested in important messages. And the Under-Manager seemed to think that this particular message was on a par with a summons to Buckingham Palace. She followed him to the Club's front hallway.

The Under-Manager disappeared into a curtain-covered alcove, and returned with a grey metal strongbox which he placed on the reception desk. He pulled a bunch of keys from his waistcoat, unlocked the box, and opened it with the élan of a quiz-show compère. He withdrew a long envelope, holding it between finger and thumb as if he expected it to burst into flames. He placed it on a silver plate, which he then offered to Lucy.

The envelope was sealed with a blob of red wax, into which had been imprinted a cursive capital M. It meant nothing to Lucy. She ripped open the envelope and turned away from the desk to shield the contents from the Under-Manager's curious gaze. There was a single sheet of paper bearing a brief message.

> *Trust me. I'm a friend. I will provide the*
> *answers to the questions you've been asking.*
> *Meet me in the equipment room of the tennis*
> *court pavilion at 1.00 pm today. Make sure you*
> *are not followed. Walk alongside, and not*
> *within, the avenue of silver birches. Burn this note and*
> *the envelope that contained it.*

Lucy's first thought was that the note must be from Julia; but then, as she re-read the strange instructions, doubts entered her mind. She should have been thrilled – she had a real lead at last – but she kept puzzling over the mystery of the avenue of silver birches. The Under-Manager coughed discreetly, his eyes straying to the paper as he loomed at Lucy's shoulder.

'Is there anything at all I can do, madam? Only too glad to be of service in any way at all . . .'

'Oh, er – no thanks.' Lucy crumpled the note in her hand. 'I'm just going up to my room. Oh yes! Could you have someone bring up some tennis clothes? Thank you. Oh – and a box of matches, too, please.'

'Only too happy to oblige, madam,' the Under-Manager said. Suddenly I'm a VIP, Lucy thought; this letter must be from someone in high places. I think I'm getting somewhere at last.

* * *

'I'm glad to see you looking well this morning.' Terence Headman's black cloak covered him from throat to ankles; his blue eyes glittered behind the grotesquely-shaped mask that covered the upper half of his face, not to disguise but rather to add menace to his appearance. Jem had some idea of the sights she was about to witness; and she was torn between excitement and distaste.

'I had a good night's sleep. I'm ready for anything.'

'I would expect no less of you, Jem. I see you have found yet another resplendent costume.'

Jem's bra consisted of two cones of red leather, each tipped with a silver spike, held in place by an excessive array of chains that ran round her torso and up to a red leather collar. She wore red lace gloves and stockings, the latter held up by chains clipped to a wide belt; also clipped to the belt were three chains between which was a tiny red leather cache-sex. 'I thought this would be suitable for a trip to the dungeons,' she said.

They were standing outside the door of Headman's dressing room in the Round Tower, in a corridor dimly lit by arrow-slits filled with stained glass in deep recesses in the walls at each end. Headman opened a concealed door in the base of a statue of a satyr carrying off a nymph, and extracted a portable phone. He dialled a number, replaced the instrument, and declared he was ready to leave.

'I'll have to blindfold you, Jem. Only Security personnel are allowed where we're going.'

'You just like to get me helpless,' Jem said with what she hoped was a betwitching smile. 'But OK – just so long as the blindfold matches my outfit.' Inwardly she cursed; she had wanted to find out the route from Headman's eyrie to the Security headquarters.

Two young Security men climbed towards them up the spiral staircase, and Jem allowed them to cover her eyes with a strip of red silk. She couldn't see; Headman pulled her hair free of the blindfold, tightened the knot, squeezed her leather-bound breasts as he kissed her tenderly, and took her arm.

They walked only a few steps before Headman pulled her to a stop. She heard him pressing buttons, and then she heard a click, followed by the swish of a door opening. So that's how to open the sealed door outside Headman's suite, she thought; the only problem is that I don't know the code number.

The little group moved forward. Jem felt a change in temperature – the air beyond the door was a few degrees colder – and then her feet were on uncarpeted stairs that spiralled downwards. Jem was grateful for Headman's hand on her arm, although she could have managed without his other, which gripped the chain between her buttocks.

Jem counted the steps: a hundred and twenty, give or take a few. She assumed that they must by now be under ground.

The floor was level, but still bare. Headman stopped again; there was more button-pressing to open a door. The group moved on.

Jem sensed that they had entered a large space: she could hear people talking nearby and in the distance, voices on radios crackly with static, the hum of electronic equipment and air conditioning. From the fifteenth to the twenty-first century in a hundred and twenty steps, Jem mused; not bad going. Orders were being issued, reports were being received. She was sure they had arrived in some sort of control room. This could be the heart of the Security network, and she couldn't see a damned thing! Her escort moved across the vast room, saying nothing except for Headman's single brusque greeting: 'Morning, Chief!'

Anderson, Jem thought. Chief Anderson. Julia's boss. In which case this must be the Rotunda – the Security base beneath the Great Hall. Is the dungeon here, too, in the cellars of the Round Tower?

No, I guess not, she said to herself as they reached the far side of the echoing chamber, because it looks like we're going for a ride. Headman lifted her on to a leather seat, and she felt him and the two guards climb on to seats nearby. There was a jerk, and they started moving forward. An underground train, Jem realised. Not much noise; probably electric. Impossible to estimate speed or distance. Where the hell are we going?

The vehicle stopped. Headman and the guards dismounted. Jem winced as fingers closed round her nipples and pulled fiercely; she had to follow the movement, and found herself falling forward, out of her seat and into Headman's arms. He kissed her again, and then pushed her away. She heard more buttons being pressed, and the slide of metal doors. Headman pulled her forward on to a stone floor, and then through a set of swing doors. She felt her heels sinking into carpet, and blinked as the blindfold was removed. The guards had gone. She was alone with the Master.

'I just hope you haven't ruined my make-up,' she said petulantly as her eyes swept across her surroundings.

The quality of the furniture couldn't disguise the emptiness of the gloomy room. It was a long rectangle, almost a corridor, in which a few armchairs and couches were all facing towards the one long wall that was not made of monumental stone blocks. Instead, this wall consisted of darkened glass. The room was a viewing gallery.

Jem found the place unnerving, but tried to look unconcerned as she deposited herself on a leather-upholstered couch. She watched Headman remove his cloak: he revealed a costume not unlike Jem's, although all in black. Chains ran round his body and met at two rings, at the centre of his chest and back; from the metal rings inset into his wide leather belt hung an assortment of whips and lengths of chain. His boots and gauntlets were of black leather, and his codpiece of fine black gauze was already stretched to transparency by the semi-erection of his twitching member. He sat on a couch behind a console of switches set into a coffee table.

'Remove that silly jockstrap, Jem, and come over here. Sit on the arm of my couch. That's my ever-dutiful concubine. Legs wide apart, you should know that by now. That's better. And now show me those luscious lips of yours . . . And open them for me, use your fingers, Jem, I want to see right inside. That's perfect.'

Headman studied Jem's vagina for several minutes. He neither spoke nor touched her. Jem stared at the top of his head. She loathed him; she knew that, but she couldn't help the feelings that his steady gaze seemed to be causing between her legs. She began to think that it was his eyes, and not her own fingers, that were separating the delicate membranes, pinching the plump flesh of her lips, pushing against the soft skin of her inner thighs. She could feel the itch deep inside her; the gradual seepage of fluid collecting into a heavy droplet at the mouth of the gully.

At last Headman moved. He removed one of his gauntlets, and placed a finger on the droplet. Jem shivered. 'What I adore about you, Jem,' he said, without removing his finger, 'is your intransigence. There are countless women here. All of them are at least pretty, or striking in their way. Some are more beautiful than you, you know. Most of them are obedient; unthinkingly obedient. Anyone can be transformed into a slave, Jem, with adequate application of fear and pain and pleasure. It's almost too easy. They obey, but I find I take little pleasure in them. A few retain a remnant of their previous selves; they obey, but they remember that they should not obey, and it causes them great shame. These I find entertaining, if only for a while. They allow themselves to perform the most indecent acts, to have humiliation heaped on them – and all the time they are blaming themselves for transgressing moral codes which have no meaning here. They blush as they are penetrated, as if it was their fault, and the penetration is thus much sweeter. But you, Jem: you're not in either of these categories. You don't need to be trained into obedience, because there's nothing you won't agree to do. You're quite without shame, and so you never feel degraded. And yet there's some resistance in you, something I can't identify. Intransigence, I called it; and yet you've never refused me. There's just something in your bearing that suggests you might refuse me, if it pleased you to do so. You obey, and yet you act as if you could choose not to obey. It that it, Jem?'

Jem's heart was in her mouth. 'It's not an act,' she said, and thrust her hips forward to capture Headman's finger in her dripping hole. Would he recognise the truth now that she had admitted it?

Headman chuckled, and wriggled his trapped finger. 'That reminds me,' he said, 'I have work to do today. And work, in the dungeon, usually entails the use of my riding crop. And a riding crop is much more effective when wet. I'll retrieve my finger, if I may, and replace it with the sharp end of my crop. And while that's going on, let's see what's happening in the dungeon.'

Headman leant forward and touched a button on the console, then turned to his task of pushing his riding crop, centimetre by centimetre, into Jem. After each push he jiggled the handle of the crop, and each time Jem's shiver of pleasure started more deeply and spread more widely than the last. She almost failed to notice that the lights in the room were fading almost to nothing, while other lights were springing into life beyond the dark glass screen.

Jem pushed her sex together round the thin cylinder of leather, gasping as her labia touched the chill corrugations. 'That's far enough,' she said. 'Let's soak it for a while, and I'll take a look at this dungeon of yours.'

The dungeon was a vast chamber, its shadowy vaulting supported by massive columns of black stone. Its walls were a maze of walkways, balconies and buttresses; Security guards stood to attention here and there. It was difficult to differentiate the floor from the walls: every corner was a black shadow, and the floor seemed to consist of a jumble of flagstoned platforms connected to each other by ramps and steps. Fires burnt in the deepest pits; on some platforms, and at the shadowy edges of the chamber, iron cages and rows of cells contained huddled and naked prisoners.

The viewing gallery seemed to be about one-third of the way up one of the walls. Near to it, presumably to entertain its occupants, other prisoners had been secured in more interesting constraints. On one platform a young woman with spiky black hair was standing sandwiched between two parallel sheets of curved wood so that she was bent forward at the waist but her back was flexed into an upright position. Holes had been cut in the wooden panels so that her buttocks and breasts protruded.

Nearby a man swathed in chains was seated in a hole in the centre of a circular wooden platform. His bare arse hung from the bottom of the platform, which was itself suspended on chains from a wheel at the apex of a pyramid of scaffolding. Cogs and chains connected the wheel to handles at the base of the scaffolding, and Jem assumed that the entire platform could thereby be raised, lowered, and turned like a carousel. Beneath the platform, and beneath the man's exposed buttocks, was another mechanism with a row of artificial penises arranged in order of size. Jem didn't like to imagine how this part of the contraption worked.

Hanging from a gargoyle that jutted from the wall near to the viewing gallery were a man and a woman bound in an embrace. Their ankles were tied behind each other's backs, and their wrists were chained together above their heads. They were sitting on a gigantic uplifted hand, part of a leering statue carved into one of the columns; and each of them was impaled on an upraised finger.

Jem was only a few metres away from them. She could see the beads of sweat on the woman's back, and the open-mouthed expression of discomfort and outrage on the man's face resting on the woman's shoulder. She saw the man try to alleviate their distress: the muscles in his arms bulged as he grasped the chains above them and pulled himself and the woman upwards. But he was unable to pull them high enough to release the stone fingers from his anus and his partner's vagina, and with a look of despair on his face he was obliged to lower both bodies back on to their impalement.

What's happening to me? Jem thought, not for the first time since her arrival in the Private House. She was appalled by the couple's moans of anguish, audible even through the thick soundproofed glass, but even more disturbed to feel her insides churning with excitement at the sound.

She might have guessed that Headman would not fail to notice the involuntary spasm of her thighs. 'You're obviously excited by my dungeon, Jem,' he said. 'It's certainly one of my favourite haunts. Have you spotted your chosen victim yet?'

'No – I don't see her. Where is she?'

'She's on the clock, Jem. And the clock, as you might expect, is on the wall.'

Jem scanned the nighted walls. Above and beyond the impaled couple, a strange machine stood on a ledge. Bound upright to the machine, with leather straps at each ankle, above each knee, round each wrist, above each elbow, around her neck and below her breasts, was a naked girl. She was dark-skinned, with long black hair, wide hips, a narrow waist, and small breasts with large, dark aureoles.

'Tell me, Jem,' Headman said, vibrating the crop upwards, towards the apex of Jem's slippery slit, 'precisely why did you request the punishment of Asmita? She's a mere junior field operative. She works out at the Health Club.'

Jem, trembling, was finding it difficult to think clearly. This was the one question to which she had not been able to dream up a reasonable answer. 'Oh – nothing particular,' she said. 'I just heard she was pretty, you know . . .'

'Don't expect me to believe that. I've had the girl researched. She's a friend of your new "bodyguard", isn't she? I suspect a simple case of feminine jealousy.'

'Oh no,' said Jem, trying to sound unconvincing, 'honestly, Master, it isn't anything like that!'

'I thought so,' Headman said, jiggling his riding crop for emphasis. 'Well, I don't mind. When I'm half-way through dealing with her, I'll tell her that the whole punishment is a present from you.'

'No!' Jem was horrified. 'No, please, Master, you can't do that! I'll do anything – '

'You will do whatever I demand of you, Jem, or you'll find yourself on the clock on the dungeon wall. But Asmita's punishment is your treat; I won't breathe a word to your victim. That suits me: I prefer to chastise the innocent, particularly when they have no idea why they are being punished. We had better have her taken down and prepared.'

Headman reached for the console intercom. Jem placed a hand on his arm. 'And why, Master, is that contraption known as a clock?'

'Because that is exactly what it is. And look: we're in luck. We're just in time for a demonstration.'

The machine on the wall was beginning to move. Jem

147

saw that each of Asmita's plump brown limbs was tied to a separate length of metal. Each leg was strapped into a concave girder that extended from mid-thigh to ankle and then followed a right-angle to support the foot. The girder holding Asmita's left leg had started to move in an arc, lifting the leg until it was almost horizontal. Jem was sure that if the girder moved any further, Asmita's leg would become dislocated from her hip; but the girder stopped moving, pointing the leg almost to the 3 on an imaginary clock face.

From the depths of the machine a lever extended into the space between Asmita's legs. Wide strips of leather hung from the end of the lever; and when it jerked upwards, although it did not strike any part of the girl's body, its tail of whips swished against the bottom of her raised thigh and the stretched membrane between her legs. Asmita, unable to move, could acknowledge the blow only with a toss of her head. After nine more strokes, the lever retracted and Asmita's leg was lowered to a vertical position.

'A quarter past ten,' Headman said. Jem had to admit that the clock was an amusing device; she suspected, from what Julia had told her about Asmita, that the Asian girl also found it entertaining.

'I guess,' Jem said, 'that at fifteen minutes to the hour the right leg is lifted to point to where the 9 would be?'

'Of course. At half past, the victim is bent forward from the waist, the legs are parted, and the whip is extended rather less. The lashes land on the lower part of the buttocks.'

'And on the hour?'

'The arms are lifted above the head – '

' – to point to 12 – '

' – and two smaller whips emerge to strike the hour on the victim's breasts.'

'Very ingenious, Master.'

'Indeed. Accurate, too. The mechanism was made for me in Switzerland. But I will have to have amplification installed if the chimes are as muted as those of your pretty rival. And now we really must bring her down and have her prepared. It's such a shame you're determined to maintain your anonymity, Jem. You could have taken her place on the clock, and shown her how to call out the time.'

Jem did her best to appear disappointed. 'It's more comfortable here,' she said.

'Your comfort is always secondary to my enjoyment, Jem. But in this case, there's little doubt that I'll enjoy the next hour. I must go and consult Asmita's file. The entertainment will commence shortly. Use this button to call Security if you want refreshments of any kind; this one turns on the sound, like this – ' the gallery filled with a murmur of noise from the dungeon – 'but be careful to keep silent: the communication is two-way.'

Jem nodded. Headman leant towards the console. 'Nyman!' he shouted, his voice echoing round the dungeon and within the gallery. 'Bring the operative Asmita down from the clock! Get her ready for punishment!'

Headman pulled Jem's face to his and kissed her fiercely as he withdrew the riding crop from her gaping sex. From its mid-point to its tip the thin leather cylinder was darkly impregnated with her secretion. He pushed Jem away, brought the crop down across the tops of her thighs, and with a clatter of chains, strode from the room.

Jem gritted her teeth and massaged the red lines that had flared across her skin. On one of the dungeon platforms a huge woman with arms and thighs as thick as telegraph poles had emerged from the shadows, cracking a bullwhip. The report echoed like machine-gun fire from the blackened walls. 'You heard the Master!' roared Dungeon Supervisor Nyman with a voice as rough as a chainsaw. 'You up there! Take her to the washroom and get her tidied up!'

Jem, alone but for the amplified hubbub of moans from the prisoners behind the glass screen, pondered whether she should allow the game to continue. But how could she stop it now, without destroying every part of her plan? She was staking everything on one wild scheme; she had no contingency plans. She had dreamt up this dungeon drama as an insurance policy to cement Julia's loyalty and, almost unconsciously, as a sort of test for Headman. But if the Master of the Private House proved to be as unhinged and

149

cruel as Jem was beginning to suspect – to what terrible danger had she exposed Julia's innocent young friend?

Jem was relieved to see that Asmita looked composed, and almost cheerful, as two guards led her to the centre of the dungeon. She looked none the worse for her ordeal on the clock; her long black hair glinted in the light of the fires and torches, and her large dark nipples appeared to be stiffly erect. Perhaps this will be entertaining after all, Jem thought, sliding into a corner of the leather upholstery and caressing the insides of her widely-parted thighs.

Nyman held Asmita's wrists in one of her football-sized fists while the two guards struggled to bring in the square wooden frame that Jem had seen used for the 'sacrifice' during the Master's homecoming banquet. They locked the wheels and then tied Asmita inside the frame so that each of her limbs was stretched towards one of the four corners. Jem's fingers encountered the wetness of her own crotch as she watched Headman place his hand between Asmita's splayed legs. He prodded, pulled and slapped the dark stretched flesh; Asmita merely smiled. She continued to smile as the giantess Nyman started to flick her breasts with a many-tailed whip.

Headman put his fingers to his nose. 'You're enjoying this, aren't you?' he said, almost to himself. 'Most people can be trained to take pleasure in a little pain, if the hurt is associated with sexual stimulation. A primitive Pavlovian reaction. But you, Asmita my dear, seem to be a natural. You're a volunteer?'

'Yes, Master,' Asmita said proudly, expecting praise.

'I hate volunteers!' Headman seemed to be shaking with sudden rage. Jem was unable to tell whether his anger was feigned, but she had a horrible feeling that it wasn't. 'Volunteers are arrogant, ungovernable and above all untrustworthy,' Headman ranted. 'You act as if you own the place. But only I, the Master, own the Private House! Do you understand?'

'Yes, Master. Of course, Master.' Asmita twisted in her bonds, suddenly confused and frightened. 'I'm sorry, Master. I always try to be dutiful. What have I done to displease?'

'What's that got to do with it?' Headman screamed. 'You're here for punishment, you imbecilic girl, not for trial, or judgement, or correction. This has nothing whatsoever to do with any misdemeanours you may have committed.'

Asmita began to sob. Headman's voice was suddenly calm and cold, and so quiet that Jem could barely hear his words. 'And appeals for clemency are pointless. Save your tears for later; I promise you you'll need them. As you're a volunteer and, according to your file, a volunteer who can stand any amount of beating, we have prepared a very special punishment for you. You'll be sorry to hear that there will be no more whipping today.'

Asmita raised her head. Her eyes were wide with fear as she saw the cabinet that one of the guards was wheeling towards her. With a lurch in her stomach, Jem considered the possibility that the cabinet contained surgical instruments; and then the thought that the Asian girl had imagined the same terror.

Headman, oblivious to the girl's whimpers, continued in the same even tone. 'Your file makes interesting reading. You are obviously a fearless young woman, in most respects. But there is a note that refers to your childhood; it suggests that you have an abnormal phobia in respect of — these!'

His hand jerked from within the cabinet and he produced a huge hypodermic syringe with a needle as long as a finger. He thrust it in front of Asmita's face.

The girl froze. Her eyes, as big as saucers, bulged. Then she remembered to breathe, and started to scream. The wooden frame shook with the violence of her struggles.

Headman replaced the syringe. 'How gratifying to discover that our records are accurate,' he said. 'Loosen her arms a little. Hold her still, Nyman, and you two, insert a cross-beam level with her thighs.'

A plank was placed across the centre of the frame, forcing back Asmita's wide hips. Her buttocks were now rounded but still soft and yielding, as Jem could see from Headman's manipulation of the big brown orbs. Asmita's screams had dissolved into blubbering sobs.

'Don't worry, my child,' Headman was saying. 'The big hypodermic was merely to prove the point, if you'll forgive the dreadful pun. I don't intend to stick it into your lovely large bottom. As long as we know you don't like needles, any needles will do. Have you heard of the Chinese art of acupuncture?'

Asmita wailed.

'I assume that you have,' Headman went on, 'and that you have understood the implications. I hardly need add, therefore, that in my opinion your backside is in need of urgent medical attention, and that acupuncture is without doubt the most suitable treatment.'

He pulled open the doors of the cabinet to reveal row upon row of objects that resembled gigantic drawing pins with slender needles and stubby heads. Asmita started to scream again. Headman tutted. 'Gag her,' he said absently; he glanced up thoughtfully to the viewing gallery, and smiled. 'No – let her make as much noise as she wants to. Now, my dear; stick your arse out for me. According to your file, that is your favourite position.'

Headman waited until the quivering girl obeyed his instruction. With one hand caressing the curves of her bottom, he took one of the pins from the cabinet. Then, after a moment's thought, he moved to stand in front of her. He remained silent until Asmita's tearful eyes focused on the object he held between his fingers.

'Don't worry,' he said, 'they are sterilised. I will insert this one in the centre of your right buttock. It really won't be very painful. But of course you will be able to feel the point as I position it against your skin. And then the sharp nip of pain as it pierces the surface. And then, of course, the sensation of the needle sliding slowly and deeply into your flesh . . .'

Asmita was frantic with fear. Jem felt sick. Headman showed no emotion; the usual half-smile was on his face as he spent more than a minute pushing the pin into the girl's arse-cheek.

Methodically and very slowly, he inserted all of the pins. He showed each one to Asmita, waiting for her to look at it, before moving behind her to press the point against her dark skin. He arranged them symmetrically, alternating between the buttocks, working his way inwards and downwards from both sides, increasing the concentration of pins towards the central crack and the low curves closest to the black sex-pouch.

Jem couldn't move. She was spellbound, watching with appalled fascination. Asmita's body was glistening with sweat, but her struggles decreased. At last Jem thought the girl might have fainted, but Headman continued in his methodical work until no pins remained in the cabinet.

He stood in front of Asmita, staring at her bowed head hanging between her upstretched arms. He grabbed her sweat-drenched hair, and yanked her head up. Her mouth was slack, her eyes closed.

Headman cursed softly, and summoned a guard to bring a bucket of cold water and a sponge. As the icy liquid trickled down her back, Asmita began to babble pleas for mercy.

Headman spoke slowly, as if to a backward child. 'I have already told you,' he said, 'there is no point in asking for clemency. The punishment is fixed; it will continue until it is ended. There is nothing that anyone can do to stop it.' As he said this he glanced again towards the viewing gallery, as if he had guessed that Jem was about to interfere. With a sigh, Jem sank back on to the couch.

'Now,' Headman continued brightly, as if offering coffee after a meal, 'are you ready for the next stage?'

Asmita merely groaned, a despairing cry that made Jem shudder.

'The next stage,' Headman said, 'is ignition. Puncturing the skin is only the first part of the treatment. This is an ancient Chinese method for relieving muscular strains. You might call it deep heating. The strange bulbous head of each pin is a sort of slow-burning fuse; when lit, it smoulders, and the heat travels all the way to the tip of the needle, which is embedded deep inside the muscle. Of course, we've improved on the Chinese originals. These pins develop a much more intense heat, and the needles themselves are very much more conductive. In fact almost every bit of the heat produced by the slow burning is conducted along the needle. Needless to say, it's agonisingly painful; but there is surprisingly little damage to the tissue. I'll demonstrate.'

He struck a match and held it to the head of the first pin he had inserted. The bulb started to smoke, and then to glow. Asmita suddenly stiffened, her body shook spasmodically, and she started to let out short, regular, panic-stricken shrieks of pain.

'Don't be melodramatic,' Headman said, rubbing his hand back and forth beneath the forest of pins. 'It's only pain. You might find you like it. You'll come to no harm. There will be no scars, which I gather is another of your curious fears. You will simply have an unbearably hot bottom for – well, for however long I decide to take to light each one of those interesting pins.'

Asmita's animal noises turned to floods of tears. She bawled like a baby, bereft of hope. Jem felt tears, of helplessness and rage, start in her own eyes as she saw Headman grin and motion to one of the guards to stroke his bulging groin.

'You'll be pleased to hear that I'm enjoying this enormously, Asmita,' he said. 'I'll start to light the other pins now. Just think, my dear, if I light all of them the pain will be thirty times greater than the pain you're feeling now.'

Asmita's sobs increased in volume as Headman touched flame to several more of the pin-heads, including three pairs that almost touched their partners across the divide between the two cheeks. Jem could imagine the threads of agony working their way into the girl's flesh. Headman's hand worked between Asmita's legs, idly at first and then with sharp upwards slaps as the girl started to scream and writhe. He waited until every pin that he had lit was glowing brightly before picking up the bucket and carrying it to the front of the frame.

'Now, my little volunteer, shall I tell you how you can persuade me to stop this?'

When Asmita only continued to shriek and buck against the cross-beam, he took a handful of water and threw it into her face. She recovered her senses a little. 'Stop it, please, please, stop it!' she sobbed. 'I'm on fire, I'm burning. I'm burning inside. Please, stop it, you must stop it, please . . .'

Headman held the bucket in front of her face. 'Cold water,' he said. 'This will put out the fire. Would you like me to pour it over your burning bottom?'

'Please,' Asmita sobbed. 'Yes, please, please.'

'And what would you do for me in return?'

'Aaah! It hurts! Anything, anything at all, I'll do anything, I can't stand it . . .'

'Anything? In that case, Asmita my dear, we might be able to come to an arrangement. Listen carefully: I want you to overcome your fear of needles.' He produced a steel needle half a metre in length. 'Although this could be said to be more of a skewer than a needle.'

Jem could hardly believe her ears. Was there no limit to the horrors that Headman could invent? Asmita was staring blank-eyed at the thin cylinder of bright steel until her mind was again overwhelmed by the pain invading her hindquarters, and she gave out a long keening cry. 'What,' she struggled to say, 'what do you want me to do?'

'As you probably know, Asmita,' Headman said conversationally, 'I admire body decoration. I'm sure you've seen the chains worn by my personal slaves, and I'm sure you've been envious of them. Your breasts aren't large, but you have very well-developed nipples. And I'm sure you've often thought how attractive they'd look if you could hang gold chains, or jewellery, from them – if only you could overcome your fear of needles.'

Asmita shook her head from side to side as she wept. Headman's voice continued relentlessly. 'Well, it doesn't much matter whether you want pierced nipples or not. The fact remains that the only way to persuade me to empty this bucket over your arse is to ask me very nicely to push this needle through your big brown teats. Beg me to do it, Asmita; and if you make it sound convincing, I'll put out your fire.'

He placed the needle across her breasts, pushing the nipples into the large aureoles. Asmita stared up at him, pain and fear momentarily replaced by an expression of simple hatred.

'Please, Master,' she said, with her voice shaking but

155

with a steady placing of each word, 'please pierce my nipples. But first, please put out the fire in my bottom.'

'Well done, Asmita!' Headman was triumphant. 'I knew you could do it. It's not difficult to defeat these irrational phobias. I knew you'd eventually beg me to pierce your flesh. I'm so pleased you've come to love needles. I'll pierce your nipples slowly and carefully, my dear, and you will say please and thank you before and after each gentle push.'

He made a sign to one of the guards, who picked up the bucket and carried it behind Asmita. Jem, blinded by her tears, could see no more. She groped for the intercom button so that her sobs would not be heard in the dungeon.

Asmita, she cried inwardly, I'm so sorry! I didn't know it would be anything like this. But I'll make him pay, Asmita. This morning's work won't be in vain. Terence Headman has been tried and found guilty. He'll wish he'd never met me. He'll wish he'd never been born!

By the time Headman returned to the viewing gallery, Jem had repaired her shattered emotions. She was sipping the coffee and reading the newspaper that she had requested from the Security guards. Headman lifted an eyebrow: he appeared to be surprised that she had not remained absorbed in the activities in the dungeon.

'I hope the entertainment was to your liking?' he said. 'Heated acupuncture needles are a useful addition to the dungeon equipment; I must use them again soon.'

'It was all very – moving,' Jem said, hoping to suggest that she had found Asmita's ordeal arousing but was too coy to admit it.

Headman smiled knowingly. 'There's nothing a woman enjoys as much as watching the suffering of a rival.'

Jem smiled sweetly. 'You're so right,' she said. 'Did you enjoy it too?'

'Of course. A pretty girl in agony – what could be more fun? I only wish it had been you, Jem.'

Here comes the difficult bit, Jem thought. 'I'll take that as a compliment,' she said. 'But my thorough lubrication of your riding crop seems to have been a waste of time.'

Headman's eyes sparkled icily. 'Not necessarily, Jem. It seems that these days I never tire of inflicting pain. Would you care for a thrashing?'

Jem contrived an expression of melting delight. 'What a lovely idea, Master! The perfect finish to an entertaining morning. I'll kneel on the couch, like this, and lean forward across the backrest.'

She parted her legs, hollowed her back, and pushed her bottom upwards to create an irresistible target. She glanced over her shoulder to see Headman stroking the tip of his crop up and down the length of his barely-covered erection. His eyes were fixed on the flawless split peach of her arse. She found herself almost wanting the pain. 'Whip me hard, please, Master,' she whispered.

Five bulls out of six shots! Julia could hardly believe her eyes, and she jumped to her feet and walked to the target. As Instructor Harrison had said, it was just like sex – a matter of technique and practice. She touched the little feathers that protruded from the darts embedded in the canvas. The air pistol was only a short-range weapon that looked like a child's toy, but at close quarters it was possible to place a dart precisely. Julia gazed at it thoughtfully, replaced it in the holster at her belt, and looked up to see Harrison beckoning to her.

'Good shooting, Julia,' he called as she approached. 'If that target had been me, I'd be so full of sleepers I wouldn't wake up until next week. Next session we'll try you with moving targets – but right now you're wanted on the phone. Chief Anderson himself.'

Julia took the receiver from his hand, pressing herself against his tunic as his fingers crept round her hip and on to her bushy mound. Anderson's voice was gruff and urgent. 'Julia? Report here at once. That woman Larson has disappeared off the screens. We've lost her.'

Julia, still savouring her new-found sharpshooting skills, nestled her head against Harrison's shoulder. 'What's the problem, Chief?' she said lightly. 'Asmita's over at the Club, and – '

'Asmita is not at the Club,' Anderson barked. 'Don't

question orders, Julia. Asmita's been taken to the – she's been taken away. Off this case.'

Julia stiffened. Instructor Harrison diplomatically removed his questing fingers. 'Asmita?' Julia was bewildered. 'Why, Chief? What's going on?'

'Not my idea, Julia. Orders from the Master himself. That's not our concern. We've lost track of Lucy Larson, that's the immediate problem. Get over here for a briefing immediately. Understood?'

'Yes, Chief.' Julia let Harrison take the receiver from her hand. Asmita's in trouble somewhere, she thought, and I've got to leave her and look for the tiresome Larson creature over at the Health Club.

'Bad news?' Harrison asked.

'I don't know,' Julia said slowly. 'But something's going on.'

In the slatted sunlight, Lucy removed her tennis shoes and tiptoed across the creaking floorboards. It was hot in the pavilion; motes of dust hung in the lifeless air. As she reached the window she dropped to her knees, and then cautiously raised her head to the level of the sill. Beneath the wooden blind was a gap through which she could survey the tennis courts: it was lunchtime, and no one was playing. The spectators' benches and the avenue of silver birches were deserted.

Lucy grinned. She hadn't been followed. This was what she called real detective work – the kind of work she didn't get half enough of in the Force. She glanced at her wristwatch: 12:56. It was time to find the equipment room, but Lucy found herself drifting into a reverie. It was very warm in the pavilion, and Lucy squatted on her haunches, resting her back against the wall and flapping her tiny pleated skirt. She felt excited, but drowsy. She spread her thighs and placed her fingers against the tight gusset of the white cotton panties: yes, she was wet again. She knew police officers who hated the tension of the job, the stake-outs, the early morning raids, the secret assignations with untrustworthy informants; but Lucy loved every nerve-tingling minute. The silence, the furtiveness, the waiting:

to Lucy it was the delicious, lingering foreplay to an explosive climax of action. Her restless fingers gathered the expanse of white cotton that half-covered her suspended buttocks and pulled it into the crack between them. She ran her hands across the exposed taut globes and buried her fingernails in the bunched strip of material, pushing the cloth into the deep tender valley. Then, with little gasps of breath, she teased apart the lips of her sex, pulling on the blonde hairs and rolling back the pink flesh, until the cotton gusset was a bunched and sodden strip almost hidden inside her. Tight, uncomfortable, but very exciting: Lucy felt that her knickers were now just like her favourite situations.

There was something else about this pavilion: it stirred a memory . . . Of course! The pavilion at school. It had been a hot, dusty day, like this one, and the room had smelt of wood and sweat and sunlight. Lucy had been playing lacrosse, and had bruised her ankle. Helen, a shy girl who was in Lucy's class but not in her sporty set of friends, had helped Lucy to hobble to the pavilion. Lucy had allowed Helen to stroke her damp brow and to place a get well kiss on the injured ankle; after a long pause filled with sunlight and anxious breathing, she had declined Helen's faltering offer of more kisses.

The two girls had done nothing else. Helen had stammered a few words and had fled, red-faced. But, Lucy realised, in a way that incident had been her First Time: her first tingling enjoyment of yearning, wide eyes, of a face gazing at her in embarrassed longing; the first time she had tasted the sweet pleasure of power over a supplicant suitor.

She stood up, and felt the thin line of her panties bite into her moist crease. She placed the palms of her hands across her jutting breasts, feeling her hard nipples through the material of the sports bra and the tennis shirt. There were three doors at the rear of the pavilion; the middle one bore a sign saying *Equipment Room*.

The door was padlocked. Almost without thinking, Lucy picked up the nearest suitable tool, a metal croquet hoop, and with one swift movement levered the pad bolt away from the wooden door. She lifted the latch, opened the door and took one step into the dark space beyond.

159

The air was colder. The rear wall of the equipment room was whitewashed brick: the pavilion was built against the perimeter wall of the Health Club's grounds. Lucy's eyes became accustomed to the gloom; she saw rickety cupboards, rolls of netting, stacks of wooden boxes – and a small cloaked figure, standing motionless in a corner. She took another step.

'Your name,' the figure said; a woman's voice.

'Larson – Lucy Larson.' Lucy almost forgot to omit her rank and number. 'Who are you?'

The figure threw back the hood of her cloak. Lucy saw an ethereally pretty face: a pointed chin, rosebud lips, wide cheekbones, startling blue eyes, a halo of long red-brown hair.

'A friend,' the woman said with a smile. 'And an ally, I hope. You broke in here like – a professional, shall we say? I want to trust you. This isn't a trick, but I must know: I think you are not what you seem, and I think that you want to find out the secrets of the Private House. Am I right?'

Lucy knew she had to think quickly. One wrong answer and she might frighten away this beautiful apparition, and lose the only real lead she had so far found. 'Yes,' she said bluntly, 'you're right. But how did you get in here – '

'Hush! It would take too long to explain. We don't have much time. They'll try to trace me and take me back. They could come at any moment. I heard that you've been asking questions. Do you want to hear what I know about this place?'

Lucy moved towards the cloaked figure, mesmerised by the sparkling eyes and aware of the woman's heavy, spicy perfume. She lowered her voice. 'Yes, of course. I want to know everything.'

'Then listen closely.' The woman spoke quickly, with a trace of an American accent. 'The Health Club – the mansion and the grounds, right up to this wall, are only a part of the Private House. The Club's a front, a cover. The House is huge, it butts on to the end of an old castle, and it's in the middle of a vast spread of land on the other side of this wall. Stretches for miles.'

'I saw a park, from the car; and some farmland . . .'

'That's all part of it. There's a complex organisation, hundreds of staff, unimaginable wealth. And they drag people in. It's impossible to escape. There are armed guards everywhere.'

'They kidnap people? And hold them prisoner in this big house?'

'You got it.'

'But what for?' Lucy hadn't known what to expect to hear, but she certainly wasn't ready to believe stories of mass kidnapping and a private army. 'Who runs this place? Terrorists? They're holding hostages?'

The woman shook her auburn curls with exasperation. 'No, nothing like that. The whole thing is run by a man who calls himself the Master. I know it sounds crazy! He acts like he's the king of his own little kingdom. The whole thing is set up to serve his sexual requirements. He's a bit weird, if you know what I mean.'

Lucy was beginning to wonder whether she was listening to the ramblings of an escapee from a mental hospital. Asmita's hints and behaviour supported the sex angle; perhaps there was a germ of truth in the pretty redhead's story. Maybe she'd been held captive so long that her sense of reality had snapped. 'I know you've probably had unpleasant experiences,' Lucy said, speaking slowly and clearly, 'but can you remember how long you've been held prisoner?'

'Two days,' the woman said, and Lucy had to admit that she didn't sound even a little bit confused. 'I'm not losing my mind. You don't believe what I told you about the Master? Take a look at this.'

The woman untied her cloak, turned, and let it drop to the floor. From her waist to her thighs her skin was criss-crossed with red weals. Lucy overcame the urge to run her fingers across the latticed perfect curves. The woman half-turned, and looked over her shoulder. 'The Master did that, about an hour ago,' she said, with a tremor in her voice that made Lucy feel weak at the knees. 'Now do you believe me?'

'OK,' Lucy said. 'Is there more?'

'Only this: the Master is some kind of big noise out in the

161

real world, I think. Someone from outside – someone with authority – has got to get inside and collect evidence against him. It's not just the wall and the guards that keep everyone imprisoned; there's also the knowledge that if one of us could escape, and could find anyone to believe the story, the Master has enough power and money to make sure the case could never come to trial. We need the help of a professional evidence-gatherer. Someone like you, perhaps?'

Lucy was lost in thought. Was it possible that Terence Headman knew that his Health Club was being used as a front for an organisation run by a man calling himself the Master? It was unbelievable. But how could he fail to know? Lucy had come to the Health Club on the trail of a handful of missing persons, and she'd unearthed a story about a madhouse – or from a madhouse. She was still suspicious of her auburn informant.

'What do you know about a woman called Julia?' she asked urgently. 'Your height and build, dark hair and eyes?'

'Be careful of her,' replied the woman, re-tying the ribbons at the neck of her cloak. 'She's in the Master's Security Corps. I don't know whose side she's on. Ours, I think. But don't tell her anything you know or suspect.'

'I wish I'd known that yesterday,' Lucy said, and then realised that she was falling in with the woman's bizarre story. 'Let's assume I'm interested; how can I get into the Private House?'

The woman laughed. 'By invitation only. You'll get in if the Master thinks you're sexy or useful – preferably both.'

'So what do I have to do?'

'Let me think. I guess you could try using Julia to carry information. Or disinformation, I should say. You're big, blonde and busty; you'd pass the physical for sure. So spin Julia a line. Tell her you're the wife of some wealthy industrialist; tell her that you're bored and frustrated, that you want excitement and danger. If Julia reports back, that little story should be enough to get you in.'

'And if I can get inside?'

'You're the expert, lady. Gather evidence, and get back

162

out with it, I guess. I'll be there, and I'll help you if I can.
But don't even look at me unless I give you the all-clear
first, OK?'

'You mean, we have to be alone to talk freely?'

'Alone, and out of microphone range, and away from
cameras. I'll tell you when it's safe; otherwise, stay in
character and under cover.'

Lucy scanned the walls. 'The pavilion?'

'Don't worry. It's clean.'

'Ah! The avenue of silver birches?'

'Video camera trained right down the middle. You
didn't – ?'

'No – I followed your directions.'

'Fine. Well, that's it. They'll be looking for you. You
shouldn't have worn the tennis outfit. They'll follow that
up. I bet when you get outside you find Julia warming up on
the courts. Get out of here – and good luck.'

Lucy made for the door. She turned back. 'What about
you?' she said.

'I'll be OK. Leave me here. Get going.'

'I don't even know your name.'

'You'll find out – when you get inside the Private House.'

'Maxine!' Julia's head was spinning. 'For goodness' sake,
Maxine, do be quiet, girl! I can't hear myself think.'

It had been another exciting, exhausting day, and Julia
couldn't decide whether or not she'd enjoyed it. From the
moment she'd woken to find Jem still asleep in her arms,
the day had seemed full of omens and portents. Her
triumphant morning at the firing range ended with the
news of Asmita's disappearance; her afternoon of
incompetent tennis against the invincible Lucy had ended
with a humiliating game of sexual forfeits in the dusty
pavilion, and Lucy's remarkable assertion that she was the
unfulfilled wife of a leading criminal lawyer.

She had returned to her room in the House, with her face
sticky with Lucy's juices and with the imprint of Lucy's
tennis racquet on her throbbing bottom, to find Maxine
bubbling over with eagerness to know the contents of the
letter that had been delivered to Julia's room.

Julia had refused to even look at the letter until she had had a long bath.

'How's the Master's consort today, Miss?' Maxine, patting talcum powder on to Julia's breasts, made yet another attempt to start a conversation.

'I've told you, Maxine, you silly goose. I haven't seen her since first thing this morning.'

'They say she's been all over the estate again this afternoon, Miss.'

'Do they. Have your gossip-mongers heard anything about a special punishment session in the dungeon this morning, by any chance?' Anderson's prevarication had made Julia fear the worst.

'I've heard it was pretty nasty, Miss. One of the Master's specials. I don't know who it was he had it in for, though.'

'And Jem was with the Master?' Julia forced herself to ask the question, dreading an affirmative answer.

'Not that I've heard, Miss. Not really her cup of tea, I shouldn't think. She was out and about this afternoon, though. She did a complete tour of the garden, and everyone came out of the temples and summer houses to talk to her, and then she led a whole crowd down to the lake and had everyone rowing about in those little pleasure-boats, you know, and then when John, the Master's chauffeur, appeared in the Rolls to take her back to the Round Tower, she pretended she couldn't hear him. She was in a boat with that bloke Sebastian, who's a servant now, and Rhoda from the airstrip who shouldn't have been there because she was supposed to be on duty, and they were all pretending that they couldn't understand John because he was talking in French, which of course he wasn't, and he was so angry he was hopping up and down on the bank, and everyone was laughing like mad, and even John saw the funny side of it in the end, and when she came ashore she told him to take her to visit the South Farm, so she never did go back to the Round Tower. I'll bet the Master was furious, silly old sod. Oh! Sorry, Miss, I meant no disrespect to the Master, Miss.'

'Don't worry, Maxine. I'm too tired to care. Shall we have a look at that mysterious envelope now?'

'Oh, yes, Miss. I'll fetch it.'

Julia opened the envelope and studied the brief note it contained while Maxine fidgeted in front of her.

'Take off your uniform,' Julia said at last. 'You're going to be a slave, just for this evening. You are required to be naked, except for collar, shoes, and chains round your wrists and ankles. I'm to take you to the Round Tower.'

Julia watched surprise, anxiety and excitement vie for supremacy on the girl's flushed face. 'Is it the Master who wants me, Miss?' the maid asked in a tremulous voice.

'Well, of course, Maxine. But I'll come with you. And Jem will be there too.'

'Thank you, Miss. I'm so excited! But will the Master want me to serve him, do you think? What will he do to me?'

Julia unbuttoned the maid's black blouse, and pulled aside the material to caress the white mounds that overflowed the corset's half-cups. 'When he sees these, darling, he'll want to do what all your boyfriends want to do. Although, knowing the Master, I imagine he might decide to tie you up first, or something like that.'

Maxine smiled happily. 'That's alright, then. What about you, Miss?'

'Me? It seems I'm going to be there in my capacity as Jem's bodyguard. I never thought I'd hear myself say it, but I rather hope I won't have to do anything but watch. But tomorrow, Maxine – when I'm feeling a bit less weary – tomorrow I'll claim these beautiful big breasts of yours!'

As it turned out, Julia found that she had very little to do. She knocked at the Master's suite, and the Master himself opened the door. He hardly noticed her, as his bloodshot eyes were instantly fixed on the bounteous charms of Maxine, quivering and wide-eyed in her slave-girl's chains. He grasped her right nipple and led her into the room, leaving Julia to close the door and stand guard just inside it.

Julia didn't notice Jem at first. She was glancing round the room, admiring the tapestries and the ornate carving of the groins of the stone arches, when she noticed a movement above the vast bed that occupied the centre of the room. Suspended from the centre of the ceiling there was a circular chandelier; Jem was tied to the underside of it, spreadeagled within the metal circle like the spokes of a cartwheel. She caught Julia's gaze, grinned, tossed her head, and raised her eyes to the heavens. Julia had to cover her mouth to stifle a giggle.

'Master! Oh, Master!' Jem's musical voice echoed in the vaulting. 'Isn't it about time you let me down from here so I can join in the fun?'

The Master's face was buried between Maxine's luscious breasts, and he seemed not to have heard Jem's question. But Maxine, sprawled against cushions on the bed, looked up to see her auburn-haired idol hanging from the ceiling.

'Oh! Miss Jem! Whatever are you doing up there?'

The Master covered Maxine's face with his left hand and with the other delivered a series of resounding slaps to the girl's pendulous globes. 'Slaves,' he said, once he had succeeded in bringing tears to her eyes, 'are to be seen, and toyed with, but definitely not to be heard. Don't speak again unless I give you permission. Miss Jem is tied up because it seems that unless I keep her on a leash she has a habit of running off; she is above the bed so that she has a bird's eye view of the entertainment she's not allowed to participate in. No doubt I will relent at some point and bring her down; I suspect that I will require her to flog you while I'm fucking your wondrous cleavage. Now stop snivelling and undress me.'

During the evening Julia stood and watched while the Master organised a succession of games. He lay on his back, staring up at Jem over Maxine's swivelling bottom and squeezing the girl's dangling breasts as she crouched over him and licked his member to its first orgasm of the evening.

While Maxine refilled his glass with brandy and soda he turned the handle, next to the bed, that lowered the chandelier, and released Jem, kissing her passionately before she had time to stretch her limbs. Propped against a pile of cushions, he sipped his drink while Maxine knelt between his outstretched legs, under orders to stimulate his flaccid organ by massaging it with her rose-tipped mounds.

Jem, in basque and stockings the colour of peonies, was told to encourage Maxine with occasional use of the Master's riding crop. Maxine obeyed her orders conscientiously, but Julia could see that she spent much of her time looking over her shoulder to smile at Jem, wiggling her plump bottom to invite another swipe. Julia began to feel decidedly left out of the fun.

The Master's second spurt came in the deep valley between Maxine's breasts, his gaze fixed on Jem as she lashed Maxine's bottom in time with the Master's grunts of breath.

As far as Julia could tell the Master's energy was failing now. After another drink, and a brief rest during which he lay with his head on Maxine's chest and with Jem's arms encircling his waist, he seemed content to amuse himself with decorating Maxine's body. He sat on the edge of the bed, and Jem knelt between his legs trying to breathe some life into his exhausted member. Maxine stood in front of him, biting her lip as he experimented with the placing of an array of bejewelled clips, silver clamps and gold chains. When Maxine was festooned with glittering chains, he leaned back to view the effect – and fell asleep.

Jem lifted his legs on to the bed, and covered his body with a blanket. He murmured something about having her flogged, and she kissed his forehead. He began to snore softly.

The three women looked at each other. 'We could kill him now,' Jem whispered, and then grinned. 'Only joking. I'm not sure I could do it, anyway. Let's go to bed.'

'I thought you'd never ask, darling,' Julia said.

'Should I come, too, Miss?' Maxine said. 'Only, I'd like to take these bloody chains off, if that's alright, because my nipples are ever so sore.'

Julia hugged Jem. She felt a wave of affection for her lovely friend and her dear maid. 'Take them all off, Maxine, and go back to my room. Stay there until I return, but don't wait up for me. I've a lot of things to discuss with Jem.'

'What sort of things?' Jem said, when her lips parted at last from Julia's. They were in Jem's chamber, in bed.

'I love being your bodyguard,' Julia said, her mouth nuzzling Jem's crinkled nipples. 'And I especially like guarding these bits of your body. Oh – yes, that's nice. Put another finger in, Jem, my sweet. You're terribly good to me.'

'What have we got to discuss, Jules?' Jem's fingers pushed more deeply into Julia to emphasise each word.

'Don't be jealous, Jem. But I'm rather worried about a colleague. A field operative. Her name's Asmita, and she's such a young thing . . .'

'I heard about that. Our glorious Master had her punished, it seems. She's being kept in the dungeon.'

'Why, Jem? What's she supposed to have done?'

'You know His Majesty. She's done nothing, as far as I can make out. I don't know what I can do, Jules. I'll try to find out where they're keeping her.'

Julia sucked Jem's left nipple for a moment, trying to order her swirling thoughts. 'There's someone else,' she said at last.

'Julia! And I thought I was the mistress of your heart!'

'Oh, you are, Jem, you truly are, you silly thing. I mean there's someone else I'm worried about. You remember I told you about Lucy Larson, the woman at the Club who was asking too many questions?'

'Sure I remember,' Jem said with a strange smile.

'Well, today she told me that she's the wife of a lawyer – an important lawyer, a fraud specialist, very well-to-do. And she said he's useless in bed, and she's desperate for some nooky, whatever that may mean.'

'She sounds like the Master's kind of lady.'

'But it can't be true, can it, Jem? Or can it? I don't think I believe a word of it. She doesn't seem to me like the bored wife of a high-flying barrister. Quite frankly, Jem, she's far too common.'

Jem burst out laughing, and then smothered Julia's face with little kisses. 'I adore you, Jules. Hell, I don't know. My advice is that you should file a report that recommends bringing her in. If she's what she says she is, the Master's gained a valuable asset. If she isn't – well, the Master and Chief Anderson have ways of detecting wolves in sheep's clothing. I guess I'm lucky the Master brought me in through the green channel.'

Later, as Julia went to sleep with her face pressed against Jem's spicy skin, she wondered briefly what her lover had meant by that last remark. Then she reminded herself to file a report about Lucy as soon as she woke up. And then she slept.

DAY SIX: *FRIDAY*

The room was still in darkness, but there were strips of grey light around the heavy curtains. Lucy fumbled for her watch and squinted at the dial. Late for breakfast again! Her head sank into the pillows and she tried to muster some enthusiasm for getting up.

Neither Asmita nor Julia had been in the Club the previous evening. Lucy had stayed up late, failing to follow the plot of a murder mystery video. She hated to go to bed alone, and waking up alone wasn't much better. And she suddenly realised she wasn't alone.

Black-jacketed figures moved in the shadows near the door. There was a click, a soft hiss that sounded as loud as an explosion in the silent bedroom, and Lucy felt a sharp pain in her thigh.

Her training took over. Adrenalin flowed. She rolled off the bed, putting the divan between her and the intruders. She clenched her fists, ready to spring into a fight. She felt something small and hard attached to her thigh; her legs were heavy, she couldn't move them; her eyes could not focus. The dark figures were closing in, but not as fast as the black clouds of sleep that overwhelmed her.

There was a knock on the door. Jem opened one eye, and reached for Julia, but she was alone in the bed. Jem was glad she didn't have to keep Security hours. She shook her head, stretched her arms, and ruffled her hair. 'Come in!' she called.

Maxine, in her maid's uniform, opened the door. 'Morning, Miss Jem,' she said. Jem grinned; the maid was shy and nervous, but kept glancing at Jem's body.

'Come here and kiss me, Maxine,' Jem said, patting the bed. The maid approached hesitantly, and sat on the edge of the mattress. Jem pulled her closer, gently tugging her dark curls until her soft lips met Jem's urgent kiss. The girl shivered and closed her brown eyes as Jem's tongue entered her mouth and Jem's fingers started to unbutton her blouse.

Jem's hands fondled the diminutive black lace cups of the maid's corset, squeezing and lifting the weight of Maxine's breasts. She placed a trail of kisses along the girl's jawline until she reached her ear. 'Julia's told me what she's going to do with these tits,' she whispered.

Jem expected giggles, or an anxious 'Will it hurt, Miss?'; but Maxine sighed and pushed her nipples against Jem's hands. 'Are you going to watch, Miss Jem?' she sighed.

'Would you like me to?' Jem buried her face in the maid's neck, nibbling her earlobe in time with pinching her nipples.

'Oh – oh, yes, please, Miss,' Maxine said between little gasps.

Jem pulled away to look at the maid's flushed face. 'Well, I'd love to watch, if Julia'll let me,' she said. 'I guess I could help. I could keep you still – hold your wrists, maybe, and sit on your face to keep you quiet.'

Maxine was speechless with joy. Jem twisted her nipples, and felt a surge of pleasure as the maid's eyes widened still further in response. 'Tell me, Maxine, where's Jenny?'

'Jenny, Miss?'

'My maid. She should be here, shouldn't she?'

'I couldn't say, Miss – honest!' The girl was patently lying, but Jem reluctantly loosened her grip. 'And I've got instructions from the Master, Miss, for you.'

'Oh dear,' Jem said ironically. 'Let me guess: he demands my presence in his chambers immediately.'

'That's right, Miss. I'm to tell him you're on your way to him, just as soon as I've dressed you.'

'I'll tell you what,' Jem said, licking Maxine's nipples until she thought the maid might swoon with delight, 'I'll dress myself, while you fetch some ribbon.'

'Ribbon, Miss?'

'Wide ribbon, Maxine. Black, if possible. As much as you can find. And a pair of scissors.'

She jumped out of bed, leaving Maxine to refasten her blouse and hurry from the room with frequent backward glances at Jem's naked form.

Having showered and applied her make-up, Jem went to the wardrobe and selected another of the costumes that Rhoda had provided. She clipped on a tiny front-fastening bra and a thin suspender belt, both in plain cream silk; then she slipped on a matching pair of French knickers and sheer stockings. She added a necklace of pearls, and earrings with pendant pearl clusters, burgundy ankle boots and matching kid leather gloves. Over the back of a chair she laid a long wine-red cloak.

She was enjoying the sensation of rotating her leather-encased fingertips round her silk-covered nipples when Maxine returned, carrying three rolls of black ribbon and a pair of pinking shears. Jem continued to tease her crinkled tips while Maxine stood uncertainly in the doorway, her eyes fixed enviously on Jem's fingers.

'Miss?' Maxine said. 'Shall I tell the Master you're on your way now, Miss?'

'I don't think so, Maxine. Close the door and get undressed.'

'But, Miss – the Master – '

'Do as you're told, girl. Take your clothes off. But leave on your corset and your stockings.' Jem cupped her silk-clad breasts and lifted them towards the maid, who gulped and hurried to obey.

As Maxine undressed, Jem watched and cut ribbon into assorted lengths. This kid's got a fantastic body, she was thinking as she estimated the amount of ribbon she would need and revelled in the anticipatory tightening of her stomach. A fantastic body, and gorgeous tits, bigger and better even than the athletic-looking Lucy Larson's pointed, thrusting pair. Maxine's body gave no hint of strenuous activity: her breasts were heavy, pendulous, pear-shaped and languorous, made for squeezing and nuzzling. They would be too soft for a riding crop, Jem considered without pausing to be surprised at her own

173

thoughts, but ideal for a thin, whippy cane. Jem pictured the pale globes streaked with the red lines of cane strokes, and then laughed softly, self-deprecatingly, when she realised where her train of thought had taken her.

'Is there – is there something wrong, Miss?' Maxine was standing in the correct position, her hands behind her back and her stockinged legs parted so that there was a hand's breadth between the tops of her chubby white thighs. With her waist clinched by the corset, her bosom and hips flared out to make a perfect hourglass shape, the curves of pale skin accentuated by the blackness of the basque, suspenders and stockings.

'Hell, no, Maxine,' Jem said, 'I'm not laughing at you. Just at me. I'm going crazy. I was thinking I'd like to cane your breasts.'

'Oh, yes please, Miss Jem. Shall I fetch a cane?'

'Not right now, honey. We don't have time. Just tell me if you like to feel those cute nipples pressed up against a cold, hard surface.'

'Of course, Miss,' Maxine replied dutifully.

'Then lie along the coffee table. No – fetch a pillow from the bed. Now hold it across that bushy black triangle of yours, and get yourself across that table.'

Maxine lowered herself on to the table top. Her head extended beyond one end of it, and her long black hair almost touched the floor; at the other end of the table her dimpled arse was uplifted by the pillow beneath her pelvis. Her breasts, flattened against the polished surface, formed circles of flesh at the sides of her ribcage. Her hands rested on the floor, and her legs extended behind her.

'Are you going to punish me, Miss?'

'Don't tempt me, girl. No, I'm going to tie you up.'

'Why, Miss?'

'You impudent servant!' Jem laughed, delivering to Maxine's left buttock a sharp slap that turned into a lingering caress. 'If you must know, it's because I'm not going to keep that date with the Master. So I'm doing this for your own protection, you see, and for the cameras. You'll be able to say that I overpowered you, and left you bound and helpless and unable to report that I'd gone out.

Now be quiet, move your legs forward so your ankles are just outside the table legs, and for goodness' sake keep still.'

Maxine bent her knees and shuffled her feet up to the legs of the table. Jem watched in silent admiration as the girl's arse curved into two soft moons and parted to reveal the funnel of pink skin at the heart of the deep dark furrow, and the plump split bulge of her sex below. She whistled appreciatively with an indrawn breath, and knelt to tie a length of ribbon between the maid's legs. She tied the ends of the ribbon tightly to the ankles, but left enough slack to allow the legs to move. She moved to the other end of the table and tied Maxine's wrists in the same way.

'If you don't mind me saying so, Miss,' the maid said, 'this isn't much good as an alibi. I mean, I can still move my feet, so I can get up. And I can move my hands to untie the knots.'

'I'm not through yet, Maxine. Now just you make sure you keep your feet and hands on the outside of the table legs, OK, and not between them.'

Jem looped a long piece of ribbon round the girl's left elbow and left knee, and pulled it tight. She did the same on the girl's right side, and then returned to the left side to tighten the loop further. She continued like this, tightening first one side and than the other, until Maxine's hands were pulled immovably against the table's front legs, her ankles were similarly wedged against the two back legs, and her elbows and knees almost met below the right and left edges of the table. The maid's arse was now even more rounded, and her sex pouch, hanging in the air beyond the end of the table, was split open to reveal the pink and glistening inner lips.

Jem wanted to get away quickly, but she couldn't resist running her hands across the taut globes, drawing a fingertip down the gaping furrow, caressing the blue-veined tender skin between the stocking-tops and the fleshy, dark-haired lips, and then finally thrusting her gloved fingers into the pale, slick interior.

'You're very wet, Maxine,' she said, tapping the first

175

finger of her other hand against the girl's stretched sphincter.

'Yes, Miss,' Maxine managed to say. 'Thank you Miss. This is lovely. And now I can't move at all.'

'Good,' Jem said, slowly withdrawing her fingers, the red leather darkly stained with Maxine's secretions. 'But there's still a whole bunch of ribbon to use up. Let me see now . . .'

She threaded ribbon from an uncut roll beneath the table top, and pulled it across the small of Maxine's corsetted back; she repeated the operation several times, and pulled the ribbon as tight as she could. Maxine complained that she couldn't breathe. Jem took no notice, and ran more bands of ribbon across the maid's back, this time looping the material under the bands that ran between the girl's elbows and knees. When she pulled the ribbon tight, pressing her knee into Maxine's spine for maximum leverage, the girl's limbs were pulled together under the table and its legs creaked ominously under the strain.

Jem stood back to admire her work. Maxine's buttocks rose like white balloons from a cocoon of black stockings, black corset, black suspenders and a mesh of criss-crossing black ribbons. Jem put her lips to the girl's split sex, savouring the salty liquid that dripped on to her tongue, picked up her cloak, and made for the door.

'Miss?'

Jem turned in the doorway. 'Yes, Maxine?'

'Thank you for tying me up, Miss. I've enjoyed it, especially as it's you that's done it, and I'm very grateful to you for trying to protect me from the Master.'

'But?'

'But he'll punish me anyway, Miss, for letting you go.' Maxine started to sob quietly, the heaving of her lungs creating no discernible movement of her tightly-bound backside.

Jem returned to the table, and ran her fingers round the bulbous edges of Maxine's squashed breasts. The maid was completely helpless, unable to move an inch. Jem realised that she could do anything to the girl. Power corrupts, and it feels kind of good, she thought. She made a ball of tightly-wound ribbon, grabbed Maxine's hair, pulled up her head, and pushed the home-made gag into her mouth. She wound more ribbon round the lower half of the girl's face.

'Still breathe OK?' she said.

Maxine nodded.

'I really have to go now, Maxine. I'd love to stay here and play, but I just can't. I'm relying on you to tell a good story, child, so you just make sure the Master hasn't got any good reason to punish you. Come and see me again this evening. If you've got stripes on that gorgeous butt, I promise you I'll count them and give you twice as many on your breasts, you understand? So you tell a good story.'

Jem stopped in the doorway for one final glance at the trussed maid, who was gazing at her with adoring eyes; then she fled.

The note must have been pushed under the door: Julia knew that she hadn't left or dropped the folded paper at the bottom of her locker. She unfolded it.

> *Dear Julia*
> *I just loved what you did to Goltz. You're*
> *terrific, and if you want to get some extra*
> *practice any time, I'll be your sparring*
> *partner. You can throw me and knock me over as*
> *often as you like. I won't mind. In fact, I'd*
> *love it. You can sit on top of me and grind*
> *your knees into my muscles and twist my legs*
> *and anything painful you want to do. Afterwards*
> *I'll lick all the sweat off your body and then*
> *I'll beg your permission to let me lick every*
> *little bit between your legs and right inside*
> *you as far as my tongue will reach.*

That was all. The note was unsigned. Julia was unsure whether she should feel honoured or uneasy. She was still trying to work out which of her fellow trainees might be her unusual admirer when the tall figure of Ruby, a willowy black girl, entered the locker room.

177

'Hello, Ruby,' Julia said, distractedly. 'It looks as though the weather's changed for the worse.'

'Julia. I'm glad I've found you alone.' Julia looked up to see Ruby staring at her; then, as if she had reached a difficult decision, the tall girl marched towards Julia and stood beside her, looking down into her face with troubled, searching eyes. Ruby's small round breasts were rising and falling rapidly beneath her thin cotton sports vest. She put an arm round Julia's waist and pulled her close.

'Ruby!' Julia spluttered, laughing and enjoying the soft full lips that the black girl pressed against hers. 'What's going on? My dear, this is so sudden!'

'The whole class is in love with you, Julia, don't tell me you don't know that. It's just that I'm the only one with the guts to tell you. The way you fixed that bitch Goltz – we all think you're the greatest.'

Julia was perplexed, amazed, almost speechless – but also rather pleased. 'Gosh, Ruby. I don't know what to say . . .' She looked up into the other woman's almond-shaped eyes.

'Just tell me one thing, Julia,' Ruby said very quietly. 'Do you ever feel naughty? I mean, as if you think you need a little corrective treatment?'

Julia felt a shiver travel down her spine, and it wasn't simply because Ruby had slipped her hand under the skirt of Julia's tunic and was dragging her fingernails across Julia's left buttock.

'Oh, Ruby . . .' Julia pressed her body against Ruby's wiry frame and waited for the inevitable. A loud smack echoed in the locker room, and a fiery glow spread across Julia's bottom.

'If I had your arse to play with,' Ruby whispered, 'I would never spank anyone else ever again. I swear it, lover.' She tried to turn Julia in order to strike the other cheek.

Julia pulled away. 'Stop it, Ruby, please. You're very sweet, and I'm dreadfully flattered, but I just can't be yours.'

Ruby's eyes narrowed. 'You chasing after that new woman of the Master's? He won't let you have her. And she won't stick around any longer than any of the others. And she won't smack your bottom like I can.'

Julia had a momentary vision of herself upended across Jem's lap, and decided that she liked the idea. 'It's not anything to do with Jem, Ruby,' she lied.

'I want you so bad, Julia you little slut.' Ruby was quivering with emotion. 'And you're trying to make an idiot out of me. I won't come begging, Julia, I won't. I'm just telling you, you'll be my naughty girl and no one else's.'

Julia stood on tiptoe and kissed Ruby's cheek. 'Don't be silly, Ruby. I'm too old for you, for one thing. You'd wear me out! And if it's true that everyone in the class wants me, just think how unpopular we'd be if I were to become your own naughty little girl.'

Ruby's face softened, and her hand stole back to fondle Julia's bottom. 'I suppose you're right,' she said.

'Of course I'm right,' Julia said, resting her head between Ruby's firm breasts. 'You've got a room in one of the Mill buildings, haven't you? Down by the stream?'

'That's right,' Ruby murmured, her fingers tugging at the tiny curls in the cleft between Julia's buttocks.

Julia moaned, and pressed her face into Ruby's right breast. 'Here's a promise,' she said, pulling Ruby's face to hers. 'Before I leave the Private House, I'll come and be naughty for you in your room at the Mill.'

Ruby smiled triumphantly, turned and strode away.

But before then, Julia thought, I'll be naughty for Jem as often as she wants me to be. I hope she wants to be naughty for me too.

A note pinned to the noticeboard had ordered all first-level trainees to report to Lecture Room 5. When Julia arrived she found that her classmates had already filled the tiers of seats: she was confronted by a phalanx of black leather tunics. Fraser and Lawrence were jostling for a space next to one of the few empty seats, and both were frantically gesturing to her to join them. Along the back row Ruby, Manfred and Violet – the latter licking her lips and kneading her leather-encased breasts – were trying to catch Julia's eye and shuffling to make room for her to sit next to each of them. Julia smiled at everyone and sat in a vacant seat in the front row; after a couple of seconds she gently removed from her thigh the hand of Imogen, the Nordic beauty who was sitting beside her and gazing fixedly at the roller blackboard behind the lecturer's desk.

Instructor Dawkin, a buxom brunette in a brief white lab coat, entered the room and waited for silence to assert itself. 'In view of the continuing absence of Instructor Goltz,' she began and waited until the cheers and whistles had subsided, 'unarmed combat training has been postponed. Instead I will instruct you in the use of the electronic contact weapon known as the buzzer. This is part of your standard equipment. Are you all in full uniform? Good. Then each of you should find a heavy cube in a black plastic case attached to the left-hand side of your belt – or the right side, if you're left-handed. This is your buzzer's power pack.'

Julia's left hand dropped automatically to the black box, and she looked up to see that the Instructor had placed a similar box on the desk.

'You will see,' Dawkin said, 'that on top of the cube there are three buttons – green, white and red – and two small warning lights, neither of which should be glowing at the moment. The green button is for use when recharging the power supply, a procedure that I'll describe later. The white button tests the power level. Would you all press it now, please.'

Julia pressed the white button on the box at her side. One of the lights glowed amber. 'If the warning light flickers or, worse still, fails to light altogether, your power pack needs recharging or may be defective. You must use the white button to test your power pack each time you put on your belt and each time you go on duty. Report a low charge level immediately. I hope that all of you have fully charged packs at the moment.'

There were murmurs of assent. 'Oh good,' Instructor Dawkin said, smiling at last. She moved to the side of the desk and leant against it so that her hip strained against the thin white cotton fabric. The class fell silent. Julia smiled, charmed and impressed by this novel method of classroom control.

'Now,' Dawkin continued, 'press the white button again to end the test, and then press the red button.'

After a brief frenzy of button-pushing, the room fell silent. Instructor Dawkin tilted her head, her eyes questioning. In her hand she held the thin cylinder of a buzzer, connected by a thin flex to the box on the desk. And on the box, the red warning light was glowing brightly.

A crescendo of baffled complaints arose throughout the room: not one of the trainees had a power pack with a glowing red light.

'The red light indicates that the buzzer is working,' Dawkin announced smugly. 'But your buzzer won't work while it's in its holster. We call this a safety measure. You have all failed to turn your buzzers on and – wait for it, you eager ones at the back – before you turn them on, you need to know how to handle your buzzers. Now concentrate: look at the position of the holster on your belt.'

Julia tore her gaze from the Instructor's pretty blue eyes that were so much like Jem's and removed Imogen's hand, which had returned to her thigh and had started to slide under the skirt of her tunic. She looked down at her belt.

'In front of your pistol holster you'll find a long, thin pouch of black leather,' Dawkin said. 'This is your buzzer holster. You'll see a hard cylinder, about two centimetres in diameter and covered with black leather, protruding upwards out of the holster. That is the handle of your buzzer. Has everyone located it?'

There were murmurs of assent. 'Good. Now, don't touch the red button on your power pack; just hold your buzzer by its handle and pull it upwards out of its holster.'

Julia joined the chorus of surprised exclamations: the lower half of the buzzer, contained within the holster, was bright red. The buzzer remained connected to the belt by a thin flex that unreeled as the cylinder was pulled away from its holster.

'The red part of the buzzer is the business end,' Dawkin said. 'Don't ever touch it. And now – holding your buzzer only by the black handle – press the red button on your power pack.'

This time every red light in the room came alight. 'Your buzzer is now ready to operate,' Dawkin said, stifling a feigned yawn. 'It will discharge electric current when touched against an earthed object or person. And now to demonstrate the various ways in which the buzzer can be used, I need a willing assistant. This is where the fun starts,' she added with a wide smile and a glance that swept across the class. 'Perhaps you'd all like to elect someone?'

Julia's heart sank. There were times when she was sure she preferred anonymity to celebrity. She had a strong suspicion that she would be the unanimous choice of her classmates, and her worst fears were immediately realised as the whispers of her name united and expanded into a rhythmic chant of 'Ju-lia, Ju-lia!'

Once again she lifted Imogen's hand from her thigh; she stood, turned, bowed to the class, glanced at Dawkin to make sure that the Instructor had taken note of Julia's most fetching aspect, and stepped on to the dais. Dawkin extended a hand, pulled Julia towards her, and to the cheers of the class pressed her lips to Julia's mouth. The Instructor had noticed Julia's cheeky bow: behind Julia's back, out of sight of the trainees, Dawkin's palm cupped Julia's left buttock and squeezed it affectionately. Julia made the quietest of moans, and pushed her tongue into Dawkin's mouth. Simultaneously they began to laugh, and the Instructor pulled her face away. 'I was hoping they'd choose you,' she said, giving Julia a final hug. 'You've got the prettiest arse in the whole of the Security Corps, and I've heard so much about you.'

The Instructor turned to face the class. 'Well!' she said, her eyes sparkling. 'I'm not surprised you chose Julia, I must say. No doubt you're all keen to see her being thoroughly buzzed.' There was prolonged shouting and cheering. 'In that case I'm going to disappoint you,' Dawkin said at last. 'Julia will be Chief Buzzer. And now I'd like a few volunteers to be her victims.'

There was a second of silence, and then hands and voices were hurled into the air as if every trainee in the room had just scored a winning goal. Ignoring the hubbub, Dawkin turned to Julia with her eyes wide in mock-surprise. Julia smiled happily and could only shrug.

After several minutes of commotion Dawkin selected Manfred and Vicki, who were making the most noise, and Imogen, perhaps because she remained so perversely silent and stared at Julia as if the intensity of the pale blue light in her eyes could start a bush fire between Julia's thighs.

The chosen three left their seats and formed a line on the dais: Vicki, small and vivacious, with brown ringlets and irrepressible giggles; Manfred, tall and burly, a comic-book superhero in cinched tunic over rippling muscles, with a bristling moustache, a face red with excitement, and an unmissable bulge contained in the black gauze pouch beneath the inverted V of his tunic front; and Imogen, with her pale skin, blue eyes, and fringe of white-blonde hair, still and emotionless except for the rapid rise and fall of her substantial bosom beneath its covering of soft, taut leather.

Dawkin picked up the buzzer from the desk and passed it to Julia. 'Hold it carefully,' the Instructor reminded her. 'Remember not to touch the red part. The class will note that this model has an especially long lead for demonstration purposes.'

Julia took the buzzer between finger and thumb. 'Look at the handle, Julia,' Dawkin said. 'You'll see that it's divided into two; it can be pulled apart. When the handle is pushed together, as it normally is, it delivers its maximum charge. Anyone touched by the red part would receive a serious shock – perhaps even a fatal shock in the case of someone in poor health. Now, Julia, pull the two parts of the handle apart, as far as they will go.'

Julia pulled. A gap appeared in the black handle, its two parts remaining connected by a metal spindle. 'The buzzer is now set for minimum shock,' Dawkin said. 'Julia, touch Vicki with the red tip.'

Vicki's eyes widened as Julia extended her hand and then, with a tentative prod, touched the buzzer against Vicki's arm, on the bare skin between tunic shoulder and lace glove. The girl jumped, squealed, and burst into a fit of giggling. 'It tickles!' she spluttered.

'Push the handle together a little,' Dawkin suggested,

'and try again.' Julia adjusted the handle; Vicki, looking from side to side as if it might be possible to conceal her movements, unzipped her tunic to reveal her left breast. 'Right on the button, please, Julia,' she said, to whoops of approval from the class.

Nonchalantly, Julia touched the buzzer to the proffered nipple. Vicki shivered violently, and her hand flew to her breast. 'How was that, Vicki?' Dawkin asked.

Vicki thought for a moment before replying. 'A bit nasty,' she said. 'But – on the other hand – rather nice too. Maybe I'd better try it again?'

Dawkin ignored her. 'As I'm sure you've all heard,' she was saying, 'the buzzer can be a source of innocent pleasure, and one of the less messy instruments of interrogation, as well as an effective close combat weapon. We'll now have another demonstration of the buzzer's versatility: Vicki, would you put your tits away and do something useful? Remove Manfred's G-string.'

Vicki made rather a meal of revealing Manfred's manhood, Julia thought – almost literally, in fact, as the girl knelt in front of him and licked his upright shaft as she peeled the black gauze down his muscular thighs.

'That's enough, Vicki,' Dawkin said. 'Water conducts electricity, you know. Now, Julia: I'd like you to use your buzzer on Manfred's cock.'

Julia looked at the young man, and saw both fear and lust in his face. Reassuringly, she used her left hand to caress his silk-smooth hardness to its maximum vertical stiffness; then, without warning, she placed the red tip of the buzzer mid-way up the veined stem.

Manfred gasped, jumped backward, stumbled, shook his head while his member twitched spamodically.

'How did that feel?' Dawkin asked.

'Like an orgasm with a kick,' he said. 'A painful orgasm. Wow! Do that again, Julia, hey?'

Julia looked at the Instructor. Dawkin nodded, and leant towards her. 'Touch his balls this time,' Dawkin whispered, as Vicki administered mouth-to-manhood resuscitation. Julia waited until Vicki's mouth had roamed all over Manfred's sexual equipment, and this time, without preamble, she extended the buzzer and brought it up sharply between his two wet, dangling testicles.

For a moment he was wide-eyed and speechless with shock. Then he howled, and hopped from foot to foot, his penis monstrously erect and swinging like a thick purple metronome. 'Julia!' he hissed between clenched teeth. 'Julia, I love you! Do it again!'

'No, Manfred,' Dawkin said. 'Enough is enough. I think the class have been able to see that the buzzer can be adjusted to give different levels of electric shock.'

Manfred shuffled towards Julia, his eyes pleading with her to use the buzzer again. She shook her head and instead grasped his thick hardness, using it to pull him to the edge of the dais. She transferred his member to Vicki's eager fingers, and pushed the two of them into an embrace. As they kissed, Julia turned them so that Vicki's back was to the class, and she folded up the stiff short skirt of the girl's tunic so that the class could see the whole of her dimpled bottom. Julia inserted her hand between Vicki's thighs, and the girl, with one arm round Manfred's body and the other hand slowly pumping his prick, unthinkingly parted her legs and pushed her bottom out to meet Julia's caress. Julia stroked Vicki's pouting sex for a few moments and then, with a wink at the spellbound trainees, thrust the buzzer upwards between the girl's thighs. Vicki's muffled shriek was drowned by the laughter of the class as her arse-cheeks contracted and relaxed in spasms like the doors of a demented lift.

'Julia!' Dawkin said, trying to sound angry. 'This is no time for horseplay. We haven't finished demonstrating the uses of the buzzer. Imogen has been waiting very patiently for her turn. Take off your tunic, Imogen, my dear.'

The statuesque blonde looked forbidding and untouchable even when naked except for her collar, boots and gloves. But when Dawkin told Julia to turn the buzzer down to the minimum setting, an expression of disappointment appeared on her pale pink lips. The Instructor ignored it. 'You will find, Julia,' she said, 'that as well as moving apart, the handle can be twisted. The top half of the handle can be turned round – you can feel a series of clicks as you turn it. Can all the class see that? Good. This controls the number and frequency of buzzes. The normal setting is for just one buzz: usually that's all you need to disable an opponent, and there's no point in wasting the charge in your power pack. Multiple buzzes tend to be for – shall we say recreational use? Imogen, would you climb on to the table – on your hands and knees, please.'

The blonde's impassive eyes remained fixed on Julia's face as the Instructor helped her on to the desk and positioned her so that she was sideways to the class. There were whistles as the trainees appreciated the firm heaviness of her hanging breasts, the slim curve of her arched body, and the round perfection of her white bottom. Julia reached out to touch the crinkled pink tips of Imogen's dangling boobs, and a smile appeared at last on the blonde's uplifted face.

The Instructor was standing at Imogen's rear end. 'Bring the buzzer here, Julia,' she said. 'You've used a vibrator, of course?' Julia nodded briefly; after just one visit to the Private House she was well acquainted with a wide variety of such implements. 'On this setting, the buzzer is very similar. I'd like you to fuck Imogen with it, please.'

The class fell silent. Imogen lowered her head so that her face was hidden behind a curtain of pale hair and her arse was lifted higher into the air. Julia touched the tip of the buzzer to the top of the blonde's right thigh, and felt a series of regular tiny vibrations in the handle as the device administered little shocks to the pale flesh. The vibrations ceased as soon as she lifted the buzzer from Imogen's skin. The blonde remained completely still.

Julia smiled at her classmates, at the same time planning her next moves. She had put on a number of performances like this during her previous visit to the House, and she saw no reason not to provide a good show for both Imogen and her audience. She ran the buzzer quickly down the cleft between Imogen's buttocks; the blonde shivered almost imperceptibly, and Julia started to concentrate her attentions on the plump curving slit, using her left hand to smooth aside the blonde curls and ease apart the quivering lips.

Imogen's interior gleamed wetly pink. Julia moved the

buzzer back and forth, sometimes using it to trace the edges of the outer or inner labia, sometimes touching it briefly against the hood of the clitoris. The blonde's body was trembling now, but it was only when Julia pushed the buzzer between the moist inner lips that Imogen moaned and started to move her hips, pushing her bottom back to meet Julia's insistent thrusts.

'Would you say that the buzzer is well lubricated now, Julia?' Dawkin asked. Julia nodded, grinning. 'Be careful not to let the moisture reach the handle,' the Instructor went on. 'Now remove it and stand back a moment.' Julia did so, running her hand across the soft curves of Imogen's buttocks, which were covered with a film of cool perspiration.

'And now the other orifice, please, Julia,' Dawkin said; and Julia applied the buzzer again, spiralling the red tip into the puckered well between the blonde's arse-cheeks, and finally pushing it gently and slowly into the round hole. She stood back again, leaving the buzzer embedded in Imogen's bottom, its tail of flex flicking up rhythmically as the blonde's body gave a little jerk with each shock.

The class broke into applause, and Julia bowed. 'Let's finish the job, shall we?' Dawkin said. 'Take out your own buzzer, Julia. Check the power. Very good. Now turn it to minimum charge and maximum frequency, that's right – and put it into Imogen.' The Instructor's calm voice was at last becoming breathy with excitement. Julia felt Dawkin's hand against her bottom, pushing her forward urgently, and as Julia lifted her buzzer between Imogen's widely parted thighs, the Instructor's fingers slid between Julia's cheeks and pushed into her humid slit.

When Julia's buzzer touched Imogen's wet labia the blonde's twitching increased, and Julia had only to hold the handle steady, lifting the red probe very gradually, for every part of Imogen's gaping sex to touch against it, each touch provoking a further spasm. 'Stick it right in!' Dawkin said, all pretence of scientific detachment now absent from her quavering voice.

'What about getting moisture on the handle?' Julia said absently, her eyes fixed on the shivering blonde's body.

'Damn it, who cares?' Dawkin said, almost savagely, and then, recovering her poise a little, she added, 'Just be careful, and remember to pull it out by the flex.'

With one finger, Julia pushed her buzzer upwards until the entire cylinder disappeared into Imogen's quivering pouch. As her finger touched the blonde's dripping lips she felt a sudden shock, and pulled away quickly, cursing inwardly because she feared the brisk movement might have ruined the finale of the demonstration. But all eyes were on Imogen, whose entire frame was now shaking rhythmically. She lifted her head at last: her lips were parted, her blue eyes wide, her face flushed and her breath coming in ragged gasps that grew louder and harsher with each spasm of her body, matching the twitching of her two tails of black flex.

Julia and Instructor Dawkin stepped forward to acknowledge the applause of the class, while on the desk behind them Imogen's gasps ran together into a long keening cry of pleasure as she experienced an endless succession of orgasms.

With the cheers of her classmates ringing in her ears, Julia's thoughts once again strayed to her new-found auburn-haired friend and lover, and she reflected that, all things considered, she was happier than she had ever been.

Breakfast.

I'm late for breakfast.

Time to get up . . .

With a start, Lucy remembered: dark figures in the bedroom, a shot in the thigh, blackness closing in.

She opened her eyes. As she expected, she was no longer in her room in the Health Club. She was on a low bed in a featureless, windowless room with grey walls. She immediately recognised it as a prison cell. She was naked except for leather bands around her wrists; each band was connected by a chain to an iron ring set into the wall at the head of the bed. Instinctively, she yanked at the chains, and was not surprised to find that the gesture was futile.

As if in response to Lucy's attempts to break free, the door opened. A man and a woman entered the room, closed the door behind them, and stood looking at Lucy. Both were tall and expressionless, and they wore similar short uniforms of black leather, with wide belts bearing holsters and strangely-shaped pockets. Each carried, from a loop around the right wrist, a short whip of plaited leather. The woman's triangle of pubic curls was exposed by the cut of the front of her tunic, while the man's sexual equipment was visible through a covering of thin black gauze. Lucy had never seen anyone dressed in such outlandish costumes, but she immediately recognised them as enforcers of a system of rules. *It takes one to know one* was the thought that flitted through her befuddled mind.

'Where am I?' she shouted, wincing at the harsh sound of her own voice and aware that she would inevitably produce a stream of clichés that her jailers had heard a hundred times before. 'You can't do this to me, I'm a – a respectable woman,' she ended lamely. *What am I doing?* she said to herself. *I almost admitted I'm a police officer. That would have blown the whole operation. What operation, anyway? Yes, of course, that's it, I wanted to get inside the real Private House. And now I've succeeded, or at least I've started to succeed.* 'Where the hell am I?' she repeated, maintaining an attitude of outrage in the absence of any other strategem.

'This is your new home, Lucy,' the man said in a soothing voice, 'and we're going to look after you. I'm Patrick, and this is Melanie. And now it's time to take those cuffs off and get you prepared. A nice refreshing bath, that's the first thing.'

They strolled to the bed and unfastened the leather cuffs from her wrists. The chains fell away. 'I don't need a bath,' Lucy said, pulling herself into the corner of the room. Melanie lifted her whip and gave Lucy a casual blow on the thigh.

'We don't want to hurt you,' Patrick said.

'But if we have to,' Melanie continued, 'we'll beat you until you do as we say. And if that doesn't work, we'll chain you up again and try again tomorrow. Even the most difficult of our new guests become more malleable after a few days with no food and without access to a toilet.'

Lucy was suddenly aware of an urgent need. 'Toilet,' she said. 'Yes, I want a pee.'

'Excellent,' Patrick said. 'Your initiation can start immediately.'

Lucy eyed him warily. Melanie stepped forward and pushed her unsmiling face towards Lucy's. 'Well, Lucy,' she said, 'you can go to the toilet – if you kneel in front of me and ask me very nicely.'

Without thinking, Lucy rejected the idea. Aghast, she stared from one to the other of her tormentors. They stared back, until at last Melanie shrugged and turned to her partner. 'Nice body,' she said. 'It seems almost a shame to mark it so soon.'

'Athletic,' Patrick agreed. 'Strong.'

'She'll need to be, if she maintains this attitude.'

'Would you like to go first?'

Melanie smiled for the first time. 'You know me so well, Patrick. We'd better chain her first, I think.'

Lucy listened, but hardly understood what she was hearing. Perhaps this is all a nightmare, she thought, or a test; that must be it. But if I have really fallen into the hands of sadistic psychopaths . . . I should have believed those ridiculous stories I heard yesterday. I thought that redhead had a screw loose, but this fits in with everything she said. And if I'm going to find out what's going on, I've got to get out of this cell, and I've got to stay in good shape, and I can't afford to waste time. And therefore – Lucy steeled herself for the logical conclusion – I must at all costs avoid being beaten and kept here for days without food. I'd be in no condition for detective work. And so I mustn't give these two any excuse.

She slid from the bed and lowered herself to her knees in front of Melanie.

'Legs wide apart, Lucy,' Melanie said with a malicious grin. 'From now on you'll never stand or sit or kneel with your legs together.'

Lucy shuffled her knees across the cold tiles and parted her long, golden thighs. Her head was bowed, not submissively but because she was concentrating on mastering her anger and the pressure of her bladder.

She forced herself to look up at Melanie's smiling face. 'May I go to the lavatory?' she said.

Melanie stared down at her, and lifted an eyebrow.

Lucy gritted her teeth. 'Please,' she added.

'Of course you may,' Melanie said. 'Patrick, would you fetch the pan?'

Lucy's head drooped. I might have guessed, she thought.

Patrick left the room and returned with a plastic bowl. Melanie took it and offered it to Lucy, but Lucy was unable to force herself to touch it. Melanie placed it on the floor between Lucy's knees.

The blush that Lucy felt spreading across her face only added to her anger. 'I can't!' she snapped. 'I can't do it like this.'

Patrick and Melanie were unmoved by this outburst. 'We can wait, Lucy,' Patrick said.

'And if we get bored,' Melanie added, 'we'll start beating you.'

Minutes passed in silence. Lucy was seething with help-less rage, torn between her desire to take violent retri-bution on her captors and her knowledge that, even if she could defy them, she would in doing so destroy her chances of uncovering the truth about the Private House. The pressure in her bladder was more than merely uncomfort-able, it had become a dull pain; and she also knew, perhaps not consciously but in the pit of her stomach, that there was something insidiously sexual about her position and about the whole business of being forced to piss in public.

The tingle in her groin came as a surprise to Lucy herself. Suddenly a stream of straw-coloured urine hissed into the bowl. Lucy was unable to control it; she closed her eyes to shut out the shame.

'At last!' Melanie's voice was loaded with sarcasm. 'Now that Lucy is quite finished, perhaps we can proceed. Come along, Lucy. And bring the pan with you.'

Fists clenched and cheeks blazing, Lucy felt herself about to burst into tears of fury and frustration.

'What's the matter, Lucy?' Patrick's voice was low and friendly. 'You must hurry up. Melanie's just waiting for an excuse to punish you.'

Lucy took a deep breath. 'I don't like being told what to do,' she said, emphasising every word.

Patrick laughed. 'Don't be silly, Lucy. You'll have to change your outlook on life, won't you? You're in the Private House now.'

Well then, Lucy thought, at least I know I'm on the inside. I'll have to do my best to put up with being pushed around by these snotty kids.

She picked up the plastic bowl and followed Patrick from the room.

Sebastian leant forward and pressed a switch on the side of the computer. The screen faded to black.

'So now you've seen it all,' he said, as Jem lowered herself on to his lap and on to his upright member. 'As you can see, there's a vast array of programs, but once you're inside the system it's all menu-driven.'

'I've worked with networked micros before,' Jem said, watching his lean face as she contracted her vaginal muscles around his thick shaft. 'I like a man who can hack his way through security codes. Now you've penetrated my system, will you select menu item one – ' she tightened her muscles again, ' – or item two – ' she rested her hands on his shoulders, lifted her body slightly, and then sank on to his shaft again, ' – or item three?' She moved her hips in a small circle.

'Any of the above,' Sebastian laughed, 'or all of them together. But not too much, my voracious darling, or I'll come immediately, and I want time to play with your silk-covered nipples first.' Jem kissed the hooded lids of his dark eyes and trembled as his fingers gently plucked at the silk triangles that covered her breasts.

'And I don't have to hack,' he went on after a pause. 'I wrote or modified most of the software. And I know all the security codes. And now you know them too.' He ran his hand down the side of her face. Jem kissed his fingertips, and looked longingly into his lined, tanned face. 'Darling Jem,' he said, 'why on earth have I allowed you to extract all this information from me? Good heavens, woman, I've even tampered with the central records file just because you've asked me to.'

Jem extended her tongue and delicately licked the palm of his hand. 'I guess you find me irresistible,' she said, wriggling her hips. The sensation of his prick inside her sent a tremor through her body, and she arched her back, closing her eyes and biting her lower lip.

She shook her head and found Sebastian gazing at her with an expression that combined wonder, devotion and desire. 'I suppose that must be it,' he said in a faraway voice. 'And stop doing that,' he added, 'or I really will come straight away.'

'Again?' Jem said. 'But Sebastian, baby, it's my turn next.'

'Precisely. So keep still, and let me do the work this time. Now then – I expect you'd like me to put this finger . . . where? Round about here?'

She felt his hand glide down her spine and come to rest between her splayed buttocks. One fingertip tapped against her anus.

'Oh yes,' she said, 'at least that finger, and maybe he could bring a friend.' She relaxed her muscles and felt the familiar exciting discomfort of her anal sphincter being widened as he introduced his fingers. She kissed his face. 'That's nice, Seb,' she said. She widened her eyes, and adopting her best little-girl voice, whispered, 'Finger-fuck my ass-hole, lover.'

Sebastian complied, his hand moving languorously as his sharp nose nuzzled Jem's right breast. He pushed aside the cream silk to take her nipple between his lips.

Between shivers of delight Jem glimpsed him grinning and heard his quiet chuckles of enjoyment. The fingers in her arse were moving faster now, and most of her breast had disappeared into Sebastian's mouth. She was writhing in frustrated excitement, her back arched, until at last Sebastian thrust his other hand into the space between their bodies, and his knuckles pushed against the top of her slit sending an electric thrill sparking from clitoris to womb to rectum. She reared up, an orgasm like a heated wave spreading to every nerve-ending in her body, and her vagina clenched Sebastian's penis, moulding itself to the throbbing hardness at her centre. Still shivering with the after-tremors of ecstasy she felt the pulses of his sperm spurting into her.

They were forehead to forehead, nose to nose. Jem opened one eye to meet Sebastian's intense dark gaze. Both of them began to laugh, and found they couldn't stop. At last Sebastian collapsed against the back of the chair, and Jem lifted herself off his prick and fingers. Sebastian lifted his hands to his face and sniffed appreciatively, as if savouring the cork of a newly-opened *premier cru*.

Jem giggled again. She was really very fond of her tall, lean, hawk-nosed lover. He was as sexy as Rudi, and as intelligent and impressive as Headman. She told herself that she must not become attached or distracted; she had work to do. 'Good of Rhoda to let us use this office,' she said.

'She's taking quite a risk,' Sebastian said, suddenly serious. 'If the Master found out, there wouldn't be much left of her to become a scullery-maid – which I imagine would be her eventual fate. I assume she simply fancies you as much as I do.'

'You're cute, Seb. This sure is a private place. No cameras or microphones here?'

Sebastian laughed. 'This used to be my office. And I was in a position to ensure my privacy.' He looked round at the blank walls. 'There's nothing left of its former glory, is there?'

Jem considered the strip lighting and the beige carpet. The room was empty except for the chair, the desk, and the computer terminal. 'This room was glorious?'

'I had it furnished in baroque style. There were several computers and monitors then, of course; but I liked the contrast between their bleak functionalism and the gilt scrolls and cheeky cherubim that sprouted from everything else in the room. My desk – Louis Quinze, very elegant – was there, in the centre of the room. There was a false ceiling and a chandelier. I used to sit on a *chaise longue* – not tremendously good for my posture, but there was room for someone else to sit or kneel or lie beside me. I dressed my staff in periwigs and satin waistcoats to suggest eighteenth century costume. There was a rota for *chaise longue* duty . . .' He shook his head slowly as he visualised the room as it had been.

Jem leant forward, held his face in her hands, and kissed his mouth. He responded urgently, and Jem was surprised and delighted to see that his limp penis was already beginning to stir. 'Tell me about *chaise longue* duty,' she said. 'You didn't have to keep both hands on your keyboard?'

'I'm a terrible typist, Jem. Two fingers. I found it helped me to concentrate if I had something to occupy my spare hand. Some of my most inspired pieces of programming came when I had my fingers inside some pretty computing trainee and she had her lips round this apparently unfailing organ.'

Jem bent to kiss his stiffening prick and inhaled the spicy aroma of his come mingled with her own juices. 'Mmmm. Gosh, it is unfailing, isn't it? But there's no more time for fun.'

Sebastian's face darkened. 'Are you returning into the clutches of our Master?'

'Don't worry, Seb honey. I can keep his mind on other things, most of the time. Today I've asked to take a look at a newcomer – what's it called, an initiation? So he's going to take me along. He says it'll be pretty straightforward. Security are in charge of this one.'

'Then it will be basic, that's certain. The Master's getting very unsubtle these days. And saying it is enough to get me executed for treason if he's in a bad mood. And he's always in a bad mood these days, too.' He sighed. 'This place used to be such fun, Jem. Never mind.'

'Maybe this place won't last much longer, Seb.'

'What on earth do you mean? The Master's got it sewn up, hasn't he?'

'We'll see. Come on, it's time to leave.'

'You're right. Thank you for a lovely time, Jem.'

'Thank you for coming!'

Chief Anderson was flustered; that could be the only explanation. He had offered Julia a chair, for one thing, and Julia knew that he wasn't the type to let his subordinates be seated in his presence. He paced around his desk, his thick fingers tapping his lips, glancing occasionally at Julia. He seemed at a loss for words, and Julia, looking at the gauze pouch swinging below the barrel of his torso, realised that this was the first time she had seen him without so much as a hint of an erection. He looked distinctly shrivelled.

At last he stopped pacing and deposited his bulk in his big chair behind the desk. 'Well, Julia,' he said, and stared at his fingertips.

'Yes, Chief?'

'I don't know what to make of you, Julia,' he said. 'Are you . . ?'

'What, Chief?'

'Never mind. If you were, you wouldn't tell me. Maybe you are what you appear to be.'

'And what might that be, Chief?'

'My star recruit, of course. A credit to the Security Corps. You've been here four days, and you're the most promising recruit of this year's intake. You've been chosen for duties in the Round Tower – over my head, I might add – and you've found a new guest for the House. And, on top of everything, your clearance level has been upped. And not just a level or two. Unprecedented.'

'My what's been upped?'

'Your clearance level, Julia. Right up to Gold. I suppose there's no reason you should know about clearance levels, as a trainee. Access to high-level files and equipment is restricted, you see. You need to know the codes and passwords. Here they are.' He pushed a plastic card and a scrap of print-out across the desk.

Julia stared at the brief list of words and numbers.

'Memorise them,' Anderson said, 'then destroy the paper. Keep the card: it displays your Gold clearance code. It's also imprinted on the magnetic strip.'

'And then what, Chief?'

'Then, Julia, you can gain access to just about every part of the House and every file on the computer system. Someone up there likes you,' he said, raising his eyes to the ceiling.

'You mean – the Master?'

Anderson nodded conspiratorially, but Julia was

196

thinking about Jem. She must have arranged this. Then another thought crossed her mind. 'Chief?' she said.

Anderson looked wary. 'Yes?'

'Where's Asmita, Chief?'

Anderson took a deep breath, and looked at the floor.

'I can find out now, Chief,' Julia reminded him gently. 'I've got clearance. Anyway, I know she's in the dungeons. I want to know why.'

Anderson shook his head. 'I don't know, Julia. I really don't. The order came directly from the Master. But if I know Asmita, she's probably enjoying it.'

And if I know the Master, Julia thought, he'll have done his best to make sure she isn't.

She realised she was thinking the unthinkable. Basically, the Master was a nasty piece of work.

Bathtime had been a surprisingly pleasant experience. Melanie and Patrick had discarded their uniforms and their severe demeanour, and had joined Lucy in the huge pool of scented bubbles. They had washed her thoroughly but gently, and when she had found herself sitting between them with Patrick, behind her, massaging suds into her breasts and Melanie, kneeling between her legs, carefully inserting her submerged fingers into all of her most intimate crevices, Lucy had started to think that perhaps she would enjoy her self-imposed undercover operation after all.

Patrick had blow-dried her hair into a cloud of spun gold. Melanie had made up her face with subtle shades of highlighter and blusher, and a touch of scintillating green above her eyes. Lucy had not protested even when Melanie methodically rubbed red-brown rouge into her lips and nipples. Patrick had dressed her in a thin black suspender belt, black stockings, and black shoes with impossibly high heels. The costume, he had told her, was the basic uniform for guests in the Private House.

Now, tottering as she practised walking in her heels, Lucy towered above her jailers. She caught sight of herself in the mirror that took up one wall of the enormous dressing room. I look quite something, she thought: tall, slim, fit, glowing with health, and definitely very sexy. In these shoes it's impossible not to wiggle my bum when I walk. And my legs seem to go on for ever.

She saw that Melanie and Patrick were encasing themselves in their sinister uniforms, and she sensed a change in the atmosphere.

'Time to start your initiation now, Lucy,' Melanie said with a twisted smile. She folded back a set of double doors to reveal a dark room beyond. 'Everyone's enjoyed watching you get ready. Now they'd like to meet you in person. Come along into the Equipment Room.'

Lucy scanned the room. There – in the corners of the ceiling – are those the lenses of closed-circuit cameras? Or are they just trying to put the frighteners on me?

Trying to project more confidence than she felt, she stepped into the darkness. Melanie and Patrick guided her past bizarre and unidentifiable shapes, and abandoned her in an empty area. She was about to set off to explore her surroundings when lights suddenly flashed on, pinning her in a crossfire of spotlight beams. The darkness around her was now impenetrable, but she could hear voices murmuring indistinctly.

More lights began to glow. Some, like cinema lights set high above her, cast a dim illumination that allowed her to see the full extent of the chamber she was in; others were spotlights, trained on the chrome and leather contraptions that surrounded her. She could make out, hanging among the spotlights, video cameras that shifted automatically to track her slightest movement.

The place was like a modern gymnasium, she thought, although she had never seen exercise machines quite like these, with chains and manacles, and none of the gyms she'd used had had seating for spectators. About twenty people, vague but colourful shapes in the semi-darkness, were sitting restlessly in the nearest two tiers of the seats that sloped up one side of the room.

'Ladies and gentlemen!' a voice boomed. 'This is Lucy, a new guest.'

The audience murmured. A spotlight threw a beam and picked out the announcer, standing only a few metres from

Lucy. He was a tall, thick-set, giant of a man, wearing only chains, a collar, and a bulging pouch of black gauze. Lucy felt imprisoned within her circle of light, and could only watch him as he advanced towards her, dragging with him his own spotlight beam.

'Lucy,' he said, his voice still loud enough to be heard throughout the room, 'welcome to the Private House. The first thing you must understand is that you are one of us now, and you can never leave. You are inside, and it is impossible to return to the outside. Do you understand?'

Lucy tried to think. Had it started like this for everyone in the Private House, she wondered. Those indistinct watchers in the seats? Melanie and Patrick? The big bruiser bearing down on her? Julia, if Julia really was an insider? The mysterious red head with the cloak and the whip-marks? And her darling Asmita? Had they all been through this ritual?

'Well, Lucy? Do you understand?'

She nodded, taking care to make a mental note that confessions made under duress are not admissible as evidence. The big man was standing next to her now; their pools of light had merged. He was taller even than she was in her heels, and she tried to stop herself being intimidated by his physical presence.

'The rules of the Private House can be summed up in two words,' he said, 'obedience and sexuality. Once you have learnt unquestioning obedience, your life will be devoted to sex. That is all you need to know.'

Lucy felt her shoulders stiffen. She'd never bothered to attend the Force's psychological warfare courses, but she had an instinctive determination not to succumb to brainwashing.

'I am your Mentor during your initiation,' the man said. 'The first lesson you must learn is respect for authority. Don't speak unless you're spoken to, and always address me as "Sir" Do you understand?'

Despite the cold tightness in her stomach, Lucy almost smiled. If only he knew how familiar she was with regimentation and the use of formal titles. 'Yes, sir!' she responded.

'Good.' He stepped back into the darkness, leaving Lucy

alone in the converging beams of light. 'Now turn your back to the audience and bend over.'

Lucy's mind raced. What exactly did he want? Was this some sort of medical inspection? She turned slowly, and leant forward.

There was laughter from the audience. 'Lucy's not a natural, is she?' shouted the Mentor from the darkness. 'Legs apart, Lucy, and bend right over. Touch your toes.'

Not medical, Lucy thought. It's a sex thing. I can't do it! I won't do it! Not in front of all these people!

She straightened, and stepped out of the pool of light. The beams followed her, trapping her again just as she was met by two young women in uniforms that were the same as Melanie's. They grabbed her; she tensed, about to throw one to the floor and break the other's arm. Just in time, she remembered that she had to avoid showing her hand too early, and she allowed herself to be led back to the Mentor.

'Don't worry, Lucy,' he said with sinister cheerfulness, 'very few novices show complete aptitude at first. You will be trained to obey.'

I won't! Lucy told herself as she was dragged towards one of the gleaming, spotlit machines. I'll never do what they want!

'This is a simple device,' she heard the Mentor saying for the benefit of the audience. 'We call it the Basic Stimulator.'

Lucy struggled, but a small army of black-garbed guards converged on her, removed her shoes, and positioned her on the polished wooden platform. Chains were looped around each of her ankles and were used to separate her legs and secure them to metal hoops at the bottom of metal uprights at the sides of the platform. Her arms were lifted above her head and chained to a metal bar that ran between the two uprights; the bar was then cranked upwards until her body was stretched taut. A second, padded bar was then inserted between the uprights, across the small of her back. Now she could move only her head, and despite her frantic movements, she could not prevent a blindfold being secured across her eyes.

She sensed that the guards had dispersed. Thankful, in a

way, that she could no longer see the audience, Lucy forced herself to remain calm and await developments. They can tie me up, she thought, and they can inflict whatever diabolical tortures they can think up; but they'll never make me do anything I don't want to.

She heard movements all around her, and suddenly a cold object nudged her between the legs: the merest brief touch of something hard against her exposed crotch. She jumped to her toes, and felt the tips of her breasts bump into soft material. She lowered herself again, slowly, and as her heels touched the floor the hard object was there again, just touching her private parts. She felt it move slightly, as if someone were adjusting it, making sure that it was positioned exactly beneath her centre, resting against the line that divided the outer lips of her sex. She breathed deeply, and concentrated on preparing herself for excruciating pain.

'The Stimulator is ready, ladies and gentlemen.' The Mentor was speaking again. 'It is a fully automatic device, with electronic sensors and cybernetic feedback mechanisms, all housed within this charming mock-Victorian machinery. I'll switch it on in a moment, and I'll turn it off again – just as soon as Lucy asks for permission to dance for your entertainment. Do you understand, Lucy? Whenever you're ready to dance for us – with some decoration, of course – just ask me nicely, and the machine will stop.'

He's off his rocker, Lucy thought. Ask his permission to dance naked, in public? I'd rather die. 'What do you mean – decoration?' she asked.

'A bum plug with a tail of horsehair,' the Mentor said offhandedly. 'It will look very fetching when you swivel your arse. We'll be expecting a dance with lots of bumps and grinds, of course.'

You kinky bastard, Lucy said to herself. You'll never get me to do that. Do your worst!

'No comment?' the Mentor said. 'In that case, I'll switch on the Stimulator.'

There was a quiet click. For a moment Lucy, muscles rigid and teeth clenched, thought nothing had happened. And then she felt it: the thing between her legs was moving, vibrating very slightly, a persistent buzz that began to tickle the curls of her pubic hair. She raised herself onto her toes, and the tickling stopped, but her nipples had again come into contact with the soft stuff, and now it, too, was moving – rotating in tiny circles, brushing against the very tips with gossamer lightness, a velvety, soft and yet tickly feeling that Lucy decided she could put up with while she tried to collect her wits.

They're not hurting me! was the thought that went round and round in her head. The sense of relief was so overwhelming that she could think of nothing else, until she realised that her nipples were hardening and her breasts swelling as the Stimulator relentlessly buffed her rouged tips. She allowed herself a smile of relief, and pushed her breasts forward, revelling for a moment in the innocuous mechanical caress.

They're not hurting me – yet. What if this is a trick, she thought, a ruse to lull me into a false sense of security? What is that thing between my legs? And as she thought of her legs, she became aware that the straining muscles in her calves were crying out for a rest. Cautiously she lowered herself from her tiptoes; and, just as her nipples dropped out of the range of the ticklish velvet caresser, she felt the vibrating object touch her lower lips and push between them.

Whatever it was, it had grown. A little bit of it was inside her now, just inside the mouth of her sex. It's vibrating, she thought; therefore, it's probably a vibrator. Perhaps they think it'll turn me on. If so, they must be really stupid. But then again, it is bloody insistent. Hard to ignore. I think I prefer the soft thing rubbing against my tits.

She stood on tiptoe again, and couldn't restrain a shiver as her sensitised nipples touched the velvet pads. She knew they were separate pads because they moved independently. They were no longer rotating; instead they were flicking up and down, the left one brushing downwards as the right moved up. She shivered again. Her nipples felt as big and hard as peach stones.

When the pain in her calf muscles obliged her to rest on her heels again, the vibrator impaled her. It was unmistakeably embedded in her slit, and now it was moving a little, up and down, forward and backward, from side to side, as well as vibrating. Lucy shook her head, refusing to admit that the machine's buzzing was beginning to set off an answering tingle in her loins. She felt hot, she knew she was blushing, she wanted to move her limbs but all she could do was to wiggle her hips, and that only increased the sweet tension building inside her. She sagged, trying to envelope more of the vibrator; and she felt something else as well.

It was in front of her; there was something just in front of her pubic mound, something brushing against the golden curls that clustered round the top of her slit. She moved her hips forward, and it touched her skin: something cool, thin and hard, moving very slowly downwards as it crept towards her. It was heading straight for her clitoris. She stood on tiptoe again, and offered her breasts to the machine.

The pads were moving faster now, catching against the bottom and then the top of her rock-hard nipples as they flicked up and down. Lucy bit her lip and told herself that the strokes were too brisk, that she wasn't enjoying the sensation.

The Mentor's voice intruded. 'How's it going, Lucy?' he said in a loud and extravagant voice, as if she were a contestant on a television game show. 'Are you ready to dance for us yet?'

Lucy had forgotten all about dancing. She had forgotten the cameras and the audience watching her every movement. Behind the blindfold, she had started to forget everything except her aching muscles, her titilated nipples, her vibrating insides. The Mentor's voice induced a sudden pang of fear.

She was no longer afraid of pain. She would even welcome it. This was going to be far worse. They would leave her tied to this machine, watching her writhe and wriggle, listening to every breath, until . . . No. It was unthinkable. Surely she couldn't, not like this, with a machine? She would die of shame. But if she didn't agree to the Mentor's despicable demands . . . How long would they leave her here? How many times could she . . ?

She set her jaw. No: she would not give in. She'd stay on the machine until it blew a fuse, if necessary.

She lowered herself on to the vibrator, guiltily aware that the device's easy passage revealed her state of excitement. She couldn't help rotating her hips as the buzzing, roving cylinder slid into her. She felt the second object probing the front of her slit, rubbing against the hood of her clitoris, each touch triggering a tremor in her entrails. And then she felt the third object, and froze.

There it was again. She hadn't imagined it: the tip of another vibrator, nuzzling the cleft between her buttocks whenever she moved her hips backwards. She clenched her arse-cheeks together, and was mortified to hear laughter as the Mentor pointed out her reaction.

She shook her head. 'No, no, *no!*' she protested; and then realised that the vibrator was still and the room was suddenly silent.

'Master!' said the Mentor. 'We're glad to see you. I was beginning to think you wouldn't make an appearance. As you can see, we've started without you.'

'That's alright, Mentor,' said a deep, powerful voice. 'I was – unavoidably detained.'

'He means it was my fault,' said another voice. 'I guess I'm just an unreliable kind of a girl.'

Lucy inclined her head. She knew that woman's voice. That was it: the redhead, the cloaked woman she had met in the tennis pavilion. She heard footsteps approaching, and sensed people gathering around her.

'A good-looking guest,' said the Master's voice, from just in front of her. 'Will she require a long training, Mentor?'

'Difficult to tell with this one,' the Mentor said. 'She's not exactly taking to it like a duck to water, if you know what I mean, but as you can see she's got loads of sexual potential. The Stimulator's working well. She's been totally resistant so far, but it's very hard to know how long we'll have to work on her before she sees reason.'

'There are no marks. Has she been flogged yet?'

Something in the Master's tone made Lucy's blood run cold.

'No, Master. Of course not. I was waiting for you to arrive.'

'Very good. Proceed with the Stimulator a little longer. I rather hope she remains obstinate.'

Lucy shuddered as a large, warm hand stroked the lower curve of her left buttock.

'May I tease her, Master?' said the redhead, giggling. 'Can I tell her what you'd like to do to her?'

'By all means,' the Master said, as his footsteps receded.

The next thing Lucy heard was an urgent whisper. 'Are you crazy?' the redhead hissed. 'What kind of game do you think you're playing? You're still stuck in the first stage. Just do what they tell you, or this initiation routine'll go on for days.'

Lucy was taken aback. 'But – but you don't know what they want me to do.'

'I can guess the kind of thing. And you're going to have to do it. Now, while you're still in one piece, or later, after they've put you through the grinder. But you'll do it. You'll do whatever they tell you. These guys have had a lot of practice. They're experts.'

'What about the cameras? They're getting this on film. If I give in . . . Well, I've got to think about my job . . .'

'You're worrying about your promotion prospects at a time like this? If you crack this place wide open, you're made. Anyhow, I can fix the cameras, if they worry you. I have a thing going with the guy who created the filing system. I can delete anything that gets recorded, OK?'

The redhead's voice seemed persuasively reasonable to Lucy. 'So – you think I should just give in and do it?'

'Yes! Goddammit, that's the only way you'll get on the inside of this operation. You're no use to me stuck in here chained to these machines for a week. Do what they want.'

'Well – alright.'

'But not right now. That way you'll blow my cover and yours with it. So make it look good. OK? Another fifteen minutes of saying no, stiff upper lip, Dunkirk spirit of defiance, and all that stuff. Then the sudden collapse, abject surrender. Can you do that?'

'If I have to.'

'You have to. Hell, you might even get to like it. Good luck!'

She was gone. Lucy heard her voice again, as her heels tapped across the floor. 'Hey, Master! This one's real pig-headed. We're going to have a whole bunch of fun initiating her, I can tell you!'

Lucy swallowed. Her mouth was dry. Another quarter of an hour of stimulation, she thought, and then I have to beg to be allowed to perform a sexy dance with a tail hanging out of my arse. All in the line of duty, I suppose. A policeperson's lot is not always a dignified one. At least I know I won't be recorded on video tape for posterity.

There was a click; the vibrator inside her recommenced its exploration of her vagina.

Jem lay on the bed in her chamber in the Round Tower. It had been one hell of a busy day, she reflected, but a successful one.

Maxine must have freed herself and then tidied the room: there was no trace of the black ribbon Jem had used to bind her, and not a speck of dust anywhere. Sebastian was a lovely man, and the information he'd provided was even lovelier. And Lucy had, in the end, succumbed very realistically to the Mentor's training methods: after two noisy and, Jem thought, genuine orgasms while on the Stimulator, Lucy had performed an arse-waggling dance of unbridled sensuality. Headman had been disappointed, but Jem had diverted his wrath and his riding-crop towards one of his slaves – the one who had tormented Jem while tying her to the chandelier in Headman's bedchamber the previous evening.

Everything is going just fine, Jem thought; so why do I have this nasty feeling that the situation is slipping out of my hands? And where the hell is Julia?

Jem was surprised by the intensity of her sudden yearning for her pretty bodyguard. She wanted to feel Julia's face between her thighs and Julia's tongue inside her; she wanted to see those dark, long-lashed eyes looking up at her.

She wasn't used to feeling indecisive. Why hadn't

Headman asked for her this evening? She was glad to be away from him, as his temper was becoming increasingly unpredictable. But she didn't like not knowing what he was up to.

Should she go upstairs and find out whether he was in his chambers? Or perhaps she could spend the evening with Sebastian? That would be a pleasanter option, but a trifle self-indulgent. Or should she try to find Julia? That might be the easiest to achieve. She picked up the telephone and dialled the servants' quarters.

'Hi, it's Jem. Yeah, yeah, cut all that stuff out. Can you find Maxine, Julia's maid, for me? Thanks, honey. Ask her to come up to my room, would you?'

Jem jumped from the bed, crossed the room to the vast, dark wardrobe, and shrugged off her silk peignoir. She looked over her shoulder and considered the reflection of her naked body. The marks made by Headman's crop were still just visible as dull red lines. No permanent damage, Jem thought; that's a relief. Just a little pink shading to make my pretty little butt even prettier!

She dabbed perfume into her pubic hair and under her breasts, and watched her nipples harden as she ran her fingernails lightly around them. Aware of the effect of the sight of her naked body on Julia's adoring maid, she decided to wear nothing but a thin leather belt buckled about her hips.

There was a knock on the door.

'Come in!' Jem called, and turned. Maxine stood in the doorway, wearing her maid's uniform.

'Close the door, Maxine, and strip. Everything off!'

The maid smiled happily, turned to shut the door, and came to stand in front of Jem. Her eyes came to rest on the gleaming band of leather slung round Jem's hips; Jem parted her legs and ran her fingertips along the belt, and as if startled into action, Maxine started to undress.

Her breasts strained against the thin material of her blouse as she put her hands behind her to untie the little white apron. She held the scrap of cotton uncertainly for a moment, and then dropped it on the floor. Jem enjoyed the blush that appeared on the maid's round cheeks as her hands went to her throat and she tried not to hurry and fumble as she undid the buttons of her black voile blouse. She left the garment hanging open as she tugged it from the waistband of her skirt and then unbuttoned the cuffs. Then, with a quick glance at Jem, she pulled the blouse from her shoulders and let it fall from her body.

She stood for a moment, the white mounds of her breasts rising and falling in the half-cups of her corset, then with one deft movement, she unfastened her short black skirt and let it fall round her ankle-boots. She smiled shyly, her eyes darting to Jem's face and away again. Jem waited, enjoying the lascivious thrills that were spreading gradually through her insides.

'Should I take off my stays, Miss?' Maxine said.

'Your what, child?'

'My corsets, Miss.'

'Of course, Maxine. I want you completely naked.'

The maid bent forward to unlace her boots, and her breasts swung free of their supports, sliding against each other and against her bare arms as her fingers tugged at the boots.

In her stockinged feet Maxine was no taller than Jem, and Jem found herself gripping the black leather belt to contain her impatience. The temptation to handle the maid's heavy breasts was almost beyond endurance, but Jem made herself watch and wait while Maxine unfastened her stockings and rolled them down her legs.

Maxine took a step towards Jem, as if to offer her magnificent bosom, while her hands were busy behind her back unfastening the hooks and eyes of the corset. She pulled the black lace and whalebone away from her front, and tossed it aside. She stood, eyes lowered, waiting for instructions.

Jem studied Maxine's body. The maid had a perfect and well-padded shape. No part of her could be described as thin, but the lushness of her breasts, the flaring of her hips, and even the rotundity of her belly only served to emphasise the incurving at her waist. There were dimples where her plump thighs joined her pelvis, and where her breasts jostled against her upper arms. Her chubby mount of

Venus was covered with a glossy forest of dark curls that disappeared into the deep valley between the rounded hills of her belly and thighs.

'Loosen your hair,' Jem said, and bit her lip with delight as the girl put her hands behind her head and her breasts rose up her ribcage. A curtain of long, wavy dark hair fell round the maid's face. Her eyes peeked out at Jem like those of a rabbit peering from a thicket of long grass.

'Come closer,' Jem said, her voice a little husky. 'Ask permission to kiss my right breast.'

The maid took small steps forward until she was only centimetres from Jem's body. Jem could feel Maxine's warm breath on her neck; their nipples were almost touching.

'Please, Miss,' Maxine said almost inaudibly, 'please may I kiss your right breast?'

'Oh yes,' Jem breathed, 'lots and lots.'

Jem closed her eyes and put her head back as the maid's soft lips touched the upper slope of her breast. The first kiss was just a brush of the lips, the second a lingering touch. And then Jem thrust her fingers into the maid's thick hair, and held her face against her body, and Maxine's kisses became a barrage of sense-explosions.

'Lick me,' Jem ordered. 'Underneath, yes, just there. Harder than that! And now the nipple, Maxine. Not so fast! Little kisses first. Very good, that's very nice. Now use your tongue . . . Yes, like that, but let me see you doing it. Good, good. Now you can suck, Maxine, and keep on sucking until I say stop . . .'

Jem's legs were trembling. She pulled back Maxine's head.

'Please may I kiss the other one now, Miss?' the maid said, her lips glistening and her eyes sparkling.

Jem shook her head. 'Not right now,' she said. 'We have things to discuss first. Tell me: what did I promise you this morning?'

'Well, Miss, you said that if the Master punished me, Miss, you'd count the lines on my bottom and give me twice as many on my tits.' Maxine grinned and cupped her hands under her breasts, lifting them towards Jem.

'Let me see,' Jem said. 'Turn round.'

Maxine turned on her heels, parted her legs, and bent forward to clasp her hands round her ankles.

Could I ever be as obedient as this girl? Jem wondered. Would I be like this, if I spent long enough being trained by those thugs in Security?

The sight of Maxine's arse drove the speculations from her mind. The beautifully smooth, white, dimpled curves, framing the deep, dark furrow and the plump sex-lips, were an enchanting sight; and the sight of pink blotches and haphazard red lines covering the pale skin sent a jolt through Jem that made her catch her breath. She had only to extend her hand to touch the inflamed flesh, and as she made contact she and Maxine gasped in unison.

'How many?' Jem asked.

'I'm not sure I know, Miss. I wasn't counting. Perhaps you'd better count them.'

Jem smiled: Maxine seemed to be able to find an infinite number of excuses for Jem to touch her. Jem's fingertip traced a faded red line from the centre of Maxine's right buttock to the satin-soft hollow at the top of the inside of her thigh. 'One,' she said, and Maxine whimpered.

Jem forced herself to count slowly and carefully, following each stripe with the lightest, most lingering of touches. 'Twenty,' she announced at last, moulding her palm to the curve of Maxine's buttock as an indication that she had finished counting.

'Is that all, Miss?' Maxine's voice sounded distinctly disappointed.

'I guess maybe some of them have faded away,' Jem said, inspecting the maid's delectable bottom more closely as a suspicion formed in her mind.

'Anyway, Miss,' Maxine said, 'that means I get forty on my tits, is that right?'

'Yes, Maxine,' Jem replied absently, her hands straying across the pink orbs.

'Is that forty on each one, Miss?' Maxine went on, almost falling over in her eagerness to look back at Jem.

'No,' Jem said briskly, removing her hands and walking away. 'I'll have to think up something a whole lot more unpleasant than that. You haven't been straight with me, Maxine.'

The maid stood upright, and whirled to face Jem; then, suddenly remembering that she had not been given permission to move, she stood indecisively, her mouth open, her protest unvoiced.

Jem, chortling inwardly, contrived to look severe. 'You've been lying to me, Maxine. The Master didn't give you that rosy backside, did he?'

Maxine's eyes filled with tears. 'No, Miss,' she said in a dejected whisper. 'But how did you know?'

'For one thing, the Master likes things regular, and those stripes are all over your arse, going every which way. For another, he'd have given you more than twenty – and at least some of them would look a bit more serious than any of those. But the clincher is that if the Master had whipped you this morning, your butt wouldn't still be glowing like a brazier. Elementary, my dear Maxine. Who did it, by the way?'

'I asked Cook to do it, just before I came up here. I'm ever so sorry, Miss, really I am. It's just that – well, you know . . .'

'What, Maxine?'

The maid took a deep breath. 'I thought you'd send me away, Miss, if you weren't going to punish me.' Her cheeks were blazing, her moist eyes were wide, her lustrous hair was wild about her face, and her magnificent chest was heaving with emotion. Jem pitied her, despised her, desired her, suffered with her, and above all felt delirious in the knowledge of her power over the girl.

'Come here,' Jem said. 'Kneel in front of me.'

A glimmer of hope appeared in Maxine's eyes. She knelt in front of Jem with her knees apart, her hands behind her back, her breasts pushed forward and her head lowered.

'Look at me,' Jem said, and thrilled as Maxine's wide eyes lifted to stare up at her face. 'What would you do for me, Maxine?'

'Anything, Miss,' the maid replied, as if the answer was obvious.

'If I told you to go to the Master, right now, and ask him to flog you all night – '

'I'd do it, Miss.'

'If I told you to jump from the window – this window half-way up the Tower?'

'I'd do that, too.'

'You'd die, Maxine. You couldn't survive a fall like that.'

'I know, Miss.' Two tears trickled down Maxine's face. 'But I'd do it, all the same, if you told me to. But please don't, Miss, not yet, please.'

Jem stroked the girl's hair. 'It's all right, Maxine, it's all right. I'd never tell you to do that. But never try to trick me again, you understand?'

'Yes, Miss. I promise, Miss. I only did it because I love you so much.'

'I know, I know. And I ought to spend all evening punishing you.'

'Please do, Miss,' Maxine said, burying her face between Jem's thighs.

'Maxine, you're incorrigible,' Jem laughed. 'I don't have time tonight. I have other things to do.'

Maxine moaned, and collapsed to the floor, raining kisses on Jem's feet.

'OK!' Jem giggled. 'OK, you win. I'll whip your lovely big titties. Just a little bit. Now kneel properly.'

In an instant Maxine resumed her kneeling position.

'Unbuckle my belt,' Jem said. As the maid's fingers tugged at the buckle, thrills of sexual expectation coursed through Jem's body with renewed force. 'Fold it in half, Maxine. That's right. Kiss it, Maxine; it's about to kiss your breasts. How many would you like?'

Maxine, trembling with emotion, was unable to speak for a moment. She tore her lips from the loop of leather. 'Forty,' she said, thrusting the belt up towards Jem.

'Twenty will be enough for now,' Jem said, taking the belt and swinging it experimentally. 'There's always tomorrow, and the next day. Stand up!'

Maxine jumped up and spread her legs as far apart as she could without falling. She crossed her arms behind her back, pushed out her chest, and gazed steadily at Jem. Her eyes dared Jem to be merciless; only her quivering lower lip betrayed apprehension.

Jem smiled wryly. 'Never thought I'd find myself doing this kind of thing,' she said, half to herself. 'Leastways, I never thought I'd get to enjoy it. You've got the most beautiful pair I've ever seen, Maxine.' Thoughtfully, she stroked the looped leather in a W beneath the maid's breasts.

Maxine's nipples crinkled and stood out stiffly from her large pink aureoles. 'Oh no, Miss,' she gasped, 'yours are much prettier. Mine are so big and fat.'

'False modesty,' Jem laughed, and swung the belt gently against the side of Maxine's left breast. The maid bit her lip, but made no other movement. Jem watched closely as the heavy bulb of flesh swung from side to side and then came to rest. A stripe of fiery pink appeared where the belt had made contact, but it faded even as Jem watched. 'One,' she said, and raised her arm again.

Apart from rocking back and forth slightly, as if pushing her breasts forward to meet the belt lessened the unexpectedness of the blows. Maxine remained still and silent as Jem whipped her. Her breasts moved, though, independently of her body, as the band of leather struck them. At first Jem's blows alternated between the two pendulous orbs. She would strike at one of them three times in quick succession, from the right, from the left, and then upwards; and then she would pause to watch the trembling flesh come to rest and blush redly, before she started on the other breast.

She continued in this way until Maxine's breasts were as quivering and thoroughly pink as raspberry blancmanges, and her arm was beginning to feel tired, and Maxine was at last beginning to utter an *oh*! of pain or of pleasure at each blow. Then she stopped, flexed her wrist, and moved to stand beside the maid.

'Keep very still, Maxine,' she said, although she could hardly control the tremors that shook her own body. She aimed a succession of swift, sharp strokes that landed across the front of both breasts, striking the proudly jutting nipples until Maxine's gasps merged into a continuous sobbing cry and the girl began to topple forwards.

Jem dropped the belt, grasped Maxine's shoulders, and

turned the girl towards her. 'How many was that, Maxine?' she said softly.

Maxine's breathing slowed. 'I – I don't know, Miss,' the maid said. 'I lost count. About ten, I think.'

Jem laughed, shaking her head in amazement at the girl's gluttonous craving and at her own bewildering lust. 'You've had enough,' she said, raising her hands to sink her fingers into Maxine's hot tormented mounds.

The maid stiffened, threw back her head, and released a long, raucous gasp of pain. Then she fell against Jem, who caught her in her arms. Maxine's burning globes smothered Jem's tight buds and their lips met; as the kiss developed into a mutual caress of hungry tongues, their hands moved downwards to paddle in the lakes of wetness beneath each other's arses.

Some time later, Jem remembered why she had ordered Maxine up to her chamber.

'Stop, Maxine,' she said. 'No, stop for a minute. I have to ask you something. Do you know where Julia is this evening? I can't find her.'

'Sorry, Miss,' the maid said, looking almost sullen. 'She popped in for a bite to eat at the end of the afternoon, and I haven't seen her since. I suppose you'll be wanting her tonight?'

'Not for what you think,' Jem chided her, mentally crossing her fingers. 'A maid in the hand is worth two of her mistress not immediately to hand, or something like that. Let's get comfortable on the bed. Looks like you need to rub a little lotion into these poor nipples of yours.'

'Shall I fetch some cream, Miss?'

'Don't bother, Maxine. I've got some creamy ointment right there where your hand is. Come to bed and rub your nipples into me, girl.'

Every door was open to her; Chief Anderson had been absolutely right. Where there were fellow Security personnel, Julia had only to flash her Gold card and they would unlock the door and usher her through it; where there were automatic gates, she had only to insert her card in the slot, or tap in a code number, and the gates would slide apart.

214

And when she had found herself in a maze of featureless corridors that she had never been in before, she had activated one of the computer terminals and had typed in passwords until the screen had displayed a map of the entire cellar network.

Thus she had reached the dungeons. Even now, at midnight, there were torches burning in brackets on the walls, and here and there prisoners were chained to humming machinery or were being intermittently whipped by tired guards. But most of the pits and platforms and galleries were in deep darkness, and anyway she had no reason to fear challenges: the fact that she was in the dungeons was in itself evidence of her high level of security clearance.

She was at the end of her quest. She stopped in front of the final door. It was set into the stone wall and made of blackened wood strengthened with iron struts. The numeral 8 was screwed into the wood at eye level. Hanging next to the door was a bunch of enormous iron keys; Julia ignored them, knowing that they were only decorative, and inserted her Gold card into the barely-visible slot below the door's keyhole. Noiselessly, the door swung away from her.

At first Julia could see nothing in the darkness beyond the door. She plucked the flashlight from her belt and held her hand across its end, allowing only a thin gleam to penetrate the darkness. The cell was small, but in all other respects it was not what Julia expected. The walls were spotlessly white, the floor tiles were clean and soft and warm to walk on; in one corner of the room the flashlight picked out a shower cubicle, a toilet and a bidet.

At last the flickering beam of light found the bed, and on it, sleeping fitfully, the naked brown body Julia had come to rescue. 'Asmita!' she whispered from the doorway. 'Asmita, wake up!'

The figure rolled over on the bed, moaned, and started sobbing. 'No, no, please,' the Asian girl murmured, 'no more, please, no.'

'Asmita! Keep quiet! It's me, Julia.'

'Julia?' Asmita struggled to sit up. 'Julia? Is that you? Have they got you too?'

'Yes, it's me. And they certainly haven't got me. I'm jolly well here in my own right. I've come to take you out of this place.'

Asmita groaned as she swung her feet to the floor. Her every movement seemed difficult. 'How?' she said in a dull voice. 'I can't leave here. You don't know what it's like. I'm only half-way through the programme. They've got another half a dozen games to play with me tomorrow. And more the day after that. And more after that. And more . . .'

Sitting on the edge of the bed, she started to sob. Julia was frantic with worry, and close to tears herself. 'I can't come into the room, Asmita. I've avoided all the cameras so far, but if I step more than a few paces towards you the lights will come on and I'll be on screen in the Rotunda. You must come to me. Can you walk?'

'Yes. Yes, of course.' Asmita stood up painfully. 'How did you get here, Julia? How do you know about the cameras?'

'It's an awfully long story. I've friends in high places, it seems, and I've been doing some homework. Walk towards me, dear, that's right. Have they chained you to the wall?'

Julia could hear a jingling of metal as Asmita took faltering steps towards her. She can't be chained up, Julia thought, she's walking away from the bed. What's that glittering on her body, though? Asmita told me she never wears – oh! 'Asmita!' she cried. 'What have they done to you?'

As the Asian girl moved out of the gloom of the cell into the relative light of the doorway, Julia could see only too clearly what had happened to her in the dungeons. Asmita turned her face away but the curtain of her long hair did not drop quickly enough to hide the tears in her eyes. The movement of her head, pulling taut one of the golden chains that connected the rings in her ears to the rings in her nipples, showed very clearly the complex arrangement of bodily adornment that Asmita had been given.

'Come closer, Asmita,' Julia urged. 'I'll take you away.'

Asmita stumbled into Julia's arms. Chains ran between her nipples, and from her nipples to her leather collar, and from each nipple to the corresponding earlobe. 'Julia – they made me ask for them, Julia.' Tears streamed down her face, and she began to wail like a child. 'They made me beg,' she gasped between sobs, 'they made me beg for every single chain. And they wouldn't tell me why. They wouldn't tell me, Julia. Why did the Master do this to me, Julia? Why?'

Julia felt her own face wet with tears. Supporting Asmita's body, she started the long walk out of the dungeons. 'I don't know, Asmita. I don't know why he does these dreadful things. Don't worry, my dear, we can take all of the chains and rings away. I'll make you as good as new. I'll look after you. I know one thing, though,' she added, to herself.

'What?' Asmita said.

'The Master won't get away with this, Asmita. I don't know how, but I'm going to make him pay.'

DAY SEVEN: *SATURDAY*

Asmita stirred and moaned questioningly, but her eyes remained closed.

'Shhh,' Julia breathed as she continued to smooth ointment into Asmita's wide aureoles. 'It's alright. You're safe. You're in my room. All the horrid chains have gone. Sleep a little longer. It's Saturday. The weekend. You can lie in.'

Julia watched a smile appear on her friend's lips. She placed a soft, lingering kiss on each dark brown nipple and then pulled the quilt up to Asmita's throat.

She stepped back from the bed and looked at herself in the mirror. Today she was off duty until the evening, and she had dressed in one of her old costumes. Apart from the tiny pink suspender belt and grey stockings, it consisted of no more than two scraps of the sheerest shocking pink silk; one piece was tied about her shoulders and ended just below her breasts, while the other she had tied around her waist to make a long, backless skirt. She turned and looked over her shoulder to admire her small round buttocks peeking impertinently between the curtains of silk, and as her fingers were still covered with the ointment she had used to soothe Asmita's nipples and earlobes, she slid her hand up her ribs and rubbed the cream into the undersides of her breasts. She watched entranced as her hips began to move back and forth and she felt her breasts tighten and her nipples brush against the flimsy material.

She glanced at Asmita, but the girl was sleeping. Julia felt a momentary disappointment: she felt like a courtesan again, and she wanted her day off to be devoted to nothing but delightful sex. She decided to telephone Jem.

'I'm sorry, Miss,' said the voice of the switchboard operator, 'she's not available today.'

Julia frowned. 'Well, could I speak to her maid, Jenny, please?'

'Sorry, Miss. No one's available. I've been told to hold all calls in and out of the Round Tower.'

The line went dead. Julia put down the receiver slowly, a fearful premonition growing in her mind. Her hands went to the bow of silk at the back of her neck, and the pink drape drifted from her shoulders. Thinking furiously but outwardly calm, she reached for her Security tunic.

The black leather uniform was strangely comforting. Julia had no idea what she might have to do, but she felt ready for almost anything. She tightened the buckles of her belt, checked the power pack of her buzzer, and retrieved from the back of the wardrobe the package that Maxine had brought to her room in the middle of the night.

The handwriting on the brown cardboard was Jem's; Julia had already memorised the disquieting message:

*If it happens that one day, maybe soon, you
can't find me, and you can't contact me, open
this box. And if you love me, please carry out
the instructions inside. I'm counting on you,
honey.*

As she tore open the parcel, Julia walked slowly to the window. In the grey light of the cloud-covered sky she inspected the contents: a signet ring, a stick of red sealing was, and a long letter.

I do love you, Jem, she thought, staring unseeingly through the rain-streaked panes; and she began to read.

The wind whistled through the battlements above Headman's chambers. Jem shivered, and Headman's hand stopped moving between her parted thighs. She tensed, and then forced herself to relax, wriggling her pelvis against his hardness. She was on his bed, lying across his lap, and she expected the spanking to start at any moment.

'Goose pimples, Jem,' he chuckled, running his palm across her bottom. 'Are you cold, my dear?'

Why's he in such a darned good mood, Jem wondered. Why's he being nice to me all of a sudden? 'I expect you'll think of some way to warm me up, Master,' she said.

'Perhaps later, my angel. But first I've got a treat for you. It's going to be a very entertaining day. Shall I play with your pussy a little longer?'

'Be my guest, Master,' Jem said, 'it's lovely.' And it was by no means an unpleasant feeling, Jem thought, to be upended on Headman's bed while his strong and expert fingers gently explored the moistening crevices of the hollow beneath her buttocks. But she could not abandon herself completely to the thrills that started to tingle in her loins; she could not forget that the telephone in her room had failed to work that morning, that Jenny had not appeared to help her dress, and that the Round Tower was deserted. Headman had told her that this was usual on a Saturday in the Private House, but Jem was still worried.

'I have a present for you,' Headman said, his thumb wriggling into her while his fingertips circled her clitoris. 'It's wrapped up and waiting in the study. Shall we go and play with it?'

Jem murmured frustratedly. 'I'm just getting comfortable,' she protested, pushing up her bottom to chase Headman's retreating hand. He laughed, rolled her off his lap, stretched, and threw aside the bedclothes.

'What shall I wear today, Jem?' he said.

'Something light and summery?' Jem suggested. 'It would suit your mood, if not the weather.'

'I don't think so, Jem,' he said, standing in the doorway of his dressing room. 'Dark and forbidding, that's my style, I'm afraid. And your present will necessitate the wearing of my dungeon equipment. One person's reward is often another's punishment, you see.'

Once again Jem suppressed a shiver of fear. 'So I'm OK in this leather gear?' she said, forcing her foot into the black cylinder of a thigh-high boot.

'That's why I asked you to wear it,' Headman said, buckling chains and belts around his grizzled body. 'We'll make a matched pair. You look very wonderful in a black corset. And there's no odour in the world that's quite as inspiring as the mingled scents of sweat-soaked leather and female sex. Don't you agree?'

'Absolutely,' Jem said, and followed him from the bedroom with a sick feeling of foreboding.

Headman held open the door of his study and ushered Jem past him. The desk had been moved aside, and in its place at the centre of the book-lined room stood a large box. It was wrapped in colourful paper and swathed in ribbons; it was obviously the present Headman had promised Jem.

It was the shape of the box that alarmed Jem. It was quite narrow, but taller than her. Images from old gangster movies flashed through her mind: hit-men being delivered, dead and bloody, as taunts to their employer. Was there a body in the box? Whose? For the first time, her fears must have shown in her expression.

'Don't worry,' Headman said impatiently. 'It's nothing too terrible. Open it and see.'

Hardly reassured, Jem stepped forward and tugged at the ribbons and paper. There were airholes in the wooden case that was revealed as the gift wrapping fell away. The box was a mock-up anyway, Jem realised. It was made of thin plywood boards, tacked together, and it couldn't have been used to carry anything. It must have been knocked together hurriedly here, in the study, around its contents. Jem was able to prise the panels apart with her fingers, and the entire structure collapsed on the carpet.

'*Voila!*' Headman murmured. 'A present from me to you.' Jem stared in silent amazement at the object standing in the middle of the room.

It was a human figure. A woman, Jem realised; the figure's breasts were visible. Almost every other part of her body, however, was encased in shining black rubber. To buy time in which to try to identify the woman, Jem walked slowly round her. The woman's mouth and jaw were visible; the rest of her head was enveloped in a latex hood. The rubber suit, which appeared to consist of one tight-fitting garment, covered her from neck to toe – apart from the two holes in front through which her breasts protruded, and a larger hole which revealed her buttocks and extended between her legs to leave uncovered her genitalia and the insides of her thighs. The flesh of her hips and upper thighs bulged out of the constricting suit. Her arms were secured behind her back with black leather belts, each wrist secured to the elbow of the other arm, pushing her torso forward. Her legs were held apart by a metal rod strapped to her ankles. She couldn't see, and Jem guessed that she couldn't hear much through the latex hood. Her skin was very pale, and Jem breathed a sigh of relief: the woman obviously wasn't Asmita, or Julia, or Lucy. She was tall and slim, and her pubic hair was pale blonde; she reminded Jem of someone, but the rubber suit made identification impossible.

'Who is she?' Jem whispered.

'One of our field operatives,' Headman said. 'She works on the outside, mainly. She's been brought back here for punishment. Her punishment is your reward, Jem. She's yours to play with.'

'Thanks a million,' Jem said, ignoring the tingle of excitement that she felt in spite of herself. 'What's she done wrong?'

'You should know better than to ask,' Headman said. 'I don't need an excuse to offer her to you as a present. But in this case, she has committed a very serious offence. A sin of omission, you might say, and one that could have had disastrous consequences. She failed to report a sighting of a woman who might have been crucial to one of my plans. But I'm sure you'll teach her the error of her ways. Shall we arrange her on the saddle?'

'Saddle?' Jem looked round the room. Headman kicked the plywood and wrapping paper aside, and dragged a metal frame from a corner to the centre of the carpet. It was indeed shaped like a saddle: a curved, concave pad of black leather, supported at an angle on a rigid framework of tubular steel. There were wide straps hanging from the mid-point of the concave curve, and stirrups dangling from the higher of the two ends.

'Help her to hobble into position, Jem,' Headman said cheerily. 'Stand her at the higher end, and then we'll tip her forward on to the saddle.'

Jem touched the glistening rubber that was stretched

round the woman's shoulder. The woman started, and almost fell, as if she had been unaware of anyone near her. Jem realised that the black suit insulated its wearer from almost all sensory input. The naked breasts and buttocks suddenly seemed horrifyingly vulnerable: the woman's every sensation would be concentrated in those pale globes of flesh.

Jem touched her again, very gently, and steered her towards the metal frame. The woman, breathing in quick, shallow gasps, took tiny steps on her hobbled high heels, until the front of her thighs touched the end of the saddle. Headman came to stand beside her; considerably less gently than Jem, he put a hand to the small of her back and pushed her forward, ignoring her wail of fear as, bound legs flailing, she toppled forward and came to rest with her pelvis resting on the higher end of the saddle and her breasts hanging over the edge of the lower end.

'Hold her still, Jem,' Headman cried. 'I'll strap her in. This is fun, isn't it?'

Jem stared at him. What had gotten into Terence Headman? Had he finally flipped? She rested her hand on the woman's craning neck, trying to impart some sort of comfort, while Headman tugged enthusiastically at the leather straps, binding the woman's arched back against the concave surface of the saddle.

'Now, Jem! I'll undo the leg separator, and then it's feet into stirrups!'

The metal rod fell to the floor, and Jem grabbed one of the woman's ankles and pulled her foot towards the hanging stirrup. She saw that Headman was simply hooking the other stirrup into the arch of the woman's high-heeled boot, and she did likewise. It was clear that the woman would be unable to unhook either her toes or her heels.

'Now we raise the stirrups!' Headman announced, buckling together two straps underneath the frame; as the stirrups rose to a level just beneath the higher end of the saddle, the woman's legs were bent almost double and her knees were lifted alongside her ribcage. Her pale, rounded, upraised buttocks almost glowed with naked defence-lessness.

'There you are, Jem,' Headman said, 'a perfectly-wrapped present.'

Jem shook her head. 'Couldn't I just have book tokens?' she said. 'What am I supposed to do with her?'

'Don't look a gift-horse in the mouth, Jem.' Headman's voice was suddenly serious. 'I wouldn't take kindly to that. You can do what you like, my dear, but I would strongly suggest that you think of something that involves both a riding crop and this young woman's arse.'

Jem tried very hard to look enthusiastic as she took the crop Headman offered her. She had been surprised to discover within herself the sexual excitement of wielding power and inflicting pain, but Maxine had been a willing and adoring recipient of her lashes, and Maxine's own excitement had been the greatest part of Jem's pleasure; this was very different. Jem knew, even as she took up a position to strike the first blow, that there could be no pleasure in beating this deaf, blind, pinioned, helpless and anonymous woman. 'What are you going to do, Master?' she said.

'Oh, I'll just sit and watch,' Headman said. 'You carry on, I won't be bored. I'll clap any particularly telling strokes.'

Headman had little to applaud. Jem wielded the crop slowly, trying to make it whistle through the air but then pulling it short to lessen its impact on the stretched pale skin. The rubber-covered woman had no way of knowing that Jem was trying to be gentle; each time the crop landed she let out an agonised shriek that flayed Jem's nerves.

Headman, however, was not fooled. He could see that each red line that appeared on the woman's arse faded by the time a few others had been laid across it, and that the tip of the crop strayed only by accident into the wide-open arse-cleft and the protruberant sex-pouch. When Jem stopped, and claimed that her arm was tired, he glowered at her.

'Don't be foolish, Jem,' he warned her. 'You've hardly touched her.' He moved his chair to a position in front of the saddle and, leaning forward, he lifted the rubber hood from one side of the woman's face. 'She makes a lot of noise,' he said, 'but she hasn't shed so much as a single tear. You must try harder, Jem. If her shouting disturbs you, I'll stop her mouth.'

He pulled his chair nearer to the saddle, until the woman's face was hanging over his lap, and uncoiled his member from its gauze pouch. It was rigid in an instant. Headman thrust his fingers into the woman's mouth, holding her head still with his other hand; then he withdrew his fingers and inserted his prick. The woman uttered a stifled protest, but the loudest sounds she could now make were low moans. 'Carry on, Jem!' Headman said.

He seemed not to care, now, that Jem's blows were as ineffectual as ever. He was concentrating on the sight of his member, buried in the woman's rubber-masked face, and the woman's breasts swinging to and fro as he slapped them.

At last Jem reached the end of her patience. She couldn't stand it a moment longer, she said to herself. There was no passion, no fun, no enjoyment in this game, for at least two out of the three participants. At least when Rudi had sprung the same situation on her . . . Her thoughts stopped in their tracks. This was almost identical to the scene in Rudi's apartment – was it really only a week ago? Could Headman possibly know about. . . ? She shook her head. It was impossible.

'Master,' she said, 'I have to tell you that I'm not getting anything out of this. Not a thing. Couldn't we just call it a day?'

Headman gave her a furious glare that only gradually turned into a sinister smile. 'I'm afraid not, Jem,' he said. 'There is considerably more entertainment to come. But if you're bored with whipping, you can stop now.'

Jem waited for the inevitable proviso.

'We'll change places,' Headman said.

Jem wanted to fight, to kick and to struggle and to inflict some damage on the man whom she now regarded as a deranged, inhuman monster, but she knew that she could not afford anything that might upset her plans now that they were so close to fruition. And he was stronger than her.

She let him seat her on the edge of the chair. He pushed her legs apart, and pulled her hands down between them. The leather cuffs round her wrists were inset with metal rings; he clipped a length of chain to each cuff, and then trailed the chains along the floor to either side of the chair, between her feet and the legs of the chair. Then, moving behind the chair, he picked up the ends of the chains. 'Now, Jem,' he said, 'let yourself lie back on the seat, slowly, while I pull the chains tight.' And as Jem lowered her back towards the seat of the chair, and her legs lifted into the air, her right arm was pulled under her right leg, and her left arm under her left leg. Her elbows were pulled into the crooks of her leather-clad knees, forcing her legs apart; as her head came to rest against the back of the chair, she heard a click behind her as Headman connected the two lengths of the chain.

Her arms were bent backwards; she couldn't move them. The backs of her knees were hooked over her arms; she couldn't move her legs, except to waggle her ankles in the air. She could roll from side to side a little, but otherwise she was helpless. With the small of her back resting on the edge of the seat of the chair, and her thighs widely parted and bent backwards, she knew that her sex and her arse were exposed in the most blatant display. Headman spent some time running his hands over her rounded buttocks, and she noticed that both his riding crop and his engorged member were twitching ominously.

With apparent reluctance he stopped mauling Jem's private parts. 'Perhaps later,' he said, and pushed the chair up to the front of the saddle, so that the shining latex crown of the rubber-suited woman was between Jem's uplifted thighs. He put his hand on the gleaming rubber sphere and pushed it down until Jem felt the woman's mouth touch her labia, and the woman's hot breath in her pubic hair.

Headman squatted beside the woman's head. 'Something else for you to suck,' he yelled, enunciating each word. 'When she comes, the whipping will stop. Do you understand?'

The woman nodded once, her chin pushing into Jem's gaping slit. Headman gripped his riding crop and went to stand behind the woman's raised hindquarters. He leered down at Jem. 'You look delightful,' he said. 'I think I'll keep you tied up for the rest of the day.'

A chill gripped Jem's heart. She had counted on being able to move when the moment came to act. The woman's helmeted head was moving mechanically between her thighs. Jem knew that Headman would flog the woman unmercifully: the fate of the woman's bottom lay in Jem's ability to come quickly, and Jem had never felt less sexy in her life. Headman uttered a wordless cry, and the crop whistled through the air.

Jem closed her eyes. Headman presented a horrific sight, his face red, his eyes bulging, his moustache bristling as he worked himself into a frenzy of whipping. Jem couldn't bear to watch. The woman had little time to explore Jem's sex with her mouth, as her head jerked violently with every one of Headman's increasingly rapid blows. Jem felt she was in a nightmare; she knew she was close to tears.

Julia! she prayed. Julia, come and take me away from this! And as she remembered her lithe, gypsy-eyed friend, and thought of lying in her arms, nipple to nipple, mouth to mouth, she felt a tiny sensation of pleasure. Suddenly she knew she could do it: she imagined that it was Julia's tongue darting in and out of her, Julia's nose butting the hood of her clitoris. She recalled the sweetness of Julia's smile; the way that Julia always pronounced every word so precisely, even four-letter words gasped into pillows in the heat of passion. Sebastian's lean face floated into her reverie; her right hand moulded itself around the shape of his lovably curved and thick penis.

Headman's hoarse cries and the thwacks of his crop hardly intruded into her daydream. She was surrounded by her friends and lovers: Julia, Sebastian, and Maxine were caressing her, urging her on, and the anonymous mouth slapping rhythmically into her sopping sex was merely a mechanical aid, a device to spark tremors through her body again and again and again until she felt the vibrations merge into a continuous shivering and a ball of heat grew inside her until she felt she would burst and then, at last, with Julia's dark eyes gazing into hers, she drew in a deep breath and released it in a shuddering, chain-rattling, chair-shaking climax.

She opened her eyes to find Headman staring at her. The woman's rubber-covered forehead was resting on Jem's pubic mound. Her body was shaking; Jem guessed she was sobbing.

'That was very noisy, Jem,' Headman said, not moving from his position behind the woman's tortured rear.

Jem's victorious smile disappeared as Headman once again raised his crop above his head.

'Now wait a minute,' Jem said. 'You said you'd stop when I came.'

Headman gave a short derisive laugh. 'I am the Master, Jem. I make the rules; I can break them. Besides, you probably faked it.'

The whip whistled, and landed with an agonising thwack; whistled again, and thwacked; whistled, and thwacked. Jem felt the tears start from her eyes, and turned her face away.

There was someone with her in the bed. Lucy moved her hand, and touched a warm, limp appendage that began to swell beneath her fingers. Where was she? Whose prick was this?

Suddenly she remembered everything. She was inside the Private House; she had succeeded. She was a trainee now; she had passed every stage of her initiation with ease. As her Mentor had promised, once the dam of her inhibitions had been breached, nothing could stop the flood. The dance had been easy, really, and she found it hard to remember why she had made such a fuss about it. She couldn't have forgotten about the silly horsehair tail behind her – after all, it was attached to a dildo embedded in her bottom – and the discomfort hadn't been all that unpleasant, it had rather reminded her to keep moving her arse, which had made the tail swish about to the evident satisfaction of the audience.

After that she had felt no qualms about masturbating under the spotlights; in fact she had taken some pride in putting on a good show. And although she had never previously fancied the idea of a man coming between her breasts, it had seemed different when it was partly a test and partly an exhibition. She had always been proud of her large, firm, golden tits, but now she had come to see them as sexual organs that she could use. The thrills that had stiffened her nipples as she had pressed her mounds round the hot, hard shaft were unlike anything she had experienced before.

She closed her hand round the organ that was now nudging her hip and opened her eyes to survey the little room that was to be hers during her training. She turned to face the man lying next to her. 'Good morning, Mentor,' she whispered.

He grunted, and opened one eye. 'Morning, Lucy. Feeling fit?'

'Raring to go,' she said. 'What's on the agenda today?'

He placed a hand over her left breast and squeezed. 'Catechism first,' he said, and she knew that her sex was already beginning to feel moist. 'What are you here for, Lucy?'

'Obedience, sir,' she said, 'and sex, please.' Her free hand roamed across his muscular torso.

'Very good,' he laughed, and looked at his watch. 'But we might not have time for the sex until later. You've got a busy schedule today. The costumes will be here soon. Go to the bathroom and get ready.'

While Lucy was brushing her teeth she heard a knock on the bedroom door, and then an indistinct conversation between the Mentor and a female visitor. When she returned to the bedroom, the Mentor was alone again, and a small suitcase was on the bed.

She enjoyed the feeling of the Mentor's eyes following her naked body as she walked towards him. I even walk differently now, she thought, it's as if I'm on high heels even when I'm barefoot.

'You're going to sample the work of a field officer this morning,' he said, pulling her on to the bed beside him.

She let him gather both her wrists behind her back in one of his huge hands, and closed her eyes as the fingers of his other hand flicked the tips of her breasts. 'What does a field officer do, sir?' she sighed.

'Field officers work with outsiders,' he said, his fingers moving ceaselessly from one nipple to the other, pinching and rolling the hardening pips. 'Either with visitors we've brought here, inside the House, or at the Health Club, or outside.'

'What will I have to do?' Lucy said.

'Just follow the script. There are full notes in the case, with your costume. You can study them on the way. These scenarios usually consist of – um, action, shall we say, and not much dialogue. There's plenty of scope for improvisation.'

Lucy giggled. She couldn't believe she had been so nervous about infiltrating the Private House. It was actually going to be loads of fun! 'Should I put on the costume now, sir?' she said, wresting her hands from his grasp and reaching for the suitcase.

'Might as well,' the Mentor said. 'Whatever it is, I doubt if it will stop me playing with your titties.'

Lucy sat between his legs, and his hands slid round her ribs to grasp her breasts. She placed the case on her knees, unzipped it, lifted the lid, and barely restrained her gasp of shock. Inside the case was the uniform of a woman police constable.

It can't be a coincidence, she thought. They've found out what I really am. Or perhaps someone's guessed or recognised me. They're playing games with me!

'Well, put it on, then,' the Mentor said, plunging his hand into the case and pulling out a black skirt that was less than a third of the minimum regulation skirt length of any police uniform Lucy had ever seen. The high-heeled shoes were completely unsuitable for police work, too; and the truncheon was sculpted into an unmistakeable shape that made its purpose very plain.

With shaking hands, Lucy started to clothe herself for whatever charade they wanted her to play.

'Julia! What are you doing here? You're not on duty today, are you?'

Damn and blast! Julia thought. The Chief's here. Doesn't he ever eat or sleep? At least he's alone. But there must be cameras in here. How can I get him out of the way without making it obvious?

'Morning, Chief,' she said. 'I shouldn't be on duty, really. But it's jolly boring in civvy street. What's happening?'

'Nothing much,' Anderson said, swivelling his chair to glance across his array of screens. 'The Round Tower's incommunicado. Master's orders. The weather's keeping most people indoors. Interesting party in one of the West Wing bedrooms.'

He pointed to one of the screens, on which Julia could make out a mound of writhing bodies. Anderson's interest was evidenced by the tent-like shape of his gauze pouch.

'Let me have a look at that,' Julia said, and came to stand beside his chair. She stepped forward a couple more paces and leant to peer at the screen. She felt Anderson's hand on the back of her thigh.

'I can see something even more interesting now, Julia,' he said. 'Don't move! That's an order.'

Julia had no objection to watching the imaginative antics of the inhabitants of the West Wing. Disobeying the strict letter of Chief Anderson's order, she bent forward a little further and shuffled her feet more widely apart. His thick, stubby fingers were soon peeling the luscious fruit between her legs, and she could feel the tip of his flicker sliding up and down the crease between her buttocks. Stimulated by the Chief's attentions and by the sight of a dozen intertwined naked bodies, Julia soon found that she was unable to control the slow writhing of her hips, and she could feel her juices flowing on to Anderson's hand.

She tore her eyes from the screen and looked over her shoulder. Anderson's gaze was fixed on her rotating rump, and his thick shaft, freed from its pouch, was standing erect in his lap. His eyes caught hers.

'Perhaps I ought to sit down, Chief,' Julia said.

'Yes,' was all he said, grabbing her hips and pulling her backwards towards him.

She settled slowly on to his prick, luxuriating in the sensation of the thick shaft pushing between her outer lips, and then widening the entrance of her hole, and then, centimetre by centimetre, forcing aside the walls of her vagina, until at last her thighs were resting on his, and one of his fingers had started to intrude into her stretched anus. She wriggled contentedly, and started to move herself up and down so that Anderson's prick slid in and out while his finger, to her delight, merely slid further in.

'Julia!' Anderson puffed. 'That's wonderful, my girl. Keep going!'

Julia bounced up and down with increasing abandon, and the Chief's gasps became louder and more explosive.

He's going to come soon, Julia thought, and she twisted her right hip into the shadow of his desk. She hoped that the cameras were unable to see her hand reaching for her belt. She shouted a word of encouragement to the Chief, increased the tempo of her bouncing and, just as she heard Anderson's anguished climactic exclamation and felt his first spurt inside her, she thrust the red tip of her buzzer against his thigh.

A few seconds later, she picked herself up from the floor.

She shook her head, and stars vibrated across her field of vision. When she lifted a shaking hand to steady her head, she found that her hair was bristling with static. Chief Anderson was slumped in his chair, his deflating member twitching and still spouting little drops.

That certainly was some orgasm, she said to herself. I wonder what the cameras made of it? The Chief's out cold, that's the main thing. I really must get on with the job.

'Wow!' she said aloud, for the benefit of anyone who might have been listening. 'That was amazing, Chief. You look completely wrecked. Let me see if I can perk you up a bit.'

She climbed back on to his lap, continuing the cheery monologue with her inert commander and feigning disappointment that he wanted to go to sleep. 'Well,' she said at last, 'if you're going to doze all day, I think I'll take a look at what's going on around the House.' And she turned from Anderson to his control console.

Having typed in her clearance code and the Chief's password, Julia contacted the first of the Security stations on her list and began to issue instructions.

*   *   *

233

The vintage bus splashed through puddles as it chugged towards the woods. Lucy looked up from the incredible script she was supposed to follow, and saw for the first time, through the rain-speckled window, the vast extent of the estate. To her left the open countryside sloped down to a river that seemed to be more than a mile away; and beyond the river there were farm buildings and fields that she could only conclude were also part of the domain of the Private House.

The bus plunged into the gloom beneath dripping trees, and Lucy shivered with the cold. The tiny black skirt was not long enough to cover even her stocking-tops, and although the black jacket covered her arms and shoulders it reached only to just below her breasts and was fastened with just a loop of braid across her straining cleavage. Only the cap, with its chequered band, and the collar and tie around her neck were anything like real items of police uniform; and they were of no help in keeping out the cold.

There were only two other passengers on the bus, and they looked as cold as Lucy felt. The athletic-looking young man was wearing only a T-shirt, a pair of tight shorts, and training shoes; his partner, a dark-haired girl with a bee-hive hair-do and garish make-up, kept trying to pull down her tight-fitting mini-dress to cover her thighs.

As they had boarded the bus, the couple had introduced themselves to Lucy. 'Hello there!' the young man had said. 'I'm John, and this is Mary. We're the victims.'

Lucy had been completely bewildered, but now that she had read the script she understood. John and Mary were two of the characters in the scenario that was about to be enacted; they were to be the victims of a burglary. Lucy, of course, was to come in to the scene of the crime and arrest the villains. But where were they, she wondered; who were the burglars?

The cold depressed her, and she was worried about remembering her few lines; but her panic about being discovered had receded. It seemed that being chosen to play at being an officer of the law was entirely coincidental. She turned back to revise her dialogue, but the bus was spluttering to a halt. They had reached their destination.

The squat, square, brick-built tower rose from a small hill that protruded from the woodland. It was surrounded on three sides by trees, and from the fourth side rain-greened meadow swept downhill to the distant river. The bus had parked next to a small door in the base of the tower, and Lucy followed John and Mary through it. The wave of warm air that greeted her came as a welcome surprise. Inside the door was a small dark hallway from which a narrow staircase spiralled upwards.

Lucy followed Mary up the stairs, admiring the movement of her pear-shaped buttocks and wondering how the small, flimsy dress stretched to cover them. John stopped outside a door when they reached a landing. 'Mary and I go in here,' he said. 'You carry on to the next floor, and make your entrance later, down the main staircase.'

'OK,' Lucy said, and continued climbing. She went through the next door she came to, and found herself on a gallery that ran round all four sides of the interior of the tower. It was unlit, but a flood of radiance spilled upwards from the floor below. Looking over the parapet, she saw below her the stage being set for the performance. Furniture was being arranged, backdrops adjusted, lights tested, cameras positioned. Cameras! Lucy fretted again. She really did not want to be photographed in this ridiculous mockery of a uniform she respected . . . But the red-headed woman, whom her Mentor had told her was the sweetheart of everyone in the House and was called Jem, had said that she was not to worry about the cameras, and that all record of Lucy's humiliation would be destroyed. Lucy had no choice but to believe her.

John and Mary were sitting calmly on a settee in the middle of the chaos, practising their lines. They had removed their shoes, and as the turmoil died down and a voice shouted 'Positions, everyone!', Mary tucked her feet under her bottom and John, pulling her towards him, started to kiss her face. The lights faded, all sounds ceased, and John and Mary were snogging enthusiastically like teenage lovers in the back row of a cinema.

'OK, action!' the voice called, and as the lights flared up John's hand stole along Mary's thigh and under her skirt, while Mary began to fondle the considerable bulge at the front of John's shorts.

In the space of the next few minutes, and without interrupting their extended kiss, the couple managed to expose most of their bodies. John unbuttoned the front of Mary's dress, released her dark-tipped, heavy breasts, and tickled her nipples into hard points; Mary untied the bow at the waistband of John's shorts, delved inside them, and brought out a large, stiff prick which she proceeded to massage lustily. John tugged at the hem of her skirt until it was round her waist, whereupon she began to shift her position on the settee to give the camera shots of her flashing thighs, of her quivering bottom, and of John's fingers dabbling between her legs.

Then the burglars arrived. Behind the settee a door opened, and two burglars tiptoed through it to look down on the oblivious couple. Lucy could tell they were burglars: each was wearing a red and black striped T-shirt and was carrying a bag labelled *Swag*. Lucy could also tell that they were the amateurs, the outsiders, the ones for whom the whole scenario had been designed. The male burglar was short and powerfully built, with a ruddy complexion; the woman was no taller, but very thin, with a pretty but lined face. They were both middle-aged, and each was carrying a copy of the script.

John cursed and Mary squealed, and both shook their heads violently when the burglars demanded to know where their valuables were kept. Predictably, the burglars' next step was to tie John to a chair, from which position he protested half-heartedly while the male burglar attempted to persuade Mary to talk. Lucy thought that his methods of persuasion were doomed to failure, consisting as they did of removing Mary's skimpy dress, mauling her naked body, spanking her generous bottom, and making use of her well-lubricated sex slot. The female burglar, meanwhile, for some reason that even the script failed to explain, had dropped to her knees before John's bound body and was masticating his exposed member like a dog worrying a bone.

The action had been continuing wordlessly for some

minutes before Lucy, in a moment of boredom, turned the page of her script and read the direction *Enter WPC, waving truncheon*.

She tripped down the stairs, remembered to drop her script, lifted her truncheon aloft, and paused outside the circle of lights and cameras. She made her entrance.

The burglars were supposed to be too busy to notice her at first, and as she strolled towards the intertwined couples, rolling her hips as she began to enjoy the sensation of being watched, she realised that the two burglars had become too engrossed in their young victims to adhere to the script. Lucy, improvising, stood above the male burglar as he thrust himself into the unresisting Mary. Lucy waited until his movements became frantic, and then tapped his oscillating bottom with the flanged head of her truncheon.

'Hello, hello, hello,' she said. 'What's going on here then?'

The burglar froze. The director flapped his hands, vainly trying to suppress the giggles that emanated from the videotape crew. The female burglar flipped through her script, and remembered just in time to remove John's member from her mouth before delivering her line.

'Oh my God,' she read. 'It's the law.'

A black-jacketed figure ran into the middle of the set. The burglars consulted their papers; John and Mary and Lucy exchanged glances. This entrance wasn't in the script. Lucy recognised the newcomer's grim uniform as identical to that worn by the guards during her initiation, and a dread premonition gripped her chest.

'Is Lucy here?' demanded the Security guard. 'Lucy the policewoman?'

They've rumbled me, Lucy thought. She looked frantically for the nearest exit, but realised instantly that she couldn't hope to overcome so many opponents.

The director had recovered his power of speech. 'What do you mean by bursting in here like this?' he spluttered. 'We're in the middle of a shoot.'

The Security guard held up a long white envelope. The red seal was prominent, and drew a collective gasp from the crew. 'Have you ever seen a Priority Order from the Round

Tower?' the guard barked. 'This overrides everything.' He turned, and Lucy shivered as his gaze locked on her revealing travesty of police uniform. 'You're Lucy?' he said. It was hardly a question. 'Come with me. You're wanted at the Keep, immediately. There are sealed orders for you there. The car's waiting. Come on – move!'

The guard grabbed her arm and pulled her towards the door. In the stunned silence behind her, the male burglar remembered one of his lines. 'It's a fair cop,' he called out, as Lucy stumbled down the rain-slippery steps and into the waiting car.

Jem was still tied to the chair, on her back on the seat with her arms locked under her knees and her sex pushed forward. Headman apparently found her rounded haunches an irresistible target, and he delivered playful but stinging slaps as he arranged a television screen on his desk so that Jem could see it between her uplifted thighs.

The rubber-suited woman was still sobbing, but was now standing, chained to a pillar in a corner of the room. With a flourish, Headman inserted a cassette into a video recorder next to the television. The screen flashed on, and he settled into an armchair next to Jem.

'I know you'll enjoy this,' he said, as numbers appeared on the screen, counting down from nine to zero. 'It's not a film, I regret to say. It's more like a slide show, I suppose; a collection of stills. But I'm sure you'll immediately recognise its significance.'

'I won't recognise a thing unless I get some circulation back into my arms and legs,' Jem grumbled.

Headman patted her sex-pouch. 'Shush,' he said. 'Lie back and enjoy the show.'

The first picture appeared on the screen. It took Jem a few seconds to recognise the three figures: one crouching, one standing, and the third bound kneeling between them.

It was not until half a dozen pictures had flashed in front of her eyes that Jem remembered to breathe again. She risked a sideways glance at Headman: he was staring at the screen, his lips white with rage. His fingers tightened about her labia until she cried out.

'Do you see, Jem?' he whispered. 'Do you see the miscreants? A brainless oaf, an incompetent field officer – and an ungrateful viper whom I invited into my bosom.'

On the screen, Rudi's face was twisted into a grin as he held the blindfolded head against his groin. Lesley's expression was serious and determined as she lifted the wooden switch for another blow. The figure between them was small and slim, but otherwise anonymous.

The rubber-suited woman was Lesley, Jem realised. She closed her eyes. How could she have been so stupid? Rudi had spoken of a business contact, a big man in the city who found him lucrative contracts but demanded control over his commercial activities and his private life. The same man had provided Lesley for Rudi's threesome. Lesley was Mike McKenzie's secretary, and Mike had said that he was sure his office was bugged, that he felt that someone was looking over his shoulder and knew everything he was doing. Jem fumed. Why hadn't she made the connection? Lesley must have gone straight to Headman and told him all about Jem . . .

But that was wrong. Lesley had been punished precisely because she hadn't told Headman. So how . . . ?

Jem opened her eyes. 'I get the picture. Alright, so you're a little pissed off. It's no big deal. But how did you find out about me?'

'No big deal?' Headman turned to look at her at last. His mouth was fixed in a grinning rictus and his eyes were glittering. 'You'll find out, Miss Darke, how much of a big deal this is.' His hand trailed along her flank until his first finger came to rest on her hip. 'The tattoo,' he said. 'Miss Morelli mentioned it in her report of course, and I've become familiar with it myself during the last few days. You've been keeping me preoccupied, Jem: I like to see every new tape and photograph on the day that it arrives, but this week I've allowed a backlog to accumulate. I didn't see these photographs until last night; and it wasn't until the final frame that I realised there was something familiar about the positioning of the tattoo on the girl in these photographs.'

'Just a stroke of luck, then,' Jem said, desperately trying to keep a flippant note in her voice.

'It seems so. I don't know what you were hoping to achieve by your deception. I can't imagine that your intentions were otherwise than to the detriment of the Private House. Had it not been for the fortunate coincidence of your tattoo appearing on these photographs, and my perceptiveness in recognising it, I might not have discovered Lesley's incompetence and your treachery.'

Jem's insides turned to water. Bound and helpless, she could think of nothing to do but to play for time. She did her best to look appealing. 'What will become of me, Master?' she asked.

'You've had your revenge on Lesley, and she has received punishment appropriate to her crime. Now I will take my revenge on you. Your punishment will be rather more severe, of course.'

Jem was becoming impatient. 'You might as well tell me,' she said.

Headman gazed at her with his ice-blue, soulless eyes. 'You're going to die, Jem,' he said. 'Very slowly.'

Chief Anderson had recovered consciousness, and glared malevolently from his chair. He maintained a continuous stream of curses, but they were rendered incomprehensible by the gag strapped into his mouth. Every now and then he would try to stand up, straining against his bonds and causing the chair to bounce up and down on the flagstones. At these times it was usually Asmita who would run to him to check the knots in the ropes, and to tease him by manipulating his exposed penis into an unwilling erection.

Julia was having fun. Asmita and Maxine, fearfully obeying unexpected orders from Security, had arrived in the Rotunda to find Julia in command of the entire Security system. They had deluged Julia with outrageous suggestions for new orders she could issue to the House, and Julia had implemented the more practical of them. Now they were giggling and kissing as they unlocked and explored Chief Anderson's Top Secret cupboards and files. Julia kept a maternal eye on them, requiring them to surrender to her any weapons they found, and demanding to know the contents of each newly-rifled hiding place.

Asmita had been subdued at first, but was now as high-spirited as Maxine, and Julia found that both of them needed frequent but considerate application of her flicker.

At last every locker and filing cabinet had been opened. Chief Anderson's office was quiet now, as Maxine's lips were busily pressed against Asmita's, and both girls were moving only gently as they lay together on Anderson's desk.

Asmita rolled on top of Maxine, covering both their heads with the veil of her long black hair. Her sari lay trailed across the floor, and her naked rump, rising and falling slowly as she ground her crotch against Maxine's thigh, presented Julia with an enchanting target.

Julia applied her flicker gently, in time with the movements of Asmita's brown body, using the tip to indicate when she wanted the Asian girl to turn slightly to expose the inside of a thigh, or to separate her legs more widely, or to lift her arse so that Julia could flicker the underhanging sex-lips. For several minutes there was no noise in the office except for deep breathing, and heavy sighs, and the soft sucking of lips against lips, and the whistle and slap of Julia's flicker.

Then Asmita lifted her bottom into the air, and Julia could see Maxine's fingers moving inside her dark slit, and Asmita's hand curled between Maxine's plump thighs. Julia stepped back, measured her aim to Asmita's uplifted arse, and delivered a rain of rapid downward strokes to the yawning cleft between the swollen cheeks. Asmita and Maxine shuddered to a simultaneous climax, gasping and moaning into each other's mouth.

'Well,' Julia announced, feeling a little bit left out of the fun, 'it's a good thing I turned off the cameras and sent most of my colleagues off duty, that's all I can say. You seem none the worse for your recent adventure, Asmita, and as for you, Maxine, you seem to have forgotten your heroine already.'

Asmita brushed aside her hair to reveal Maxine grinning sheepishly at Julia. 'Me and Asmita are just good friends,' the maid giggled. 'I couldn't ever forget Miss Jem, Miss, any more than you could. Should we do something now, Miss? I mean, Miss Jem is alright, isn't she?'

241

'Don't worry, Maxine. We're ready to move when the time comes. I've sealed off the Round Tower. I've sent all the guards off duty, or out to patrol the perimeter. Jem's a very clever lady. Everything's under control.'

'Are you familiar with an instrument known as the Little Ease?' Headman's question was punctuated with pants of breath as he tugged a large contraption into the centre of the room.

Jem's line of sight was blocked by her left thigh. 'I thought I was already in it,' she complained. 'I was hoping for something a shade more glamorous than the death of a thousand cramps.'

'I like to keep you tied up. You're at least as decorative as usual, and considerably less dangerous. Be content that you are about to change your position.'

'Oh goodie,' Jem said. 'Carry on talking about the Little Ease, it'll help to keep my mind off my aching muscles.'

'I rather doubt it, actually. The Little Ease was all about aching muscles. It was a form of imprisonment used, reputedly, in medieval times. The cell was very small, and was designed to accommodate just one prisoner in such a way that he could neither stand straight, nor lie, nor sit, nor move his limbs. It must have been excruciatingly painful. I suppose the prisoner would eventually lose consciousness.'

The conversation was failing to melt any of the ice that had formed in the pit of Jem's stomach. 'And you're going to keep me in one of these cages?' she asked in a small voice.

'No.' Headman was still busy with the equipment in the centre of the room. Jem could hear little taps and clinks, as if he were assembling small metallic parts. 'I have to make a compromise,' he went on, 'between my determination to provide you with the most lingering punishment I can devise, and my aesthetic revulsion at the idea of seeing your half-dead body slowly rotting away before my eyes for weeks on end. I want you decorative and sexy even in your death-agony, Jem.'

'Difficult to arrange,' Jem muttered. She was feeling faint now.

'I have created a modern version of the medieval cage,' Headman said, but to Jem his voice was distant and indistinct. 'Jem? Don't pass out on me now, Jem. On second thoughts, I suppose it might make matters easier . . .'

Jem was floating upwards, she was sure of it. She was in a deep, dark well, and she was floating up to the expanding circle of light . . .

She groaned. Every limb ached. But she was no longer tied to the chair. She could flex her muscles. She could stretch. It was ecstasy just to extend her arm . . .

'Exercise while you can, Jem.' Headman's voice brought her back to reality. Where was she? In his study, at the top of the Round Tower, about to be killed. She was naked. She was kneeling, her knees widely parted, not on the floor, but on a raised sloping platform, soft under her knees. Her feet were not touching anything, were just hanging in the air. Her hips were resting against a padded bar in front of her; she felt another padded bar against her back, and her arms were resting on a third. She was imprisoned within a framework; but she was comfortable. She opened her eyes.

'I can move in this thing,' she said.

Headman was gazing at the computer screen on his desk. Jem noticed fine wires and thicker cables that snaked from the framework that surrounded her and were gathered together into a box next to the screen.

'Of course you can move, Jem,' Headman said. 'The question is, will you want to? This is a modern instrument, and I haven't turned it on yet.'

Jem noticed that her neck was surrounded by a wide collar; she could see its edge, like the rim of an Elizabethan ruff, moving whenever she moved her head. 'What's this thing round my neck?' she said.

Headman sighed. 'You're determined to interrupt my preparations, aren't you?'

Yes, Jem agreed fervently but silently; in this situation, every second counts.

'I'll explain briefly,' Headman said. 'Although you will

243

find out soon enough how the mechanism works. Attached to your limbs and body are sensors that detect movement. Your movements are translated into electronic signals, the power of each signal depending on the amount and speed of each movement you make. The electronic impulses are then fed back to the collar round your neck. It works on the principle of the iris valve. And the greater the impulse it receives, the more the valve constricts. In other words, the more you move, the more you strangle yourself.'

The small part of Jem's brain that wasn't overwhelmed with panic admired the elegance of the system. 'And if I keep still,' she asked, although she already knew that she wouldn't like the answer, 'the collar loosens up again?'

'I'm afraid not, Jem. It's on a ratchet. It tightens, but never loosens. I'll switch it on soon and you'll find out how it works.'

'Don't bother just on my account,' Jem said. 'So all I have to do is keep completely still? This is a really nasty machine. I take it I'm allowed to breathe?'

'You'll find you can breathe gently. There are no sensors attached to your ribcage or stomach. And you're quite right, to stay alive you simply have to remain motionless. It's quite impossible, of course, however strong-willed you prove to be. I will derive my entertainment from watching you gritting your teeth and fighting the imperative urges of your aching muscles. And, of course,' he added, picking up his riding crop, 'it will be most enjoyable trying to make you move.'

He smiled, and pressed a button on the box on his desk. Jem felt nothing but a slight vibration from the collar resting on her shoulders, but she knew that the machine was now working.

Suddenly she was almost overpowered by an urge to finish it now: to flail her arms and legs wildly, so that the collar would squeeze quickly, tightly, fatally, the whole thing over in a moment, Headman cheated of his fun.

She resisted the urge.

Maybe, she thought next, maybe if I'm really fast I can get my hands inside the collar, pull it apart, or wrench it off, or stop it closing, before the feedback mechanism clamps it shut round my neck. How fast would I have to move? Surely I can react more quickly than a hydraulic system?

But I don't know anything about this thing, she made herself think. I don't know how fast it reacts, I don't know how strong it is, I don't know whether it's protected against interference. She had a sudden vision of razor-sharp blades on the collar's outside surfaces; of her blood-dripping hands raised in front of her screaming face as the collar squeezed inexorably.

She didn't try to grab the collar.

She was tempted to move just a little, though; to lift just one finger, just to make sure that Headman wasn't bluffing, just to find out how much the collar would tighten. She told herself sternly that she couldn't risk the slightest movement: she'd find out soon enough whether Headman was bluffing, and if he wasn't, the lifting of one finger could lose another few seconds of life.

Jem remained completely still. When the tip of Headman's riding crop touched the lips of her sex, she turned her shudder into a contraction of her diaphragm.

'Very good, Jem,' Headman said. 'I can see you're determined to live as long as possible. I'll make sure the small remainder of your life is full of pain.'

The crop sang as it fell.

Crouching in the shadow at the base of a stone column, Lucy consulted her instructions again.

Look for two tapestries: shepherds being seduced by nymphs, and the flagellation of a nun. Between them is an archway. Through the archway you will find a short corridor with doors on each side. The third door on the left is a weapons store. Take whatever you need.

She took a deep breath, straightened the cap on her head, and stepped gingerly into the vast and gloomy void of the Great Hall. The tapping of her high heels echoed from the overarching vaults, and she froze in mid-stride, waiting to be apprehended. But the huge hall was deserted, and no one challenged her as she crossed the stone floor and disappeared into the side-chamber between the tapestries.

She still had no clear idea of what she was doing, or why. She was simply following the instructions that had been handed to her in the half-ruined castle to which she had been driven at break-neck speed. The note, which she still carried in her hand, told her that she had a clear path to the Master's den, and that she would find evidence against him there; it told her which doors were unlocked, where the few remaining guards were stationed, where she could find weapons. She had no way of knowing whether the instructions came from Jem, the Master's auburn consort, or from Julia, whom Lucy suspected of being a representative of a faction within the House staff. They could even come from the Master himself, or his Security Corps, who might be toying with her and drawing her into a trap. So far, the instructions had been accurate; all she could do was to follow them, and remain alert.

A slim iron bar was resting against the padlocked door, almost as if had been left there for her to find. She used it to break open the padlock.

The weapons in the store room were mainly useless: ornate swords, a multitude of whips, strange electronic gadgets. She chose a pistol in a holster, identical to those she had seen clipped to the belts of the Security guards. It was only an air-pistol, she realised, and useless for long-distance work; but the feathered darts were supposed to contain a strong tranquiliser, and she reasoned that she would be as well armed as any opponent she might confront. She discarded the holster, gripped the pistol in her right hand, and made for the main staircase.

Could it be blood that was trickling down the insides of her thighs? No, Jem thought, it was just sweat, the same as was collecting in the hollow of her back and tickling the lids of her eyes. She checked the urge to shake her head, and instead blinked slowly.

She hardly felt the individual blows now. Headman was wielding the riding crop like a madman, howling curses at her as the leather sliced into her flesh. She had flinched, to start with, at the most cruelly-placed of the strokes, and the collar had tightened each time until it was now a rigid ring of pressure around her neck. As the pain became undifferentiated, a blazing area of agony, she found that the torture of her buttocks and thighs and sex drowned out the anguish of her aching arms and legs, and she was able to keep still, absorbing the pain as it grew. It took her several seconds to realise Headman had stopped whipping her. She shut her eyes, and opened them again, staring straight ahead at the centre of the door, resisting the temptation to turn towards him, and dimly conscious that she had survived, she was still alive, there was still hope.

'Magnificent!' Headman gasped, catching his breath. 'I always knew you were special, Jem. I haven't enjoyed a flogging as much as this for months. I think you might last all day, my dear. I trust you're enjoying your last sensation-filled moments?'

Jem managed to remain silent.

Headman laughed. 'Well done, Jem! The longer you can keep still, the more fun I can have with you. Your arse is more than a little sore now, my dear. Should I apply the salt water compresses now or later? Later, I think; just before I start on your breasts. For now, perhaps we should see how you're enjoying this experience.'

Jem almost wanted him to hurt her again; as the pain behind her dulled, she became aware of the rigidity of her limbs, and the trembling in her thighs and arms that she could not control. The collar tightened fractionally; swallowing was painful, and deep breaths were impossible.

Her hindquarters were numb; she didn't realise that Headman was touching her until his fingers were inside her vagina, circling as they pushed upwards. She remained impassive; the sensation was nothing compared to the pain, except perhaps a useful diversion from concentrating on remaining motionless.

He was kneeling beside her now; she did not dare look at him, but she could feel his breath on her back. His other hand stroked the fronts of her thighs, and then moved between them, tugging at her sodden pubic hairs. She winced, but stayed still; she could bear it. His fingers were at the front of her slit, infiltrating between her lips, searching for the tiny button of her clitoris.

His fingers found the round nodule. She couldn't ignore the sensation. His fingers moved erratically, touching, tapping, circling her clitoris. Tremors rippled unbidden through her insides.

I can't become excited, Jem thought wildly, it's not possible, not like this.

The reaction's physiological, she realised, as a tingling warmth spread through her stomach and she felt her nipples harden. This isn't desire, it's an automatic response to stimulation. How long can I keep my body still? How long before I lose control?

'Do I sense a weakening of your will-power, Jem?' Headman asked softly as his fingers established a regular rhythm. 'I've found your soft spot, have I? Your Achilles' heel is between your legs, it seems. Your sexuality will be your downfall, then. I think I've found the means to make you move. You'll die ecstatic, Jem. As you come, you'll go.'

Jem knew he was right. She knew her own body; she knew she was building up to a shattering orgasm, and that when it came she would be unable to control her involuntary spasms of release. And then the collar would close remorselessly, biting into her neck, and she would be killed. Like a fountain leaping higher and higher, lust expanded inside her. She couldn't help it; she was going to come . . .

She stared at the door, trying to concentrate on anything but pain and constraint and sex; and she thought she had imagined the two heavy thumps she heard. But there was no mistaking the loud crash that followed a few seconds later.

Headman's fingers stopped moving. Jem, choking as the collar tightened a little more and she tried to still the tempestuous gasps that wracked her body, hardly heard his exclamation of rage through the dizzying mists of interrupted sexuality that were slowly clearing from her mind.

Headman stood up, still shouting. Another crash; and the door flew open.

In the corridor were the slumped bodies of two of Headman's elite bodyguards. Standing in the doorway, with a pistol in one hand and an iron bar in the other, was a blonde Valkyrie in laddered stockings, a tiny skirt, a brief tunic and a policewoman's cap. It was Lucy Larson.

At last, Jem thought, the cavalry's arrived.

'Hello, hello, hello,' Lucy Larson said. 'What's going on here then?'

Headman was furious. 'What the blazes do you think you're doing?' he yelled. 'No one has access to these chambers without my permission. I remember you: you're new here, aren't you? You were initiated yesterday. You've made a big mistake, my girl, and I can promise you you'll pay for it. Now get out and report to the dungeons for punishment!'

Jem couldn't believe her eyes. Lucy, accustomed to obeying orders, had started to turn as if to leave; but she kept the pistol trained on Headman.

'You're the Master?' she said uncertainly.

'Yes,' Headman said through gritted teeth.

Lucy lowered the pistol. Jem almost screamed with frustration. 'Don't I know you?' Lucy said. 'I've seen you in the papers, haven't I? The business pages. Oh my God! You're Terence Headman! I'm sorry I disturbed you, sir. You must be a very busy man. There must be some mistake. I was just following these instructions – '

Jem could stand it no longer. She had to risk speaking. 'Lucy!' she hissed, trying to keep her jaw still. 'He is the Master. He's behind it all. He's murdering me. This machine is strangling – ' Her words ended in a rattling gasp as the collar clenched her throat. She couldn't breathe.

It seemed that *murder* and *strangle* were words that Lucy understood. The pistol flicked up, there was a loud pop and a hiss, and Headman had no time to dodge the dart that embedded itself in his shoulder. Before he had crumpled to the floor, Lucy had jumped to the desk and had switched off every control she could find. Jem felt the collar's vibration cease, and just as she began to lose consciousness she felt Lucy's fingers tugging at the stubborn mechanism; and suddenly she could breathe.

* * *

Lucy's training had not prepared her for the situation in which she found herself. She had no idea what to do.

She was in the topmost chamber of a medieval castle, surrounded by ancient and futuristic instruments of torture. Sleeping fitfully on the floor was one of the country's better-known property tycoons, dressed in nothing but chains and bits of leather. Collapsed against a bookcase, and swearing softly in an American accent, was a half-strangled and devastatingly beautiful woman wearing a leather corset and thigh-length boots. Lucy looked from one to the other, and then caught sight of a third figure: a woman, chained to a pillar, with everything except her erogenous zones enclosed within a rubber suit.

Lucy began to feel disoriented. She clung to one indisputable fact: she had caught the famous Terence Headman in the act of committing a murder. She'd got him bang to rights, and that meant at the very least a commendation, and perhaps promotion. *Chief Inspector Larson* – yes, that sounded right. And she deserved it. Headman was beginning to groan; he was waking up.

'He's got the constitution of an elephant,' Jem said in a hoarse voice. 'Quick, help me get him on the Saddle.'

Lucy snapped out of her daydream. 'What? Him? He's no problem, I've got him covered. Look, are you OK? You're very pale. Would you like to sit down?'

Jem tried to laugh, but it was obviously painful. 'Sit down? That's the last thing I intend to do. I'm OK, I'm just not used to being killed. But we have to immobilise this bastard. He's big, strong, clever and vicious. Let's put him on the Saddle.'

Lucy shrugged, and pulled into the centre of the room the metal and leather contraption that Jem had indicated. Together, the two women managed to drape the semi-conscious Headman along the concave leather surface.

'Fasten the straps across his back,' Jem gasped. 'Put his boots in the stirrups and pull them up tight.'

Lucy felt she was losing control of the situation. 'This man is my prisoner,' she said. 'It's against regulations to use unnecessary restraint on a suspect.'

'Suspect!' Jem screeched, and massaged her throat.

'Listen, lady, this guy's a killer. Anyway, I'm willing to bet that doll's outfit you're wearing doesn't come equipped with handcuffs.'

Lucy shrugged again, and secured the straps across Headman's back. 'All right,' she said, 'you've got a point. But the minute he wakes up, I'm going to arrest him, caution him, and read him his rights.'

'You can read him what you like,' Jem said. 'Just make sure you get his reply on tape.'

'And where am I supposed to find a tape recorder in a museum like this?'

'I'll find the tape machine; how about you unzip the rubber queen? Her name's Lesley, and she's a witness. She won't have heard much, she's seen less, but she's felt plenty.'

Lucy had a great deal of difficulty with Lesley. The rubber suit was not easy to remove, and the unfortunate blonde seemed to be delirious once Lucy had peeled it from her body. Lesley, too, refused to sit down, which Lucy found exasperatingly incomprehensible until she saw that Lesley's bottom was only slightly less raw than Jem's. The girl refused to believe that Lucy was a policewoman, but took no chances anyway and would not disclose more than her name and address.

By the time Lucy had found a scrap of paper on which to note Lesley's particulars, she became aware that another conversation was going on in the room. Headman had woken up.

'I'll give you half,' Headman was saying, his voice still thick and unsteady. 'Half of everything, Jem. Think of it. We'd make a good team.'

Jem was shaking her head in disbelief as she stared down at his bound form; Lucy began to think that her grip on the situation was slipping again. She marched towards the Saddle.

'I'll take over now,' she announced. 'You,' she added, nudging Headman's ribs with the point of a shoe, 'stop trying to bribe a witness. Terence Headman, I am Inspector Larson, on a special assignment for the Missing Persons office. You are under arrest.'

She charged Headman with every offence she could think of, while Jem impatiently tapped what appeared to be a riding crop against the edge of the desk.

'I demand to speak to my solicitor,' Headman said when she had finished, and Jem snorted in disgust.

'He's got a point there,' Lucy said, and then raised her eyes to find that Jem was pointing the pistol at her. 'Put that down, dear,' Lucy said. 'You've had a very trying ordeal, and – '

'Cut it out, sister,' Jem said. 'We'll do things my way. Turn on that tape machine, keep your ears pinned back, and take notes if you want to. Terry baby has a choice: he can either spill the beans about this whole set-up, and let the law take its course, or else I'll give you a dart, police lady, and he can take his chances with me while you're asleep. I'll be just as gentle with him as he was with me.'

Lucy started to protest, but Headman cut her short. 'I'll talk,' he said. 'I'll give all the information you want to hear. I don't want to be left alone with Jem.'

'This is all very irregular,' Lucy grumbled. But Jem had the pistol, and a taped confession would wrap up the case. She pulled a chair up to the desk and turned on the tape recorder.

Jem's arm was tiring. Headman's revelations had been given grudgingly: Jem had been obliged to jog his memory with the riding crop at frequent intervals. The police-woman was making it very obvious that she was getting restless, and kept asking whether it was really necessary to go into such detail about the administrative systems within the Private House. Jem tried to ignore the interruptions, and continued to ask Headman about the location of deposit boxes, the names of secret bank accounts, and the exact relationships between the shell companies and subsidiaries of Headman's business empire. Headman's muscular buttocks were a flaming network of raised weals, and his answers came in broken sobs, but at last Jem had all the information she wanted.

There was just one more part of the plan to put into operation, as far as Jem was concerned; but at that moment three Security guards appeared in the doorway, their pistols drawn.

'Thank God!' Headman cried weakly. 'What the hell kept you? Guards, these two women are traitors. Keep them covered and get me off this contraption now!'

'I'd love to keep them covered, Master,' Julia said with a smile, 'but I rather think we'd better leave you where you are. Are you alright, Jem?'

Jem could have wept with joy. She couldn't speak for a moment, and could only shake her head and grin stupidly as Maxine and Asmita closed the door and covered the room with their pistols and Julia stepped towards her. She fell into Julia's outstretched arms. 'We did it, Jules,' she whispered, burying her face in Julia's dark hair. 'We did it!'

As if from a great distance, Jem heard Lucy's shrill voice. 'Julia!' Lucy shouted. 'Asmita! For goodness' sake find a telephone and call the police. Any police! Just dial 999. Tell them Inspector Larson wants a car and a detective team immediately. Julia! Are you listening?'

Julia pulled away from Jem. 'I'm yours, Jem,' she said. 'We're all yours now. What shall we do?'

Jem closed her eyes and summoned her last reserves of strength. She wanted nothing but to sink into a soft bed with Julia and a large pot of soothing lotion, but she had new responsibilities now. She pointed the riding crop at Lucy.

'Inspector Larson, you have no authority here. I have videotape of your initiation, and I guess your dramatic performance this morning, in that ridiculous costume you're still wearing, is also on tape. I'll bet your superiors would find it entertaining viewing.'

'But you said nothing would be recorded!' Lucy said. 'You said you could wipe everything!'

'Sure, I can. But I prefer not to. This way I can ensure your co-operation. We'll find you a job in the Security Corps, maybe; or you can work on the outside, as a field officer. But I think you need a whole lot more training first.'

Lucy could hardly find words. 'But – but what about – I mean, bloody hell, I've made an arrest, and we've got all that information about the Private House, and – '

'And it will be very useful,' Jem said. 'The Private House will go on, boys and girls. Business as usual, but under new management. And one more thing: from now on, I guess you all better call me Mistress.'

EPILOGUE

Simon Warbeck glanced up in annoyance when he heard the door close. His expression changed to one of shock and embarassment as he recognised his visitor.

'Inspector!' he stammered. 'I didn't expect – I mean, you're back again. I thought you weren't coming back to Hendon. Didn't you say – '

'You don't sound very pleased to see me, Simon,' Lucy said. 'Didn't you enjoy my last visit?'

Lucy gave him several minutes to think about her previous visit, and was gratified to see a bright pink blush appear on his cheeks and spread gradually up to his receding hairline, across to his freckled ears, and down to his wrinkled collar.

'Yes,' he said at last. 'Yes of course. It was great fun. I'd never done anything like that before.'

'I know, you told me,' Lucy said. She pulled a small cassette recorder from her handbag. 'I thought you might like to hear the edited highlights.'

She watched his eyes dart from the cassette recorder to her face, and then to the four corners of the small office, as if seeking an escape route.

Lucy grinned. Confrontations of this sort were becoming almost routine, but she found that her enjoyment of them was as keen as ever. In fact, as she gained in confidence with each figurative notch she carved in her cassette recorder, she found that she was increasingly able to relax and take her pleasure during the first stage of each operation and also to revel in the one-sided power games of each second stage.

The Simon Warbeck operation was in its second stage.

Acknowledging the fearful technician's protests with no more than a careless smile, Lucy locked the door, swept a heap of print-out off the side of his desk, and placed her cassette recorder in the space she had created. She pressed the *Play* button.

Warbeck stared at the hissing machine as if it were a bomb about to explode. But, Lucy thought as she unbuttoned her skirt and let it drop to the floor, in a way that's exactly what it is. She walked round the desk, discarding her blouse on the way, and stood next to Warbeck's chair.

She leant forward to switch off his computer terminal. Warbeck's proprietorial concern for his software overcame his fascination with the hissing tape, and he turned to find himself gazing into the golden valley between Lucy's lace-supported breasts. He gulped.

Lucy removed his spectacles. His eyes swam weakly. *My name's Simon Warbeck*, the tape machine suddenly announced. *What can I do for you?*

Lucy ran her fingers through his thin strands of hair, and then pulled his head forward, crushing his face between her jutting mounds. She heard her own voice emanating from the tape: *There are lots of things I want you to do for me, Simon. But first I'd like to do some things for you.*

She unclenched his fingers from the computer's mouse and pulled his hand towards her. She used his inert fingers to ruffle her blonde pubic curls, then momentarily opening her thighs, she imprisoned his hand in the moist, warm hollow. 'We had fun last week, didn't we, Simon?' she breathed, her lips touching the top of his head.

Warbeck only whimpered and nodded, burying his face more deeply in her cleavage. Lucy let him remain there as the tape continued to spout its crackling record of their last encounter.

They'd done another good job at the House, Lucy thought. The Security sound engineers had edited out most of the chit-chat and every mention of Lucy's name; but the conversation still sounded realistic and fluent, and it gave the impression that it had been Warbeck who had seduced his anonymous female visitor rather than the other way round. Every word and sigh was audible, and the engineers

256

had amplified the sounds of rustling clothes, of lips against skin, of fingers dabbling in well-lubricated orifices, so that the taped conversation could be taken as nothing other than a record of a frenzied orgy.

The reality had been rather different, Lucy remembered. Faced with Lucy's stockinged, knickerless legs and warmly inviting bosom, Warbeck had reacted like a rabbit trapped in the headlights of a car. It was only after Lucy had half-smothered him between her tits while whispering lewd suggestions and coaxing his shrivelled member out of its Y-fronts that he had started to appreciate the erotic possibilities of the situation. *You've locked me in your office, Simon*, said Lucy's voice on the tape, not exactly truthfully, *and you've found out I'm not wearing any knickers, you naughty man. What are you going to do next?*

Don't stop – don't stop touching me there, said Warbeck's plaintive recorded voice. *Let me play with your titties.* Lucy felt his fingers move between her thighs, and detected an unmistakeable twitching in the front of his trousers.

Judging the time to be right, she released his hand from captivity, swivelled his chair to face her, and slowly lowered herself on to his lap. *You've got such lovely big titties*, Warbeck's amazed voice was saying from the tape as Lucy pushed forward her chest and unhooked her bra. His eyes bulged as the lacy cups fell away and Lucy's pink-tipped breasts were revealed.

'You had so much fun with these last time,' Lucy, said, pulling his hands against the firm flesh. 'Would you like me to rub your willy in between them again? Or should I send this tape to your wife instead?'

It took several seconds for Lucy's words to permeate Warbeck's breast-fixated consciousness. In the silence, his recorded voice was pleading to be allowed to spurt all over his visitor's face and titties.

'What?' he said at last, lifting his gaze from Lucy's chest. 'My wife? The tape? You mean – ?'

'I'm blackmailing you, Simon,' Lucy said, delighted with the look of abject confusion on his face. 'I want you to agree – on tape again, I'm afraid – to do the things I want you to do. If you co-operate, my breasts are all yours; if

257

not, I expect your wife will want an explanation when she receives a copy of the tape we're listening to now.'

'What do you want me to do?'

'I want you to tell me how to access HOLMES; how to add, delete and alter records; how to use HOLMES to pass information to local police forces.'

'But you're not on the list of permitted users. You haven't got an entry password!'

'Silly!' Lucy said, unzipping his trousers. 'I'll use yours!'

'But I can be identified! They'll think it's me tampering with the records!'

His penis was as limp as stewed rhubarb. Lucy tried to restore its circulation. 'Well,' she said reasonably, 'I don't want anyone to know I'm doing it, do I? Anyway, why should anyone check up? You technicians are dipping into the system every day, tinkering with the software and so on. It's almost entirely undetectable.'

'But if someone did find out . . .' Warbeck began, his protest fading as Lucy's agile fingers elicited a swelling reaction.

'Don't worry,' Lucy told him. 'I can patch things up in an emergency. You'd be surprised how many people I've recorded on my little machine. Superintendents, Chief Constables, all sorts. I'm sure I can persuade your superiors to overlook any small misdemeanours you might commit – as long as you agree to do what I tell you, of course.'

'And if I don't agree?'

Lucy released his throbbing organ, and cupped her breasts in her hands. 'No more rides in the valley of fun for your little willy,' she said. 'And unfortunately I just don't have the same influence with your wife that I have with Superintendent Mosley. I expect she'll get a copy of the tape on the very day that you get the sack.'

'You can't do this to me!'

'Oh yes I can, Simon. And I can do this, too. Isn't that nice?'

Julia stood at the open window, the autumn sunlight warm on her naked body. The gardens of the château were spread out below her within a complex pattern of box hedges, and beyond them russet-leaved woodland sloped away towards the river Bandiat, glinting in the sun as it made its way towards Angouleme.

'Come back to bed, *chérie*,' said a throaty voice, breaking into Julia's quiet contemplation of the landscape. 'And bring your flicker with you.'

Julia turned, and smiled at the woman lying propped on an elbow in the middle of the vast four-poster. For a few moments she remained by the window, studying the woman's calm, aqualine features and her pale, slim body. Then she walked to the chair on which she had abandoned her clothes, and picked up the short whip of interleaved leather strips. The woman smiled briefly, but otherwise remained expressionless as she turned on to her stomach and lifted her slender buttocks into the air.

Julia shook the flicker, flexing her wrist, and felt a corresponding vibration in the wet, tender hollow between her legs. 'I thought I'd had enough,' she said, strolling towards the bed. 'And your tongue must be exhausted.'

'She is exhausted,' the woman replied, her voice muffled by the pillows. 'If you want her to do more, you will have to use some force . . . Please,' she added with a giggle.

Julia looked down at the flawless cream curves, separated by a chasm as dark and deep as her own. The woman wriggled her rump expectantly, and Julia smiled delightedly as the pert hillocks of flesh oscillated before coming to rest.

'Move your legs apart, then,' Julia said, touching the tip of her flicker to the insides of the woman's blue-veined thighs. The woman moved her knees, and Julia climbed on to the bed to kneel between them. She inserted the end of the flicker in the puckered funnel of dark skin between the pale orbs, and the woman shivered. Maintaining the pressure on the flicker, Julia leant forward to inspect the dark, downy fruit that nestled below the swelling buttocks.

She forgot the temptation, which had seemed so irresistible only a moment earlier, to criss-cross the creamy mounds with a pattern of pink stripes. She was lost in the musky odour of the woman's sex, and lay face down between the outstretched legs to push her nose into the welcoming slit. Her tongue darted forward, licking more and more deeply into the moist opening, savouring the changes in flavour as the sharp tang of the outer lips gave way to the heavier, sweeter saltiness in the depths of the woman's vagina. She felt the contractions of the woman's inner muscles, and stretched the tip of her tongue forward to hunt for the woman's clitoris.

'Now it is your mouth who will become tired,' Julia heard the woman's low and richly-accented voice complain. 'You are my guest, and it is me who must give enjoyment to you.'

'I'm . . . enjoying . . . this . . .' Julia said, plunging her tongue into the woman after each word. Then she sighed, and pulled herself up to her knees. 'But you're right,' she said decisively, and slapped the woman's right buttock. 'Come on, turn over. Let's get the talking finished now. Then we can spend all evening having fun.'

'We can talk tomorrow morning, *chérie*,' the woman said, rolling over to gaze up at Julia with disappointed eyes.

Julia smiled and shook her head. 'Tomorrow morning we will feel rested, and full of energy – and we'll just start playing again. And then it will be time for me to go home. Let's conclude the deal now.'

'As far as I am concerned,' the woman said, pulling Julia down to lie beside her, 'we have already agreed on the business. Your *Maîtresse* wants to start her affairs in this country; she wants a – what is the word?'

'A base. An operational centre from which to expand.'

'*Exactement*. I have this château, and my girls and the other staff. She has the money, and a big organisation – and an enchanting ambassador. Of course we must do it.'

'Then let's open that bottle of bubbly,' Julia said, returning the woman's gentle kisses. 'We'll drink a toast – to *le Château Privé*!'

On the screen, a naked silver-haired man knelt on a bed between the uplifted knees of a flame-haired young woman. The soundtrack of the film had been turned off, but the woman was clearly talking to the man, smiling and pouting as her hands caressed his shoulders and her shins stroked his thighs.

The man smiled, and pulled aside the woman's only garment to reveal her small, pointed breasts. His face sank towards them, and his stiff prick was visible for a moment before it disappeared between her thighs.

A third figure come into view: a slim, lithe young man, naked and with an erect, slender penis. The woman spoke to the older man; he stopped nuzzling her neck, and looked over his shoulder to look at the newcomer. The young man spoke, gesturing at his own body.

The older man nodded, and turned back to face the woman. She arched her back and opened her mouth as he thrust his hips forward, and then her hands stroked down his back as he rested his body on top of hers and began to move against her gently and rhythmically.

The young man climbed on to the bed at the feet of the couple. He pulled apart the older man's legs and knelt between them; and at the same time the woman's hands converged on the older man's buttocks and separated them. Without any preamble, the youth leant forward, taking his weight on the one hand he placed on the bed and using the other hand to direct his member at the centre of the older man's slowly moving arse. His prick penetrated slowly, as he lowered his body only a little each time the older man's thrusting buttocks lifted towards him.

The screen went blank.

'Damn!' Jem exclaimed. 'What happened?'

'Sorry, Mistress,' said the Security guard standing alongside her. 'The tape ran out. They took rather a long time getting down to it, if you see what I mean. And as the camera had been set up on a timer, and it was in a hotel room – well, we couldn't do anything about it.'

'I can't imagine there was much more to see,' Jem laughed. 'That tape alone will be extremely useful. Well done, Anton.'

The Security guard smiled and blushed. 'Thank you, Mistress. The field operatives deserve the praise, not me.'

'Nonsense, Anton,' Jem said, reaching out to run her

hand down his muscular thigh. 'Give me a kiss, darling, and then flicker this slave for me.'

As Jem lifted her mouth to meet Anton's gentle lips, she saw the petulant face of her slave Sharna between her thighs.

'Why, Mistress?' Sharna asked. 'What have I done wrong now?'

'Nothing much,' Jem admitted, pulling away from Anton's embrace. 'I just love to watch you being flickered, that's all. And I didn't tell you to stop licking me when the video stopped, did I?'

'No, Mistress,' Sharna agreed reluctantly, 'but my knees are getting stiff. I've been down here for hours.'

'Impudent little kitten!' Jem said softly. 'I'm real glad you're my slave, Sharna, you're just perfect. Flicker her, Anton, just a little. Stick your butt out, Sharna, and don't stop licking until I tell you.'

Jem lounged on the couch and watched through half-closed eyes as the quiet swishes of Anton's flicker landing on Sharna's arse matched the thrusts of the girl's tongue between Jem's legs. Anton's strokes became a little stronger, and Sharna started to shift her bottom from side to side very prettily, Jem thought. At the same time the movements of the girl's tongue became less regular, providing a hint of unpredictability that started to lift Jem towards another climax. Sharna was licking faster and faster now, and her bottom was jiggling delightfully under Anton's whip; Jem surrendered to the jolts of pleasure that merged within her to create a feeling of warm, satisfied pleasure – a slow, relaxed orgasm that seemed to Jem to sum up her feelings about being Mistress of the Private House.

'That's enough,' she said to Sharna and Anton. 'Thanks, both of you. That was quite something. You can both go now.'

The Security guard and the slave looked crestfallen at being dismissed; but they know better than to protest, Jem thought with satisfaction. 'Teri!' she called; and as Sharna and Anton cast their last backward glances from the doorway, a figure dressed in a maid's uniform emerged from the shadow between two bookcases.

'Teri,' Jem said, giggling as the maid approached, 'are you ever going to look right in that costume?'

Terence Headman made an unlikely-looking female domestic. He was clean-shaven now, his short greying hair was hidden beneath a wig of blonde curls, and his arms and legs had been depilated; but in stiletto-heeled boots he was taller than the tallest of Jem's Security guards, and the blouse of black voile was stretched across his broad shoulders.

'I'm sorry, Mistress,' he said, standing beside the couch with his head lowered, his legs apart, and his hands behind his back. 'I always endeavour to please.'

'And you do please me, Teri,' Jem said. 'Why, I'm almost glad you tried to kill me, because it's so much fun getting my own back. Are you happy, too?'

Headman took a deep breath. 'Yes, Mistress,' he said, as if repeating a litany. 'I'm happy to be your maid. I'm happy to serve you in every way. And I'm very happy to be displayed in the stocks each evening at dinner, as a visible reminder of your authority and power.'

Jem felt the thrill of pleasure that she felt whenever her maid Teri expressed her gratitude and happiness. Jem lifted the hem of Teri's short black skirt. 'No sign of an erection,' she said gleefully. 'Oh dear, Teri, that means yet another whipping for you after dinner tonight.'

'Yes, Mistress,' Headman said. 'Thank you, Mistress.' A pained expression appeared on his face. Jem thought he might be about to cry. 'If there's nothing else, Mistress,' he said, 'might I be excused?'

'Absolutely not,' Jem said. She was determined that he would not enjoy the satisfaction of private grief. 'Julia's not home yet, Sebastian's just left for New York. I'm lonesome tonight, Teri, and I want you to keep me company. I like to watch you suffer.'

She put her hand under his skirt again and pulled him closer to her. She felt his manhood begin to pulse, and she used her other hand to play with his balls, watching the changing expressions on his rouged face as she caressed, slapped, pinched and squeezed his sexual equipment. 'Good girl,' she said to him as his member continued to swell and harden.

She released his testicles and reached for a telephone. 'Rhonda?' she said into the receiver. 'Hi, kid, it's me. I'm in the Round Tower. Send over one of your biggest boys, would you? I want someone to sodomise Teri while I play with his prick. Thanks, doll.'

Headman had closed his eyes. 'Open those peepers, Teri,' Jem said. 'If you're about to start blubbing, I want to see the tears. I want to taste them, Teri. I don't think I'll ever get tired of humiliating you. This is going to last forever, Teri. Now bend over the arm of this couch, across my lap. Let's get your arse ready for a good long fucking.'

His penis in her hand was still long and firm. He's getting to like this, Jem thought; and when he likes it, he won't be any fun any more. And maybe that's just as well: I'll never admit it, but I'm getting bored with revenge. I guess I've always had more fun with Julia, and Sebastian, and Maxine and my other slaves, and with new recruits.

She squeezed his prick. 'Did I ever tell you your trouble was lack of ambition, Teri?'

'Many times, Mistress,' Headman said. 'But I never tire of hearing it,' he added quickly.

Jem smiled happily. 'Good. Now where was I? Unambitious and parochial, that was your regime here. You though you were a big shot, Master of the Private House, but how many cabinet ministers did you have on the books? How many dukes and duchesses? How many overseas branches?'

'None, Mistress,' Headman said, beginning to breathe heavily as Jem worked her hand briskly beneath his bent form.

'That's right, Teri. None at all. I'm different, Teri. I want power, in addition to unlimited sex and wealth. Now consider the silver-haired guy we just saw in the video.'

'Who was he, Mistress?'

'The British Ambassador in Paris, being turned into ambassador sandwich in a hotel room. He'll be a reluctant ally, no doubt, but I think the video guarantees his co-operation. He'll be useful to Julia's plans in France.'

There was a knock on the door.

Jem squeezed Headman's penis hard, and stroked his

blonde curls. 'That'll be some big bugger come to fill up your butt,' she whispered. 'Poor Teri. You saw the Private House as the end of your dreams. But it's just a beginning, for both of us. Come in!'